ARRAS OF YOUTH

Oliver Onions

ARRAS OF YOUTH

London

MICHAEL JOSEPH

To

MONICA

from her Grandfather

First published in Great Britain by
MICHAEL JOSEPH LTD
52 Bedford Square
London WC1
1949

This edition 1973

© 1949 by Oliver Onions

ISBN 0 7181 1147 8

Printed in Great Britain by
Hollen Street Press Ltd at Slough
and bound by James Burn at Esher, Surrey

CONTENTS

✤

That boy within us who is said to be the father of the man shall sooner look into the future than, arrived at its estate, he shall recall the morning brightness he has left behind. Robert Gandelyn was in fact in his middle years before it occurred to him that as juggler, clerk, lover, and soldier as it suited him, he had an account of himself to give at all.

There were good reasons why it should not be set down by his own hand. No sooner, however, does another hand attempt it than a somewhat curious question arises: Can that properly be called a sequel which, while subsequent in date of publication, at the same time predetermines events to come by a good twenty years?

The conditions were strict, the period itself settled in advance. Many things were already precluded, others would have been a contradiction of the man himself. In short, it began to look as if it could not be done.

Yet, if the truth inheres, there is usually a way. He first showed his face in a Tapestry he shared with others. If now he could be granted a scrap of Arras all to himself he might occupy it after the fashion of the Prodigal in the illuminations, gadding, returning, as many Prodigals as might be, yet each of them himself.

Arras, moreover, has a running border, alive with the idiom of the time and strown with the broken meats of history. Occasionally its self-occupied little figures wander into the picture, and a beginning has to be made. So let the first of these strayings be the dying verderer-knight, opening his eyes only to close them again for ever. He was seized suddenly, on a journey. An abrupt halt had been called and a tent hurriedly erected. The headland was high over the sea, and the thin ridge of trees that crested it sloped at all seasons landward, like these italics. It was early of a spring twilight, and the promontory's underlying chalk was just beginning to give back the light of the day in a tender mirage of bloom.

Sir Matthew

The dreaming swan that paddles in his sleep
Stationed in love as the dark stream slips by
Lets only water go; alas who keep
Station in running years! Invisibly
Open the dripping floodgates of the locks,
The one-way locks, back to no river-head,
But grave upon grave, box after lowered box
Discharging to this estuary of the dead!
O springing rills of him whose daily theme
Was ever with her service interwove!
O ebbing tide of him whose nightly dream
Still, as the swan's, is reflex of his love!
Open the gates; better to be at rest
Than dream a song beside an empty nest!

I

The clerk he had called for had come, and with his coming he had made signs that all others were to leave him. He lay on the sparse grass, with a horse-blanket folded under his head, and dropping the tent-curtain the clerk had lighted a lantern and hung it on the hook of the pole at the foot of which the saddle-baggage lay. The growing flame showed the flaccid mouth on the blanket and the youth's own face, fastidious, difficult, dark, and apprehensive of the spiritual ordeal so plainly before him. The stricken man was speaking of his will.

'You will find it in my closet, in the chest that is bolted to the floor-beam—there is a stone in the wall—'

'Rest a little, sir. This will pass,' but the head on the blanket was slowly shaken.

'To Netherby twenty shillings for a hundred Masses—twenty times a Requiem and twenty a Placebo and Dirige—'

'To-morrow, sir—try to sleep a little—'

'Loose my neckband—'tis you are the sir now, Robert—I would die as I was born, naked Matthew,' and the loosening of the neckband easing him a little he went struggling on. 'Men make wills but cannot stay for the carrying out of them. To the prisoners of York five pence—and to Efga Hartlip thirteen-and-fourpence—'

'Sir, I know none of that name. If it is in the will—'

'Late of Beverley—lift my head—nay, go get the candles—'

But with the candles the youth also brought wine, and a few sips of it seemed to revive him, for presently, bare-

throated and uncovered as to his shoulders, he was fretting
and fumbling to gather his clothing about him again.

'Green oaks go by the score—you see more unlawed
mastiffs than there are rabbits in the garths—even as I lie
here the rascals are at it—'

'Sir Matthew, it is not the moment—'

'But another assize is due and they shall smart! Leave
this other business!—bid Stephen Hurst get me home to
Newbiggin!'

The candles had been set on prickets where he could see
them, but now at the sight of them a fanning of harp-
strings started forth from his jaw and twitched down to his
collarbones. His voice broke querulously.

'Why are these candles here, and what is that in your
hand?'

Seldom did Robert Gandelyn carry the object now in
his hand anywhere but in his breast, and his nervous fingers
made an imperceptible movement. Unction was always
delayed as long as hope remained. Young as he was he
had seen men die before, and many conceived themselves
to be dying who were only in fear. But from the mori-
bund man throttled sounds were breaking, and the
small wooden crucifix was back in his hand again, and
now that the ordeal was upon him the novice shrank no
longer.

'*Te, Deum, commendamus*—' the solemn words sounded
muffled in the closed tent, but the other sounds grew
louder.

'He should have stayed in Guienne—in three months
he'd wearied of her—silkier hair never spread pillow—her
voice was like marrowfat in your ear—'

'*Requiem æternam dona eis, Domine*—'

'But out of his house he drove her, and her with
child—' he was on his elbows now, veins swollen and eyes
bolting. 'Nay, stop the assize! An oak or two—are you

there, Robert? As you live and I die—I charge you seek
her—seek her and tell her—'

But it was never finished. There came instead the harp-
strings, the convulsion, the choke and the falling back of
the head on the blanket like a spent loggat. Dazed that
already the ordeal should be over the ministrant was on
his feet again. Slowly he covered the naked shoulders. He
placed the crucifix on the breast, blew out the lantern on
the tent-pole. But the four candles he left burning, only
snuffing them mechanically with his long fingers before
dropping the curtain of the tent behind him.

The men of the meinie had lighted a fire of brushwood
and were cooking their evening meal. They looked up as
he passed, but turned to their spits and broaching again,
for all they knew of this moody young sir who had been
quartered on them was that he was newly back from
France, that time seemed to hang heavy on his hands, and
that as he idled about Newbiggin's peel and courthouse or
walked through its village alone he muttered more to himself than he talked to any other. A glance at his face had
told them all they wanted to know, and their backs were
to him as he walked along the wood-end to where the
horses were tethered. There he stood looking in despite
at his own hands, as if he would have disowned them.

Finger-sleight at such a moment, and not with any
common object but with the holy crucifix itself! But if he
had sinned it was too late now. He had never performed
the Rite before, no such thought had been in his mind, and
if to have practised oneself in the back-palm was a sin the
devil had claimed him long ago. He ceased to frown at his
hands. Suddenly standing there by the horses he raised a
dark and page-cropped head and his voice at the same
time.

'Stephen Hurst!'

The business for which they had turned aside was a wreck, still far away down the coast. It was not easy to see what title the dead verderer-knight had had in it, and notwithstanding his advancement in the Forest service he had been unable to read the record of his own assize, but for this lack the man who now advanced amply made up. Put Stephen Hurst into his household gown and baldrick, with a few jacks and sallets behind him, and he would carry things off with a bluster; but now he had removed his baldrick, and in his hand he carried bread and a spitted bird.

'We thought as much when you came out for the candles,' he said as Gandelyn took these without a word. 'What sort of end did he make?'

But Gandelyn, setting his teeth into the bird, did not at once answer, and when he did it was to ask a blunt question in return.

'One Hartlip by name,' he said. 'He'd be some neighbour of his as I take it?' and the steward turned a broad and showy beard.

'What name?'

'Hartlip. He'd been in Guienne. There's an Efga Hartlip too, late of Beverley. Who's she?'

Slowly the beard was stroked. At one time Stephen Hurst had been a pantler. Now his beard proclaimed that he had risen in the world.

'Hartlip you say? Now should I have remembered that name in a month of Sundays! And Efga it was, to be sure!'

'I'm to seek her. Where am I to look for her?' but the beard was still stroked.

'To think o' that coming back to him in his end! And did he give you any indications, how to know her when you saw her?'

'Briefly, she'd hair on her head, and a voice she used to whisper with.'

'And wi' that he'd gone?'

'Wi' that he'd gone.'

'Think o' that!' the steward mused. Then after a remembering silence, 'But if it's hair you say, it wasn't a deal of hair they'd left Efga Hartlip the last time I saw her! They'd scraped her as you'd scrape a pig, to the scalp—but there, she'd been warned, and them that won't be warned must be disciplined. Still, think o' that!'

Yet when at last it did come out, no story could have been more commonplace. In the Forest four verderers went to the Regard. A verderer presided over his own court, one of the four had died, and because of his juris-diction it was settled practice that no verderer must be under the degree of a knight. Into the vacant place Matthew Poole had stepped, out of his woodcraft and long experience, and now as Gandelyn listened the rest followed almost of itself. A husband away in Guienne, silky hair and a voice like marrowfat, a forest-knight riding by with a new pair of spurs to flesh—just another barefooted woman in her shift with a candle in her hand, whipped three times round the church to the chanting of the Miserere, to show her face in the parish no more.

'And her husband?' Gandelyn asked when the steward had finished.

'He cast her off, as I would ha' done.'

'What, to beg her bread?'

'Or win it she knew how.'

'What of her babe?'

'Nay, seek her midwife while you're about it. I cannot tell you.'

'And him? Did he do nothing?' and the cropped head was turned for a moment towards the tent where the candles burned.

'I did hear he was in Swaledale at the time. They say she painted that that they'd set on her cheek, but the paint was worse than the scar, and it may be I'm thinking of another,' and Gandelyn stood with his arm flung over a horse's quarters, silent and frowning.

For the journey he had put on a russet habit divided for riding, with a sort of capote that he could draw forward over his head. His pouch and poniard were at his belt, and now, the dreaded Rite over, he was restless on his own account. A month ago he had never heard of this Sir Matthew Poole. Since then it had been Robert this and Robert that, never had he been so be-Roberted in his life, and now on his conscience was placed this last dying injunction. Out in his exasperation he broke.

'Why must he saddle me with it?' and as it was not for Stephen Hurst to tell him he would live and learn he only hoisted his burly shoulders.

'What, a month in his house and you haven't guessed that?'

'Not I, and would I had never seen him or his house!'

'He was for getting you into his own service. He'd have had you at his elbow to jog him at the assize and be a pair of eyes and ears for him in the Forest. Would all were as smooth for me now as he'd ha' made it for you! And you've passed his soul on, but I have his body to get home, and the sooner he's in the chaplain's hands the sooner we shall all see our beds again,' and back to the fire Stephen strode, leaving Gandelyn to follow or not as he list.

The dying evening was cloudless and serene. Gulls wheeled in the infinity overhead, and as still the light faded from the sky the chalk beneath the promontory's short herbage woke to haunt the air with its mirage. The men's weapons, a nondescript assortment of gisarmes and pikes, had been stacked against a tree, and if a man would know the minds of his own servants let him die and come back again but for half an hour. Already they were mutinous. Pricking up their ears at the news of the wreck they too had reckoned on a few pickings and were returning empty-handed. Their long day in the saddle was likelier to be three back, with a dead man to carry and useless horses to lead at a walk, hastening a little it might be over the unfrequented places but dropping to a funeral-pace again for every company that passed and every hamlet they came to. Slowly Gandelyn had followed Stephen Hurst back to the fire. A score of yards away the crack of the tent showed where the candles continued to glimmer. No ear but his own had heard that last choking message, he had given no undertaking. As for the thirteen-and-fourpence, they are little the poorer who never know that they might have been better off. But suddenly unseemly words reached his ears. The men were for getting the dead man home with the least trouble to themselves. Their voices were loud as they spoke of trussing him to a horse, depositing him in some church, loading him on the first cart going their way. But when all was said the man had been a knight. Not for one yard of the way was he going to be hustled home after such a fashion, and suddenly Gandelyn again raised his voice.

'Stephen Hurst!'

'What now, Master Gandelyn?'

'The night will be a short one and we start early. Let these be getting their rest now.'

And with that he took charge. Not a voice was raised in reply as he rose. From the weapons stacked about the tree he chose a short boar-spear, and that night, long after the retinue slept, with the candles still glimmering in the tent and the chalk-ghost from the ground, his nimble fingers were busy with poniard and twine, turning it into a ceremonial cross.

Who goes so slowly home who only a sunrise ago set out so full of life? Only Matthew Poole, his bier of horse-blanket and spear-shafts, fashioned as best they were able. Four carried, the four who rode behind led each an empty horse, and every two hours they changed places. Only Stephen Hurst rode all the way. Over rough and broken ground, with the shifting dead-weight under the blanket to be shaken back again at every jolt and stumble or a thrust of the nearest knee, they cursed the burden of him, and long before midday of the first day had ceased to speak of the two days of it still ahead.

They had scattered their fire early, but the wind had woke as early as they. First they tied stones to the corners of the blanket to keep it from carrying away, but that only added to the weight, and at one point, where a boisterous gust swept up a gully from the sea, the mutiny had all but broken out. Any might carry who wished. Half of them were for deserting. But from his horse Stephen Hurst pointed to the slender figure that walked ahead, and the dissent died sullenly down. They bound the blanket to their burden with ropes instead, knotting all to the litter as if Sir Matthew Poole and his bier had been one faggot.

To his boar-spear cross Gandelyn had bound a heavy streamer of black. But at this too the wind tugged and tore till the staff in his hands quivered as if with life, and always he had bragged of those sensitive hands of his, that they could distinguish between the weight of one feather and another. But scarce a morning had passed before the staff of a pound or two was as heavy in his fingers as if it had been moulded of lead. They cramped themselves to it as the toiler's fingers grow to his hook, and with the same slender muscles constrained to the same unvarying posture the numbness crept and spread. Every stumble and trip added its twinge, and voices behind him seemed to reach him from a great distance.

'I'd as lief have our burden as his,' he fancied he heard such a voice sometime that afternoon. 'He cannot change about like us.'

'He's young enough. Their prayers support them.'

'Is he a priest? He's little more than a lad.'

'He was priest enough to put this one away.'

'They say there's a difference between a live weight and a dead one.'

'Nay, we ha' the dead one,' and the voices died away.

So again came the bloom and magic of the twilight, and the evening and the morning were the first day. But the second day was not like unto it, for that secret of the chalk-refraction, so lovely at fall of eve, changed by day to a fritillary-dance of outcropping flinders and shards in a tossing, moving world of windbowed tussocks and bents and a myriad florets. Their shimmer brought on the tears like lime, and the black-draped cross became something to rest his reddened eyes upon as the land began to undulate and sway. From time to time the sagging of the cross brought him from his doze again, to see not chalk but sheep, sheep in countless multitudes, and far-off inland woods that seemed to advance and retire into the pale distance as he blinked. The sheep did the same, approaching and pattering away till half the wold seemed to be on the move with them, and suddenly they were real sheep, for they baa-ed. He had not noticed the lessening of the wind, and it startled him to find a horse suddenly at his side and to hear Stephen Hurst's voice in his ears. Stephen's finger was pointing.

'Seeing you at your meditations we let you alone, but look,' he said, and from the saddle shook an arm that did not feel the touch.

Sir Matthew was no longer bound to his bier like a faggot. The high wolds lay behind them, outspread before them lay the Vale they had crossed two days before, cultivated, sappy, lush, not chalk-casting back the light now, but drinking it in as a mother nourishes the milk in her breasts. The inland woods had crept forward, patched and diversified where they broke into tracts of tillage and

dotted with villages and spires. Here and there the sail of
a ship moved so slowly along its waterway that it seemed
to be standing still, inland ships, tacking and poling their
way between meadows and cultivation, their wharves the
byres and barns. But it was at none of these things that
Stephen Hurst's finger was pointing. It was at something
close at hand, toilsomely moving athwart the slope to meet
them, and against all nature that too was a ship.

Yet it had neither sails to drive it nor did men with
quant-poles urge it along. It moved on the wheels of a
wain as broad and long as a floor, and it was drawn by a
score of oxen. Half a dozen men were in charge of it, and
it seemed the end of the world to see a ship there, being
driven across a hillside like a plough.

'It's a Noah,' Gandelyn heard the steward say, 'but
we're a long way off Corpus yet.'

But it could only be a Noah, stripped and stowed for
travelling. The pavilion-like structure that made a stage
of its stern was fresh and shining with new paint. Its pole-
mast had been unstepped and lashed along its waist, and
the dismantled halves of its round topcastle had been
recently decorated and gilded. But it was no moment to be
wondering what that galleon would be like with her mast
upright and her splendid sail set, the Cross and Keys
perhaps, the Mitre borne aloft by angels, the IHS, the
Holy Face itself. A players' booth lay directly across a
funeral procession's path. Not a man had bared his head,
and in the presence of the dead, one sweating fellow was
bawling aloud at the top of his voice.

'The devil take them that sent us this gait, and these
bullburnt cattle too! Kick that stone out o' the way, Jonas,
and give that wheeler a prod!'

But he drew startled back from a black-draped cross,
held shakily out at arm's length by a sacerdotal young
figure that thrust the emblem almost down his throat. To

drowsy words in Latin the goaded beast responded with a windy bellow; then, with both prayer and progress at a standstill, the bellow died away on the hillside as there stepped forward a tall, limber-built, jauntering man who, doffing a feathered cap till it swept the ground, uncovered the crown of a half-bald head.

'Sirs, your forgiveness! You were flush in the eye of the sun and these meant no irreverence!' Then, as he swung his body round as if a king should bid his subjects bend, 'You, every man of you! Uncover yourselves, and stay so till I bid you move!'

Yet save by its own picked way such a structure could hardly be moved on land at all, nor on water neither, since the floor of a wain was its only bottom. If it was to be turned there would be a pole to rig and the oxen to unyoke, and such were the address and tact of the tall man that, seeing the youth with the cross, he whispered to the steward only.

'Who is it you bear?'

'Sir Matthew Poole,' and though it was plain that the questioner had never heard of any such knight he crossed himself none the less. Then he looked up at the man on the horse.

'Peace be with him, but you see how it is, sir. We're for York and the Guild of the Lord's Prayer, and we cannot be dancing a jig with this every half mile. Would it serve if these got down on their knees and stayed so till you were past?'

And for all his sleepiness the cross-bearer heard. His eyes never left the black streamer, his lips were not seen to move, but Stephen Hurst took it that the man was to be more fully questioned, and his hand sought his beard again.

'You have the manners of a player. Is it Noah you play?' and again came the regal gesture.

'As you see, sir. She was built in Brid, this last winter.

Riggers from Hull and gilders and painters from I cannot tell you where—would they flung their money about on actors as they do on gear like this!'

'We're long enough off Corpus yet. Are these your company?' and at that the man came near to raising his voice.

'These my company! God forfend! York's a long way off too! *These* my company! These are but waggoners and labourers.'

'And who might you yourself be?'

'A poor actor and reciter of verses, sir, Robin Crosby by name. It may be you've heard of him they call Two-ways Robin, that can play two men at once, so that you'd say a man was fighting a combat with himself?'

'To be sure, to be sure,' and Stephen's ear was inclined for a moment for further instruction. Then, turning to the actor again, 'And what do you play besides Noah?' he asked.

'Besides Noah? As it comes, sir, as it comes. What hits their fancy in one place mightn't in another. Only Robin Hood pleases all. With my own company I could give you Jacob and Esau, or the Three Kings, or Baalam and his Ass, or Herod, or twenty more. Would I had 'em with me now! But who wants York's money must do as York says. It's a pageant-master they want, not actors. But I shall come up with them again in the summer. Am I to bid them turn the oxen, sir?'

Wherefore, so let it be. Leave had been asked, every head was bared, at a sign from the actor every man was sinking to the ground. Had they been common packmen or clothiers—but it was only the church giving way to the church, a funeral to the Guild of the Lord's Prayer. With one hand behind him Gandelyn made the sign. The men of the meinie took up their burden again, and Sir Matthew resumed his homeward way.

II

Husbandry, industry, peace. A few weeks before a cham-
paign black with burnings and for three days on end as
silent as the grave; here spring-ploughing, lambs nuzzling
beside the ewes, sails on the waterways and the knocking
of the loom: how well they knew their business who when
they made war did so in somebody else's land!

But less now than ever must any decorum be lacking as
the stripling with his cross went before, the bearers and
the led horses followed, but always the big man with the
beard and baldrick rode. Another day was drawing to its
end as they reached a scattering of huts set in a waste of
cracked mud and reeds. It was a sometime squatting that
beyond the marsh grew to a sizeable hamlet, and here
Stephen Hurst called loudly to a grey-bearded man who
carried a lamb under his arm. The place he sought was
nearly a mile further on, a wayside chapel with a lych-gate,
and under its pent the bier was set down. The men lighted
their fire, and perhaps it was the one who had shown
understanding about the boar-spear cross who stood
looking down at Gandelyn where he lay among white
dead-nettles in an angle of the chapel's buttress.

'Stiffly, young sir,' he said. 'It may be now a horse-
litter's to be had, then we can all ride,' but Gandelyn
answered with his eyes closed.

'There must be no unseemly haste. Has that steward got
his baldrick on?'

'Ay, and to-morrow should see the end of it.'

'For you, but not for me,' Gandelyn replied, and his
comforter turned away.

For now he too must turn to the works of peace, not the

husbandman's part or the craftsman's, but that of the clerk and factotum of the law. 'Men make wills but cannot stay for the carrying out of them,' the dying man had said, and no restful prospect loomed up before Gandelyn now. The administration of wills devolved upon the church. From where he lay among the dead-nettles he had only to lift his head and he could have seen the bier under the lych-gate and the men about their fire. But his closed eyes saw Netherby instead, Netherby where he had had his schooling and like a truant must now present himself again with his report of Sir Matthew's end.

Haughty Netherby by its stream, with its parent-house at Citeaux in France and its lesser monasteries stretching like stepping-stones across Northumbria to Scotland and its lands and possessions stopping only at the Welsh Marches and the western sea . . .

Lofty Netherby, like a bride in her wedding-robe of stone and her chapels for her handmaids and the Sacraments to veil the majesty of her face . . .

By now its bell would have rung for compline and at midnight brother and monk would be out of their beds again. To-morrow or as soon as might be he must be there, but first the will was to find. It was in Sir Matthew's closet, in the chest that was bolted to the beam—there was a stone in the wall—

Suddenly, slipping back among the nettles, he slept.

And now the sun is hardly above the horizon before Sir Matthew takes the road again and out of the arras-border and into the pattern they spread, the little things, the domestic things, the crowing cocks and the raked-over fires, the half-awake villages and townships, the lant-tub slopping and splashing its way from door to door. Past farmyards and turning water-wheels Sir Matthew jogged as the sun climbed higher, backwaters sudded with the grease and ley of the washings, and the 'Addle-and-*tak't!*'

of the loom as the galley-baulk rocked and the treadles
clattered and the flying shuttles cracked. The midday rest,
and early in the afternoon Great Kirby lay behind them,
Little Kirby, Ness. And at Thorpe the worst was over, for
word had gone ahead and there they found the head burgess
waiting for them with a horse-litter. It had two horses, one
before and the other to push behind, and now for the first
time Gandelyn too rode.

But still past those who stood in their doorways or
uncovered by the way he carried the streamered cross.

Where there are sheep there are starlings, and towards
evening they began to darken the sky with their multitudes. In wave after wave they came over, so closely packed
that now and then one of them fell to the ground, maimed
or stunned with the crowding of its fellows. Two men had
gone before. They returned, and beyond a chattering ford
there waited those come out to relieve them, with Newbiggin's priest at their head. Now against its darkening
hillside Newbiggin's prick-eared peel might appear at any
moment, and the only new thing about Newbiggin was its
name. There under the foothills it had stood before the
streams had been diverted or the busy Vale parcelled out,
and in course of time its village had grown up behind it, a
church, a few yards and kilns, and a single steep street.
Suddenly under another canopy of starlings, the tower
appeared, a gaunt eaveless landmark sticking up like a
pig's ear, windowed as ascending levels, its court in its
yard below and its ramp of stone steps ascending direct to
its first floor. On either side of this the stay-at-homes of
the household waited in attitudes of mourning. SirMatthew
was home again.

Newbiggin's industry was tiles, but every tiler and his
wife had pressed into the courthouse yard, while over their
heads the church bell tolled every minute. It was in this
same courthouse that Gandelyn was to have sat at the dead

verderer's elbow, whispering to him who was building
what, where he had got his green oaks from, whether his
mastiff had been lawed and who had been selling venison
lately. But by this time he was lying flat on his back in his
chamber next to Stephen Hurst's. It had once been Newbiggin's cellarage, long since converted into living-quarters
and offices, and gladly would Gandelyn have slept, but to
the tolling of the bell and the voices from the yard outside
there was now added the voice of Stephen Hurst, a head-
servant suddenly without a master. And as Stephen had
carried no burden he was fresh and vigorous for counsel.

'It's each of us for himself now,' he was saying, wiping
a few drops of wine from his beard. 'Matty Poole had all
the luck of things, old Sir Walter dying when he did and
all waiting to be stepped into, and I'm not saying he didn't
know his business. But Poole was the sort of man who'd
never own to being in the wrong. He should never have
fallen out with them at Netherby over Pennypocket bridge
the way he did.'

Gandelyn, testy with drowsiness, only muttered, and
the steward quaffed again.

'Granted he was in the right of it. Granted it was
Netherby's upkeep. But it could have been settled in a
friendly way, instead of having them up in his court like
common poachers.'

'I know nothing of it.'

'So now which of them will you be seeing at Netherby?
But no matter which. Barring they bring it up themselves
say nothing of Pennypocket, nor ever at any time make an
enemy when you can make a friend. There'll be changes
at Newbiggin too. They'll advance him from Knares-
borough belike or maybe some man from Elmet. Would
I'd had a start like yours! Letting alone he wanted you
himself, the newcomer'll be to put into the way of things,
and that's where *your* door opens!'

But Gandelyn, shifting from this position to that, found only aches in them all and scarcely heard what golden opportunities were now his as the steward filled his beaker again.

'How did I start? By studying his ways and being fore-seeing of them. The hour he liked his morning wine, I saw it was there. If he was to his ride his horse was at the door. So do you with this new man when he comes. If he's to set rights let it be only in small matters he can pass on as his own. This young clerk that's here now, find some way to get him out. Whenever a thing turns out well, see it's by *your* counsel, and if it's wrong say you feared as much. The more middling they come from the more they like their persons respected. I mind before I came to New-biggin—

But Gandelyn had heaved his stiffened limbs up from the pallet. There was no need to go outside and up the ramp, for an inner stairway had been fitted, and the will was in his closet, in the chest that was bolted to the beam. Up the ladder he dragged himself, mounting to the floor above. Here alone two symmetrically-placed windows gave to Newbiggin's twisted frontage a semblance of balance, and the closet lay in an opposite corner. A candle stood on a ledge and he lighted it and lifted the curtain that hung over the low entrance. There in its accustomed place the chest stood, and raising the candle he began to peer about the stone surface of the wall.

But a child could have found the place by the pawings and fumblings all about it. The stone was pivoted and worn, it swung aside at the pull of his fingers, disclosed the recess. With the key in his hand he turned to the chest beneath. It was of oak, almost the length of a man and banded and nailed with iron, and it had a staple and a ring at either end through which a pole could be passed should it ever have to be unbolted and carried away. It stood some inches from the wall by reason of the depth of its lid, and the heavy cover jolted back to its former marks and chippings. But his trouble was wasted. He had not even to lower the candle. All that its flame showed him was packed and folded clothes.

Yet two objects lay on top of the rest, the first a small key and the second a small flat package separately wrapped in linen. Disturbing the order of the garments as little as possible he began to lift them out, laid-away cloaks and gowns, hose and a short velvet mantle. It might be that other articles lay beneath and the will among them. But soon the garments gave way to household stuff, sheets and napery and the like, and he turned to the linen packet he had set aside. As he opened it there almost rolled from his palm, but was deftly caught again at his finger-tips, a feminine gimcrack of filigree-pierced silver, dull with tarnish, round and hollow and light. It was a perforated musk-ball, and that from which it had kept the moth away was a child's unfinished garment, with a needle and an inch or two of thread still sticking into the beginning of an embroidered letter. What the letter was to have been he could not tell, for if there had been pencilling to guide it it had long since vanished away, and as he stood there look-ing at it there reached him again the note of the Newbiggin church bell.

Now however it told him by far the likeliest thing to have happened. It was the practice among those not content with the security of their own houses to lodge their valu-ables in some nearby religious establishment with a strong-room, and it might be that this was what Sir Matthew had been struggling to tell him in his extremity. If therefore the will was at Netherby the smaller key would be that of the box or casket in which it had been carried there. It was intricate in shape, not flat, but fitting some keyhole in the shape of a shallow S, and he examined it attentively before tucking it into the satchel at his waist. Then slowly he replaced the garments in the chest, folding the unfinished bit of embroidery in its linen again. Closing and locking the chest he returned the larger key to its niche. Now, if he could, to catch up for some of his lost sleep.

But Stephen Hurst's question—what now?—was more pressing than he had at first supposed. Except as the bearer of a few letters, now delivered (for as the Lord John's poursuivant he was his runner and letter-carrier too), he had been given no orders. At Newbiggin he had been instructed to wait, the Lord John was presently following, and were he now to return to France he might well miss him on the way. But he was taking no advice of Stephen Hurst's. As for the dying knight's injunction, that he was to seek out some strange woman and tell her he knew not what, he must first hear what Netherby had to say. The tolling of the bell had ceased, no sounds came from the courtyard outside. Beyond the curtain the steward snored loudly. But still Gandelyn lay awake.

Then, without knowing how he got there, he was back on the wolds again with his boar-spear cross in his hands. There was no light in his basement chamber; the light about him was that of the chalk-blink and its dancing that turned to sheep, its fluctuations to inland woods that came and went. He heard voices, and suddenly from the mirage there emerged Stephen Hurst on his horse, pointing to a ship that toiled across a hillside, its hull a waggon floor. And Stephen was not alone, but conversing with a tall jauntified man who said he was an actor and whose feathered cap swept the ground. They were for the Lord's Prayer in York, he said, and they played not only Noah but Baalam and Herod too. His name, he was saying, was Crosby, the one they called Two-ways Robin, who could make himself two halves and back again, so that those who saw him had the illusion of a man fighting a combat with himself.

Now how in the name of counterfeit, Gandelyn wondered as he tossed, did the cunning fellow contrive to do that?

III

In the cool parlour at the end of the chapter-house passage Brother Isidore thrust the paper under Brother Baruch's nose that he might see for himself. It was a parchment engrossed *In Terra de Gower in Wallia*, and because of it not only Brother Baruch but the precentor too, to say nothing of three of the scriptorium clerks, had been kept on the run half the morning.

'It is, I repeat, a copyist's error!' the sub-prior petulantly repeated. 'Our own Brother Francis is continually making them! For "commons" only read "commote" and see how plain the sense at once becomes!'

Brother Baruch only shook his shaven head in its muffle of unbleached wool. It might or might not be as the sub-prior said.

'Yet see how dearly this error cost our unhappy brethren of Valle Crucis! "Commons," observe, is an English word for an English thing. But a commote—do you yourself know what a commote is?' and again Brother Baruch tried to get in his word.

'Not I, learned brother, and to speak for a moment of another matter—' but he was overridden.

'It was a Welsh cause, that should have been tried in a Welsh court. Yet here we are prayed to take cognisance that "commote" is a word unintelligible in the courts of England. At once the argument is wrested not to what a

commote is but whether this English court *knows* what
it is . . .'

Brother Baruch sighed. Meekly he suggested that it was
a long time ago, but all he got was a smart rap.

'Not so, when these precedents still govern us. I say
nothing of a second flaw, that this bailiff, being provided
with a chancellor, had not the power to write to the bishop
direct—'

'Briefly, brother—'

'—as instance our own Pennypocket bridge. There was
little or nothing amiss with the bridge. I hastened to give
orders about it. Yet this petty forest-court amerced us!
But he overshot himself over our sheep-fold! Over his head
to the Duchy I went, and now we rent and keep it for ever,
as they say for a song!'

With this Brother Baruch managed to get his message
off his tongue. There was news of this same knight, he
said, and the sub-prior's head stiffened in its corolla of
wool.

'News of Matthew Poole? Now what?'

'Only that he is dead,' and first there was a moment's
silence and then a quick flicker of the blue-veined hand
over the woollen tunicle.

'Poole dead! . . . Who brings this news?'

'One schooled in our own lay-school, Robert Gandelyn,
who left us last year. You set him under me for his
copying.'

'A spare, overshot youth with a dark and attentive eye?'

'He has been waiting at the streamside this last hour.'

'Poole dead! . . . And as I remember we have his will.
Refresh my memory of this youth.'

Briefly it was done and the hand moved over the tunicle
again. Asked who was in attendance at the strong-room
Brother Baruch answered, 'Brother Zachary.'

'Then return this to its shelf and tell the youth I will be

with him when I have knelt,' and with the *Quare impedit* in his hand Brother Baruch retired along the chapter-house passage again.

It was the hour between sext and nones. Across the footbridge Gandelyn could see them at work in the kitchen-gardens, bare-armed in their brown scapulars, their skirts corded up and their hoods fallen back, resembling so many pied and busy birds as they weeded and hoed and tended the buds on the walls. They worked in silence, for few sounds broke Netherby's round-the-clock stillness but the brief and frequent bell, the processional psalm, the Service and the singing of the birds. But from over by the guest-houses the sounds of the world could be heard again. The masons were at work on the new central tower, and why ask for more when at Netherby two worlds met in one? Architect, artist, scholar; butcher, baker, carpenter, craftsman; lawyers, administrators, soldiers at need; what was wrong with young Robert Gandelyn that all this had not contented him?

But now he had a hangdog sort of feeling, as if there had been some covert guilt in growing up at all. Urchins he did not know shuffled their feet in that schoolroom and scribbled on the archway walls. Nor had he ever before seen the treasury with one iron-scrolled door half open and Brother Zachary's tall death's-head figure standing there formidably on guard. He felt his shoulder touched. As suddenly obedient as if he had never left the place he saw Brother Baruch, with no recognition in his eyes, since he was not alone. The strong-room lay between the vestry and the great nave's southern aisle, and the sub-prior must have taken the short way through the church. Of itself, Gandelyn's body doubled in a deep inclination. By the time he was upright again neither of the other brothers was to be seen.

As the scrolled door closed behind him he was at first

aware only of a dim grey loftiness, shut off midway by a massive iron grille. On the hither side of this grille wooden benches were set against the walls, and whatever was to be distributed was passed through the middle grating. But the chamber beyond it was furnished with an oblong marble table, inlaid like a chessboard with black and white squares, and the dim rest was a receding vista, racked and shelved with ancient books and stacked-up chests in recesses, many doubly and trebly padlocked. For here, in the monastery's secular heart, reposed its archives, its muniments, its all-embracing deeds and charters, the Chapter Seal itself.

But the private coffers stood in a bay apart, and a tall chair stood before the marble table with two lesser ones for the tellers. With the small crooked key in his hand the sub-prior had moved away, and Gandelyn could see him in the middle distance, fumbling with the coffer, taking out and returning this object or that, and finally standing long with a document in his hand, his brow knitted as he mastered its contents. Then he returned to the table. Seating himself in the high chair he made a sign that Gandelyn might take one of the lesser ones, and when he had done so spoke with the paper folded in his thin blue-veined hand.

'I am told you performed the last rites for this deceased knight,' and Gandelyn inclined his head.

'At his request, father.'

'As in the circumstances was laid on you to do. He died confessed?'

'So far as he was able, father, which, however, was only in part.'

'Explain.'

'His breathing was difficult. It was difficult to follow him. It seemed to me there were things he would have added to his will.'

'Things of what nature?'

'Of a charitable nature, father, those in prison, other things,' and with that Brother Isidore opened and attentively scanned the will in his hands.

'The Masses and the Commendation, they are here. The way to Newbiggin church to be mended, it is here. Such prisoners as may lie in York—it is all here.'

'And yet, father—'

'Indeed, he makes no bad end after all, and you did well to acquaint me with speed.' Then, as if all that was necessary had been said, he looked for the first time at the messenger in the teller's chair. 'I am told you are newly back from France?'

'A month ago. . . . But his breathing, father—at the end his gullet was heaving like a frog's—'

'Last year I was myself in France. I took the place of our Lord Abbot at our annual chapter at Citeaux, where as you know all of our Order must yearly attend. Did you visit Citeaux?'

'No, father.'

'Nor our brethren of Pontigny or Clairvaux?'

'Father, I was with the armies, far from these places, and touching this will I seek a direction for myself also. This that to my thinking he would have added concerned a woman by the name of Efga Hartlip, on whom thirteen-and-fourpence was to be bestowed. I was to have given her a message also, but in that same moment he'd gone.'

'You cannot deliver a message you never received, my son.'

'Yet *in extremis*, father, his very last breath—it sits on my conscience—'

'It is a matter for the chapter. It shall be borne in mind. Account your conscience discharged. And this key you may leave with me,' and he made a movement as if to rise.

Gandelyn's heart sank. So dismissed, so lightly set

aside! But it was not all. A pair of chill eyes was searching his face.

'Did you know this woman?'

'No, father.'

'Or anything concerning her?'

'At that time nothing, father.'

'Then sponge it from your mind. And yet—' and Gandelyn knew in his heart what was coming, '—these are small matters, of momentary importance. My son, why did you not remain with us in our House and take our vows?'

Yet how many answers could Robert Gandelyn not have given to that! In the very act of submission, always his mind had been tempted elsewhere. Daily, from his place far down the echoing nave, he had edged himself behind some pillar the better to see without being seen, the far-away brothers in their stalls, their demeanours and differences and likenesses, the abstracted eyes and nodding heads of the monks in their lesser seats. Like dotted mushrooms their shorn heads had always seemed, the blanket-white of their wool as if snow had drifted and thawed in the great grey place. And even then it had been the inclination of his nature that others should be made to titter while his own face showed never a sign. With a handkerchief round his hand and two dots of Brother Baruch's ink for eyes, how the lay-school rabble had giggled at his mammet, turning now this way and now that, expounding, exhorting, deploring! But let the Lord Abbot be officiating and ah, how his own eyes had shone! The lofty mitred head, the stiff and glistening chasuble and the great golden crozier held aloft—almost he forgot the sub-prior, still waiting for his answer.

'Why had you to stray? Now it may be you have seen the grossness and folly of the world. It is not too late. Netherby's arms are still open to you,' and at that the young man broke desperately out.

'Reverend father, I came here to tell you my heart! I cannot reach so high! Try as I will it is all above my head! I cannot feel the love for all that we are commanded! Even this Sir Matthew, though I would do his errand, wrecks so far away were no business of his, yet flushed with greed—' but he was interrupted.

'A wreck? What wreck?'

'We never got as far, but this steward of his would have bawled them down, and already I've noticed this of men, that in their hearts they like best those that daunt them most,' and the cold eyes were bent on him more particularly.

'You speak observingly for one so young.'

'He wanted me for a spy in his service, to get them into his court, and I'll profess no love for a man that sees another's wife, and waits till he's off to Guienne, as Uriah the Hittite was had out o' the way—'

One finger of the blue-veined hand had a heavy ring on it. The tips of the others were tapping softly on the marble table. 'Less hotly, my son. But continue.'

'Then, when he should have been standing by her in her trouble, making himself business away in Swaledale—out on the roads she was flung. . . . Nay, father, since I'm unfolding myself, it would have shown a better grace in him to go on forgetting her than only calling her to mind when the sweat of death was on him!'

And who shall say that in monasteries too there are not minds as subtle as any in the outside world? The fingers on the marble table had ceased to tap.

'Who, my son, is your informant in all this?'

'His own steward, Stephen Hurst.'

'Ah! I remember him. There was some trifling matter of a bridge. But tell me this: with our Lord Abbot himself bearing no ill-will for that, why should you show yourself so spleenful in things that happened before you were born?'

Who either shall say that they do not serve the best who do so in their own way? By joining himself to these of the Lord's Prayer—he knew not how to frame his request, but the anger died from his voice.

'As we carried him over the wolds, father, we met with a certain company. They were neither church nor lay, yet in a manner both.'

'What is one to make of this?'

'Though secular, they knelt decently and devoutly as we passed. They were for York and the Corpus plays, father. And the goldsmiths lend their jewels and the church its vestments and ornaments. Oh, father, if it would but lend me, the least of its sons!'

But the rebuff was prompt. 'We of Netherby meddle not in such things. York does as it will.'

'Yet in the church's name, father—it might be that a letter from you to present me—' but he got no further, for the sub-prior had stiffened like a rod.

'What! You leave us and then come suing to us for favours! It is too high for you but *we* must stoop! Peace, enough! You have brought me your message and the key. What of Newbiggin itself? Its furnishing and moveables? Is it well or ill appointed? Did he live in lavishness? Of all this you say nothing.'

And there could be no second interview. By whatever device the precious moments must be lingered out, and there on the table lay the will, with a seal dangling from its inch or two of silken cord. The key shaped like an S lay by it, his only help was in his wits, and feverishly he began to improvise.

'Had the armies been anywhere near Citeaux, father, how I should have run to knock at its gate!' (Oh, something, but what?) 'Or Pontigny or Clairvaux either, to close my eyes but once under roofs so blessed!' (*Ah!* It was a saucy prank, but it would delay him!) 'As for Newbiggin, father, it is but a rude house, but if it is your wish I should prepare an inventory—' (What runaway fingers could do with a crucifix they could surely do with a key.) 'I could return with it to-morrow or the next day—' (Always by word or gesture turn their attention somewhere else, never had his stealing fingers been busier.) 'He has good clothes in a chest—many a poor soul would be glad of them—'

But Brother Isidore was on his feet. With the will clasped to his tunicle he was looking for the key that had lain by its side. Then, concluding that he must have left it in its lock, he moved away.

But at a far quicker pace he was back again, searching first the table, then the floor beneath it, while Gandelyn, in sudden fear of what he had done, stood with his hands clasped in trepidation over his breast.

'A key. A few moments ago I had a key. It was lying on this table.'

'Dear father—'

'I said a key. Here in my hands is the will but not the key of the box I took it from.'

'Most reverend father—I was at my wits' end—it is a small skill, but it is all I have—open the will, shake it—'

There was a slight slipping sound, but no key fell clinking to the floor. Yet the unfolding of the will revealed it, deftly tied to the cord of the seal, and at so impudent an affront to his person the sub-prior's lips moved in ominous silence.

'So,' he said at last. 'It is these pickpurse tricks that are your gift! But marry, we have an answer to that! Under our chapter-house there are certain cells, but these are only for the lighter offences! Beneath the infirmary is the lyng-house, and none may approach him who lies there, but his bread and water are let down to him by a cord and there the least imprisonment is for a year!'

And Gandelyn blenched. The lyng-house was for felonies and blasphemies and above all for contempt of the Rule. Even the choristers never spoke of it but in a whisper, nor did they ever say of the sub-prior (as they did of some) that occasionally of a cold morning he celebrated in his bed or ever slipped past the porter's lodge after compline, not to be seen again till prime. Brother Zachary was not far away. He had only to clap his hands; and the delinquent broke out in a shaky voice.

'Father, it is not as you think! I could as easily have stolen that ring off your finger or the will itself! It is that there must be things, secular things—I know not what they are but things you would have done such as you yourself may not do—ever you would find me faithful, and I cannot think our Father in heaven made even such an instrument as I am but He had a use for it—'

The sub-prior of Netherby did not clap his hands for Brother Zachary. He looked instead at the beseeching young figure and saw a face still smooth but troubled and earnest, a weather-browned and somewhat irregular face, mobile to conceal and quick to substitute. Then he began to do an absentminded thing. This was to unfold the will again and to re-read it, mutteringly and half aloud, over again from the very beginning.

'The Commendation to be full, both before burial and afterwards in anniversary . . . The Masses, he says a hundred, that is to say, in each of our other establishments also . . .' Then, with hardly a change of tone, 'In France. Whom did you serve?'

'The Lord John, father.'

'Colleges—but he neither founds nor endows any. As for the road to Newbiggin church . . . what are your present orders from the Lord John?'

'None, father, since any wind may blow him home again.'

'Yet I find here nothing expressly to Citeaux, nor to Clairvaux, nor to Pontigny. This is surely an inadvertence and an omission. . . . What was your employment with the Lord John?'

Then, a few more questions answered, he rose and walked away. Gandelyn heard the turning of the key as he replaced the will, after which he began to pace the vista back and forth, many times, till Gandelyn wondered whether he had forgotten him. But when at last he returned to the table his manner was resolved and austere.

'I thought it well to leave you for a little time. Have you used it in humbling yourself?'

'Never was I humbler, father.'

'Brother Baruch has reported you as of a good discretion, also some of your answers to myself have not lacked acumen. It may be that France has matured you somewhat beyond your years. But pertness cannot go unpunished, so do you submit yourself to my penance?'

'I am a son of Rome, and your son.'

'It is true there are things our Lord Abbot would be informed of that cannot be watched from within these walls. The will you have brought me in no way concerns you. None the less it provides that one shall go to York, on foot for sign of penitence, where fivepence is to be bestowed on the prisoners in its castle. How if I appoint that one to be yourself?'

First Gandelyn's heart stood still, then gave a bound. To York, he!

'Hear me before you answer. As for these other matters, they are meat that is useless to us served up on a cold dish. Therefore, though you go afoot, that is not to say that on sufficient occasion you might not mount a horse and ride your hardest.'

Gandelyn could scarcely believe his ears. A breathless 'To do what?' was on his lips, but the churchman, with a

quick glance about him, sank his voice as he drew nearer
in the high chair.

'Listen attentively. If you must speak, speak low, and
after this forget. This that I tell you now is for your
guidance.'

The laws of the Forest dated from Knut. The First
William had more immediate things than forest laws on
his hands, but not so the Second, he who died by the Forest
arrow. With John all came to a head, but only that another
order might begin, and it was this history that Netherby's
sub-prior unfolded to Gandelyn at Netherby's exchequer-
table that morning, in the hour between sext and nones.

But again these things touch Gandelyn's own story only
as the small activities of the border, where the little figures
plough and scatter the seed and shake their rattles to scare
the birds away. For Rufus a prone body, a tumbled-off
crown and an arrow, but into the same cramped space
other figures press and jostle. A ragged starveling in
brown, plainly of no degree, is seen raising his hand
against a forest-officer in green. It is his right hand that
he raises, and the significance is that if he raises it a second
time not the hand but his life will be the forfeit. The laws
were hard, the punishments cruel. Even when it ceased to
be death it remained banishment. The Forest was still the
King's.

But always there are more little figures in brown than
forest-officers and kings, and generations ago these had
squatted and scratched their plots, claimed custom, been
entered as copyholders on the manor-rolls. Now, with
loud Lancaster crowing England's skies down, they would
strike a blow for what they had won, and little the settlers
of Netherby Forest cared for the parchment that had made
them and their rights and their service over to the Duchy
as long ago as the Third Henry. Grown unruly and bold,

many even held themselves free to go to certain fairs without payment of the toll, a moiety of which by ancient deed was Netherby's, and it was at this point that the sub-prior's lowered voice became audible again.

'Yet we are loth to invoke the law against men of no substance, nor would we use avoidable force,' but the young man answered him eagerly, impetuously.

'Tell me what you would have done, father—'

'If we could answer that by the letter we should have little use for eyes abroad.'

'You would know who these men are, their ringleaders, their numbers, where they assemble and in what array?'

'We would know what is necessary to be known. Bring us that and few questions will be asked you as to how you came by it,' and at that Gandelyn came near to laughing outright for joy. *This* is a penance, that of all commissions he would the most gladly have embraced!

'Father, never was heart so lightened as you have made mine! For many months such things have been my trade, and you may account it already done!' but he was sternly rebuked.

'What of your own unaided strength?'

Down on his knees Gandelyn sank to the treasury floor.

When he rose from them again Netherby's bell was ringing for nones.

Jan Schmidt

They kept a corner for the household pet
Who graved the marble of the funeral-stele,
The little friend, the kid, the marmoset,
The linnet in the cage, the dog at heel:
The quail he matched to win a purse of gold,
Her fountain's carp she fed with crumbs of bread:
Proportioned sorrow, such as each could hold,
Lightened this last sad office for the dead.
But now our world has learned a double grief
No consolation comes of simple things:
We bear the hookèd cross of unbelief
And know not heaven save on an engine's wings,
And hearts crack twice under their weight of ill
When lesser grief makes greater greater still.

I

In a small clearing where two leafy rides met an ale-stake stood. It was no more than a hut of daubed wattle with a garland for a sign, but it had an outside bench, and on this Simon Grindrod the watcher of Pennypocket ride was wont to stretch and regale himself whenever his duties brought him that way. High among these he accounted the espying of strangers, and on that midday, at his length on the bench, his eye was cocked up over his pot at a face he didn't know.

But dressed as the man was dressed his name mattered little. He leaned on a white-painted staff that ended in a cross, his travel-worn gabardine was of a special cut, and stitched to its upper sleeve was a conspicuous yellow cross. By these signs all who saw him might have known how pressing his business should have been, and from his bench Simon Grindrod addressed him authoritatively.

'And when, might one ask, did *you* leave Durham?' and as the man seemed one whom hardly a dog would have called master, he answered as those do whom anybody might stop and question.

'Two days ago, friend. I'm but buying bread for my way,' and Kitty-à-Wood, blocking the door of her stake, had the bread ready in her hand. But the charcoal-burner and the two alder-seekers who lay on the grass with their backs to the wattles only settled themselves more comfortably to watch the baiting.

'Where did you sleep last night?' the watcher demanded, and the man, shifting uneasily, would have left without his bread, but was stopped.

'No such haste. Sanctuary-men cannot come and go hereabouts as they please. How many days were you given?'

'Five, sir.'

'For what port?'

'They directed me to Hull, sir.'

'And what are you doing off the highway, you that may sleep no two nights in the same place? You are started off with your bread and meat. Neither have you walked from Durham here in two days,' and the other whined expostulatingly.

'Friend, I did not say so. I bestowed my bread as I went, and thrice kind hearts gave me lifts on the road,' but now Simon had heaved himself from his bench and in his forest-green stood rufflingly before him.

'What's your name?'

'Schmidt, sir.'

'An outlander's name. Ha' you but the one?'

'Jan Schmidt.'

'Some Jew belike or a felon. Well you know this road goes nowhere near Hull. Into the Forest you come i' your Cuthbert cross and out of it you'll go some sort of a palmer, or another o' these with a tale they're back from France! What have you on you under that Durham rig?' and now the man began to whimper outright.

'Sir, you'll find neither bird nor egg on me—dressed as you see me they conducted me to the boundary of the diocese—gladly would I have stayed with them but my thirty days were up—'

And his staff and yellow cross should have been his protection, but now the men on the grass were egging on the sport, and stripped and searched he would doubtless have been but for help just round the corner in the very moment of his need. A few yards beyond the stake the trees closed in again. They were breaking into spring leaf, among their twinkling greens and golds little was visible till it moved, and there was a parting of branches. Like some Mercury alighted from nowhere there stood under the alestake garland a slender figure swathed in a russet cloak, with bright and dark-dancing eyes that swiftly took the whole scene in. Gandelyn's journey-boots were on his feet, he had cut himself a hollystick to walk with. The woodland was a flush of the hues of spring, and for half the morning he had out-carolled the birds to think that there were those in the world who were their own masters all the time! . . . From face to face the brown eyes darted. The sanctuary-man—poor devil! That fat forester, now which of Poole's rascals would he be? Ah! This must be the Pennypocket purview, and if so its watcher would be Simon Grindrod. From his potterings about Newbiggin's courthouse he had gleaned a little here and there, and a good fling of the heels on a merry morning does any man good. The brown cloak that enveloped him to his chin suddenly split in two. There shot from it an arm as rigid as a fingerpost, directed straight at the sanctuary-man, over whose unlucky head a second storm of upbraiding now broke.

'Álehouses again, Jan Schmidt! So this is the dance you lead me! Where have you been these two hours?'

But not for a moment did he give him time for any gaping 'Sir, I know you not.' With his hollystick he took a cut at the white staff on which the other leaned, almost bringing him to the ground.

'Straighten yourself before an officer of the Forest! A courteous good-day to you, forester! Saw you ever such a cartstail of a face? But from now on I'll not have the ramskite a moment out of my sight!' and next the brown eyes lit on Kitty-à-Wood in her doorway. 'Mother, how much ale has he had?'

But the man had asked for no ale, only for the bread that

Kitty had ready in her hand, so now for another fetch while the music was still in his heart.

'Have his fingers touched it?' he cried in tones so horror-stricken that the bread almost dropped to the ground.

'Nay, let him take it and begone—'

'Or yourself when he gave you the penny?'

'Marry no—'

'Yet let me see the penny!'

But the devil must have been in the penny, for suddenly out of Kitty-à-Wood's fingers it melted as if into the air, and the young face worked fearsomely up and down as springing forward he snatched the penny from Jan Schmidt's yellow cross. It was plain sorcery, and even the charcoal-burner and the alder-seekers stood open-mouthed.

'Ay, stand back, nor touch him, any of you! O the wickedness that is in this man! He can addle eggs with squinting at them—see the basilisks in his eyes! Three brockets he's cast blasts on since he left Durham, and if you see his left thumb begin to waggle and his lips mumbling strange words in the name of all the angels stop your ears—'

But Simon Grindrod too had all sorts to deal with, and somewhere he had seen that cropped head before if he could but remember where. And the difficult part of a jape too is sometimes how to get out of it again, and now as the forester stood paunchily before him he spat as it were upon his luck-penny. It was all to be learned at New-biggin, these and their petty filchings and back-money and the extra toll-pennies they extorted whenever they were two or three to one traveller. (And Matthew Poole had wanted *him* for this beggarly service, Stephen Hurst had counselled *him* on how best he could feather his nest!) Now the forester was asking who *he* was that he should come between an official and his duty, and suddenly he slapped his hand rememberingly upon his brow.

'Ha! This should be Simon Grindrod, of Pennypocket! Well met, Simon, for now I can relieve you of one of your duties! As for this man, evil as he is, grace has yet been shown his miserable soul. A while back he healed one of our lay-brothers of a palsy, which is a gift he has when the devil's out of him, and for this our Lord Abbot interceded with them of Durham for him, and the safe-conduct of him has been turned over to me—' but the forester was having none of such a tale.

'I know not who you are, young sir, but I'm the watcher of this ride and I ha' my duty to do—' so now for a little magnificence, and Gandelyn drew his cloak about him again with hauteur.

'Yet have a care how you detain him, and me with him! It's none of your duty, Simon Grindrod, to be lolling on alestake benches, drinking with colliers in the morning and stopping a man that has but five days to get out of the realm!' and the forester spluttered.

'You say? You say?' and now the quicker it was brought to an end the better, and Gandelyn drew himself up like a princeling.

'What, Sir Matthew Poole scarce dead and this is the horse his lackey would be riding! Caught with birdlime on his fingers, prying into an alewife's takings—'

'Now by Saint Harry—'

'To say naught of the two turvers you billeted on the widow-woman and her lying sick in her bed, nor of Dick o' the Vale you threaped out of half a web of cloth, nor of Will Rabey and his three sheaves of corn! And now you'd—' but he judged it was enough. Suddenly his voice was the voice of a monarch. 'Mother, take this man's penny and let him have his bread! It shall be reported forthwith! Give him half a dozen eggs too and let this pot-belly in green pay! . . . Jan Schmidt—six paces in front of me—march!'

There was a thwack as the hollystick swept Simon's pot of ale from the bench to the ground, and from start to finish the frolic had taken exactly a quarter of an hour.

Out on this ruthless art, that like the pelican must vuln the breast that is its source! Scarcely was his performance over before he saw thirty ways in which it could have been bettered. What, a word like basilisk and no better done with it than that! It should have been brought out with a gnash and a rolling of the eyes and a baring of the teeth, so—and softly, not to attract the attention of the man in front, '*Basilisk!*' he hissed as the green wood swallowed them up. And so with the blasts on the brockets and the curse on the bread. But among so much bad it was the management of his cloak that had been worst, and suddenly the sanctuary-man, glancing furtively behind him, might well have thought he had a lunatic for his protector, for there was Gandelyn, making goblin-flaps with his cloak and grimacing fearfully as he enacted it all again. But it was the end of the antic. His captive carried the bread, but he himself had taken charge of the eggs, slipping them into his hood. Cloaks with eggs in them should not be flapped so, and crestfallen he lengthened his stride.

'Have a look what's happened inside here,' he muttered.

Not until some minutes later, when the ruin had been attended to with scrapings of twigs and wisps of grass, did he add, 'And now—good morrow to you, Jan Schmidt, supposing that to be your name!'

No name could better have fitted a figure so small, shuffling and nondescript. He wore no cap, Durham had cropped him close, and his shent poll was a new springing of stiff grey bristles. He had a short prominent nose beaked like a bird's, but the mouth beneath it was gap-toothed and sunken, so that nose and stubbly chin made as it were a pair of pincers. The legs under his gabardine were thin and bandy, he had stuffed his shoes with hay, and his little blue eyes were almost lost in the wrinkles that puckered them. His manner of answering was as if a dog wagged its tail.

'The first water we come to we'll give it a washing. Jan Schmidt is my name, blest friend and helper in my need,' and Gandelyn gave a shrug.

'Nay, I care not for your name. But garbed as you are, is it not as that man said, that you'd have been better on the highway than straying off into woods like this?' and the answer was a deep and dejected sigh.

'Sir, cannot you guess? What's a man like me to do? Oh, be thankful my lot is not your own!'

'Then if not Hull where then are you making for?' and now the sigh seemed to break his very heart.

'Before I'd opened my mouth, sir, that forester'd seen through me like glass! As clear as day he'd seen through me, that cannot find the heart to dissemble like some! Poor lollbrueders such as us—' and Gandelyn looked up from his egg-smirched hood.

'Poor what?'

'When he said one man goes into the Forest and another comes out—nay, then he'd said it all!'

'I mean the word you used. Poor something.'

'Poor cellites, sir—we are from Ghent—'

'No, the other word.'

'Lollbrueder, sir? It is a lay-hospitaller and a singer of hymns for the dead.'

'Say it again,' and when the foreign-sounding vowel had been repeated, 'Lollbrueder. I have never heard of them. Are they of Rome?'

'Assuredly, sir. When they would have shortened our habit holy Gregory himself said we were to be let be. In our own country we are permitted a chapel with a bell.

But here the ignorant, taking the word to mean a lollard, cast stones at us and set the dogs on us as heretics.'

'Loll-*brue*-der. It is strange I should not have heard of them. Did you say they are from Ghent?'

The leafy ride they had entered ran straight, now a friendless man had met a friend, and bit by bit as Gandelyn questioned him out came the rest of his lugubrious story. By trade he was a weaver of fine woollen cloths, but they were for shrouds for corpses. Besides singing hymns for the departed he laid them out and washed them, not as the Lord Abbot washed the feet on Holy Thursday, feet already washed, but as he found them. He dug graves, and lacking those of his own kind to bury became a cadaverator of diseased animals, lighting the pyres in desolate places by night. In short, the sunny ride so began to take on the shades of a Maison Dieu that out of the very excess of the gloom the droll side began to peep forth again.

'Think o' that!' said Gandelyn, as Stephen Hurst had said before him. 'It's Lollbrueders for mirth! And what prison did you break out of that you should be seeking sanctuary in Durham?' but the gravedigger only sighed out his midriff again.

'They can make light of such things who have never known them, sir,' and Gandelyn broke into a laugh.

'Who, I, who not a week ago stood on the edge of a lyng-house? Come, loll us a hymn as we go,' but with an appealing look Jan Schmidt showed the loaf of bread under his arm.

'Since yesterday, sir, I have fasted. But for you I should not have bread to eat now, for I am forbidden to beg. If I have your leave—' and without waiting for it he began to cram himself as if he had not eaten for a week.

But he could talk as he munched, and now it appeared that even in his extremity he was not without his plan.

Not a word did he let fall of whatever his offence had been; now, penitent, he wanted no more than to make a fresh start in his own trade, in some place where nothing would be remembered against him. The place he had in mind was Beverley, and at the name Gandelyn pricked up his ears.

'What place?'

'Beverley, sir. There they suffer neither coroner nor sheriff to meddle in their affairs. All they ask of a man is his trade, if he shows himself diligent and of good conduct they have made grithsmen of some, and some have even risen to be burgesses of the town.'

'So! And when were you last in Beverley? Making shrouds for the Black Death?'

But the quip fell flat. In cutting Jan Schmidt's hair Durham had cropped to the wood, of humour he had none, and seeing the heavy sum in arithmetic he made of it the jester was at trouble to keep his countenance.

'Nay, young sir, you misreckon. Few live to such an age as that would make me. The Black Death was nearly a hundred years ago,' and Gandelyn chuckled softly.

'No matter. So it was, but let it pass. I was only about to ask you whether in Beverley you'd ever heard the name of Hartlip spoken.'

'Friend, I have not been in Beverley these twenty years.'

'Have you not? Well, twenty might be about the time. Say twenty.'

'Hartlip. What sort of a man and of what trade?'

'Not a man. A woman. Leastways if there was a man he'd be in France at the time. But some of them don't grieve long in loneliness, so for discipline they say they branded her. 'Tis certain they wealed her back for her.'

'A woman's back, sir, would be work for another woman, as it might be one of our own schwesteren. Yet

stay a minute. Somewhere I did hear of such a one. Later
she took up with healing too, though in no such way as we
account lawful. Had she any name besides Hartlip?'

'Efga.'

'Skilled in herbs?—But it has gone from me, and they're
strict in Beverley, and a likelier place to find that sort
would be somewhere in the Forest,' and from the rate at
which he went on tearing at the loaf there would soon be
scarce half of it left.

But there are outcasts so despised that what hardship
will not wring from them they will yield up of themselves
at a befriending. Heartened by his meal of bread he knelt
at a brook to swill it down with water. At the brook he
also washed Gandelyn's hood, wringing it out again and
making himself his clothes-horse till it should have dried.
He still walked a few paces ahead as he had been ordered,
but now it was to put the boughs out of his benefactor's
way and to warn him of stones and roots across the path,
and at one of these services Gandelyn stopped suddenly in
his walk. As another whipping bough was held aside,
Gandelyn saw that the puckered eyes were moist with
springing tears.

'Now who's mare's dead?' he demanded, and at that Jan
Schmidt broke completely down.

'Oh sir! The more I think of it the more it comes over
me, all I have to bless you for this day! Like an angel
dropped from the skies you appeared in my need! But oh
sir, sir! Why had you to use my good name like that?' and
Gandelyn could only stare.

'*I* use your good name!'

'Miscalling me, and saying I was a swillpot and telling
them I cast spells on brockets! The brockets, sir, as all
dumb animals, we can but commiserate with them, and
rarely do I eat of their flesh, but to say the devil was in
me, sir, and lay on me the wickedness of sorcery—'

And at that there broke from Gandelyn such a laugh as he had not laughed for a year. It was not to be believed! He laughed, he laughed again, and it was minutes before he could get his breath.

'Nay then,' he gasped at last, 'I cannot have done it so much amiss after all! Addling eggs with squinting at them! Her in the doorway dropping her bread as if it had an adder in it! Those oafs on the grass—that forester when I knocked his pot of ale over—' and again he laughed till he was weak.

'And I healed no lay-brother of any palsy, sir, nor have I any such skill—'

'Ha ha ha!'

'And as for finding pennies in my sleeve—'

'Ho ho ho!'

'And then as we came away, and looking round I saw you with your teeth bared like fangs, raging about you with your cloak—'

'Oh my sides! What, like this?' and he set himself as if to perform the antic all over again.

'No sir, not even in jest—I beg of you—'

' "Basilisk!" There's a word should have a jape to stiffen the hairs on your head—'

'If indeed any Lord Abbot ever intervened for me, sir—' and again Gandelyn held his sides.

'No more, Jan Schmidt, no more! If you can do this on dry bread and a swill of water what would you not do on a peppered haunchbone and a bellyful of ale! My ribs, my ribs! . . . Yet set your face again as it was a moment ago—nay, keep it as it is—ho ho ho. ho ho!' and up against the lollbrueder he reeled as further from Pennypocket and the Vale they continued to wend.

II

His final instructions had not been given him by Brother Isidore. Judge of his consternation when, presenting himself at the appointed hour in the sub-prior's cool parlour at the end of the chapter-house passage, he had found it as hot as a furnace with the irascible presence of Netherby's Lord Abbot himself. And here was a churchman of another colour, and he had heard the blusterous words even before Brother Baruch had opened the door.

'Men! Anyone would think we lacked men! There are two hundred men at Cawood now! In Hexham there are twice as many! Brother, your law takes too long!'

'Men at sixpence a day each,' but the captious legal voice had been borne stormily down.

'Six apple-pips! Stop work on the tower! Put a few masons into breastplates! Did Bowet stand looking at sixpence a day? Sick as he was, he had himself carried on his litter to Berwick! With their weapons in their hands he blessed them, and these were tough Scots, not a rabble of market-rogues and sheep-stealers! One can wait for ever for your law! This—' and round with a glare he had suddenly swung, '—is this the youth?'

'This is he.'

'They tell me that in France you served with the lord John. Served him how?' and Gandelyn had trembled at the knees.

'Most reverend father and lord, in carrying his letters and privy messages.'

'No more?'

'In certain watchings and listenings for him that may not be spoken of—in mingling with all sorts and finding out what I could——'

Ten minutes had sufficed. At the end of them his capacity
had been conceded.

'Then see if you can do as much for our holy House!
Sixpence a day! Word shall be sent to Hexham within the
hour! Brother, let Cawood hold itself in readiness! Then
instruct this youth particularly in his part. If he bears himself well in it, well. But let him beware how he bungles it.
We want none that come running and whining back to us
with a tale of failure, for we shall know neither them nor
their names! Enough, about it,' and, sweeping his robes
together and fuming like a thurible, out of the parlour
Netherby's metropolitan had thumped.

And truly a man might boast that he mingled with all
sorts who could take up with such a companion as Jan
Schmidt, but now for an hour past his captive had also
been his guide. The way by which they had left the clearing
swung back so clearly in the direction of the Vale again
that they had left it, and up rough and rising ground had
taken a bridle-path that led ever deeper into the thickness
of the wood. But Jan Schmidt seemed in no doubt as to the
way, and for some time past Gandelyn had been wondering
how, entering the Forest one man, he intended to leave it
another. It was of this very thing that his guide suddenly
spoke.

'You'll be asking yourself where we're making for, sir,
but have no fear,' he said. 'There should be a mete-post
hereabouts, and unless God's taken him one dwells hereby.
I'm never in these parts but I visit him. He is of our own
persuasion, but so far gone in years that no man knows his
age—'

But he broke abruptly off, his wrinkled eyes hard fixed
on something ahead. In the same moment Gandelyn too
saw it, the mete-post of which he had spoken, and such
posts marked the boundaries of purviews and preserves
and it was a grave offence to disfigure or remove them.

But a disfigurement such as that that the next moment came into full sight was hardly less heinous in the Forest than sacrilege in a church. It was still the middle of the fence-season, of all the beasts in the Forest the hart is the noblest. None the less, where the slender upspringing bracken should by now have stood almost knee-high, tramplings and signs of a mortal struggle showed where a staggard of the fourth year had been newly slain and decapitated. The maned and antlered head, hacked raggedly off, had been stuck up on the top of the post itself, and the dried blood and mucus about the dead nostrils were already a crawling of black flies.

It was the open derision and challenge of the affront that had set Gandelyn's eyes so suddenly a-stare. It is the craft of the poacher never to leave such traces behind him. But the next moment he was looking not at the head but at Jan Schmidt, for the lollbrueder was moaning and wringing his hands like a demented man.

'Wah wah!' he wailed. 'What a sight, what a sight!' and so toppingly was the object lodged on its perch that as a bird alighted on an antler-point and began to preen itself it looked like falling to the ground. Now Jan Schmidt was running this way and that as if to see how far the traces extended.

'See, his morning fumets still on the ground!' and picking up his gabardine to his bandy knees he sought to scatter the droppings with his feet, while Gandelyn watched him with half-closed and suddenly suspicious eyes. All this to-do over a dead staggard!

'And you a cadaverator, Jan Schmidt!' he thought, but Jan Schmidt was looking anew at the clotted nostrils and the great hairy ears and redoubled his wah-wah-ing.

'It is not to be made light of, sir! Would I'd a spade to bury it! Do you see aught of an arrow about? Wah-wah! Let this be found and within an hour we shall have the

posse out with horns and dogs, and a proclamation and
every man's house entered! Great and small will be
questioned alike—they'll have holy Joachim out of his
cell—as for a poor wretch like myself, safe in no place—
wah wah!'

But Gandelyn saw none to question nor anywhere
houses to enter, and he knew nothing of Jan Schmidt more
than Jan Schmidt himself had told him, and now if he
feared only lest his own skin should be scratched gladly
would he have been rid of so whimpering, spiritless a
fellow. 'All sorts,' was easily said; and now by the look of
it the wood seemed to be thinning to some crest or top,
and he spoke with sudden asperity.

'Say when it's your pleasure we should make a move,
or do we stand looking at this cabbage of a thing for the
rest of the day?' he cried, and giving the fumets up as a bad
job Jan Schmidt sighed deeply, gave the head a parting
groan, and took up his Durham staff again.

He had guessed rightly about the wood. A little higher
up it ended at a ridge, and spread out below them lay a long
oval dell or glade through which a streamlet ran, with a
grassy track at its farther side. A high cliff-like scar closed
its upper end, and from the falling away of the land they
seemed to have crossed some ridge or divide, and hence-
forth the ways would run not east but southward and to
the west. No sign of house or hut was to be seen, yet Jan
Schmidt seemed to be attempting some sort of a toilet,
shaking the stickings from his gabardine and scraping the
fumets from his shoes.

'Is this where he lives?' Gandelyn demanded, and Jan
Schmidt looked up with a momentary start. His thoughts
must have been elsewhere.

'Sir?'

'This Joachim you say they'll have out of his cell,' and
the toilet was resumed.

'It is in yonder rock, sir, where he lives on roots and sorrels and water from the stream. He's a hermit this many years, if he still lives, and never do I pass this way—'

'What place is this?'

'—it may be he'll not remember me, so if of your goodness you'd suffer me to go down first—' and picking up his gabardine and using his white staff for a third leg he took his request as granted and began to pick his way crabwise down the slope.

Gandelyn needed no telling that a hermit's life was the holiest of all, so holy that great prelates put on their lowliest weeds and went on arduous pilgrimages to kneel before them; but Jan Schmidt had not fled to Durham for nothing, and now Gandelyn had a number of reasons for keeping him well in sight. The rock rose sheer, and at its foot grew a thorn bush. Before this he saw Jan Schmidt sink to his knees and so remain for some minutes. Then, rising, he thrust his cross upright into the bush. He disappeared, and Gandelyn came to life. His own active legs made short work of the descent, and advancing cautiously he peered in.

But a look and a whiff were enough. If Netherby's fretted fane had failed to keep him he found little to delay him in this gloomy fastness of a rock. There in its heavy twilight the anchorite squatted among his mastications and throwings-away, and the lollbrueder was on his knees before him, feeding his co-religionist with morsels of bread. He had a glimpse of a dim vastness of unkempt beard, the toothless orifice that pouted like that of a fish for the crumbs, the spillings, two blue eyelids dropped like cockleshells over purblind eyes, and in that same moment something else caught his eye. The holy man still had his natural needs. Through the vegetable fermentation a shuffling path had been swept to some yet inner portion of the rock, and from this there emanated the odour of some latrine or jakes. Also along this path something was stealthily advancing. He saw a pair of beady bright eyes, a pointed and whiskered nose, a tail—

Rats too, by the Rood! How long was it since he had hunted a rat? A year fell from him in a moment. His holly-stick was in his hand, lightly he leapt, struck, missed and sprang again. Have at you, my whiskered Monsieur!

But the two leaps had sufficed. Straight past the hermit and his devotee they had landed him in a rock-chamber, irregular, lofty, and by far more commodious than the outer cell. From a crack high above his head a dim greenery of daylight trickled down through ivies and bryonies and tangles of brambles. But it was on what had been done in the face of the rock itself that his eyes were fixed in fascination.

So *this* was what they called a catacomb! Yet Brother Baruch, who had seen many of them, had always spoken of them as vast labyrinthine places, their galleries extending for miles underground, ghoul-haunted, their ancient masonry fallen in, silent cities of the dead over whose ruin the myriad living feet unheeding moved.

This gravedigger and his trade!

Yet when Jan Schmidt dug a grave it was in loam or clay, whereas here the loculi were chiselled in the rock itself. When Joachim's time came he had the choice of no more than four of them, two above and two below, and no sanctified bones rested in them now. The first object on which his eyes alighted was a net, with a tangle of ropes and pegs for setting it. This, being bulky, occupied the whole of one of the lower recesses. The adjacent one showed a spring-trap with its cords loosened about it, a large flaying-knife and a number of crocks and pots. Greases? Limes? Soot for the face and scents for snares?

Then he looked higher and up crept one of his eyebrows. Soho, friend lollbrueder! Into the Forest one man, out of it another—it was as simple as that!

For there they were, thrust into the upper loculi, the wherewithal to turn a forest-dweller into a swineherd or a hay-ward, a mendicant or a friar, a women even, for hoisting himself up by his fingertips he saw a market-woman's cloak, half hidden under a man's leather jerkin. That grizzled head that Durham had cropped was not so wooden after all!

And as suddenly as he had seen he was aware of flatness and disappointment. A few nets and greasy disguises, the petty lawlessnesses of the Forest, the poor man's need of something for his pot, the Simon Grindrod work, the ignoble part that Matthew Poole would have fastened upon himself: did his discovery amount to no more than this? And as he stood there, disillusioned and thumbing his jaw, he was aware of Jan Schmidt behind him again, his face drawn to its most lugubrious furrows yet.

'He knows!' he all but wept. 'I had to tell him! Oh that more misfortune should light on that venerable brow! But let them come with their dogs. They'll but find him as ever, at his prayers,' and slowly Gandelyn's eyebrows began to twitch.

'So! He knows!'

'Yet his first thought was for the schwesteren. And pray God that feast of bread doesn't lie too heavy on his stomach! So I left him to sleep while he could.'

'As who would wake him! And yet, Jan Schmidt—'

'Sir?'

'For one that's said his farewell to the world isn't his wardrobe a thought more extensive than you'd look to to find in a Forest? You've but to cry "Joachim, shop!"—' but at the irreverence the lollbrueder trembled all over.

'Oh sir, speak not so lightly in this hallowed place!'

'Schwesteren too if that's a woman's cloak I see on the shelf there—'

'No more than four of them, sir, that bring him his food, for he's nigh blind and only comes in here to his stool—' but Gandelyn could hold in no longer.

'While the tidy lads come tiptoe past him, and back in their ploughing-smock again the next morning, and that's the way staggards' heads get on poles?' and it went home, for now Jan Schmidt tried to pass his confusion off with flattery.

'One can see your eyes miss nothing, sir. There at the alestake, when up out of the ground you popped, "There's a young gentleman that sees all," thinks I, "yon forester, them on the grass, her with the bread, all!" But, sir,' and his voice became that of one who has received some deep inner wound, 'have I hidden aught from you? Freely and of myself did I not confess my simple plan? And now have I not brought you to the place itself?' and again Gandelyn considered it.

'So you did, Jan Schmidt, so you did.'

'And now, if you're so minded, cannot you tell whom you will? Did you rescue me from one to betray me with the pack of them on my heels? Oh sir, it's little you know of the ways of this Forest if you think we've not been followed! That sinful head on the post—oh, Jan Schmidt, Jan Schmidt, trust none, old or young!' Then, as he ceased to wring his hands, 'Friend, this gabardine on my back would make any housewife a good kirtle. If there's six-pence in the bargain I'll make it good when I get back to my trade again—' and Gandelyn first grimaced, then bustled.

'Have done. If it's your skin you're shaking for you can keep it unwhipped for me. And I'd not ha' missed seeing this jakes of yours for a book of ballads, but I've smelt fresher places, so let's be about something. Which of this

finery are you fancying for yourself?' and up shot his stick
and down a bundle of it came. 'How say you to the king
of the charcoal-burners or a knacker's apron? Come, all's
at your choice!'

But no gear for Corpus was here, chasubles lent by the
church or crowns from the goldsmiths' guild. The Lazarus-
garments lacked nothing but the fleas, and as Gandelyn
turned them over with his stick Jan began to shuffle out of
his Durham gabardine as if time now pressed. Now for
high spirits Gandelyn might have been back at the alestake
again.

'Come, your pick, where you will and all a price!' he
broke out. 'Here's a ditching-robe of the finest—or in that
leather jacket that hugging the goodwife you could be one
of these blades back from Picardy with twenty dead French-
men to his score—' but the fugitive shook his melancholy
head.

'Merry sir, what it is to be young!'

'Out o' these pots I could paint a fine festering sore on
you or a boil that wouldn't heal—' and now with his lean
hams tucked up under him Jan Schmidt sat in nothing but
an old patched shirt with a bladder tied about it such as
serves the poor for a purse. He was drawing on a pair of
leather-seated breeches that laced at the knees, and also to
his hand was a square of frieze with a hole in it like a
soldier's cape. When Gandelyn asked him why he preferred
these before the rest he answered between tugs at his laces.

'It's plain you've never sat on a loom-bench, young sir.
With bones as sharp as mine weaving comes heavy on the
seat. You say? The jerkin to go with the breeches? Not in
the Forest, sir, never in the Forest. Jerkins smack too
much of weapons. I count not that poniard of yours, which
suits with your degree—and for gravedigging what's
handier than a soldier's cape, that you can turn till the
mud's dried off it again?'

At last he was ready. On his shorn head was an olive-green cap of fustian, but the breeches only showed his thin legs more warped than before. The head-hole of the cape almost let a shoulder through too, and now he began to wah-wah again.

'Would that shameless head were buried! It cannot be but in a place like this there must be a spade,' and hardly had he spoken the words before he found it, a short one such as miners use, which he slipped out of sight under his cape. Even Gandelyn did not see him slip anything else out of sight with it, and now that he was ready he had only one more request to make.

'Never, sir, shall I receive our Joachim's blessing again. Approach the mete-post warily, sir, for we know not how close behind us they are. In five short minutes I'll be with you—I feel my tears rising to think I shall see him no more—'

So if five minutes were any good to him for God's sake let him have them, and he left Jan Schmidt once more among the garbage, bare-headed and on his knees.

The mete-post was still as they had left it, and down on the nearest tussock Gandelyn placed himself to wait. As well be eating his supper while he was about it, and his viands were in his pouch, leathery to look at but rich with compressed nutriment, deer's meat wrung of its blood and dried. A little was due to co-religionists who would never meet on earth again, and perhaps the schwesteren had arrived with the eremite's own earthy repast.

Then, to save Jan Schmidt's time, he began to cast about for a suitable burial-place for the head. But beneath its leaf-rot the ground was matted with tough roots and stones, and finding himself back at the crest again he made a box of his hands, set his knuckles to his lips, and blew a hollow fluttering call. No call or other sound answered it, and down he sat again.

Perhaps it was the white cross still sticking in the thorn-bush that first brought the surmise to his brow. To be sure, with a green cap on his head and a pair of leather breeches on his buttocks Jan Schmidt would be best without a Durham cross now, yet somehow to see it still in the bush had seemed an earnest of his presence. Now, his eyes suddenly glooming darkly over, Gandelyn was striding back down the hillside again at thrice his former pace. This time he made no bones about looking boldly in. There in the twilight the hermit still nodded among his roots and leavings. But neither bruder nor schwester was with him, and at a bound Gandelyn was once more in the jakes behind.

He had left the place a disorder of scattered garments. Now all had been put methodically back into the loculi, with the exception of one implement. It was the spade all the to-do had been about. There among the weeds it lay, with the rat once more peeping brightly from behind it. And one other tool also had gone. It was the flaying-knife he had last seen among the pots of grease and powder. Armed, Jan Schmidt had shown him his heels and his leather backside, and there was no reason why he should not have been on his way for the best part of an hour.

Washburn-in-the-Forest

So little learned, to close the book on learning,
The armour watched to leave the high emprise—
The wings, the vision, yet already turning
To seek the own-truth in another's eyes—

And so to glimpse the wherewithal to measure
All truth too true for use, too high for guide,
Too pure for currency, unspecied treasure
No man has change for and so waves aside—

Count not the gain but in the rich alighting
Nor loss but riches missing of their hour;
All yellows mingle in this dusty plighting
Of pollen pulsate at the first-seen flower;
Kiss and be done, and so on neither's head
The lack, the mask, the sword hid in the bed.

Never had humiliation so stuck in his throat. He, the spirited one, the leader, himself led by the nose, out-wheedled, out-contrived, packed off to eat his supper among a staggard's fumets, while this crottle of a fellow slipped like a grass-snake away! Jan Schmidt, the scavenger, the butt, witless, humourless Jan Schmidt, for whom like Herod in the play every cowclap he got in the face was as good as a rise in wages!

Yet come to think of it, which is the fitter instrument for the work that some hands must do that others may be kept clean—the lancegay lad with a wit sharpened at both ends, to be seen and noted and remembered when he is seen again—or him of the shadows, the swallower of every indignity, the letter-laugh so long as the laugh is his in the end? Have done, Robert Gandelyn, if this is to be your trade! Eat you peck like the rest of us, and learn from your master how it is done!

But he had little time in which to rage. Flushed with mortification he had wandered off down the streamside, knowing nothing of his whereabouts except that that thin grassy track must lead somewhere. It was the evening stillness, before a frog drummed or a warbler cleared his throat. There was scarce wind enough in the glen to have drifted a spider's filament across his face. And suddenly all this evening quietude was shattered by the winding of a horn.

The blast was as long and sustained as breath could make it. When it ended it had not finished, for three short blasts followed it, then again the long note and the triple

alarm. Such a commotion could only mean that the head
on the post had been discovered, and it was no business of
his to advertise his own presence. Columnar trees closed
the glen's lower end as Joachim's rock the other, and
swiftly he made for the shelter of them. But scarcely for a
score of yards did they hide him. A vista became golden
ahead, an effulgence and a dazzling met him full in the
eyes, and he stood still, blinking and peering about him.

Woodsmen had been at work, felling oaks. Strown
about a clearing eight or ten of the giants lay scattered
among their sawn-off butts, and it was the season of the
year that loosens the cortex from the underwood, yet
where the breadths of bark had been flayed away the
milky glistening had creamed over again within the hour.
The greater branches had been cut again and dragged
aside to make working-room, and in the tangled rampart
of brushwood that ringed the clearance in a thousand birds
were busy. The suspended dust of the massacre spun with
the globules of midges that made the air a dance and maze
of gold, and as Gandelyn stood there, with the ichor of the
sap and the tang of the sawings in his nostrils and the
sound of the horn still in his ears, there detached itself
from the sun-shot tangle a small figure, the figure of a
naked child.

As naked as at her birth, which might have been two or
two-and-a-half years before. Now she was of an age to
walk with a sort of stumbling firmness, and round-bellied
as a tuber, mired to her crumpled knees, she was plashing
through a puddle where trampled debris and flakings of
bark made a quag of the stream. It was hardly to be supposed that a truant so small was not being looked for.
Beyond the maze of brushwood there was an agitation of
yellow as the tufts of a palm-willow moved. There the seeker
stood, and Gandelyn was looking at the child no longer.

Yet surely such a figure belonged to no Arras, but

rather to the border where the geese are driven and the poultry fed, the scanty patch tended and the lesser animals are prepared for the pot. In threadbare sacking such as that across her shoulders those who work among the bark carry their gleanings away, and their hands are imbrued with the tan and for strangers they have hostile looks. But she had not seen him yet, standing motionless there where so few strangers came. Her eyes were ranging for the child, and she opened her mouth as if to call. Then out of the quag the infant paddled, in that same moment she saw the intruder. Into two eyes lost in the colour of all else about them there leapt a pale and grimy glare as she bounded forward. Protectingly she snatched the child between her knees. He had a momentary glimpse of two uncovered shoulder-blades, a breast-channel, and again the inimical glare. Then the sacking was wrapped close about the child.

At any other time he would have found twenty things to say. He was not there to steal the child. If it was the horn it could hardly be any concern of hers. Aptest of all, which was the truth, he could have told her that he had missed his way, would be glad if she could tell him his whereabouts, and it was for this last that he was opening his mouth. But in that self-same moment, before he could get a syllable out, commotion was upon them. There was a rending of branches, men's voices grew loud. There crashed from the brushwood and bounded into the clearing a great unlawed mastiff, with a hot and cursing man struggling to check it by the tree-rope wound about his waist. They were the returning woodsmen, five or six of them with axes and irons, swarming into the clearing and vaulting the fallen trees in their haste, and as they ran the man with the mastiff bawled to the girl over his shoulder.

'Away with you home, Echo! Tell Efga to get summat for this brach o' mine, a swaddling for his feet or a brew to stretch him out sick!'

With the onrush of the men he had placed himself at her side. She too must have loosed her hold on the child, who finding herself at liberty again had tottered off to the nearest bole, shedding her covering as she went and as naked as before. But as the other sounds diminished the silence of the clearing was tingling now with a name. It was not one of the commoner names. He had heard it first from the dying Sir Matthew. Next Stephen Hurst had known it, and even Jan Schmidt had had a fancy he had heard it before. Now he heard it flung over a man's shoulder as he ran.

But now without her sacking the girl stood in her smock and petticoat only, and she had stuffed a handful of this last into her waistband, showing her scratched ankles and feet as bare and mired as the child's. Turban-wise about her head she had wrapped a breadth of old poaching-netting, hiding her hair completely, and instead of glaring palely at him now her eyes were shifting evasively from his cloak to his boots instead. Her arms, stalk-white where they issued from her torn shift but bark-smirched from the elbows down, seemed the slighter for the topheaviness of her head-wrapping, and now that he had heard the name he had given a quick, foreknowing and intuitive gasp. He found his voice.

'Is your name Hartlip?'

The long muscle started out from her ear to her neck-pit as swiftly she turned her head. 'Judith!' she called sharply.

'And is Efga your mother, Efga Hartlip, sometime of Beverley?'

For if so one of his errands was unexpectedly accomplished; but even when he had repeated his question she still watched him with that look of half-animal wariness. The child, intent on her small affairs, had clambered to a stump, but still the forest-girl's eyes were on him and his cloak. Best to take matters into his own hands. Her piece of sacking lay only a stride away, and stooping he picked it up. Not a fingertip came near her as he dropped it over her shoulders, but from her lips came a muted little sound. At the worst he could only be wrong, and the gold was shifting from the glade.

'I come from a place called Newbiggin. I'm seeking a woman by the name of Efga Hartlip. If that's your mother, take me to her.'

Again her lip trembled. Then she fell back, for one dressed as he was dressed to go before.

It was with its burn and its washing that Washburn-in-the-Forest began. Not far below the clearing the meander from the rock he had left was joined by a fuller stream. The confluence of the two was dammed, with planks for crossing, and a higgle-piggle of props and poles on the farther bank made a drying-ground for the clothes. But no women knelt on the flat stones, and with the way to lead she had picked up the child, whose face looked solemnly back at Gandelyn past the bunch of netting on her head. But her burden was not far to carry. Suddenly across a plank there dashed a gaunt dishevelled woman with a flame of red hair, who broke into a torrent of loud words, but stopped in the midst of it on seeing Gandelyn. As she snatched away the child she kicked the plank away behind her, leaving it half in the stream, anchored only by its peg. When presently Gandelyn asked the girl how far it was to her mother's she answered that it was at the other side of the town, but of town saw he none.

Then at a break of the sunken bank he had a glimpse of it, getting on for a quarter of a mile away. A darkening common was irregularly dotted with isolated trees and dwellings of wood; apparently Efga Hartlip lived in its very last house, and suddenly the girl quickened her step. In time past some seeker for peat or gravel had dug a deep excavation into the streamside. This some later occupant

had enlarged, shoring it up with wood and adding a roof,
and alongside a small herb-patch an outhouse also ran.
Where two boulders split the stream was a stake with a
hand-rope. The girl gave a call of 'Mother!' Then as lightly
as a deer she was gone.

And now he felt like an actor whose opening lines,
rehearsed a hundred times over in his fancy, had vanished
in the moment of his need of them. If only he could have
come with the thirteen-and-fourpence in his hand! But at
least he had another message for Efga Hartlip that in
nature she could scarcely refuse to hear, and as he waited a
light appeared in a small window, only to be immediately
hidden again by the drawing of a thick curtain. It must be
the way of Washburn-in-the-Forest, he thought, to let the
stranger wait. But at last a door opened. The girl called
Echo stood there with a candle to light him across the
water, and his first glance showed him that her shoulders
were no longer bare. At some time or other a forest-guard
had cast away an outworn livery-jacket, and probably by
way of Joachim's jakes it had come into her possession.
She pointed to the rope. He made his way across, and as he
set foot over the threshold something brushed across his face.

Except for a dull smoulder from an earthen hearth the
girl's candle was the hovel's only illumination, and by its
light he saw the object he had walked into. It was a bundle
of dried herbs hanging from a hook, and the whole of the
low ceiling was a grove of similar bundles, that one spark
from the candle would have set ablaze like tinder. As she
shielded the flame with her hand he saw that rickety
shelves sagged with their load of medicines and simples,
as well as less pleasing things, small specimens and flay-
ings, a bat, a lizard, the bones of birds. And now that he
remembered, he had been told that this woman he had
come to see had taken up with healing, though in no way
that some would have accounted lawful. Probably he had

been kept waiting, not only that the daughter might array herself in her jakes-jacket, but that the other also should be ready with her stock-in-trade, and next his eyes fell on the red glimmer on the hearth. An iron crock hung over it by a chain. About it were scattered various pipkins and an iron spoon or two, and in a high-backed chair, before a three-legged table, there awaited him the mistress of the establishment herself. (Since when, he wondered, had witches made their abodes by the side of running water?)

But he was little prepared for what happened next. A motionless black shape between the arms of the cratch had moved, but no face was turned to meet his. It was a half-face only, its other half cut vertically off in a black bi-section, and its single eye was fixed on him as, in a voice he judged to be feigned, she asked him who he was. As startled as if he had seen an apparition, he could only stammer.

'Madam—my name is unknown to you—'

'Are you a priest?' for now the eye was on his hood.

'It is in a sort priestly business, madam—' but an exclamation cut him short.

' "Madam!" That I should live to hear that name again!'

'Madam Hartlip, if you are she—it is no easy matter brings me here—' and the voice in which she took him up was not in the least like marrowfat.

'If it's priestly I warrant it isn't! She says you are from Newbiggin?'

'I am from Newbiggin, madam, and I fear my news—' but there emerged from the black folds that enveloped her a hand far too white ever to have toiled.

'Folk come to me for what hasn't happened. That that's happened is anybody's news. I will tell you your news now. It is that Matthew Poole is dead, and all the Forest knew it ten days ago.'

And that was indeed part of it, and he might have known that it was already abroad, and now he was past his first shock at that half-moon of her face and the place in which he found her. It stiffened him that, knowing that Matthew Poole was dead, she betrayed so little sign of emotion.

'Madam,' he began again, 'I was alone with him when he died. Among other things I was charged to tell you that a certain sum of money—' and her quick start at the word stiffened him still further.

'A certain—? Echo, a stool for this young bachelor!'

'Falling sick on a journey, and having his will on his mind—'

'Sit you down. Sit you down! You said money—you *did* say money?'

'The sum he had in his mind, as wishing to bestow it upon yourself, was thirteen-and-fourpence. This I reported, as was my duty, urging all I could upon those in whose hands it rests. Full weight is to be given to it, even though in the will itself—'

It was the left half of Efga Hartlip's face that was the hidden half, but she still had the use of both her eyes, and slowly she had half risen from her chair. Nor had he forgotten her hapless story, which indeed he had often pondered. High on the walls of Newbiggin's church the cool spandrils were painted with the Seven Corporal Acts of Mercy. There the fatherless were fed and the stranger sheltered, the sick visited and the needy refreshed. But down below this same woman had had it laid on. Thrice round the church, barefooted and with a candle in her hand she had been scourged, and now she had sunk heavily back into her chair again and was muttering.

'What! Has this church not finished with me yet!'

'Madam—'

'His wish, but not in his will! . . . Where is this will and in whose keeping?'

'It is in Netherby's strong-room, madam, and to the utmost of my poor power—'

It was the bitterer that it did not break out. The girl, placing the candle on the table, had retired into the shadows again. Suddenly the white hand caught the candle up and thrust it before his face.

'Put that hood back! What is your name?'

'Robert Gandelyn, madam.'

'Aged what?'

'Coming nineteen,' and having satisfied herself that there was such a trusting young fool as this in the world she slapped the candle down on the table again and the next moment there was a crystal in her hand.

'Not in the will! . . . Peace while I peer! What's this I see? A strong-room? Nay, was ever such a place! Plate and jewels and agnuses of gold—chalices for the altar and great ewers—but thirteen-and-fourpence for Efga Hartlip, that would but ware it on her sinful pleasures! But maybe such a fleabite's got pushed away into some corner—' and she made a mock of turning the crystal this way and that in search of it. 'Nay, I see it not! I see nought of the thirteen-and-fourpence that would have put her daughter into some decent household, with seemly folk, and taught broidery or some honest occupation—' and out of the shadows came a full-voiced wail.

'Mother—do not start it—' but it only became the louder.

'No, not set up in some quiet town to ply her needle, not as long as there are pigs in the Forest to tend and all Washburn to fetch and carry for and everybody's pot to scour! Not while there are whips to buy, for sinners, and churches to paint with holy pictures—' and now round she turned on the messenger himself. 'And have you sought me out for this, young man, to tell me a tale of a will with all left out of it and priests that say it shall be borne in mind?'

And even Stephen Hurst had asked what sort of an end he had made, and her hardness revolted Gandelyn, so now to finish. In his pouch was something that even Netherby could hardly claim, and as he rose and drew forward his hood his fingers went to the buckle. Without a word he placed it on the table before her, and as if by some miracle it might have been the thirteen-and-fourpence after all her fingers went to the linen wrapping. The next moment, rigid as death, she was gazing at it out of the half-eclipse of her face. It was the unfinished garment he had found in the chest that was bolted to the beam.

And now he knew what that initial was into which the needle had been left sticking all these years. But the baby Echo had never worn that garment. Year by year she too had grown up, first an uninhibited infant, as uninhibited as the infant Judith who by every token was a female child, then, an infant no longer, had begun to imitate the ways of any a few months or a few years older than herself, and so to that day when suddenly and mysteriously she had needed no more telling. But again from the shadows she had started forward with a cry.

'Mother! What is it?'

Now Gandelyn saw the rest of Efga Hartlip's face. She petted and farded it—somewhere he had heard she had even tried to paint it—but the falling forward of her head had disarranged its wrappings. Straggles of iron-grey hair escaped from them. He saw the blanched cheeks and blood-less lips, satiny-faint in its pucker the other cruel mark. She had thought it was all behind her when she had come to Washburn's very last house. Now for her livelihood she interpreted their dreams, cured dog-bites with pennyroyal and a hair and quinsies with lard from a stuffed and drawn cat. Doubtless they believed of her that at night she turned herself into a hare, re-entering her human shape the next morning.

But for the church that had disciplined her she would have mingled graveyard moss with curses and spittle, and tremblingly the bloodless lips moved.

'It was—for a christening—'

'Quick, catch her, sir—'

' "E" for—as it might have been—'

'The hartshorn—' and the girl in the forester's jacket sprang to get it.

It was she too who, with her ear at her mother's lips, presently had to interpret the whispers that were inaudible to Gandelyn. Efga Hartlip's eyes closed, her fingers trembled over the tiny garment, and the younger voice was less loud as she passed the broken murmurs on.

'She wants to know when you left Newbiggin.'

'Tell her six nights ago.'

'She's asking you if the little chamber at the stairhead's still the same,' and he nodded. It was used for saddlery and harness now, but best say it was still the same.

'The swallows outside, she says—'

'It's too early in the year yet, but there's their nests,' and next it was the little garden by the well. It was long since Newbiggin had had a garden, and now the porch of the courthouse covered the well too, but out of common pity he answered that never had he seen garden more beautiful, and now the girl herself faltered.

'She wants to know where you found that—that that you brought—'

But he was spared this last invention. Suddenly Efga Hartlip slept in her chair.

To see wise-women into their beds was no business of Gandelyn's. Again the girl had tiptoed away, and a half-door beyond the hearth evidently led to the sleeping-chamber they shared. She dropped the blanket that closed its upper half, and again he looked round the kitchen at the herbs hanging from its ceiling, the huggermuggery of its shelves, the iron spoons on the hearth, and back at the sleeping woman. The single window was latticed but unglazed, and so that the curtain that closed it should not blow inwards a number of stones from the beck had been set along its ledge. Suddenly he started on his stool as one of these rolled to the floor. The curtain was being poked or picked at by somebody outside, and the next moment he was on his feet. The outer door had opened, and into the kitchen there stalked the great mastiff he had seen that afternoon among the fallen oaks.

Almost before he could hood himself his master followed. He too was the same man who had bawled over his shoulder as he ran, and now he was to be seen as a huge lurching fellow with a thick throat and bulging choleric eyes. The mastiff, advancing straight to Gandelyn, began to snuffle him up and down, turning to his master for his instructions, but the man was staring in a half-wit's stupor at Efga Hartlip's uncovered face. Only with the lifting of the curtain and the return of the girl did he swing angrily round.

'What did I tell you about this brach o' mine, Echo Hartlip?' he demanded. 'Ha' you got that poultice ready?'

But the girl who was at everybody's beck did not reply, and the nosing dog was waiting only for a sign, and now the bull-necked fellow was glowering at Gandelyn.

'Who's this you ha' here? I tell you my dog shall be lawed for no man! I'm leaving him with you, and if they're here before morning see he's covered up i' your bed! Let be, Cham!' for the animal had given a dangerous growl. 'Strangers i' Washburn! And up at the rock a flaying-knife's missing, and a green cap and a pair o' breeches with a leather arse! My dog maimed! Not while my name's Will Acle! And what's smittled *her?*'

But at his raised voice Efga Hartlip had opened her eyes

again, and in a trice her hands had flown to her face-cloths. She had started from her chair and was on her feet, bale blazing from her eyes as she pointed to the door. Hurriedly crossing himself the man fell back, and with a deep 'Woof!' the animal too cowered backwards to the door.

Five minutes later Gandelyn had besought the shelter of their outhouse for the night.

II

But not to sleep in that tumbledown shed that ran from the dwelling to the babbling beck. By the light of her candle the girl had moved a litter of sacks and pots and implements from a trestle with two planks on it, and the business he now had in hand was not to be done with every eye on him and every tongue asking who he was. At one end the broken roof-boards admitted light enough, and nothing fell with a clatter as he slipped from his planks to the ground. Noiselessly he unhooked the door and stood listening. Indoors, all was quiet, the gurgle of the stream loud as it lapped and chattered past the boulders. He closed the door of the shed behind him, his fingers found the rope, his feet the stones. Then he climbed to the level of the other bank.

The moon, in its first quarter, had already left the sky. In a few hours the sun would be on his way again, but now only a starry mid-while suffused the sleeping earth. The settlement lay a quarter of a mile away on his left, and out towards its common he struck. But he had scarcely gone fifty yards before he stood still again. In the distance, isolated and alone, there burned a light.

But as he drew nearer to it no light could have been milder or more reassuring. There is no community that

settles as Washburn-in-the-Forest had settled, son following his father's trade and his son his again, but here and
there in the generations it provides its own artist-crafts-
man too. So, with no better tools than his fellows, Woodcutter Wilfrid had set up the carving before which he
presently stood. The saint was to be known as Hubert by
the dog at his feet, the hunting-horn at his waist and the
milk-white stag in his wooden arms, with the crucified
Figure between its horns. A shallow pent kept the rains
from him, and the storm-lantern beneath it beamed harm-
lessly down on the couching wooden dog and the children's
posies of wilting spring flowers.

And here too on hunting-mornings the lords of the
Forest assembled with their spearmen and beaters and
dogs, and amid leapings and bayings hurried through a
prayer that their hunting might be blessed; but seeing so
christian a thing as a shrine Gandelyn was wondering
whether Washburn might not possess a church also, and
turning his back on Hubert he scanned the starry vault for
the shape of some spire or tower.

But he saw none, and with Hubert to watch over them
Washburn's men were less to be feared now than their
dogs. Already one animal knew more about him than he
had any liking for, and now in the grey stillness of the
mid-while the dwellings he was approaching seemed inky
islets afloat of themselves, each under its separate oak.
Outside their doorways stood sheaves of withies for
basket-weaving, hives for bees, a cobbler's bench or a
wood-turner's wheel, but of a sudden he dropped flat on
his face. He had stumbled upon something that had set up
a noisy jangling of iron. He held his breath, waiting for
other sounds, but no dog barked, no bolt was shot back.
Washburn slept with a good conscience, and they said the
clank of iron kept the fox away. Rising again, and avoiding
outhouses, he moved on to the other dwellings.

There were perhaps thirty of the houses, but to have seen half a dozen of them was to have seen them all, and already he knew he was wasting his labour, for the economy of the place was simple enough. The more active of the men would be woodsmen, with their secondary occupations as might be. The main of their business would be the timber, its haulage and the bark, oaks for the knees and ribs of ships and the frames of houses, the bark for the tanners' pits and yards; and because of the game these last would be elsewhere. Naturally there would be more or less of netting and snaring, sudden commotion when a horn blew, hurried hidings away, a covering up of traces, and by the time the posse arrived every man at his lawful occupation again. Let those who were paid to stop it earn their wages. None of it was in the least what Gandelyn had been sent out for, and·with a glance up at the Plough he struck across the common, this time with Hubert and his light behind him.

So satisfied was he that there was nothing more in Washburn-in-the-Forest to detain him that he almost missed the wheelmarks at his feet. Yet they were hardly to be missed, for at that point they turned back again in the direction from which they had come. Where a few meagre birches had been hacked at for firewood a light structure of poles and roofing stood among tracks of backings and wheelings and turnings. The ground was a litter of broken bark, the spillings no doubt from the sacks carried on backs and shoulders, and for a moment he had a picture of a forest girl, with a clump of old netting bound about her head and bits of bark lodged in her scantly-sufficient garments. Apparently this was some sort of a terminal depot. At the shed's end a broken old cart stood, left to fall to pieces of itself, and a burnt patch on the ground showed where the carriers were wont to light their fire. Beyond that the wheelmarks converged into a well-used track, and as he stood there, picking out these indications by the wan starlight, for the second time since he had set out he saw ahead of him the glimmer of a light.

But Hubert's mild light stood still, whereas this was a light that moved. It was true too that shrines were not always fixed, for Brother Baruch had told him how the shrine of blessed Gilbert had been carried from place to place, and Brother Baruch knew all about blessed Gilbert, having himself come from the same village in Lincolnshire. But this light, still a furlong or so away, was being carried close to the ground. Intervening objects made it erratic, and at moments put it out completely, and in Gandelyn's nocturnal experience to come upon a man dazzled by his own light was to have the advantage of him. If it was the light of more men than one they were certainly not Washburn men, for by twenty signs he had satisfied himself that these were all in their beds. With infinite heed of snappings and cracklings he advanced along the wheelmarks.

Alas for his disillusion! Suddenly the light disappeared. He stood at the corner of a long low building with a plain central doorway, over the lintel of which was a niche with a slender cross. And he knew that they were to be found everywhere, these hospitals for travellers where the houseless might find a shelter and the hungry pottage and bread and the infirm might even remain till their hour came. Often the rich preferred them to the inns, but this seemed to be one of the humbler establishments. Its door was closed, but it had a porter's aperture, through which he peered. No porter dozed in his chair, nothing moved, and he continued along the frontage to where it ended in a scattering of sheds and possibly a kitchen-garden. Whoever was carrying the light was entering the premises by the back way.

But no door opened or closed. Indistinguishable in the starry greyness a tumbling of miscellaneous objects lay about him, the hospital's domestic discardings, its supplies of fuel, rough mounds, with sheds beyond. Further he could not see, and yet at this hour of the morning somebody was awake, moving about with a lantern in his hand. Past hummocks of earth, stepping over this and that, nearer to the sheds he continued to pick his way.

Then of a sudden he heard a faint metallic clink. It was followed by another, and then by the scraping of a spade. The next moment he saw the light again, not directly, but this time raying dimly up from the ground itself. Somebody was digging a grave.

In an instant he was again flat on his belly, all a-tingle now with exultation and the divination of first intention. In hospitals more than in other places folk were likely to die. He knew there were schwesteren in the neighbourhood, and nobody asks a woman to dig a grave when also passing that way there is a lollbrueder, on his way to Beverley, his trade at their service. The ramparts of earth—what he had taken to be a kitchen-garden—again he heard the clink, the scrape. The upraying from the ground showed him a barrow, battens, a measuring-line, a small pile of clothing. Up came another spadeful, he saw the end of the ladder that projected from the ground.

Softly now, Gandelyn—your hand on the rung and then the quick upward heave—

Without a sound he accomplished it. Then, rising to his feet, he tossed a clod down into the grave.

Jan Schmidt had just put down his spade to take up a mattock. The clod took him in the mid-ridge of his ropy back, which stiffened as if instead of a morsel of earth a paralysis had descended upon him. So suspended were his faculties that for a moment he even seemed about to resume his occupation. The lantern between his bandy legs shone on the leather seat that should have been polishing a loom-bench. He was stripped and shirtless down there, but he had kept his green fustian cap on his head. And as still he remained without motion there reached him from above a civil-spoken voice.

'You're at your work betimes, Jan Schmidt. Who's dead now?'

In removing the ladder he had leaned it against the rampart of upthrown earth. As well sit as stand, and there at his feet lay Jan Schmidt's shirt, his soldier's cape, and the flaying-knife from the jakes. Down on the ladder he sat.

For the young their shining moment of triumph, for the old their sheepishness and discomfiture. Hardly had Gandelyn made himself at his ease before the tension ended. Looking shyly up from the grave Jan Schmidt spoke.

'It's to be seen, young sir, you haven't heard the rule of these places. Always there must be a grave in readiness and another half-dug. The one that's ready, if you'll but turn your head you'll see it, not four paces behind you.'

But—carry no weapons in the Forest and that flaying-knife naked there on his shirt? Gandelyn turn his head, and a mattock slipping suddenly in Jan Schmidt's hand and himself coming by a wipe with it? Jan Schmidt was more than ever to be watched, and in case of surprise the edge of the barrow was a more convenient seat than the rung of a ladder. When he had changed his position he took up the flaying-knife and dandled it lightly in his hand.

'Fie, fie on you, Jan Schmidt!' he murmured softly. 'No weapons in the Forest!' and the gravedigger, looking furtively up, saw the knife daintily balanced on one of Gandelyn's fingertips. There was a flick, it turned a small somersault, and then a second glint joined it. The anlace Gandelyn carried at his belt weighed only a few ounces, the other a pound or more, but as they began to curtsey and dance in the air like ill-assorted partners, Gandelyn gently counted their capers and curvets.

'Ten, eleven, twelve—oh Jan Schmidt, your angel at need, sent to you from the skies, and you use him after this fashion!—Thirteen, fourteen, fifteen—packed off to eat his supper with a staggards' droppings for sauce! And now you cannot look me in the eyes for very shame, but must go on patting and scraping and patting again while you think of some new fetch!—Twenty-one, twenty-two, twenty-three—'

And how if Gandelyn had been at the mete-post when the keepers had come upon that tell-tale head, and where had Jan Schmidt put the new edge on this whittle and sharpened it to such a point? What of the rest of the trickery that even now for a moment reddened Gandelyn's cheeks again? Thirty-six, thirty-seven, thirty-eight, he counted, but so he could have gone on till the sun rose. Forty-one, forty-two—ah, Jan Schmidt thought he had massed that one, but here it was see, behind him—and now Jan Schmidt himself had laid both the spade and the mattock aside. Down there in the grave he admitted defeat, awaited Gandelyn's pleasure, was ready to sue for terms. There he stood with his green cap resting against the earthen wall, his tough and wizened body showing its every rib and strand, lately sweating and now beginning to shiver in the night air, and again the captive looked beseechingly up.

'Sir, I own to it all. I was for shaking you off, yet not as you suppose. As for your finding me here, sir, I have to spend the night somewhere, and what should a grave-digger be doing but working off his supper and his bed with the little he has to give? It is here that the schwesteren live, sir, fetching the wood and water and making the beds and emptying the night-pails.'

'Do they so!'

'Before the lark the poor souls are up, toiling and moiling all day, and then Joachim's food to take to him,

that's nearer six miles than four if you reckon it both
ways—'

'This is a trim edge you've put on this weapon of
yours.'

'—And as for the freedom I took in leaving you, think
no more of it, sir, since the first thing in the morning I
should have been seeking you again,' and Gandelyn looked
up from his trying of the edge of the knife.

'Think o' that! And where would you have looked for
me?'

'At Mother Efga's, sir and friend,' but the rest of the
answer was cut off by a cough.

And what great perspicacity was there in it after all?
Gandelyn himself had been the first to speak that name,
and had been answered that such were likelier to be found
in the Forest than in a settled town. Twenty other things
he had told him too, and now it occurred to him that any
time this last quarter of an hour his prisoner had only had
to raise his voice and the whole hospital would have been
running to see what was happening out at the back there.
Now that he had him what was he going to do with him?
Again the night air started the cough. He wanted no man's
death on his conscience, for a turning of the tables he had
not looked for Jan Schmidt was taking it not amiss, so
truce. He rose from his barrow.

'When do those of your trade call a grave half-dug?' he
asked.

'Sir?'

'Your pardon if I don't turn my head. You said one was
finished behind me. One would say the one you're in was
reasonably advanced. How if I were to throw you down
your shirt?'

One look of gratitude settled it.

'Indeed, my old bones don't take to it the way they
used to,' Jan Schmidt sighed.

'And your cape. But what of this?' and nothing could have been more shamefaced than the foolish glance Jan Schmidt gave to the newly-whetted knife.

'As you please, sir. I have seen what you can do with knives. Trust me or trust me not.'

It seemed pledge enough. If there was to be talk between them it would be freer without sleepers to disturb. Down into the grave went the shirt, the cape, the knife. Then he lowered the ladder also.

'Your scalado, monsieur,' he said 'Montez.'

The morning star queened it alone in the sky. It was the darkness before the dawn, the hospital lay a mile out of earshot behind them. There was an earth-bank over a dry ditch full of last year's leaves, and on this a young man and an old man sat side by side before a bird yet moved in its nest. But it was the young man who was silent while the other, with never a 'sir' or 'young master' now to break his tale, unburdened himself of the bitterest and the most sustaining that his life had taught him.

And Gandelyn himself had travelled as far afield as Burgundy, but never had he been within half the breadth of Europe of some of the places Jan Schmidt's wanderings had taken him to. The son of a poor schoolmaster with an immoderate family, off the lot of them had started, quartering themselves wherever they went upon cellites as poor as themselves. Dragging from town to town and from country to country, with one dying here and another lost sight of there, as far east as Bohemia they had wandered, and back again to Flanders and Brabant. Rome had no time for a following so obscure, they troubled Rome as little. Back in Ghent again, his kin he knew not where, young Jan had learnt his trade of weaving, and hearing of some crossing to Essex had joined himself to them. It was in Essex, later, that he had dug his first grave, and Gandelyn

no longer mused that if there was a trade lower than a
gravedigger's it was the hangman's.

'And I was hotter in blood in those days than you see
me now,' the suddenly-tired voice at his side went on.
'Not hot for such things as are common to youth, but over
things that truly concerned me not, the rights and wrongs
of things as I saw them all about me.'

And now out these came too, the indifference of lassi-
tude, the small injustices slothfully endured, the petty
extortions and wringings, the two hens at Easter, the dozen
eggs at Michaelmas, where a man's corn must be ground.
In England, moreover, he was an outlander, and because
he was a lollbrueder mistaken for a lollard, and so to the
stone-throwing boys and the dogs, as before—

'And you English, you bluster among yourselves, and
vow you'll have no more of it, but none will start it, and
all goes on as before—'

'Keep to the tale, Jan Schmidt.'

So one day in Essex the tax-collector had met with the
accident, and there had been something of a hue-and-cry
about it, but by that time Jan Schmidt had been well away
in Lincolnshire. But in Lincolnshire also tax-collectors
went in fear of their lives, and lawyers slept uneasily in
their beds, and at the manors and courthouses where the
rolls were kept the guards were doubled. Plainly he had
cast in his lot with malcontents and unruly men, and
Gandelyn interposed a meditative word.

'And who met with the accident in Lincolnshire?'

'A name you wouldn't know.'

'So a few more such accidents and there was nothing for
it but Durham and its night-knocker?'

But instead of answering Jan Schmidt did the last thing
in the world Gandelyn would have thought it in him to do.
Placing his clay-stained hand on the young man's knee he
broke suddenly down in a voice strangled with emotion.

'Oh comely youth, that two days ago these eyes of mine had never seen, what is this you have done to me! The gifts and grace that are yours by nature—that in you that for two days has warmed this old heart like the sun itself— oh suffer me this once to speak to you with the freedom and loving-kindness of a father! Cannot you have wit but you must burn your tongue with it? Cannot you set traps but your own foot must be the first to step in them? Mettle- some, unbroke—' the hand trembled and worked on the knee, '—oh while there's time—me, I must go on my way—but you—oh, have nothing to do with it, now nor at any time, root nor twig!'

Gandelyn, affronted and embarrassed, would have drawn away his knee, but the lately-whining voice only shook the more.

'Root nor twig! What is it you seek? Cannot fifty years of bitterness reach out to twenty that knows nothing of it yet? Never will you content those you serve, for what they want they know not themselves! Bring them good news and they'll feast you, but bring them bad and hungry you'll go till you can bring them better! In six short months cannot you see what your study will be? What will it be but what they most want to hear? Is somebody living that should be dead? You'll be ready with it, the net he's in he's bound to be ta'en to-morrow! Is he dead that should be alive? Though I washed and buried him yesterday I shall vow I never saw him in better health! Sent out to watch you'll find yourself watched by them sent out to watch you again, and hearing only lies, lies will become your meat and your drink and the air you breathe! Oh gentle-hearted and merry youth, I have but to look at you as you still are, naught misshapen and all the sweetness of life waiting for you like honey in the comb—oh, it's then I could wish the next grave I dug might be my own!'

And what could such an outpouring mean but that his

own errand was guessed and that Jan of Ghent was seeking
to parley, to divert, perhaps to forestall? And now the
dawn was at hand. Out of the receding night glimmers of
woodland and heath and pasture were beginning to emerge,
birds cheeped, a faraway cock crowed. The crooked hand
still trembled on his knee, but suddenly Gandelyn saw Jan
Schmidt as he had seen him at first, full of fawnings and
wiles, different in nothing but the soldier's cape and the
green cap on his Durham-shorn head. The light broadened,
from a craggy eminence that overtopped the western mists
the first ray of the sun struck a silver glint. In a few
minutes it sparkled like a diadem, and now for Jan
Schmidt's answer. The most baffling of answers is to say
nothing at all, and suddenly Gandelyn raised his finger
and pointed.

'Yon lump of limestone in front of us, Jan Schmidt.
What place now might that be?'

Very slowly the hand was withdrawn from the knee.
The gravedigger's voice was scarcely to be heard as he
replied.

'That, young sir, is a place they call Aptrick.'

'They rise early in Aptrick,' for the silver crag had
houses on it and from their chimneys thin smoke was
rising.

A short back-snuffle came from Jan Schmidt's crooked
nose. Then slowly, ache by ache and pang by pang, he
made shift to pack it all back into his breast again.

'You cannot answer me but so, sir?'

'To be sure I can. Who's these that are making for
Washburn-in-the-Forest so early?'

On the morning air was borne a light jolting of wheels,
which as they drew nearer could be seen to be those of a
low tumbril or cart. To either side of it had been fixed a
light frame like that of a hay-wain, and it was drawn by
three strong dogs, the foremost of them on a trace. In

token that they were licensed for such work they wore brass collars, irremovable except by a file, and as they were for draught their feet had been let alone. The men who accompanied them were four in number, and from the sound of its jolting the cart was empty.

'What are they fetching?'

Now the facile 'sirs' returned in a flood.

'They're tanners, coming for a load of bark, sir, and by your kind leave, sir, I think I'll go back with them and try to get an hour's sleep. It was but my guess you might be at Efga's, but say it's so. Your best way back will not be round past Hubert's, sir, but make for those birches, and keep on till you come to a claypit—'

He was still pointing out the way when the men came up.

And Gandelyn took it, and this time Jan Schmidt had not misled him, for it brought him out by the beck-side at a point only a little lower down the stream than that by which he had left. He reached the boulders and the rope-way. From the closed door and the undisturbed curtain he judged that the mother and daughter still slept. But as he too stretched himself on his two planks again and in three minutes was fast asleep he was played a naughty trick.

For between Arras and the wall there is a dark and narrow cat-walk where those on hidden business move. Stealing like shadows by night, emerging from the morning mists before the rest of the world is astir, rarely are they taken (as they say) 'with the manner,' backbear or bloodyhand. Gandelyn slept, but from a grave behind a wayside hospital there was being lifted at that very moment and placed in a tumbril, with bark-strippings to cover them, a load of pikeheads and whinyards, arrow-heads and bags of bolts, as heavy as three strong dogs could draw.

III

He was awakened by a flurry and a squawking outside his shed, that died away again, and back into slumber he dropped. When next he opened his eyes it was with a feeling that the morning must be far advanced, and slipping from his couch and unlatching the door he found himself looking into the yellow eyes of a goat tethered to a large stone. Fresh feathers strown about the chopping-block showed where somebody had been killing a hen. Refreshed by his sleep he now only needed a pool in which to duck his head, and there were signs that the sun-dappled nook he found, hidden from eyes on the opposite bank by alders, had been used since he had returned that way from his nocturnal prowling. Then, finding Efga Hartlip's door standing open, he stepped to it and looked in.

The night before the place had not lacked of mysterious-ness, but now in the daylight it showed dingy in the extreme. But somebody, as if aware of this, had already been abroad, a great armful of opening purple lilac had been carried in, and of this a display had been made. A great bunch of it crammed into a crock left room for little else on the three-legged table by the hearth. Sprigs of it had been set among the stones on the window-ledge, and now the glitter of the stream on the dancing water outside set the ceiling-herbs too softly a-ripple. Last night he had been offered nothing to eat, now amends were to be made. Over the fire the crock bubbled softly, whatever was cooking in it was beginning to smell appetisingly, and with her back to the door the girl of the oaks stood at a kneading-board, mixing something in a wooden bowl. She still wore the forester's jacket, but her turban of netting had gone. Its removal showed her nape, its hair divided behind and set in a flat round over either ear, and though she had changed her kirtle her feet were still bare. As his shape darkened the doorway she gave a quick turn.

When one has not eaten for eighteen hours there is no trick like the old trick. Probably they had been ashamed to bring out whatever bowl of whey or scrap of salt fish their own last night's supper had been, and now Gandelyn had advanced.

'It's time I was getting on my way, but I couldn't leave without a thanks for my bed and paying my duty to your mother,' he needs must say.

Her bare feet must have been still chill from the cold woodland water, and now he saw that at her neck something glinted. It was the silver musk-ball, scrubbed and scoured and threaded on a string. But the spoon in her hand was suddenly still. He had scarcely heard her voice the night before, but now it was almost startlingly strong.

'But she said I was to kill the hen! She said I wasn't to wake you, because you'd come all the way from New-biggin castle, and I was to milk the goat and make a chervil sauce, and she wants to know about the little garden, and she's getting up now—' and sure enough from behind the half-door there came just such sounds and stirrings.

So as the events of Washburn-in-the-Forest that day are to be related almost hour by hour, let them begin with the ruminative conversation Gandelyn presently held with the family goat outside.

Already the animal had made away with the hen's head. Now she was straining at the stone to get at the feathers strown about the chopping-block, and Gandelyn, seating himself on the stump, addressed her with suitable consideration.

'Think o' that, Nan! Newbiggin castle! It seems we're risen in the world before we know it! . . . Newbiggin castle and its garden! Think o' that!'

He gave himself to reflection for some moments, click-clicked once or twice with his tongue, tossed the animal a tail-feather, and went on.

'And how do you find life in Washburn-in-the-Forest, Nan? Mind you, say not a word about my having been out of my bed last night! . . . And when they've naught to offer you for your supper overnight they kill you a hen for your breakfast instead! Hens in Lent! Yet boiled, with a chervil sauce. . . . Has Echo a light hand for milking you, Nan?'

The animal made a snatch, which he put aside with a mild reproof.

'None o' that, Nannie Hartlip! We know a goat will eat anything, but not my clothes with me inside them! . . . And as it might be one lady speaking of another, you've a lump of stone round your neck, but it's musk-balls this morning for Echo! Musk-balls—rabbit-nets—but New-biggin castle! That pig's ear of a peel! Think o' that!'

But who in his senses sits talking to a goat? The animal made another snatch, this time at his hand. With a 'Plague take you, you yellow-eyed brute!' he let fly a kick at it, then was on his feet. When your presence in Wash-burn-in-the-Forest is already known there is open virtue in showing yourself, and a stroll up the stream would give him an appetite for his lenten fowl. He continued however to talk, not now to the goat but to himself.

He saw the chatelaine-like figure in the doorway as he put his hand to the stream-rope. She had placed herself there as if to receive some guest of high distinction, of her last night's perturbation there was no sign, of the char-latanry of her trade no trace. Like a matron she stood there, her face-cloth in its place, her white hand emerging with such an air from her black garments that for a moment he wondered whether he was being invited to kiss it, and as she greeted him he could well believe that her voice had once been honey-sweet.

'What's this I hear of your leaving us? You must be about your business? Tut, what's a day! Indeed it was a shameful lodging to have offered you, but poor come-down folk can only offer what they have, and truly a week would scarce be too long for all I long to hear!'

The repast too was all but ready. The crock of lilac had been moved from the three-legged table and on it had been set knives, spoons, two small drinking-cups of horn and a larger one of pewter. Platters were keeping hot on the hearth, the place was hot and homely with cooking, and Echo Hartlip was preparing to dish up the fowl. Now she no longer wore even the old green jacket from the jakes. The garment she had exchanged it for was probably some old laying-by of her mother's, a faded crimson surcoat from which the fur had been picked to trim up something else, and Gandelyn was looking at it as if for some future conversation with the goat about it. But on either side of the high chair the stools were set, he must prepare himself to sing for his supper, and in her most gracious voice Efga Hartlip was asking him how he had slept.

'Like a bear in a tree, madam,' and once more her uncovered eye melted with memory.

'Ah, could you but guess the music of that "madam" in my ears!' Then, the little sigh of luxury over, 'And of what did you dream, Master Robert, as you must suffer an old woman like me to call you?'

But he answered that the dream that is told before noon never comes true, and nobody remembers last night's deers-meat when to-day's boiled fowl and sauce mingle creamily together. The mead to edge the appetite for it, Efga Hartlip said, was of her own brewing, and of whatever it was made it tingled in the blood like a cordial. At first Gandelyn fancied it had a faintly earthy taste, but this passed on a second draught, and now he was busily engaged in not-looking at Echo Hartlip. It was only natural that her own eyes, so rustically instructed, should in turn be furtively watching her mother's every movement, and now the kitchen's mistress was loud in her admiration of it that one so young should already have been in France.

'Scarce nineteen, there's advancement!' she flattered him. 'My first husband served in France too, but at getting on for twice your age he was no more than a poor captain of archers! Tell me, is His Grace of Bedford still with the armies and are we still routing them?'

So little however were we routing them that the subject was best not pursued, and as for his own prowess, it is approved modesty in the young that they should speak as if a man might go through twenty wars and come by nothing worse than a sprain or two or a bruised elbow. Therefore, leathering meanwhile into his food, he answered belittlingly and charmingly.

'Madam, there's times you'd scarce call it a war at all. A skirmish or so when they bethink them, then another of their solemn truces—and yet I'll not deny it's an entertainment, with its junkettings and jauntings and the prettiness of it all,' but the chatelaine shook her head in its cloths as knowing better.

'Nay, nay, Master Robert, women as we are we cannot be put off with that for a tale!' and gaily he protested.

'Yet I assure you, madam, though I'm no more than a prentice and a poursuivant, scarce a year in the field, what with their défis and challenges, their gages and gallantries, and the courtly form of it all—' and off at score he went, anything rather than that little garden that had once flowered by Newbiggin's well and the little bedchamber where now the saddlery was kept. The girl was eating little for her watching her mother, of the mead she took only small and bird-like sips. Only once did she flush a little. 'Echo was born in Newbiggin,' her mother had said, and even her flush was only a flitting and a passing, for her natural complexion seemed able to carry an old crimson surcoat or the forester's green as indifferently as it carried the seasons of the year. Once she opened her mouth. She wanted to know what a poursuivant was. It was of her mother that she asked it, but he took it upon himself to answer her directly.

'A poursuivant, Mistress Echo—' he began, and was about to say that a poursuivant was not quite a herald and yet somewhat more than a common runner, but for some reason or other he turned to the mother again. 'Let us say, madam, it's another of these truces and a tourney's to proclaim. You'd never believe the pomp and the punctilio of it! "In the name of God and Saint Denis and our most puissant king"—or if it isn't him it's him of Orleans, or our right trusty cousin of Burgundy, or some other—'

'You cannot be liking your mead, Master Robert, for you scarce sip of it—'

'—and then on the appointed day comes the tourney, all the helms with their plumes and mantlings, and the silk housings of the horses and the flashing of the armour and the trumpetings and gallopings up and down—'

'Are the poursuivants in armour too?'

'No, madam, though I'll not say but once in a while there isn't a shirt under their tabards somewhat heavier than you ladies might like to wear! But the pick of it comes afterwards, when they all sit down to meat together in the château or maybe some great pavilion pitched in the field. Marry, the compliments and the courtesies and the pardon-me's as they ride every tilt over again! "Noble sir, had I that horse of yours I'll wager a thousand livres—" so as like as not he gives him the horse, and then in no more than a month or two they're breaking one another's necks again—'

Brightly too he knew all the time what he was doing. Like a peacock he was spreading his tail, strutting, showing his paces—

'She wants to know what they have to eat in the pavilion—' and by this time he was in full song. Long were they to remember how one day there had arrived in Washburn-in-the-Forest a young stranger in hide boots and a russet doublet, nothing out of the common in the face perhaps but with an air and a way all his own—

'To eat? Ah, there's a picture indeed! To eat, Mistress Echo? Why, there's roasted cranes, and sucking-pigs gilt all over and pasties with lozenges of gold—there's custards-royal half as tall as yourself—' but now Efga Hartlip's half-face was laughing.

'Nay, do not shame us, Master Robert, for a poor boiled fowl's all you're getting here to-day!'

'—and great cakes with "Te Deum" scrolled over them, and then maybe another sucking-pig or two, and beef with their mutton, as they say they always eat it in the Duchy—' which of course was meant to be preposterous, so that when the laughter was over decorum had to be restored again.

'Yet at Newbiggin we kept a good table too. We'd no custards as tall as Echo, but seldom fewer than a dozen did we sit down, and often twenty or more—'

But at that moment something seemed to have happened to the girl. In the act of raising her pipkin of horn to her lips she suddenly coughed, put it unsteadily down on the table again, and jumping hurriedly up half ran to the outer door. Her best kirtle was becomingly longer than the rag she had worn in the oak-glade, and he saw its flurry as she caught it up and the gleam of her bare ankles as she disappeared. Then, looking inquiringly at Efga Hartlip, it seemed to him that she showed annoyance but no great perturbation. She merely let her go, and as the door closed again leaned confidentially towards Gandelyn and whispered in his ear almost as if the two of them had been of an age.

'Take no notice. Say nothing, neither now nor afterwards. Rarely does she drink of anything but water. A clean-eating girl like Echo—their stomachs aren't used to it the way a man's is—'

But on a quick thought he had sipped of his own mead again. There was no doubt about that faintly earthy taste, and mushrooms he knew, and puff-balls and toadstools and the night-shining agarics with which he had smeared spectral shapes on Netherby's dormitory walls.

'Has she run out to be sick?' he demanded, but the hand that had held the crystal was placed for a moment on his sleeve.

'When she comes in just go on talking as if nothing had happened. She'll be none the worse and she'll know better another time,' but now he had made his guess.

'What was in that mead? Truffles?' but the mistress of the kitchen only placed her finger on her lip.

'Say nothing. Indeed I have heard it said that truffles put a man on his horse and a woman into her grave. They shouldn't meddle with such things that don't understand them, and I was in my bed when she came in and didn't rightly see what it was she had in her hand. Yet I'm vexed too, for we had but the one pig. A rare snout for truffles he had, but he had to be killed last autumn because of a fever, and even so, Master Robert? There's worse eating than truffles. Ssh—let on not to see her—'

But as the shamed girl passed quickly through her face was averted. Again the skirt she kept for high days was caught up as she passed through the half-door and closed the inner curtain behind her. So of that day's onrush of events in Washburn-in-the-Forest let her disappearing heels be the second hour.

There should be trout in the pool under the alders where that morning he had dipped his head. If deer roamed the wooded hillside behind him it would be here they came down to drink. But now the morning glitter had left the water, its sheen was no more than the upside-down of the sky, and only where the alders overhung it did its pebbly bottom seem to rise half-way to the surface. He gave a moody kick, and at the scattering of earth the pool was a mirror no longer.

So this was what they meant, this loosening, this release, this warm stir of burgeoning, and it was he, the tall leader, who all the time had been the backward one! *This* was the wantonness that had set the choristers off in their corners, the soldiers at their fires, and had brought the forbiddance to the brothers' faces, that the fairer the seeming the apter it ever was for the bearing of the devil's message!

He was trying to remember exactly what had happened. His guide had deserted him, and coming suddenly upon her in the glade he had just opened his mouth to ask his way. For answer he had had certain glimpses, certain items, and a grimy glare. What had this to do with an alder pool and himself standing on its bank, restless as he had never been restless and a stranger to himself?

But with the choristers it had never lasted long. He had only had to set his candle-end on the dormitory floor and start the hand-shadows leaping on the wall and in five minutes every urchin had forgotten all about it. The brothers were old men, their minds on another world. As for the soldiers in the field—but another kicking up from the ground broke the pool as he put aside the soldiers in the field.

But how now, with scarce a glimpse or item to be seen? She had put on her mother's left-off surcoat, changed her working-petticoat for a kirtle that made a trammel about her heels. Must his thoughts be flushed because she had

cast aside her head-net and a silver musk-ball now rested
in that notch of her throat? And say she had been down to
this very pool that morning while he had slept?

But he knew that he was looking into its shallows for
the whiteness that Actæon had seen, that hot and ruddy
David had seen, and this time no kick shattered the surface
of the pool.

Of all the watching saints it was blessed Monica who
came to his aid. He gave himself a shake, the phenomenon
passed, and the next moment he was broadly smiling
again. Blessed Monica also, sent down into the cellar for
the wine, had swigged it on the way, made herself tipsy,
perhaps eaten truffles too, yet for all that she had triumphed
over sin and now sat in glory for ever. At once the fair
phantom ceased to beckon, the world took on its right
proportions again. Echo Hartlip, too, sipping an un-
accustomed concoction, had had to jump suddenly up from
the table and run for the bushes. He saw it as we see things
only twice in our lives, beginning and end in one, prophecy's young eye and again when all is over. A waif of
the Forest, out of an unknown bed, a stray of an unguess-
able inheritance! In an hour he would be gone. He was
only there for a last look at this Washburn-in-the-Forest,
if possible from an eminence. A few yards down the pool
the bank was broken with pockings and patterings. With
another laugh for blessed Monica he gave a kick that
shivered white phantoms into a thousand fragments. Then
he followed the deer-tracks up the hillside.

It was thinly wooded, the trunks rubbed and nibbled as
high as the animals could reach, and soon they began to
mingle with an undergrowth of budding crab and pear. Its
short steepness ended at a flattish top scattered over with
gorse and brambles, and at one point among these a refuge
had been set. It was a pen of stout upright posts, wide
enough to admit a man edgewise but too narrow for an

antler-branched head, and on moon-flooded October nights, when the stags battled and belled, it was there for the foresters' own safety. Across the plateau the trees began again, and he was making for them when suddenly he came upon as pretty a sight as eye could wish to see. Emerging from a brake a fully-grown hart had raised his head guardingly into the air. Behind him there followed a dainty-ambling doe, sagging heavily with her June young, yet secure in that fierce protection of her male. This time Gandelyn smiled gently. He knew nothing of October jealousies, but it had his high approval that so nature had ordered things, and he would have done the same himself. He was down-wind, the snuffler did not nose him, and when he looked again they had gone.

Soon the trees began to close again over his head. The summit he had reached seemed to be some spur that fell away again to a parallel valley with its stream, and he was ankle-deep in the rot of last year's under-vert and up-springing new growth. Lacking Jan Schmidt's guidance now he must fall back on his own wits, and all at once a look of attention became fixed on his face. From some-where there had reached him the sound of bells.

To be sure there was nothing alarming in music so gentle. In the Forest it was the stealth and silence that were the offence, always those on honest errands gave frequent warning of their approach, and what could be more frequent than bridle-bells, that jangled with every movement that was made? It might be he was in some portion of the preserve over which its owner still had curtailed rights. Some company, unfamiliar with the region, might like himself have missed its way. But it was none of this that had brought the quick look of attention to his face. It was many hours since that first blast of the horn. From whatever cavalcade the sounds were coming it was a numerous one, and say even that it was the full

Regard, that every three years must answer it to the
Duchy that no nook or corner of the Forest had gone
unvisited. Even so the bells were too numerous, their
jangling too continuous, and now he had reached a point
from which he could look down.

There, as he had surmised, lay the second valley, its
stream a hundred feet beneath. Along the hillside below
him ran a shelf or ledge, and the riders were just beginning
to come into sight. If they were the Regard the four
verderers would carry the silver horn at their waists and
the enamelled Huberts about their necks, and would be
attended by their wardens and deputy-wardens. But they,
if any, would know every ride of the Forest and every
winding of its ways, and something had gone amiss.
Along a track only fit for mules far too many were picking
their way. Something of greater import was afoot, among
themselves they were wrangling, and the watcher,
dropping to a cover of bracken, had crept close to the
edge. Suddenly a voice the iron ring of which brought his
heart half-way to his throat clashed like the closing of a
steel trap.

'Christ's Thorns! So this is your forest-watching when
there's none to watch yourselves! 'Tis well I came!'

And Gandelyn knew that voice. In all England and
France there was not such another, and now numbers were
coming into sight, and if the man also had a sword-cut so
coinciding with his mouth and jaw-furrow that it pushed
as it were his smile to the other side of his face he was the
one on earth whom Gandelyn desired next to see only in
the presence of his own lord John. Immediately below him,
mounted on the biggest horse of all, rode a short, strong-
shouldered man of a swollen and violent complexion, its
congested blood the blood of the least knightly Gaunt who
ever bore that crest of kings. In France he was the soldier
they knew as The Cooper, for with the Oise to cross in

force at a point where no more than a handful could find a footing he had undertaken to find a way. Falling a mile or two back, for a fortnight he had made the nights clamorous with the hammering of a thousand barrels for a bridge, and now, while those who pressed about him were resplendent in doublets of cramoisie and sewings of gold, he had scarce changed out of his working-clothes. Save for the embossed red lion in his round red cap he was still dressed in his armour-rubbed under-leather, and again his camp-roughened voice snapped.

'Bring me the chart, that I may see for myself where in this accursed Forest we are!' but a soft and practised voice answered him.

'My lord, we are skirting a place called Washburn-in-the-Forest, not worth turning aside for—' but another swollen oath cut him short.

'I called for a chart!'

'Indeed, my lord, they follow their peaceable trades, and as for the chart, it was your lordship's orders that he in whose charge it is should stay on post at Pennypocket—'

'Sir Maris!' and then another voice.

'Nay, my lord, my writ ended when we set foot in Nidderdale—'

'Then who is verderer here?'

'He was Sir Matthew Poole, my lord, but he died some weeks back,' and now the oath was a harrowing one.

'What! One misbegot loses a chart, and another's writ runs out, and a third cheats me by dying! Would I'd had a few of you in France! And then I warrant you'd ha' found yourselves daybed jobs in some pleasant château or lining your pockets among these hucksters of the Staple!'

But Calais and its Staple settled it, for now Gandelyn's young face was black with his ugliest memory of all. He had been the bearer of a letter to this very man from his own lord John. In Calais he had found him, dining with the merchants, and dropping to his knee, in fealty he had kissed his letter's seal before delivering it. Even the bearded merchants had blenched in silence at the next. Breaking the seal the earl Philip had read the letter with a purpling face. Then he had moved his buttocks in his chair and handed the letter back to its bearer. That was his answer to the lord John, and again that same voice of the camp cracked in Gandelyn's ears.

'Is there not one man here can show me my way through this stew of Yorkshire woods and streams?'

None dared to tell him that only his own headstrongness had brought them there. Hurriedly they consulted. Yes, there might be one—the late verderer's steward—

'Then in God's name bring him here!' and the intermittent jangling of the bells became a carillon as the horses tossed and champed and the word was passed back for the new guide to be summoned forward.

Stephen Hurst's baldrick was newly furbished. His beard was combed, his clothing point-device, personal port and duteousness were mingled in the obeisance with which he stooped.

'Are you this steward?'

'Of his household only, my lord,' was the scrupulous reply.

'That is to say another mouth to feed. How well do you know these parts?'

'Indifferently well for one who is no forester, my lord.'

'The less like then to have been bribed. Hearken. Since daybreak these have wasted my time as they waste their own. At Pennypocket they bring me two hare-pipes and a sulphur-candle. A mile back it was a washerwoman's petticoat from a cave and a gabardine with a yellow cross. Which way does this Washburn lie?'

'It is direct over the hill, my lord. Keeping to this ledge, but singly and in file and then about again, it might be a cast of three miles or less.'

'Villainy's in the air, yet never a villain caught! Who's not well-affected with twenty hours' clear warning? It is weapons I seek, not nets and limes and candles! Were you in this verderer's confidence?' and Stephen Hurst stood stroking his beard with careful judgment.

'There are things I may not speak openly of, my lord. Yet were I to say Yes it would but be that often he spoke as your lordship speaks, that even the best of men are to be watched. I have indeed heard whispers of weapons.'

'Then I'll visit this Washburn they give so good a name! If they have chimneys a pole or two shall be thrust up them! I mistrust them that all speak too well of,' and as if it came over him again that he was being contrived against he raised his voice anew. 'Chimneys did I say? As many haystacks as there are they shall be thrown down! I'll have their middens turned over and their beds shaken out! They shall have a taste of the Picardy stuff, and if I find but one unlawful weapon, one pick-bill or aught such as soldiers carry in their hands—'

And at that moment he chanced to look up. A young chestnut-frond, its still-folded leaves drooping like a bird's claw, had moved. Stephen Hurst had come forward on foot, but the soldier, swinging sideways from the saddle, caught him roughly by the baldrick.

'*Eih!* Saw you that? There, fool, where the leaves are still moving! In brown and eavesdropping! With my eyes I saw him! I see where none of you's a mind to look! And this your innocent Washburn!' and out in a torrent cracked his orders. 'Sir John Boles, prick ahead and cut that man off! Those afoot, up into the wood and scatter wide! Steward, get you one of those horses and ride with me! Spied on! Listened to! Pass the word back—into the wood every man and catch me this knave in brown—'

The words were hardly out of his mouth before the steep bank was a swarming and clambering of men.

IV

Not a woodsman had left for the Forest that day. The visit of the Regard was their sole spectacle and contact with the world. For safety they had had ample warning, and when an offender has been smartly dealt with by an underling it heartens him again to see his persecutor at the finger-snap of those more exalted than himself.

But from the very beginning it looked little like the ceremony of former years. There advanced into the open space about Hubert no herald-like minion with his silver horn and stately gazehound held in a leash as symbol of his office. Instead there came tumbling in twos and threes down the wooded hillside more strange liveries than there were foresters in the accustomed green, and lacking orders these stood in small assemblies about the washing-stones, while at their own doors the men of Washburn looked warily and watchfully on. Only Will Acle, as big as a house and as timorous as a hare, wandered from group to group, his mastiff nowhere to be seen. The hour was now three in the afternoon.

Before half-past a breathless lad came running up with news they were on their way. A very little later and they heard the approaching bells, and the men at the washing-stones, most of whom were armed with short spears, thrust away the food they were munching. The tintinnabulation grew louder, and from behind Hubert's copse they suddenly emerged into sight. Not four verderers in green, but three only rode ahead, the office of the fourth supported by a saddled and riderless horse. Massed behind came, besides the haughty four of the Regard with their attendants, such an assemblage of velvets and sayes and colours of nobility as surely visitation had never seen before. To

left and right of Hubert they unfolded themselves like
multicoloured wings. Spearmen and men-at-arms were
manœuvring over half the breadth of the common. Reckoning in the first-comers, it was an encirclement, and
directing it, riding a huge horse up and down in front of
the array, was a bullfronted man in chafed and soiled
leather who looked like a groom but spoke with the
ringing voice of a commander. For form's sake he issued
his orders to the officers about him, who interpreted them,
but low mutterings came from the men of Washburn as
their purport became clear. The common was to be
quartered up. No house was to be passed by. If any engine
was found inside, were it but a mousetrap, it was to be set
outside its door. If any man resisted he was to be bound.
Then a horn sounded as if for onset, and Washburn's long-
to-be-remembered visitation had begun.

Espied then up in the wood, himself expressly sent out
on the same errand, surely, surely Robert Gandelyn should
have started up from his covering of bracken, declared
himself, and at once have placed himself at the general
disposition? Alas for duty, ay me for an honour forsworn!
He was doing no such thing. Stealing from tree to tree,
listening, hiding again, he was making his way back to the
streamside. First and foremost in his mind was that two
women must be warned to keep within doors.

But he reached the kitchen some time later only to
intrude on a small domestic difference. All traces of their
meal had been cleared away, the lilac still strowed the
windowsill, but—stretched on a bed of sickness, Echo
Hartlip? There at the window she stood, angrily picking
the purple-black buds to tatters. She wanted to go out and
see what was going on. Evidently her mother had forbidden it, and now the nape between the two flat plaits
was as obstinate as the flower-stalk that the gale only

bends. That back that so straightly supported it could have carried bark all day without tiring, and had the visitation come only a few weeks earlier the man she called father would have been riding that fourth horse that now none bestrode. Rebelliously she flung the stripped flower-head out of the unglazed window.

'I shall be seventeen come Midsummer—' she cried, and the mother's single eye gave Gandelyn a beseeching look.

'See what you can do with her, Master Robert,' and crossing to the window he attempted it, speaking gently and persuasively in her ear.

'Be guided by your mother, Echo. There's little to see. As like as not they'll be off and away before you'd time to get there.'

'I want to see them!'

'Bide in quiet where you are—they'll never find a place hidden away like this—'

'I want to see the verderers on their horses—'

'I'll tell you all about it—your mother cannot be left alone by herself—come now and do as she bids you—' but even as he spoke the confused sounds across the common became a hubbub, with dogs that barked and again a horn snapping out. He was half-way to the door when suddenly she raised her eyes. First she would have his promise.

'You'll come back?'

'Stay you here—yes, I'll come back—'

'On your knightly faith?'

'On my knightly faith——'

'How long will you be?'

'Not long—' and in a moment he was gone.

It was the men in green who had found. From all quarters of the common there were runnings and gallopings towards the dwelling where the clanking iron kept the fox away, and with the men of Washburn looking sullenly on half a dozen foresters had flung themselves on a struggling, man who was bellowing aloud in a half-demented voice.

'My brach shall be hambled for no man—'

But three or four others held a great midden-soiled mastiff pinned to the ground. On his knees Simon Grindrod was binding its muzzle about with a cord, and a dozen other dogs were whimpering and whining piteously, starting forward and cowering back again as if at some remembered pain, while again the man's voice was raised.

'Never has he smelt blood—he's harmless as a wean—'

But Simon Grindrod had one massive paw in his grip and was turning the integuments back to the quick, first one paw and then the other, and now the red-faced Lancastrian had galloped up, and no warden or ranger spoke for him now.

'Silence that man!' for Will Acle's voice was raised till it cracked. As well too that the animal was muzzled and its master gagged, for it was as much as three of them could do to display the great paws for Philip of Gaunt's inspection.

'All six as sound as trenails, my lord—'

'Where was this animal found?'

'At the back of yonder biggin, my lord, in a cess covered over wi' hurdles and withies.'

'Deal with it,' and the apparatus was at hand.

But the gagged man was stronger than the six of them, and with all that weight of men on him had struggled to his knees and was plunging forward like a baited bull. It was minutes before he could be brought down again, and it was to a fresh panic of dog-fear that there was brought forward first a foot-thick billet of wood, chipped like a butcher's block with old incisions. Kneeling, Simon Grindrod put out a hand behind him. A broad chisel was placed in it, then a heavy mallet of wood. A second man knelt on the heaving ribs, a third gripped the great pad. There was a short dull blow, but the animal's howl of anguish was throttled in the tightly-corded muzzle.

'Over with him,' and at the second blow dog and master lay shuddering alike.

'To which of these houses did this cess belong?'

'Please you, my lord, it's one they use among 'em.'

'Set a seal on the door.'

Now the fourth horse that should have carried Sir Matthew Poole was no longer riderless. With charts lost and writs run out and only one man not a numbskull to help at need, Stephen Hurst had been ordered to mount it. He was now a galloper, riding back and forth with this order and that, and when a man has been put off with a harepipe or so and a candle or two and a washerwoman's cloak, what is a single unlawed dog but a whetter of the appetite for more? The earl Philip had tasted blood, and the bridle bells broke into another jangling as he wheeled his great horse wrathfully round.

'These petty assarts and pilferings! Where is Sir Maris Hurd? That eavesdropper in brown I had to spy out for myself! Is he caught yet?' and again the soft placating answer came.

'They're hard on his heels, my lord—any minute will bring him now—'

'This Forest reported an armoury and all you bring me is a dog! Fetch me the headman of this place!'

But though Washburn children already born lived to see their stream bridged and a toll of its own, and a smithy where the bark-shed stood, and many other signs of progress, a place still so unincorporated lacked even a headman. The best they could bring him was their oldest inhabitant on his two sticks, and as the first question that was put to him was the question he expected he answered it aright.

'Your name?'

'Raistrick o' the Vale, great sir,' the quavering voice replied.

'Where is your roll?' but the second question fared less well than the first.

'A turner of wood, my lord, but my wheel has been my son's this many a year.'

'Which of these houses is yours?' but now the ancient began to waver on his two sticks.

'As I live, dread sir, neither staggard nor hart—'

'He's very deaf, my lord, you must raise your voice—' and the dotard was waved angrily away.

A pace or two behind him Stephen Hurst sat on the verderer's horse. A man of mark and promptitude he looked, and on his mettle with his fine beard, his baldrick and his bold-ranging eyes. Such a man would far liefer kiss a hand of the blood of Gaunt than count the chattels of a dead forester, one stroke of good fortune now and Stephen need never look behind him again, and zealously his eyes were scanning the common's every coming and going. Beginning with the houses nearer the watercress beds the inquisition had moved to the dwellings among the oaks, but with the expedition of the dog the women had fallen back. Now they were gathered by the washing-stones and the drying-poles, and Stephen had been quick to see that there two others had joined them. Their habits were of dingy blue with cords at the waist, the head-dresses that hid their faces too were blue, and coming suddenly upon so large a concourse of men they had faltered and stopped. With the other women gathered about them one of them was pointing and gesticulating, as if to make clear some narration. Stephen had closed his horse up to the earl Philip's side. At the worst he had nothing to lose, and he lowered his voice as if to confide something of import.

'If I might venture a word, my lord—'

'Now what?'

'Cast your eyes over yonder, my lord. There's two there in blue would seem to have a deal to say.'

'I see a gaggle of women.'

'One would say nuns by the look of them, but I've known even them fond of the sound of their own voices. Have I your leave to see what's in the wind?' and at the earl Philip's impatient sign the man who sought a new master rode curvetting away.

As it had chanced, truant Gandelyn was now a prisoner of his own making. The order to seal the house had caught him perilously close to it, with small chance now of getting away unseen. But it is odds that a house sealed at the front usually has a loose shutter or so at the back, and the proscribed dwelling had an upper floor. Here its inner frame of timbers leaned together, but between them and the outer wall was a space. An airhole pierced it, and it was at this that he had posted himself, all the safer now for the seal on the door. The branches of the oak limited his view annoyingly, but his ears eked out the glimpses he had between the leaves, and so he had to make the best of it when presently the two schwesteren were ushered forward by Stephen and brought before the earl Philip.

And Stephen was not browbeating a handful of fishermen out of their wreck-pickings now. Stephen was a politic man, who never made an enemy when he could make a friend. The soldier left such petticoat stuff to him, and things that would have to be left for some other time deepened the suddenly remembering look on Gandelyn's face as he heard and partly saw him, gentling the frightened religieuses as he gentled the neck of the animal from which he leaned.

'Never tell me, good sister!' he was saying in the voice that made Gandelyn so suddenly thoughtful. 'A holy man at his prayers! Think of that! But it is my lord's hope, and the hope of all these gentlemen of the Duchy, that amends

E

may be made. Should your nunnery be in need of some small alms, and the holy mother would graciously accept of it—'

There was an elder of them and a younger. The elder was telling over a paternoster and did not raise her eyes, but it was the younger who over by the washing-stones had done the talking and the pointing, and she looked up for a moment under her blue headgear and down again.

'We are of no nunnery, sir, but of the hospital. We had been up the glen with his food, as we daily do—' and Stephen's voice became more gentling still.

'Which heaven will reward you!—but a hospital? In Washburn?'

'It is back from the roadside, sir, a mile and a half away—you will see a graveyard—' and now with the schwesteren up had come the rest of the women, and out broke half a dozen of them at once.

'The poor souls cannot take Holy Joe his handful of beans but they must be had up before strangers and questioned!'

'On their feet all day and no sleep o' nights—'

'Come to this of old Margaret—' but the other had now finished her paternoster, and it was a different voice that reached the listener in his wall-cleft.

' 'Tis not for her to speak till her elders have had their say. Old Margaret must have her eggs at night, and now three of our best's ta'en to laying away—' and with scarcely a bell tinkling now, Stephen's voice could be plainly heard.

'Ah, once hens take to that—'

'But I had a couple laid by, and at night we always use the back way as being nearer the shed where we sleep—'

'To be sure, nearer the shed where you sleep.'

'And the eggs were ready-whipped, and there was this light, dimmering up out of the ground, but we're used to gravedigging at night, and Jan has to have his lantern to work by—'

'Not so fast, good sister. What time of night would this be?'

'I cannot tell you the hour, sir, but when of a sudden this other starts its twinkling—'

'Another? What other?'

'This at first I thought was a Peg-o'-Lantern, but it was two knives spinning up and down, and him that was tossing them was counting out how many—ten, eleven, twelve—'

'And well it's to be believed, the turn it gave you! Knives! But a bit more in order. Are you saying there were two of them digging this grave?'

'Nay, only one was digging, and all had stopped by this. But we durstn't go out, so we prayed a while, and Margaret cannot get through the night without her eggs, so I unbolted the door, and round we both went the other way to find Sim the porter. Then Sim got his lantern too, but by the time we got to the grave there wasn't a soul to be seen, and Sim was jealous something was wrong, so down the ladder he gets him into the grave, and picks up the spade, but hardly three scrapes had he given—'

The next Gandelyn did not see. It was the face of the Cooper of the Oise, its vessels standing dangerously out. But he heard the oath and the rearing of the horse that set other horses plunging and rearing too, the fracas of the bells, and again that voice as if an anvil had been struck.

'Hardly three scrapes . . . what, woman? Rouse me not— for the love of God madden me not—'

'Oh, I faint—'

'*What was in that grave?*'

'First Sim found a bill and a scythe-blade—'

'Flames of damnation!'

'Then he fetches out a bag of bolts, and then some side-swords, and that isn't all neither—'

'*More?*'

'Nay—for almost before a cock had crowed all had been ta'en away again!'

And now fierce question began to follow fierce question like the shaken-out links of a chain.

'There? And gone again?'

'Oh, support me—'

'This gravedigger, have him here before me, and now!'

'Nay, sir, he stayed but the night—'

'Him you say was with him!'

'We know him not, nor could tell even his face—' and all that had gone was nothing to the next fierce order.

'Seize and bind every man in this place! Your pretty Washburn! . . . Sir John Boles, to that hospital yourself and see none comes either in or out! Where's that man that was gagged?'

'Under guard, my lord.'

'Rope the others to him! What one knows they all know! Up into their lofts! If aught's found locked break it open! Sir Ranger, who's your trustiest man and hardest rider?'

'I have both, my lord—'

'Then let him not draw rein till he gets to York, where room's to be made in the gaol on my information! Then count the rascals! Stay, he shall have my letter and seal for it! Carry me over a table and chair to yonder Hubert! The Duchy flouted, in *my* person! On their own common I'll make this a day of doom for them all!'

It was plain that the prisoner in the sealed house would have to remain where he was until darkness should enable him to steal away, but there was no urgency about his thoughts now. There would be to-morrow, and many morrows after that in which to ponder all that he had just heard and learned, and still from his coign in the wall he saw the carrying out of the furniture for the earl Philip's drumhead court. Already they were running to execute his orders, and the air rang with the wild cries of the women as their houses were forced, their cupboards ransacked, spearheads thrust into their bolsters and bedding. Now and then scraps of thoughts came of themselves. In the very act he had caught Jan Schmidt but no more than quicksilver had been able to hold him—with the Aptrick men fetching all away in broad daylight still dust had been thrown in his eyes—and all the time Jan Schmidt, with his crooked hand on his knee, had movingly besought him to have nothing to do with it, root nor twig. But enough. From somewhere below him there came a piteous whimpering. It was the maimed dog on the ground, whining for water. Yet to break a seal from the inside might be even more conspicuous than to force it from without, and at that moment there passed the lattice a sentry's head. Descending from his niche he stretched himself on somebody's bed below as again the dog howled. The hour was now five in the afternoon. At six he heard the most anguished outcry of all. It was the women, turning their backs even on the rifling of their homes to troop at a run across the common. They were marshalling the roped men for driving away. The gag had been removed from Will Acle's mouth, and he was again crying to heaven that his dog should be lawed for no man.

By a little after eight o'clock stillness reigned in Washburn-in-the-Forest once more.

No sorrier sight of evening beauty could anywhere have been found. Flooded and separate in the sunset light, every croft and house and dwelling stood forth illumined like cloth-of-gold. Every shadow stood directly behind the object that cast it, the bold-topped oaks seemed stitched with a needle to the clear amber of the sky. Over by

Hubert's copse the chair and table of judgment stood alone
and empty, unclaimed by any owner. Pigeons crooned,
rooks filled the air with their confabulation. But the
women, clutching their children to them, had set out after
their men.

But they had not been suffered to follow them any great
way. Apparently at the hospital they had been driven back,
back to the ruin and spoliation of their chattels, back to
their husbandless homes. Some with sudden outbursts of
clamour, some weeping in silence, they could be seen
returning in the distance, and Gandelyn, at liberty again
but keeping prudently out of sight, saw hobbling alone
across the common old Raistrick of the Vale on his two
sticks, carrying Hubert's storm-lantern in his hand.

And for the cost of his oil they passed the cap round
among them, and his yearly coat of paint was a common
charge too; but to reach up to the pent-roof was more than
Raistrick's old limbs could manage, and the returning
women were now drawing near. Suddenly striding man-
like towards him came the gaunt bedraggled woman who
had snatched the babe from Echo Hartlip's arms, and she
was Jemima Hackett, and Forest and Vale alike knew her
story. One day, when her eight-year-old son should have
been in for his dinner, he had been missing from his home
by the watercress beds. Only late that afternoon had he
been found, under the water by the weir-post, his drowned
face a purple bloat when they had cleared the ruffle of
green away. She had borne little Judith since, but there-
after had never been quite right, and little she cared what
of herself she showed as she snatched the light from old
Raistrick, clambered up to the pent, and set the lantern on
its nail.

And now in their desolate plight Hubert and his light
became a beacon and a summons to them all. They had no
other council-chamber, always it had been there that their

men had discussed whatever affected them all alike. Now again they broke down into sobs and lamentations as the sun sank and the bronze tops of the oaks glowed redder than the dishevelled fiery cross of Jemima Hackett's hair. They too would have many days in which to weep, and now the children, ignorant of all, were at play among the spillings and the spoilings long after they should have been in their beds. Nor was it ever a good omen when Jemima Hackett's thoughts ran on children.

'Have done, Jemima,' a woman suddenly said, but Jemima had begun and was not to be silenced.

'Never stranger set foot in Washburn but it was pepper in the nose for somebody!' her strident voice mounted. 'Folk we know we know, but foreign vagabonds—'

'Whisht!'

'—like him that was seen at Pennypocket two mornings ago wi' Durham's badge on his arm—'

'Ha' done, Jemima!'

'But for him, and Simon Grindrod and his pack on his heels—'

'Peace we say!'

'I'll ha' done when I'm finished! And up at the oaks last night there was another, and that wagtail Echo Hartlip was with him, and off to their biggin by the streamside they went—' and now that it was started others joined in.

'Ay, and Will Acle told us what he saw there, that curst cow and what we always said she had on her cheek—'

'And this morning, just as I was getting the dinner out o' the pot, in rushes my Samson, crying out he'd been set on by one that called himself Giant Jawbone—'

Seldom they say do listeners hear good of themselves. Gandelyn, lurking in Hubert's coppice, had clean forgotten the foolish little incident that had interrupted his morning's walk in search of an appetite for his fowl with chervil sauce. Near the washing-stones a pebble had shot suddenly across his path. He had spied the culprit behind a gorse-bush but had walked on, then swiftly wheeling had had him by the ear. It was only a lad with a sling and a pocketful of pebbles, and he had contented himself with a few grimaces and a tweak of the youngster's ear, but now on the lips of an angry mother it was less diverting.

'Giant Jawbone he said he was, and he emptied his pockets of all he had and made as if to hang him in his own sling—'

'And them two at their business in the wood, and me hunting everywhere for my little Judith, the same as I did that other time—'

'Us that tries to keep our bairns in innocence as long as we can—'

'Hanging about the wood-edge at the end o' the day, I've seen the doxy, and told my Edward if he sees her there again he's to run straight home and tell me—'

But it was at the next that the sudden silence fell. A woman who had not spoken lifted a pair of red and weeping eyes.

'With all that's fallen on us this day, how comes it there's one house i' Washburn hasn't had a finger laid on it?'

And there were reasons in plenty and they knew them all. It was the very last house in the village, scarcely to be called a house, so dug into its bank that none but themselves would ever have supposed it to be there. That house alone had been overlooked, and they were women beside themselves, powerful-bodied and vengeful women, and again it was the virago's voice that supplied the spark.

'How long is it since that Newbiggin whore came here wi' her bastard at her apron-strings?'

'Eight year.'

'And when she came, with scarce a bundle to her hand or a string to her clouts, did she meet with aught but kindness?'

'We were over-kind—things were given her to set her up—'

'That table she eats off was given her, and young Dan turned her stool legs himself—'

'Many a bridegroom would ha' been fain of the place she had but to step into—'

'And we ha' rents to pay, but has Efga Hartlip ever paid a penny?'

Not one penny had Efga Hartlip ever paid.

'Scarce before midday is she out of her bed—'

'And that froward young besom—'

'Old Dan's the one to tell us what to do—'

For old Dan Raistrick on his two sticks was some sort of a descendant of Wilfrid the Woodcutter himself, and had known that hovel by the stream a couple of generations before Washburn had ever set eyes on Efga Hartlip and the black eclipse of her face. He remembered Tom Locksley the gravel-screener who had built its outhouse, and before that it had been old Huddy, searching for top-coal. But for his sudden death a verderer-knight this woman called her husband would have been among their persecutors that very day. But when old Dan was brought forward it was only to mishear them again.

'Ay, his lantern must be kept alight—I cannot reach up to it myself, but it must be kept alight—'

'Tell us what we're to do, Dan—'

'Ay, Woodcutter Wilfrid was a Washburn man—in my young days I knew them that had spoken with him—'

'He hears you the best, Jemima—' but the dotard quavered on.

'Wet or fine, always at it they say he was, whittling away with his chisels and a sharp little axe he had—and the next to come was William Huddy, and after him Tom Locksley—'

And the old man would not be with them much longer,

so heed the prophet while he is among you. Suddenly it
seemed to them a vile and a monstrous thing that an abode
with such associations should be profaned by Efga Hartlip
and her godless practices. But before any of them could
speak again half a dozen of the elder children could be seen
running towards them and calling as they ran. Young
Samson Strong, clutching at his mother, was pointing with
his slinging-hand.

'Mother—look, look!'

In the western heavens the last red bars still glowed,
but that was not the redness at which young Samson
pointed. Only old Raistrick on his two sticks did not run
to where no saint or copse shut out the light, and the
direction and the distance were enough. The redness was
the sullen smouldering of smoke where the earl Philip left
his beacon behind him. The roofs of Aptrick on its limestone crag were alight.

There their men too, were bound and compelled to
look on—

They might have been their own roofs, and presently
the oaks catching, and the common ringed with a forest-
fire that roared as it ran—

Those powerful-bodied women of Washburn-in-the-
Forest were enduring no more, and Jemima Hackett's cry
was that of her wound torn open again.

'You children, get you home and wait—'

'Nay, not with Hubert's lantern, Jemima!' but as
Jemima clambered down from the pent again the lantern
and her incendiary head made one flame together.

'Her and her afterbirths in jars! . . . them that willn't
follow me, let them stay behind!'

And Gandelyn had the start of them with a scant three
minutes to spare.

Corpus in York

Now the church nave's become the cambio,
And some may kneel but all must live by bread,
What of the wares, and how's a man to know
These lusty living from those noisy dead?
'Past twelve o'clock, a vessel in the bay,
And not a slut woke from her slumbers yet!
Hark where they come, their pockets hot with pay
They must be shut of or three suns be set!
Bestir you, hussies! What, you'd pick and choose
Of this town-tunic or those fingers tarred?
Go wash yourselves! Into those dainty shoes
And busk you blithely when the cash is hard!'
Who said it, and to whom? I cannot tell,
And yet it clangs loud as the market-bell!

I

A stream-rope hurriedly cut to gain a few minutes in which to pack a hasty bundle for flight; infuriated women seeking another crossing, Jemima Hackett with her lantern stumbling through swirling water; ceiling-herbs and shelf-sweepings to burn by the chopping-block, a tethered goat looking on—with its tale to tell Arras can stay for none of these things. For many days it had not rained; now it must needs come on. The roof of an open bark-shed where wheeltracks turned drummed to a vertical downpour that hissed greyly on the ground and drubbed on the cart that had been left to fall to pieces of itself. Such questioning as was to be done Gandelyn did in the fewest words.

'Where in York do you want to go?'

'It will have to be Thomas Twentyman's, by the Skeldergate postern.'

'Is he akin to you?'

'By marriage, no more.'

'What's his trade?'

'A fishmonger.'

'York's two long days' walk away.'

'Beggars cannot be choosers.'

It was neither the time nor the place for more. He showed them their end of the bark-shed and from his own lay in the darkness, listening to the unremitting rain. There had been only one thing to do and he had done it. Now this Thomas Twentyman was to find, and he supposed he would do that also. At a guess all roads would lead to York, and for York he had letters. They were two in number, and in a way one of them concerned these enforced companions of his, since it was to the governor of York's gaol, where under a will fivepence was to be bestowed upon the prisoners there. The other, the Lord Abbot's letter, was for the Archbishop himself and he knew nothing of its contents. In the house with the seal on the door he had provisioned himself for his own journey, for food left there would only be food for the rats and mice. Into his pouch he had therefore thrust half an oaten cake and a thick slice of cold gammon in case of need. These two had set the best they had before him, now he must do as much for them. So, couched on the bark-strippings, he waited for the dawn.

It came with tumultuous beauty, for the rain ended as abruptly as it had begun. The sky was a rolling of blue and white, the deluge had brought the fat earthworms from the ground, and every creature that had a voice seemed to be raising it at once in a brilliant and steaming world. Diamond-drops twinkled on the eaves and flashed at the alighting of every finch and thrush. Quietly, in case they still slept, he made his way out to the broken cart and looked west. There it was, Aptrick's crag still sullying the distance with its smoke. He made what toilet he could and then returned to unpack their breakfast.

But it almost dropped from his hands when in answer to his call they appeared and he saw what Echo Hartlip had done to her appearance. It was the bundle, both for her mother and herself, so hurriedly caught up as they had fled. Her feet were shod for her journey. No old green jacket sagged from her shoulders now, but the outer garment in which the bundle had most likely been wrapped, an old silk shawl from better days, green as to its ground but patterned all over with pinks and pomegranates and small gambolling animals. Old laying-by as it was she defied the morning in it, and yet it gave him a check, for nothing in it was proportionate. Besides its fruits and flowers stiff little Persians hunted gazelles in its folds, but the pinks and the pomegranates were larger than the bowmen and the gazelles. She too seemed over-aware of it as they ate in silence, they their oatcake and gammon, he the dried deersmeat he said he preferred. Whether they had seen Aptrick's smoke he could not tell, and nothing was said of their own ejection or of that upward flaring of ceiling-herbs and simples with a yellow-eyed goat looking on. Nor after breakfast did they linger. They had a long, long way to go on foot before any faraway glint on the horizon would become a greyness of walls and spires and two white towers reigning like twin kings side by side—the York where Echo Hartlip was to seek employment, the York where Thomas Twentyman the fishmonger was to be found.

So therefore let their wayfaring be depicted, seen as the singing birds might have looked down on them, three plodding earthbound figures, keeping together in artificial expanses that wind and turn, best to be recognized by their colours, one in inky black, one in russet, and the third in a pomegranate shawl, following themselves, preceding themselves through a packed and economical little world where one thing must stand for a multitude. Sometimes the three become two awhile as one turns aside to ask for a direction, then three again, till with night two of them lie under Gandelyn's cloak. As for Gandelyn, he needs no cloak. He is warm without, for his gleam of prophecy is over. Now all is as it comes. And so at break of dawn on again.

But track begins to converge upon track, and the miles bring company, so that to mount a small hillock is presently to see them in the distance, closing in as if of a sudden all the world was minded to go to York at once. Dotted over the plain move horsemen two abreast, riders

between bulky panniers, footfarers like themselves with
their budgets on their backs, their destination almost in
sight. And the reason? Why, man, the reason is Corpus,
when to England the foreign merchants come, lords of
commerce from Italy and the Levant and as far away as
Muscovy, their coffers and saddlebags stuffed with gold.
They come for wool and wool-fells, woven cloth and
leather and lead, and where the great staples are thither
flock the lesser businesses too. They make their own
roads, the clothiers, the merchants, the tradesmen, the
vendors of petty wares; they trample and widen them, the
mendicants, the hawkers, the friars with their pokes and
begging-staffs. And besides those going to York there are
those coming out of it, the returning drovers and purveyors, the inn-touts, the vendors of images and tokens.
By the morning of the second day the city was in sight, a
few more hours and it was no more than a mile or two
away. But now also came frequent congestion and stoppage.
Some said York's gates had been temporarily closed, since
when a city has admitted more than it can well accommo-
date it must cry halt until it has digested what it has.
Others said that soldiers were on the move, and yet others
knew that neither was the reason. Always when the foreign
merchants came York was studious to display itself at its
best, and here they were, the disreputables who had been
turned out till Corpus should be over. About a hip-roofed
inn many booths and huts had been set up. The place had
the look of an encampment, where drink and victuals were
to be had, for the moment there was no going forward,
and about the hip-roofed inn cattle and human beings
pressed confusedly together. Among swaying beasts and
staling horses, the known women, the abram-men, the
pickpockets, those who a week ago were in prison, were
eating and drinking and trafficking about the booths and
stalls. And it was here, amid the noise and sweat and the

vinegar of the pigs'-feet and tripes, that Gandelyn's eyes fell first on the tall horseman and then on his equipage.

He was a proudly-erect but ageing cavalier, grey-bearded and nobly moustachioed, and his high turban of blue velvet had a great cluster of rubies in the middle of it. His tasselled gloves were triple-seamed, his sword pommelled like a sword of state, and his somewhat sorry white horse so resplendently caparisoned that wherever he had procured the animal it was odds its housings had crossed the seas with him. Behind him three jades, also hired, were harnessed to a hooded palankeen. It was every inch of five yards long, plumes nodded over its arched hoopings, its wheels were carved and painted, and doubtless the cavalier had paid a rich man's price for its hire. It was not to be supposed that prey so tempting had not attracted every rogue who could get near, and the corner of an embroidered curtain was timidly lifted as a great goitred bawd of a fellow with a tray at his breast bawled out at the top of his voice, extolling the virtues of what he had to sell.

'My flies of Spain!' he was bellowing in tones that could have been heard a quarter of a mile away. 'Old men gi'en back their prime again! New bones for gaffers' backs, my Spanish flies, my flies of Spain!' he bawled with his goitre ashake as he thrust his packet under the signor's beard, who lifted it haughtily aside, for of our language he did not know one single word. 'A packet would fell an ox, so no more than a pinch of it, i' white wine, or if you haven't white red, or water, and if you haven't water, God bless you! Brides and bridegrooms, buy my flies of Spain!'

And now his great voice had set them all off at once, never was such a din, and a juggler had begun to toss his coloured balls into the air, and the bewildered signor might well have thought the English were all lunatics together as now to the babel were added the noises of

hollow thwackings. A lean spidery fool in a chequer of red
and sweaty white, whose face looked out of an oval with
asses' ears, had a bauble with a bladder on it, which
rebounded from heads and shoulders as he laid about him.

'Brawn and pigs' feet! Brawn and pigs' feet!'

'Any pies, any pies—'

'At the *Rose*, lodging for man and beast—'

'Quicker than quickmatch, my flies of Spain!'

Hours ago the plodding of one of the three had become
no more than a footsore dot-and-carry. Efga Hartlip, who
lay in her bed till noon, had broken down, her daughter
too was wearying under the double weight, and the black
and the pomegranate dragged along together like old
Raistrick on his two sticks. Now half York's spires seemed
to have concealed themselves again behind long grey walls
only a couple of miles ahead, and all at once there had
come a rude diversion. For a moment the elderly cavalier's
hand had gone to the hilt of his curved sword as another
boor, approaching the palankeen's curtain, had made as if
to pry within. In that same moment the buffoon with the
bladder, joining forces with the vendor of flies, ventured
on a grossness that exceeded all bounds, and there was a
glint of steel as Gandelyn whipped out his poniard. A short
pop and the bladder exploded at its point. With glaring
eyes the youth looked round for some constable or any of
the civic power, but saw none. Then with a stride he was
at the Italian horseman's side, a hand on his tasselled glove.
He too had ladies under protection from such outrages.

'Signor—'

The foreigner started as if at some fresh affront. Looking haughtily down however he saw only a dark, angry
young figure who had addressed him in his own tongue.
Yet Gandelyn's own skill in languages stopped at his
church Latin, his army French and 'lollbrueder,' and at a
loss, he stammered.

'Non   Italiano—Français—moi,   Signor,   je   suis
Anglais—'

So let it be put into his own speech. The privacy of a
foreign lady travelling in England had been invaded. It
should be reported to high quarters in York forthwith.
But the linguist himself was also *gentimment accompagnée*,
by a widow lady *en deuil* and a virtuous *bachelette*, her
daughter. With words, expressive face and pointing finger
he explained as best he could, while the visitor from over
the seas never removed his eyes from him.

'Her husband, signor, was a knight. In York they seek
their kinsfolk. They have been placed in my care till
better can be found, the elder has fallen lame . . . these
canaille—'

In short, he was asking that they might be permitted to
ride in the palankeen. There was room in it for ten, and
the matron inside, again peeping round the curtain to see
who was speaking to her husband, had said something in
Italian. Further words passed. The signor turned to
Gandelyn and nodded in assent. There were movements
behind the curtains as the waiting-woman passed to the
opening, which was behind. With no more speech
Gandelyn beckoned forward his shrinking charges and
handed them in.

The interior of the palankeen was honey-coloured and
rosy with a silky half-light. Heaped up luggage had been
rearranged by the waiting-woman to make room for the
newcomers, and now she and her mistress had resumed
their former places at the vehicle's forward end. The taut
drum-hoops of the roof vibrated with the rumbling and
jolting, but the side-curtains that fluttered from their
valances were in gentle and continual motion with the air.
Let it therefore be set down that in no less state than this,
in the Year of Grace 1441, between Whitsuntide and the
Feast of Corpus Christi, there rode into York two women

by the name of Hartlip, while their squire and rescuer walked with his hand on the rail behind.

For there was no riding for Gandelyn. As a penance he had been ordered to York at a footpace, meditating as he went, wherefore he walked for the most part with his eyes on the ground, though to a walking-pace all were now reduced. But he smiled as he walked, as a musician smiles who hears music without instrument or score, tapping with his finger to the harmony within. Did he however chance to lift his eyes (and he had been at some little trouble about his adjustment of the two rear curtains) he could see part way into the palankeen's veiled interior. A yard beyond the curtain was a corner of a shawl, in which among overblown pinks and pomegranates stiff little bowmen hunted white gazelles. No harm in that, and it was amusing that when a fold of a shawl moved of itself a little Persian bowman peeped out, and when it moved again was back in his ambush once more. He could see her hands, busy with her bundle, drawing on a pair of faded gloves, and down dropped his eyes to the ground again. When next he looked her hands were in her lap and the Italian lady was pretending to be reading a little book. Now it gladdened him that he had given not only help but pleasure too. Anybody could go to York, but not everybody could ride there in a plumed and painted palankeen, with a foreign lady of high station for company and a moustachioed cavalier on a red-caparisoned horse to clear the way for them in front.

And where shall a fairer city be found than York in the spring, a city of fourteen thousand souls, enthroned where its three ridings meet, a capital city, a seat of government and ecclesiastical rule, cleansed of its harlotry and vice when from Italy and Muscovy and the Levant the rich merchant-magnificoes come to trade? With every step you drew nearer its grey walls the flowering burgeoned. Ings

and leasowes were white with daisies, ditch and marsh
yellow with kingcups. Whitsun was over, Corpus now a
matter of days, York itself at hand. Lest the bawds and
prostitutes should creep back again searchers and scruti-
neers had been posted at every Bar, and in York from
bustling street to quiet garden or leafy close was seldom
more than a stride. Blossom of pear and bud of apple
looked over walltops, overhead in the streets still swung
such Whitsun banners as it had hardly been worth the
trouble to take down. Some accident had separated the
Signor Battista from the guides who had led him through
forest and fen, but here at Monk Bart they awaited him.
His inn was the *Bull*, near Mint Yard. Along Goodramgate the palankeen rumbled, plumes, carved wheels,
occupants and all.

The inn was approached by an archway. The chamber
over it was probably a through-chamber with casements
opening on both yard and street, and these resounded with
cries and 'Whoas!' for the turning and manœuvring of so
lengthy a vehicle. But it was accomplished without mishap.
Under the arch the honeyed interior was suddenly
darkened. Then slowly half a curtain was drawn aside,
from within.

It was Brother James who had so often smiled over his
crabbed breves and semibreves, hearing a music that was
not there. Sometimes too Brother James had watched
young Gandelyn's brown eyes fixed on the lesson's hour-
candle as the flame crept down to its notch, flickered,
passed it, and burned on, with nothing to show that an
hour had just died but another hour had been born. The
Signor Battista had reached his inn, but nobody had
reserved a lodging at the *Bull* for the wayfaring three.
Presently the Signora's woman would be unpacking trunks
and hampers, shaking out garments, preparing her
mistress's bed; but let Echo Hartlip put on what gloves

she pleased her hand was still the hand that had stripped
the bark and scoured out the pot. Her mother was to
provide for, she would have to traipse York for the best
employment she could find, and for their arrival she had
gathered her bundle to her on the seat and with one hand
was adjusting the shawl about her face. The other still
held the curtain she had twitched aside. Then a trousered
twinkling little Persian withdrew himself slowly into his
fold. As if the moment of suffering had come, he saw the
quivering of her outpushed lip, the tear at stand in her eye.
Then the twilight lifted again and the wheels of the chariot
ceased to turn.

In the yard all was a running of ostlers and porters and
the touts who had followed behind. They were the first to
descend, and under an upper gallery was a bench. He took
them to it, and leaving them there entered the inn. Efga
Hartlip would have to get to Thomas Twentyman's
though she dropped.

They were busy in the inn and it took him some time
to get his information. When he returned they were still
there, and he stooped and picked up Echo Hartlip's bundle.

'Come,' he said.

Only twice before had he been in York, but everybody
knows the way to Coney Street. 'Thomas Twentyman the
eel-catcher?' they had said at the counter; 'over Ouse
Bridge to the Skeldergate and then ask the first you meet,'
and the Coney Street in which they stood was multicoloured with banners. On their poles they rose at the doors
of the great inns, they swung from gable to gable across
the way, they were draped from balconies, banners of this
and that and everything, devices of church or benefaction,
insignia of the military orders, of the guilds and corporate
bodies, the arms of resident families. It was still afternoon,
but the siesta was over and in the streets the visiting
merchants were taking the air. Impassively in their cloth-

ing of other fashions they kept their faces until some
English friend or host appeared, when magically they
became all animation and pleasure. But two of the three
lagged while the third retarded his pace to theirs, and if
this was Coney Street what of Ouse Bridge, when after
nearly half an hour they had managed to get so far? The
timbered buildings that rose on the bridge's either hand,
the chapels, the beamed guildhall and all who jostled and
shouldered one another there? But as long as he was by
let none in York suppose that two women went unpro-
tected! For the younger of them set no guard on herself.
She had parted the shawl again, this time to look at the
wonder of the shops, the mercers, the glovers, the jewellers
the drapers, the tippets and turbans of the foreigners, their
chains, their clasps. Men were more numerous on Ouse
Bridge than women, and he was glad when they had
finished with it, for past it there was more elbow-room.

Then again he saw her countenance change. In the
Skeldergate were the set-back houses of the wealthier
citizens, each with its glimpse of orchard or peep of
paddock or the leafy top of a garden wall. But beyond the
postern Foss and Ouse met, and it was there, hard under
the Old Bail wall, that Thomas-Twentyman lived. Dropping down to the river was a rutty path. On the stream at
which it stopped hoys and barges were moored and small
boats moved in and out. The muddy foreshore was given
over to wharfingers and fishermen and the trades of the
waterside, and where their huts and sheds ended a short
row of double-storied buildings leaned against the wall of
the Bail itself. They were patched up of many materials,
with oars standing at their doorways and nets stretched
out to dry. The lower chambers seemed to be carpenters'
sheds and repositories for old stores, and Gandelyn hailed
a man who was melting something at an outside fire. The
house at which the tinker pointed was the furthermost of

the row, a rickety stairway ran up its outer wall, and at its corner a waterbutt caught the rain from the roof. All smelt of fish and tar and mud and waterside discardings, and across the river with its moored barges the castle rose on its monticule, making with the Bail a *tête-de-pont* to guard either bank.

Thomas Twentyman was not in his dwelling. Looking into his lower room Gandelyn saw an iron cauldron on three short legs over a half-extinct fire, wicker pottles and traps, nets hanging from nails. As the herbs had dried on Efga Hartlip's ceiling, so here several sticks of eels depended by the gills, most of them still alive. Now the tinker had gone in search of Thomas Twentyman himself, but only a week before it had most unhandsomely happened that Thomas had been smartly fined for selling his eels direct to the cooks of the inns, for he was no more a licensed fishmonger than he was mayor of York and its fourteen thousand souls. From a pile of rotting cordage he advanced, small and skinny and weatherbeaten, in a pair of great wading boots copiously slashed to let the water out again. He had a pair of empty eel-sticks in his hand, and his voice was querulous and inhospitable as he came up.

'You've gotten me wrong. I'm Thomas Twentyman o' Ouse-bank. Where do you say you're from?'

'Washburn-in-the-Forest.'

'Isn't that where them prisoners was marched in from? You cannot be put across here. All that side's guarded. Yon's the prison, but you'll ha' to go round by Castlegate.'

And even when it was explained it was no more than Gandelyn had already guessed. Because, many years ago, Thomas Twentyman had married a woman long since dead, he did not therefore hold himself beholden to all or any of the same name. First he protested he had nowhere to put them. When next he learned that they had no money he flung up his arms to their pits, for half a shirt, his slashed boots and the breeches he had tucked into them were the whole of his clothing.

'The hangment, what next! I tell you I ha' no more than kenneling for myself! Try Clementhorpe yonder. Over the meadow and past them cows. There's no bull and cows wean't hurt you.'

But if only for the night the man would have to do something, and Gandelyn had stepped to the stairway that climbed his outer wall. Mounting it and looking in he found a sizeable loft, neat enough, for the rougher a man's occupation is by day the more likely he is to redd himself up at the day's end. Eels wriggled from the ceiling beneath, but the upper room had a bed, a hearth with a small stock of hardware set tidily out, and the table from which the eel-catcher ate. The square window at the end looked not towards the boats and the castle but over the meadow where the cattle grazed. The place would have to serve for lack of better, and descending again Gandelyn made short work of the eelman's protestations.

'Talk of all that to-morrow. Two days these have been on their feet and are like to drop.'

'Eh? This'un told me they rode into York in a coach!'

'That's as it may be. Money I know of is on its way to them and they know none in York but you. By the look of you a night in your boat'll do you no harm. Make that room ready for them or it may be you'll hear further of it.'

And whether it was the hint of money to come or the tap of authority's rod he had so lately received, Thomas Twentyman grumblingly did as he was bidden. Gandelyn, moreover, stayed to see it done. Nightly Thomas and the tinker sought the same alehouse together, and down to the boiling-shed came what he needed for his evening dressing. Up the stairs the others passed, but with all now done that he could do Gandelyn still lingered. The day was dying, the cattle in the meadow returning to their byre, the Clementhorpe's almshouse losing itself in the shadow of the Old Bail wall. The weary two would be quickly into bed, and having closed the door upon them he next took a turn along the foreshore where the scatter of lights rode on the water. So Washburn's prisoners had arrived. He wondered whether the Washburn men would be any better for the benefaction of the late Sir Matthew Poole. Then he idled as far as the meadow, but there was little to be seen that way, and returning he stood by Thomas Twentyman's waterbutt, where in the upper room the candle had been set down on the window ledge. He could not see its flame, but it may be that he too thought of Brother James's hour-candle, burning down to its nick, flickering, and then burning steadily on. At one moment he fancied he saw the shadow of a head, combed and dressed for the night. Then the candle went suddenly out. Always some monastic lodging for rest and prayer could be found for any who could say he was a scholar of Netherby, and an hour later he had found one, within a stone's throw of the Pavement. But the lantern that burned on All Saints throughout the night closed an eye as much as he.

II

In the summer York threw open its gates with the first ray of the rising sun. The day after the day now dawning would be the vigil of Corpus, the solemn Thursday on which the Body of Christ was carried with processional prayer and incense and chanting through the city, and to-day was therefore the last general market for three days to come. Gandelyn too rose while the fraters of the hospice still slept, first making sure that his letters were safely in his belt-pouch. That for the Archbishop was thick and formidable-looking, and he hardly dared to hope that in a missive so weighty there might lurk some small commendation of himself to these players of the Lord's Prayer. He might be required to wait in York for a letter to carry back, but that remained to be seen. Out of the hospice and to the broad Pavement he stepped.

Already they were assembled in groups there, the market-gardeners and purveyors of the countryside who had journeyed all night to await the raising of the Bars. In the grey light they were unpacking their poultry and vegetables and panniers of eggs and hampers of butter, talking to this official or that acquaintance as they waited, for until the bell should ring for the opening of the market York did its public business in a public-businesslike way. No ounce of commodity must be offered for sale till it had been tested, tasted, weighed, the weights with which it was weighed weighed also. As well as the gates, Ouse too was watched for every bale or cran that entered or was unloaded. Lest cook or innkeeper should have set some unlicensed hoarding by the searchers and inspectors passed in and out of the inns, examining cupboards, peering under bulks, checking the stock in the back premises. Indeed, some said that to sell a pound of butter it took four clerks to every salesman. But let them be careful in whose hearing they muttered that York was governed to death and that but for a little complicity here and a little eye-shutting there its business would never have got done at all. The country folk ate their breakfasts as they stood, but the light on the roofs was beginning to catch the banners and the opening shops below. It was far too early for Gandelyn to be delivering letters, so in and out among the inspectors and their clerks he idled, stopping to watch them as they lifted cloths and looked under scales, checking and comparing with the lists in their hands. Then, leaving the

Pavement, from street to street and market to market he began to pass, from the quarters and sides and mountains of lesser flesh of the Shambles to Foss and its fishmarket, thence to the cornmarket with its eggs and cheeses and sacks of corn and meal. He wished he had money of his own to spend, but he had no more of it than might suffice him for some sudden emergency. Money, moreover, suggested some precise sum, thirteen-and-fourpence say, and after an hour or so of it he had begun to weary of all this provender for York and its fourteen thousand mouths. In a narrow and deserted street of storied wooden houses he dipped under a carved lintel and found himself in a close with a church in it and a beggar already shaking his dish on its steps at the sight of him. A procession of collegiates not yet in the tonsure was just shuffling in. He followed them, and in a candle-glimmering half-darkness sat down to muse while York entered on another day.

It was from the walls that the city could best be seen, and what a city to show to the stranger within its gates! The market-bell had rung, the inspectors had retired to their offices again, the Pavement was a brawl of buying and selling. Under the banners of Coney Street the merchants in their best clothes greeted such of their foreign guests as were yet abroad, and now it was what-you-would for courtesy and compliment, proper pride yet distinguished consideration for the other. If one had not his clerk with two languages with him another had, so if Genoa or marbled Venice had better to show than York let them be hearing about it! Si, si, signor, that is our Minster, but Saint Mary's is older, and when you have seen our city its abbot has prayed us to dine at his house! This is our river, the Ouse (explain to these gentlemen, Ned; this is my clerk, who speaks excellent Italian). Our northern rivers, signor, are like the fingers of my hand, thus: and a

finger for Aire and another for Wharfe and a finger apiece
for Nidd and Ure and Swale. *Perdona mi?* Excellently com-
pared, as it might be your own Adige and Tagliamento
and Po! That is my poor house, under the spire of Holy
Trinity, and when we have seen the Minster I will take
you there to meet the ladies of my family. Saint Mary's
has Roman pavements—but who are we to speak of pavements to those who have trodden the pavements of Rome
itself? . . . So the courtesies were bandied, with much
praising of jewelled dagger-hilts and admiration of rings.

And now Gandelyn, coming out of the church again, had
bethought himself of the Signor Battista. The Signor
Battista was lodging at the *Bull*, the commotion of arrival
had left little opportunity for civilities, and the least he
could do would be to call upon the signor, thank him for
his graciousness to a knight's widow *en deuil* and a virtuous
bachelette, and to trust that his own lady had recovered from
the fatigue of her journey. To the *Bull* therefore he made
his way, lingering for not more than a moment as he
turned into the shadow of its arch.

The wooden gallery that ran round three sides of the
yard was a stir of chambermaids and domestics about their
morning duties. In the farther stables horses were being
groomed, ostlers carried hay, lads buckets of water. Tilts
and waggons had been backed under cover, and among
them the palankeen of yesterday projected farther into the
yard than the rest because of its unusual length. The
servants of the inn had been too busy to take in its flowered
curtains yet, and had not one of them moved he would
have passed the vehicle without a glance. But he stood
suddenly still as some motion within caught his eye.

For half the morning he had been dawdling about
markets and sitting down in churches to kill the time.
Now, with the Archbishop's letter in his pouch, he had
only come to pay his duty to the Signor Battista. But he

had taken a quick stride to the curtain that had moved. He plucked it aside. Then he fell back. There in the same corner as before she sat, to all appearances as if she had spent the night there.

She had made herself a bodkin with a small splinter of wood, and with this she was pushing and poking at her nails. He spoke sharply.

'What are you doing here?'

She glanced rebelliously up, popped a finger into her mouth, and did not answer.

'Where is your mother?' and when it did come her answer was no more than two words long.

'In bed.'

'Does she know you're here?'

'She was asleep.'

'And how long have you been up?'

'Hours. I've been for a walk.'

'This is not your carosse and you've no business in it.'

'I didn't know anywhere else to go.'

'But I took you and your mother to Thomas Twentyman's.'

'He went out with that other man. He forgot we were there. Then when he came back he was so drunk he fell down the stairs,' and his brows came together.

'Take that finger out of your mouth and don't speak in a mumble. What have you been doing all the morning?'

'I went to that Bridge.'

'Has either you or your mother made any plans for yourselves yet?'

'We've only just got here. But now I'm going to see if she'll make herself a vowess.'

'A *what?*'

'A vowess. The priest gives them a ring and a veil and then they're vowesses.'

'You said "now" you were going to ask her. What's the meaning of that "now"?'

'And being a vowess isn't the same as being a sister, because sisters have to live there but vowesses can live where they like.'

His frown had darkened. A vowess, Efga Hartlip, whipped thrice round a church and told to show her face in the parish no more! . . . 'And you that's lived in a forest half your life, where did you get all this of sisters and vowesses?' and to that her answer was prompt and startling.

'A gentleman on Ouse Bridge told me.'

'A who? A what?

'A very respectable gentleman, and it was his gown I noticed, and we were both looking into the same shop, and he asked me in what he could help me.'

'He—' but better wait till his voice shook a little less.

'And he praised my shawl, and said he had a friend a pardoner just back from Rome, and a girl with makings such as he saw in me—'

How ardently he desired to meet this kindly gentleman of Ouse Bridge should fortune ever bring them together! Not a day in York yet, unable to read or write and with employment to find, how long would it be before its Babylon swallowed her up? His foot was on the palankeen's step, and two chambermaids on the opposite gallery had come to a stand with their pillow-carrying and were watching with their heads smilingly together. Her talking-to would be better administered inside than out. In he stepped abruptly and the door-curtain fell to of itself. He was too perturbed to notice that he began with the very words her mother had used to himself.

'Echo Hartlip, how old are you?'

'Seventeen come Martinmas.'

'Have you been baptised?'

'No.'

'How then come you by the name of Echo?'

Her answer was to begin prodding again with her bodkin, and he too made a fresh start.

'This Newbiggin castle as you call it. Do you remember anything of it?'

'It had a great hall, and always a good table kept, and a beautiful garden, and my father was its knight . . .'

'That's your mother's remembering, not yours.'

'You said so too.'

'Leave that for now. Perhaps I did, but it's not the same. Newbiggin isn't a castle and never was. It was just a strongpoint for soldiers to fall back on in the old days. It's been a prison since then. With its court in its yard it might be a prison again.'

But he saw plainly it was useless. Those who had called Matthew Poole knight had looked no higher than his new-gilt spurs, she had grown up in her fancy, and it was not for him to tell her that those who lingered about Ouse Bridge were likely to follow those who were turned out of the town when Corpus came. She had sought this palankeen only because she knew of no other place in York in which to rest her feet. Again its interior was soft with light, the yard was a coming and going of feeding, grooming, washing the road-dust from the vehicles. Briskly with the scolding then and get it over.

'Echo Hartlip, you're a very disobedient girl.'

'Nobody told me not to.'

'You're old enough to know without telling. And those nails you're fiddling with, you've been biting 'em.'

'Two got broke.'

'Then let 'em grow again, and you'll never find yourself work in York with a face like that. Moping won't help. They like them with cheerful faces. Straighten yourself up and let me see you laugh.'

'What for?'

'Because it's better than crying. Because a laugh

does you good. Because everybody likes people who laugh.'

'There isn't anything to laugh at.'

'There's always something to laugh at. Make a face and laugh at yourself. Laugh at that Italian lady in the corner peeping at us over her little book. Laugh at her woman seeing we don't run away with their baggage. Laugh at me. You make *me* laugh!'

But instead of laughing she turned in her corner, covered her face, and burst into a torrent of tears.

So when, in his experience of the world, had young Robert Gandelyn sat in a closed palankeen before, staring in dismay at a young woman who, bidden to laugh, suddenly buried her face and shook with passionate convulsions? Alas for the peacock and his tail, alas for gallantries and struttings and the gilded viands of France! At first he could make nothing of her broken sobs.

'Judith was lost—I was looking for her—'

'Tut, what's all this?'

'Jemima Hackett never gave me none but foul words, ever—and then Will Acle came in and he started, but you opened the door, and they always know when things are done in a noble way—'

But he could not stop the sobbing from the corner in which he had placed himself, and he had crossed to her side.

'And him with the great neck was bawling, and you stuck your dagger into the other's bladder, and then you spoke foreign to the gentleman on the horse—'

So let those who must go about the world doing things in too noble a way see what they bring upon themselves. But at least something could be done about that too-talkative shawl of hers, yet when he took a little Persian between his thumb and finger to draw it aside she only wrapped herself up closer in her corner.

'Listen, Echo,' and the sobbing ceased for a moment,

for at the same time he had given the tip of her ear a gentle tug. 'Something will have to be done. It's to be seen something will have to be done. But this morning I have business on my hands, and first I must take you back to your mother. Then if Thomas Twentyman's no help it'll be for her to try some other place. My business is at the Minster. It shouldn't take me long, so if you'll come along with me and wait for me in the church—'

But the sentence was never finished. At that moment the whole palankeen gave a heave and a lurch that flung them in a lump together. There was a flooding of water on the wheels beneath them, followed by a second bucketted cascade as the curtains were flung aside and a splashing mop was thrust in. Little doubt but the chambermaids of the gallery knew all about it, for there three or four of them were, tittering together, while the yard seemed half full of people who rocked with laughter.

And his boots were of hide, so that he could laugh too, but she had jumped angrily up. Out of the palankeen in her shawl she sprang. Still laughing, across the yard and under the archway he led her away. But now his duty to the Signor Battista would have to be paid at some other time.

III

The Minster nave was thronged that morning with all sorts. So interwoven was the religious rule with their lives that its celebrations affected them as little as the lives of the streets, and they used the place for traffic, gossip or prayer indifferently. But beyond the transept she was little likely to be molested, and now his manner, too, was businesslike.

'They'll soon dry on you. Kneel down under the window in the sun. Echo Hartlip, do you know what a promise is?'

'Yes.'

'Then you're to promise not to move from here, nor to speak or let yourself be spoken to by none.'

She nodded, and with a frown to impress it on her he left her there to dry.

At his hospice he had made certain inquiries, and had been advised that it would be best to ask for the Archbishop through the precentor. His quarters were to be approached by a small door beyond a buttress of the southern wall, immediately within which wound narrow winding stone stairs, and these five minutes later he was ascending. At a low panelled door on a landing he knocked, waited, knocked again, and then made bold to walk in. The apartment was small and sunless, and it seemed to be both the precentor's chequer and his repository for stores. Facing him was a long narrow oak table on which stood piles of singing books, supplies of parchment and ink and other clerkly apparatus, and at it sat a soberly-clad student or amanuensis of much his own age. This youth looked up as underlings do who are left in charge.

'Your business?'

'I bring a letter for His Grace the Archbishop.'

'His Grace is not in the cathedral. He is at Bishopthorpe.'

'His suffragan then.'

'At this hour he is not to be seen,' and at that Gandelyn judged it well to be brief too.

'Then be so good as to take me to the precentor,' he said, and the youth rose and went out.

The occupation at which Gandelyn had interrupted him was the counting off of sheets of paper from a pile. He returned, took no further notice of Gandelyn, and resumed his occupation. His air of self-importance was not much to Gandelyn's liking, but you never knew, and he was getting tired of watching his laborious way of counting when the door by which he had gone out opened again and the precentor stood there. He was thin and for severity of mien all that a precentor should be; Gandelyn dipped his knee and watched his face as he presented his package.

'This,' said the precentor, looking up from it 'is Netherby's seal.'

'It is from there I come, sir. My instructions were to deliver it to His Grace himself, or if that might not be, to his suffragan,' but he found the precentor as little accommodating as his clerk.

'Corpus is upon us. There is not time. Both have a thousand things to do. Let it suffice that I am York's precentor.'

'Then, reverend sir, my protection for my return?'

'If you mean your receipt for this—Peter, a taper, wax and our seal,' and sitting down at the table he wrote it there and then. But it was no more than a receipt for a package, and Gandelyn demurred.

'Sir, with all respect, the letter is not yet even read. Its answer may press. It may also be that in it is a post-scriptum concerning myself and what next I am to do in York.'

'Where in York are you to be found?'

'I lodged last night at a small house behind All Saints on the Pavement.'

'Then return there and wait. The letter shall be in the suffragan's hands after nones. If there is anything in it touching yourself you shall be informed at your lodging,' and with no more to say the precentor retired to the inner parts of the Cathedral again.

Those who cannot have the crumb must make the best of the crust. Gandelyn's acquaintance in York was all to make, the more people he now knew the better, and if there was a year between himself and this young scribe at the table he had the advantage of it. A little familiarity then could do no harm, and uninvited he placed himself on the bench at his side.

'I can show you a handier way of counting paper than that, Peter,' he said. 'What's your other name?' and for answer he had a stare.

'My name's Oates. Who are you?'

'I've been in scriptoriums too, and you do it this way,' and taking leave to stretch across him he showed him the circular movement with the thumb-nail that fans the leaves out so that they can be counted a number at a time with ease. 'Would I could have handed that letter to His Grace himself! Is Bishopthorpe where he lives?' and the youth's own thumb began to circle.

'Ay, that's a short way of knowing how many beans make five,' he conceded. 'What's your name?'

'Robert Gandelyn, of Netherby as you may guess, but newly back from France, and now in need of help in a little matter that's much on my mind. How well do you know your way about York?'

They are often the most impressed whose own emulousness is touched. Peter Oates could not boast that he had been in France, but did he know his way about York? Ay, that he did, he was presently declaring, and for his years few better! Besides his clerking for the precentor he was a collegiate of Saint Leonard's, and to help himself out with his studies hired himself as a tutor to the children of the wealthiest houses. At busy times he gave a hand in the offices of merchants and lawyers too, and as, in short, he was the very man Gandelyn was looking for, straight into it he plunged.

'You heard me tell the precentor this letter might have a postscriptum touching myself. Well, for a start (for there's other things too), I want to know where I shall find a lot that call themselves the Guild of the Lord's Prayer.'

So when your luck comes let it not slip through your fingers.

'What, them that Robin Crosby's sweating and cursing over?' Peter exclaimed, and Gandelyn nodded.

'That's the man,' and Peter's tongue was loosed.

Not only was Master Crosby to be found at Roger Wymark's great house next to Holy Trinity in Micklegate; it was also at this same house that Peter himself attended, thrice in each week, to teach the mercer's children their ciphering and Latin roots.

Was ever then such fortune? Gut fish and skin Thomas Twentyman's eels! Sleep in his loft, for him to come home drunk and fall down his outside stairs! Wealthy mercers had households and wives. These needed sempstresses and maids, nurses, keepers of linen and caretakers of wardrobes. Exulting, Gandelyn was on his feet.

'Think you I should find Master Crosby at this house now?' he cried.

'Ay, and till nightfall and by lantern-light, the muddle they're in!'

'And if there's aught for me in this letter, who'd be the one to let me know?'

'Myself most like.'

'Then it's a chance I'll be seeing you before long, Peter,' and with a triumphant wave of the hand he was off.

The two were approaching the bridge before he spoke.

'Are your legs dry yet?' he asked her.

'No. The sun went off them, and you told me not to move,' and out broke his laugh.

'We shall have to get you a pair of boots like Thomas Twentyman's, that let the water out again! I meant you weren't to get into talk with the first you met, not that you mustn't move a yard to dry your legs!'

'Where are we going?'

'Wait and see.'

But already apprehension was in her eyes. She no longer looked at the houses that bulged out storey upon storey like the sternworks of great ships. He had said nothing to her yet of his conversation with Peter Oates, collegiate, tutor, clerk-at-large, with his foot in a wealthy mercer's house. The way they were taking led back to Thomas Twentyman's again.

But no Skeldergate postern came into sight. Instead he had taken the turn into Micklegate, where ahead of them Holy Trinity's spire pierced the blue, and suddenly he stopped, with an arm across her stopping her too.

'Hark . . . Yes, this'll be the place,' he said.

But it was none of Holy Trinity's music that had caught his ear. He had stopped before a closed double door strapped with blacksmith's work, and he picked up a stone to knock with. After a minute or so a guichet slid aside, an eye appeared, a few words were exchanged, and a panel within the door opened. Instantly the music grew louder. It was not continuous, but a medley of sounds like those of a fairground, of tuning fiddles, nackers, the trill of a pipe or the strumming of a zither, intermingled with a distant confusion of voices. Ahead of them along an enclosed alley a patch of sunny green showed. Then from the alley's end all could be seen.

Mercer Wymark's private pleasance seemed to have been turned into a carnival. A spacious lawn was crowded with all manner of people, and in the middle of it, for token that the family was not childless, a small quintain had been set up for exercise and play. But only its upper half could be seen for the heaps of gear that littered it about. Coffers stood open, discarded garments lay on the grass, with harness, cords, properties and all the apparatus of those whose toil is the entertainment of others. Unsmiling priests, costumiers and tiring-men for the nonce, moved here and there with vestments. These they were draping upon the smiths and saddlers and weavers and fullers who for a day would enact the great of the world, doffing their costly borrowings when Corpus and its pageantry were over. Grave officials looked on, the guild-masters who paid, the craftsmen and foremen, councillors, the privileged, with here and there a foreign guest. Only the more distant portion of the lawn had been roped off for the mercer's domestic privacy. And over all, shadowing and close at hand, the spire of Holy Trinity tapered into the blue.

But it was to what was drawn up under the elms that Gandelyn's eyes had instantly flown. There in a row they stood, the chariot-stages that to-morrow would pass in glorious procession through the city, from Holy Trinity to Skeldergate End, back again along Skeldergate to Ouse Bridge and by way of Concy Street and Petergate to the Pavement, stopping before the greater houses, a dozen stations in all and to each station its play. He counted them. Six he made them, so probably they would be joined by others, and there under the elms they glittered with the arms of the city and the badges and insignia of the guilds, petticoated with curtains to hide the wheels and axles on which they moved. Short ladders led up to the level of the stages, and his dark eyes shone with his inward picturing of it all—Isaac upon his face that he might not see the cruel knife in Abraham's hand, the Shepherds talking their grass and sheep as they waited for the Star to rise, while on the next waggon the carpenters set up the gilded pillar for the Scourging and the Cross for the Body Itself—

But Echo Hartlip was shrinking back from a Herod-like figure that grimaced and mowed as he practised his part alone, his vizage painted black that all might know his soul was damned. Another, hideously masked and gloved with fierce talons, clashed his pincers together, to be mocked by a sudden cockcrow. And last of all Gandelyn saw the chariot that, too lofty to go under the elms, stood by itself in a space apart. It was the Noah. Now they had got up its splendid sail, its gilded topcastle rode its mast like a golden crown upon a sword, and the rehearsal was already in progress. Noah was adjuring his wife to leave her spinning or at least to bring it with her before water destroyed the world. But saucily she was answering him back, and as Gandelyn dragged Echo Hartlip forward some cue must have been missed, for with a clapping of his hands that brought all to a stop there bounded to the stage as if at a handspring a tall and jauntering and storming figure.

'Dolt! Mudhead! Ape! Is it so you are going to shame us to-morrow before all York? What rhymes with bowers and towers but showers? Back to the levins and cataracts again! Now—"*Both balls and bowers, castles and towers*—"'

And Gandelyn's heart gave a sigh of content. At last, at long-last, he had found him.

But now the trouble was to get speech with him, for Noah was only one of them. Next it was the turn of the pleading Isaac, and after him of the Shepherds, and for mounting stages he disdained ladders, but put as it were a finger on an edge, gathered his feet up under him, and was there as lightly as a bubble that bounces from the back of a hand. He was the actor who could make himself into two men, the one fighting a combat with the other, and when he had finished with the stages there was still no rest for him, for if it was not a councillor in furs it was a priest with a garment or a messenger with a paper, and suddenly a voice spoke at Gandelyn's elbow. It was the voice of the porter who had admitted them.

'You'll never catch Master Crosby by following him about, young gentleman. If I were you I'd place myself over yonder and wait till he comes,' and he pointed past the quintain to a thick box-hedge by the rope that shut off the private garden. A tunnel or arbour had been cut through it and a small table and stool placed within. The table was littered with papers on which objects had been placed to keep the wind from carrying them away, and like a cock-bird on a nest the player's tall feathered cap sat on a pile of accounts and bills.

Gandelyn too had rehearsed his part. The last time he had seen this pageant-master he himself had headed a slow procession with a black-draped cross in his hands, but he was skilled in lighter accomplishments too. Modestly yet deftly he would advance these. His actual experience might be scanty, but always he had felt it in him, and (he would say) it was because he had heard of Master Crosby's own resounding fame—but he never got a quarter as far. There came with long strides across the lawn as it were a skip-jack of wires and springs, who took not the slightest notice of the two standing there by the hedge, but placing himself at his table clapped a hand feverishly to his fore-head. It was a steep, smooth, harassed yet calm-looking forehead. It had tufts of brown hair to right and left of it, but up its middle a habitually-sweeping hand had worn a polished path. It swept it now as placing himself on his stool he began to rock himself gently back and forth. Gandelyn's shadow darkened the opening of his arbour, but the shadow made no difference. Still he rocked, and when he spoke it was without even looking up.

'After Corpus,' he said to whomever it might be.

'Master Crosby—if I might have the favour of a word with you—'

'After Corpus.'

'I am just now from the Cathedral—'

'After Corpus.'

'—where I was the bearer of a letter. I have some reason to believe that it might contain a small commenda-tion of myself—'

'After Corpus, after Corpus, after Corpus,' and as a parrot could have said as much he sought another way.

'The last time we met, Master Crosby, you were at the head of a team of oxen. You had a dozen men with you, and though I spoke not a word, nor was then to be spoken to, they uncovered their heads. You did the same, and bade them get down on their knees till I and what I had with me had passed,' and at that the surprised actor did look up.

But it was not at Gandelyn that he looked. Echo Hartlip, standing a little back, was watching the coming and going about the quintain. Suddenly she gave a violent start as she heard a peremptory call that could only be directed to herself.

'You! Standing there! Uncovered heads, say you? That that's on *her* head, bid her take it off! Put it on again! Look up—look at that spire, look at aught you like! Stay, take this!' and among the objects that weighed the papers down was the wooden platter that had evidently served him for some hastily-snatched meal. On this he clapped his feathered cap. 'Here's her dish and here's the head on it! You that spoke, take it to her!—now, wench, back, ten yards! Higher, higher, so all behind can see! Now walk!'

Gandelyn had raised a protesting voice, but the eager actor was half off his stool.

'Stand you out o' my light! After Corpus! . . . By my box of paints and beards, Salome! . . . Again! And again! Never mind your face, just walk! *Salome*, or I never played Herod yet!' Then, for not only the eyes in the bald brow but the man's whole mind seemed to be made of bits of looking-glass that flashed in a trice from one thing to another, 'Is she your wife?'

'Master Crosby, for I'm given to understand that's your name—' but down came a hand on a flutter of papers.

'Where did you light on her? Where do they make them like this? How comes it that I . . . but no, never, never again!' and sinking back to his stool he began to rock again. 'Their Guild of the Lord's Prayer! (After Corpus, after Corpus!) Not a penny to call their own, not a chamber to meet in, all their wares a gilded scourging-post and a

handful of masks and pincers for the devils! Nay, for the
Descent itself they grudge you half a dozen devils! Never
again! I'll sing my way along the roads, but no more
Guilds of the Lord's Prayer—no more, no more!'

It was only the beginning of his tirade. Next, out went
a long arm to the groups about the quintain. Never a song
or a line among 'em, yet because they paid they were for
managing all—the best stations before their own mansions,
the pick of the lines omitted for fear of giving offence, this
and that written in because some rich old usurer must be
flattered—

'And you cannot have Noah without animals! Animals
eat, and am I a pageant-master or a chandler? But no more,
no more! We'll see this Corpus over, but never again! Did
you say you were wed?'

'No.'

'Not a word would she have to speak, not a word! She'd
be to loosen and supple and torment a bit, but for a singing
of motion and movement such as not one in ten thousand
sees till the right hands have brought it out—*then* they
see—nay, I cannot hear myself speak for that prater over
yonder—'

For now from the gilded topcastle across the lawn could
be heard the mouthing voice of him who had been cast for
the part of the Almighty Himself—

> 'Noah, to thee and to thy fry
> My benison give I
> That ye shall wax and multiply
> And fill the earth again—'

But at least it served to flash that looking-glass of the
actor's mind elsewhere, for again his hand swept his
elderly-young brow as he looked at Gandelyn for the first
time. Then he began to pick up his scattered bills from the
ground again.

'But neither finger nor foot can be lifted till after Corpus,' he said at last. 'Yes, I call you to mind now. You seemed but a lad to be in charge of a weight like that, and I'll not say I haven't given it many a thought since, you coming on us right out of the eye o' the sun with that in your hands. 'Twould make a scene. Seek me in the *Keys* the day after to-morrow. Now I've got the *Descent* and the *Kings* at Master Campion's, then to the guildhall, then . . . and if I'm asleep when you come see you don't wake me. Eh? Can you stop here a bit? Freely. You'll find a tent with food in it. Did I say after to-morrow? Three days might be better—no, she hasn't that wedded look yet—' and bundling his papers together he crammed them under his arm, spilling them behind him as he swept prancingly away.

And so much for his hopes of Robin Crosby. It was the dazed girl who watched his dancing feather grow smaller across the lawn, for Gandelyn, turning his back, was gazing moodily into the shut-off garden beyond the hedge.

Mercer Wymark's frontage on Micklegate was ornate with timberwork and grotesque spout-heads, but its back part was wholly domestic. It had a pleasant open gallery for rainy days, and its garden had a dovecote and pigeon-spotted flags and hutches for pets. On the gallery three children were at play, two boys and a smaller girl, and Gandelyn's acquaintance in York was rapidly extending. He knew the tutor of these children. He knew the Signor Battista at the *Bull*, had spoken to York's precentor, and now had made himself known to the one of all he had most desired to meet. And what the better was he for it? Worse, worse. Save for 'After Corpus' the pageant-master had deigned his own merits scarcely a word.

But her? It was bitter, but it had to be faced. She could not read, she could not write. Thousands of young girls in

York could feather and boil a hen as well as she, the mistress of this house would have her pick of those who could count linen or sew a seam. Now she had stolen away from her mother at daybreak and a distracted Efga Hartlip would be seeking her. From the direction of the dovecote a man-servant was advancing towards him. If she wept, let her weep. This time he took her neither by the shoulder nor the hand.

'Are you ready?' he said, and they turned away from the priests at the quintain, the fiddlers, the nackerers, the damned and the redeemed and the Noah with its rainbowed sail.

It is the moment of its nappening that changes the whole event. They had reached the outer door again, the porter had his key in his hand. It was as if of an afterthought that, placing it in the lock, he glanced first at Echo Hartlip's shawl and then questioningly at the silent youth at her side.

'Would this by any chance be her they're ringing the bell for?' he asked, and for all his moodiness Gandelyn's heart gave a jump of new anxiety.

'Eh? What bell? Who's ringing a bell?'

'For sure. You'd hear little wi' the racket that's going on in yonder. The bellman's out. It seems some wench is lost. She'd some sort of a shawl on, but I didn't rightly catch it all. But we all know Thomas Twentyman,' and he felt his arm agitatedly seized.

'Twentyman the eel-catcher? What of him?'

'Nay, nowt of Thomas. But if it's the same they're ringing for she's not to go back there. She'll find her mother wi' the sisters at Clementhorpe,' and he opened the small door within the greater one that led out to Micklegate again.

IV

Efga Hartlip had a daughter to marry if she could. Her opportunities had been few, such another as this was not likely to occur again. She was a clean-living girl, inexpert but yet with the makings. If young men were too wrapped up in themselves to notice it it was well older eyes should see for them, and a poursuivant, at nineteen, was better than a middle-aged captain of archers. Then a tired mother could rest from her troubles too.

The rest had not been difficult to bring about. The girl had never seen such a city as this before, to arrive in it at pageant-time was to enter it by gates of gold, and after a little headshaking and protestation that she was too old for such things she also had allowed herself to be persuaded. She would have to be out of bed a little earlier than was her habit. Anything else was her plain duty as a mother.

The sun rose that morning without a cloud in the sky, the larks sang as they had sung in the days of the innocency of the world. One would have said that York itself had hardly closed an eye, for as early as four o'clock the city was awake and astir. By five the chariot-stages stretched from Holy Trinity to Micklegate's towering Bar, and it was at the peril of his pocket and his good name among his fellows that any guildsman was absent from his post that day. As banner-bearer or horse-leader, sub-constable or clearer of the way, play by play each had his appointed place and duty, for the goldsmiths the *Kings*, for the hosiers and dubbers *Moses and Pharoah*, the smiths for the *Crucifixion*, for the *Flight* the farriers and loriners. Instruments tweedled and skirled as the players mounted by their short ladders to the stages, for weeks past every station of the itinerary had been proclaimed. First after Holy Trinity came Martin Pocock's tall house in the Skeldergate, and despite the early hour Martin's house was already packed with guests to the second gable, tossing down sweetmeats and little cakes to the rabble beneath. But after that the procession went no further in that direction. Martin's house was near the postern, and at the postern was a space in which it could turn itself round. As moreover the postern was already half-way back to Clementhorpe it was there that the three were standing, the same three as before, one of whom already spoke of turning about. The last public procession Efga Hartlip had seen had been too much her own, and a tremulous sigh escaped her. A murmur that had once been marrowfat came from her face-wrappings. There, she said, she would leave them, to be alone with her thoughts. She gave them her sad half-smile, and side by side they watched her cypress-like figure till a towering stage hid it from their sight.

In all the tales he had ever heard young people fretted and fumed because mothers would *not* leave them. They watched them with a hundred eyes, and there was something odd in it that between being alone with her yesterday and being alone with her to-day there should be all the difference in the world. At first he thought it was in part her shawl. It caught the eyes of talkative gentlemen on Ouse Bridge and set the chambermaids of the *Bull* a-titter. But no sooner had Robin Crosby seen it than he had ordered her to take it off, and for the greater part of that night, with All Saints lantern burning over the Pavement and the breathing of the stranger who shared his cell in his ears, he had seen the pageant-master's looking-glass eyes, dancing excitedly over her as if shawls and kirtles and what-not were so many encumbrances and superfluities. He had thrust his feathered cap into her hands and commanded her to walk. '*Salome!*' he had exclaimed, and had asked him where he had found her.

Twice too he had asked them if they were married.

What play was being performed before Martin Pocock's great house he could not have told. Whatever it was it was over, and from the balconies plaudits and small gifts were showering down. A horse's cheek was against his own, already the procession was on the move again. In such a press she would have to be held in safe keeping. Since her mother's departure they had not spoken twenty words.

But now with Ouse Bridge ahead the progress slackened rather than quickened. A bridge with shops and chapels and a great guildhall on it already carries burden enough, and constables were placed there to see that not more than a stage or two at a time with its following should pass. It was like to be an hour before the last of the procession was over, and she had asked him why the old man was killing the young one and what the ram was doing on the stage. Yesterday they had eaten for nothing among the mummers, but to-day they had brought their provision with them. So, the Bridge at last passed, to the Minster to eat.

And to-morrow there would be no setting foot in the great place for the solemnity of the Body, but to-day in all York there was no quieter retreat. There are, too, cathedral windows so thunderous with their lapis-lazuli blues and sullen with their ruby reds that they have more of Sinai in them than of sun, but that before which they sat themselves down was not one of these. In passing the altar he had made her dip her knee in that genuflexion that for a moment sets each soul apart and alone, but in the window now before them all souls seemed to meet together again. Lucent with its ambers and pale greys and greens, fivefold it mounted to the very roof, its leaded compartments gathering together as if in one flat glass picture-book all that the players were playing outside. They would be every one to teach her. Why, she did not even know the story of Isaac! In the other transept, where she had dried her drenched legs, the sun had moved on, but here it stood still, the lustrous *summum bonum* of all suns since Eden.

So with her eyes on the windows she listened dutifully as he murmured and pointed, just a girl in a thrown-back coloured shawl, just a youth with a cropped head and a pair of knee-boots of hide, in York's north transept in the Year of Salvation 1441.

But as they sought the revels outside again it was the turn of the pigs. York and its regulations for its fourteen-thousand souls! . . . Offal in the river was bad enough, unled horses a danger to the street children at play, but ever the pigs topped all. An unclaimed pig found straying on the walls was four trotters in the sergeant's pocket, and as they left the Minster a pig at large had trespassed almost into the Church itself! With every householder making holiday others too had broken loose, and along a nearby alley they were advancing, a dozen of them, a Gadara of pigs, rooting and grubbing, their backs grimed with garbage. Let her not get her legs against those bristly sides! Clutching her kirtle to her she had made a huddle of herself, and he saw that what she had dried yesterday was her lumpy leg-wrappings of taffeta or what-not, bound with a ligature that tucked in at the knee.

But no sooner had the agile actor seen how she bore herself upon them than he had clapped his cap on a bread-board, thrust it at her, cried "Hold it higher so all can see—now walk—*Salome!*"

The swine passed on. The alley was a short one, and at its end the strident sounds of the pageant could be heard again in the street beyond. For hour after hour it would go on, the day would be over before all York packed the Pavement to rejoice at the happy ending. Isaac was not killed, Noah's wife was finally persuaded into the ship,

Christ descended into hell but on the third day He rose again. And there were no pigs on the walls.

That portion of York's walls began at Lendal. Thence they ran north to Toft Green and south to the Old Bail, and she need have no tremors about the Skeldergate postern now that her mother had been given the shelter of Clementhorpe. The watchman came and went, but not too frequently, and from embrasure to embrasure they could pass, looking now outwards over York's wide plain, now down upon the banners themselves, into gardens and closes, with the topmost blossom sometimes almost at their feet. And now he had seen what happened to those who went about the world doing things that everybody else did but doing them in too noble a way. He still felt the small rub of it that all that he himself had had had been a dismissing 'After Corpus—come and see me at the *Keys*, and if I'm asleep see you don't wake me!' They had turned southward to where Micklegate Bar reared its twin towers, grim with what still hung among their swinging irons and chains. There a few steps descended, but only to rise to their former level on the Bar's farther side, and it was time he was showing his paces again. At an embrasure he suddenly stopped, confronting her.

'What's this on your neck?' he asked her.

She stared, not understanding. Surely he, the bestower of it, could not be asking for his musk-ball again! But still his eyes were on the pit of her throat.

'No, not the silver thing—the ladybird, at least it looks like a ladybird,' and picking it off he showed it to her. She had not noticed that in his palm was a small box. The object between his long fingers was small and crimson and glittering, and he was looking at her with accusing eyes.

'Echo Hartlip, you found this in the Signor Battista's waggon! It's a ruby, and it must have dropped out of that jewel he wears in front of his turban!'

'But—but—I ne'er saw it before!' she exclaimed, in bewilderment, but next the back of her hand was tapped, the ruby had vanished, and he was passing her the closed box.

'What's inside's yours if you can open it,' he said, and leaned his elbows on the embrasure to admire the beauty of the sky.

But try as she would she could not open the box, though half a dozen times he did so slowly before her eyes, each time passing it back to her again. And suddenly when he passed it to her it was not a box at all, but a small wooden top spotted like a dice and a small spindle to spin it by. But he must have something level to spin it on, so a niche with a stone seat had to be found, and how was a girl of the Forest to know that both the top and his ruby-box were outrageous cheats? For the one had a leaden pellet that when it dropped into its hole locked it fast, while the trick of the other was in its spindle. It was a spindle that worked either way. Twirling it by one end he could have spun double-high for a week together, but if he gave it a push as he passed it to her she could spin none but the lower numbers, and out of this a merry little thought was born.

For had Robin Crosby found her for himself in the dusty sun-gold and midges of an oak-glade? Had *he* brought her all the way to York, put himself to trouble about her, so craftily considered that to do next?

Twice the actor had asked if they were married—

So say now he were to spin his cheating little top not to mystify her, but for those rosy forfeits of a summer's day that whoso wins wins, and she who loses is not a pin the worse? There they were, her half-parted lips—no bell-man would ring his bell for her to-day, no mother be anxious, for her mother knew who she was with—

But as suddenly his heart failed him, and so that his

flush should not be noticed he pretended to be looking under the seat for the top. So much for the forfeits. Call the top and the ruby lost, and along the circuit of the walls they resumed their way.

Three times during that long afternoon they descended from the walls, making their way by empty streets with shuttered shops, wandering at large, guided by the music and the lulls ahead. But now she was sated by the very newness of it all. Abraham's ram had reminded her of the goat by Washburn's stream-side, she no longer wanted to know why the old man was killing the young one. Seen from the walls the distant meads about the Archbishop's palace were a sight to behold with their pavilions and tents for the accommodation of His Grace's noble guests; but in the place she had grown up in only the children and the old men remained. If a score or so of ragged woodsmen had to be brought into York they hurried them through in the quiet hours and by ways where no banners waved, and even at Clementhorpe she had only to lift her eyes to see beyond the shipping the castle on its monticule and the sentries pacing the bank where no ferry might land. So noting her silence back he led her to the walls again.

But now to think of Washburn was to think of its women too, and he too remembered again those powerful-bodied furies who had lashed themselves into a frenzy against her and her mother alike. Traitorous little questions began to stir. Could they not have made a bonfire of those witch-craft herbs but they must call the daughter wagtail too? With his own ears he had heard them say that she lingered about glades at the end of the day, in such a sort that their still-innocent sons had to be warned against her. These things too walked by his side as from Lendal steps to Toft Green they erred. Chastity enfolded her again as they wandered back to Lendal once more. It was a tossing and a misery, so down into the streets where other things were to be seen.

Fourteen thousand souls can have enough even of pageantry. Never however do they weary of themselves, and now they were breaking up into bands, kind seeking kind. She had to be protected from swayings and jostlings, and as once more they came upon the Noah Gandelyn was at odds with him who played the patriarch himself. His cubits and measurements, his clowning with his pitch and tar, his apeings and mouthings as he shaped the ark's doors and windows faster than the gabble of a line!—'What rhymes with bowers and towers but showers, fool?'—No wonder the pageant-master had called him mudhead and dolt! Did Robert Gandelyn want to be an actor after all?

But he was only the more resolved to see Robin Crosby at the *Keys* the day after to-morrow, and his arm was still protecting her as they ascended to the wall for the last time. That only is fear that a man is afraid of, and what sort of an evening was this to be doing things in too noble a way? All day the cuckoo had been calling if only his note could have been heard above the din of the pageant. On such evenings new moons are lost in light and when the eye seeks them again they have set. He knew she could show temper when she chose, but she had confided herself softly to his arm without speaking. The pageant-master had said he didn't want her for her words, and at last out he came with his grumble.

'I'm nobody,' he chafed. 'All I've been at the trouble of learning is nothing. I'm just a mudhead and a dolt!'

By daylight her eyes were a sort of light hazel or tan. As she lifted them in the dusk they seemed to have hardly any colour at all. 'Who are you talking about?' she asked.

'I mean it's you he wants, not me.'

'Do you mean that man we saw in the garden where all those people were?'

'Yes. Him with the air in his boots. The famous After-Corpus-Crosby.'

'What has he done?'

'Nothing. I'll tell you after Corpus.'

'But you just said—'

'After Corpus.'

'I don't think I like him. He stares at you, and jumps up and points, and tells you—'

'After Corpus.'

'Then are you going to see him?'

'I'll tell you when this watchman's got past.'

But the watchman took no notice of them, and now they no longer had the walls to themselves. Two by two York's lovers were seeking them, and the watchmen were used to those pressings together till two shapes became one in the embrasures of the walls. Northward the woods of Gaultres were sinking into shadow for the night, already they had missed the final assembly at the Pavement, and lights were beginning to appear in the town below. One embrasure was as good as another, and at Lendal, because of Ouse, it was necessary to come down to the level of the streets again. But at Bootham the walls began their other circuit, and there were fewer flowery tofts and gardens now. About the Minster pressed closed shops and lock-ups, the dwellings of the poor, huddles of sheds and backs, and over the roofs towards the Pavement rose a dim halo of light. Soon Robert Gandelyn would find a couple in every embrasure he came to, his boldness had returned, and he had resolved it should be in the very next one they reached. It chanced to be near Bootham, where those who had died of long-ago plagues had been buried outside the walls. His throat was constricted, his mouth dry, yet above all he must appear to be playful, happy, gay. She was only saying how vexed she was that he had lost his little box with the ruby in it, but for all that she had found no ruby in the palankeen. His lips were at her ear.

'Lost?' he whispered. 'Put your hand here in my breast.'

She hesitated barely a moment, then did so.

'Now tilt your head back . . . shut your eyes . . .' (Had he not been told that all the joy and sweetness of life were waiting for him like honey in the comb?)

There was neither witchcraft nor sacrament in it, potion nor prayer, only two young people, on York's northern wall, a very long time ago—

And so often had those who passed seen that lifting of a face, the bending over it, the sudden stillness, that hardly the oldest of them sighed to think what the world was coming to.

But once they had given up their wall-niche near Bootham they found no other. The brighter part of the town was behind them, the walls were populous now. Her hand still remained where he had placed it, his own was at the musk-ball at her throat, and walking so they turned the farthest angle of the wall, with the Minster too now behind them. Monk Bar, by which they had entered York, also lay behind, and where the walls finally ended the marshy Foss alone was York's southward defence. There the kingcups grew, and on the ings and leasowes was room for a hundred lovers. He knew not how it was with his heart, nor cared so long as his tongue did what was required of it. His young madam he was calling her now, not that it seemed to matter what he called her, since for answer she only pressed herself the closer to him. Where the walls ended at a garth with hawthorns they descended, but the hawthorns were scattered out over the ings, and a distant hum of music stirred the air. At the Pavement, with All Saints' lantern for light, they were nackering and dancing. He found a patch under a hawthorn where the daisies slept, and well he knew that the musk-ball's proper place was nowhere near that uncovered whiteness of her rounded shoulder. But she herself had been the first to show it when she had dropped her bark-sack over the child, and he murmured with his mouth against it.

'Little apple—I want to eat you—'

As the shoulder did not reply his lips moved to her ear.

'Whose young madam are you now?'

'When you kiss me—'

'Then call me Bobbie again—'

'Bobbie—'

Then the deep sigh, the man-of-the-world, the heart-break.

'After Corpus . . . we'll find a church . . .'

And surely in York there were churches enough to marry them.

V

The rumour began at daybreak with a watchman on the walls. Chancing to raise his eyes to the north-west he saw two specks in the misty distance, that presently became two horsemen at full gallop, making not for Micklegate, their directest way in, but holding straight on to the palace of the Archbishop himself. This man, coming off duty, told his fellow, who again told his neighbour, and before the sun was well up it was all over the back parts of the town. They who had galloped in were from Ripon, thirty miles away.

The mumming and the fiddling were over. Already the bell of Saint Mary's was reminding York's fourteen thousand souls that, corporate in its Elements, to-day was the Day of the Body Itself, with processional candles and holy pictures, the relics in their precious caskets, the chanting priests and the acolytes censing the streets with the aroma of purification. Other bells too began to be heard, lesser bells, calling the priests and deacons to their several churches. But the rumours only gathered particularity as they ran. It *was* Ripon, open on every side, for such a thing would have been impossible in a city with gates and walls. There had been a clash. Fifty had been slain, five hundred, half Gaultres was in flames. Some, mounting to the walls, swore they had smelt the smoke borne on the wind, and not an hour ago many had seen for themselves two more horsemen, pelting for York in a lather and making by way of Bootham straight for the house of the mayor himself.

So as they say, the better the day the better the deed. Gandelyn stepped from his hospice to the Pavement. Until that morning it had gone completely out of his mind that he was the bearer of a second letter, the one for the governor of the prison. No rumours had reached him yet. The stones of York's walls did not whisper their secrets nor the daisies open their eyes to tell of what they had dreamed, and as he lifted his heavy eyes to the empty market-stalls it seemed impossible that there should have been dancing and nackering there the night before. He was to see her at mid-morning if Clementhorpe's rules permitted it, and it eased the heartbreak to be about something. He was glad the castle was not to be approached by Ousebank and its ferry, but only by Castlegate through the town. Even the challenge of the guards at the gate would bring back the everyday feeling of life again, and to Castlegate he directed his steps.

But the governor was not immediately to be seen, nor was he the only one anxious to see the governor that morning. Twice he had pushed himself forward, saying that his business was urgent, but later-comers were passed through before himself, as many came hurriedly out, and it was nearly half an hour before with a gruff 'This way' **he** was marched along a chill and dank-smelling corridor **and** shown into the governor's room. He was an elderly,

grey-haired, sad-eyed man, forever harassed between con-
flicting orders, and one of his hands already had a paper
or list in it as he held out the other for Gandelyn's letter.
He broke the seal, read it, and then looked up with a smile
that somehow seemed the sadder for the relief of it.

'Sit,' he said civilly, pointing to a stool, and then read
the letter again. 'I get few letters worth a cup of wine,
but—' and he rose and from a closet got the wine himself.
'Do you know what's in this letter?'

'Sir, I do, for at the instance of our sub-prior I penned
it,' and the governor did not put the letter down till he
had read it for the third time.

'Would I had more such! I know not who this knight
was, and the wretches are leaner than rakes at the best,
but 'tis a poor way to make them leaner only to make
room for more!'

'I do not follow you, sir.'

'Nor may it ever be your lot. Prison walls do not
stretch, yet still they thrust them in.'

'I know nothing of it, sir, save for thirty I heard of a
short while back, and it may be they will not come within
the scope of this benefaction.'

'Ah! You speak of them the Duchy had in from the
Forest! Know you anything of them?'

'Nothing, sir.'

'Nor I, yet they did not look to me worse than most,
and, neither tried nor charged, they are an inch in Ouse-
water already. Release one—make room for three—for a
holy day this is a bustling one!' and he sighed. 'Anon,
Jenkins, bid him wait but two minutes! It shall be acquitted
to your reverend sub-prior when it is received, rest this
good knight's soul!—That call means still more to come—'
and seeing him so pressed Gandelyn finished his wine,
took his receipt for his letter, thanked the governor
miserably, and left him to his grimly-humane office.

How he longed now for the simple goodness that seemed
to breathe from other hearts! Even Sir Matthew Poole was
'this good knight.' This tired and harassed prison-governor
could show compassion for the wretched in his charge. But
in escaping out of the house with the seal on the door he
had not even thought to leave Will Acle's brach a bowl
of water, and before he could even pray again he must now
find one, no older than himself, who of all in York could
best be his help.

For he was not so simple as to suppose that he could
walk into the first church he came to, call for its incumbent,
and require of him that he should marry them forthwith.
He would be asked how long he had been resident in York.
They would want to know which citizen of worth he knew
to be his sponsor, some man of substance whose name was
on the rolls. There would be banns to proclaim, a score of
questions regarding the woman and who she was. Only
Peter Oates could tell him these things, Peter who taught
Mercer Wymark's children their Latin roots, Peter who
knew priests and lawyers and York's every in-and-out.

But on that day least of all was he likely to meet Peter
Oates hurrying along Micklegate to the house with the
quintain in the garden, and he had only to walk a mile or
two out of Monk Bar to where the prostitutes and the
vendors of the flies of Spain plied their trades and he would
find a dozen hedge-priests and friars ready to marry them
for the price of the wedding-ale. But as he drew near Holy
Trinity they were singing the *Miserere* within. '*Wash me
thoroughly from my wickedness and cleanse me from my sin.*'
At the corner of Clementhorpe's meadow was a dark
coppice of elders. Whether he would ever see that coppice
again as she had clung to him last night with her face
turned up, or whether in his dreams he would ever cease
to see it, he did not know. '*Behold, I was shapen in wickedness and in sin did my mother conceive me.*' It had been long

after compline before they had parted, and of her mother neither of them had spoken. *'Make in me a clean heart, O God, and renew a right spirit within me.'* She had said she would be at the top of Micklegate steps by mid-morning, but how if she was prevented? Moment by moment more people filled the streets, hurrying pastors, collegiates, lay-clerks like himself. More guards than usual seemed to be assembled in the archway of the Bar, and as he was not returning to his hospice he had brought his cloak away. He drew forward its hood, lest like the mummers in the pageant his sin should show on his face. He stood for a moment with his hands clasped. Then he mounted the steps.

For a moment he could hardly breathe for the lifting of the weight from his heart. Just as at the *Bull* he had found her in the same palankeen, so in her shawl she was sitting in the same niche where he had mystified her with his little top, alone, her head erect, contentedly waiting. She heard his step, raised her eyes, was on her feet, broke into a little run. It was his miserable self who like one of York's busy-body inspectors had been lifting corners, peeping and nosing lest in the presence of his officiousness some hungry mouth should eat. Black faces for the damned, white faces for the redeemed? No brother had ever told him that there were wall-pictures far more ancient than those of New-biggin church, in which the black meant no more than that the man was a man, the white that a woman was a woman. He could only stammer.

'I thought perhaps—you mightn't be here—' and her voice was as he had first heard it, strong, a little loud.

'I've been waiting, and nobody's spoken to me—'

'I mean—last night, when I left you—?'

'My mother let me in.'

'Your mother?'

'She had to go to bed when they all did—they have to

there—but there's a little door by the scullery and she left it open.'

'But that wall?'

'I climbed over it. I can climb trees. But I've found a better way now.'

'Of getting in and out?'

'In the mornings they ring a little bell, but she isn't used to getting up so early. So she goes out, and gathers a few herbs, and leaves the back wicket open. And now she knows I'm with you, and I shall say I've been to church, and if they find out . . . oh look, quick! What is it?' and jumping up she strained half her length over the wall.

Still a mile away to the south a concourse was slowly advancing. They were on foot, but it was from Bishopthorpe that they were winding, and there was no need to ask who they were. That day the pavilions and tents that made a fair of Bishopthorpe meadows were empty. Here they came, His Grace's proudest guests, in their velvets and their cloth-of-gold, with their collars and jewelled chains and their attendant gentlemen behind. They came on foot who had horses at their command, to bend their gartered knees with the lowliest and humblest. But in an hour or two the grooms would follow with the horses, and they would ride back, for in the resumption of their greatness the Body was doubly praised. It was hardly to be supposed she knew all he meant when, again in an embrasure with her, he found her hand and lifted it to his lips. He was as he was, she too, and the world had managed to rub along that way for a very long time.

But far more swiftly than those who advanced from Bishopthorpe there had now arrived in York a chandler (or some said a butcher and others a maker of spurs), hot from Ripon, where he had seen for himself. While York had had eyes only for her pageant, some hundreds of men, armed with pikes and bills and whinyards, had forced their way into the open town, thrusting officers and constables aside, vowing that their grandfathers had paid no toll and neither would they. Unfortunately the eye-witness had himself disappeared, but that only left each man the freer for his own tale. Now a different one was on every tongue. The outlaws had split into bands, each of them larger than the original force, Westgate and Bondgate had been sacked. Two burgesses had been bound and beaten, with the wakeman for makeweight, and when the Ripon men had rallied and driven them out they had set about the raiding of the Liberty at large, Stainley, Brampton, Conyers and Wath, as far away as Pateley Bridge, which was the last that had been heard of them.

And York, that could turn out its prostitutes and bawds, could not stop every idle tongue, yet such rumours must be put an end to. Too many foreigners were in the city, and some went so far as to say that too many of these great folk together never made anything but mischief yet. The Signor Battistas themselves were the perfection of courtesy and understanding. In Livorno and Venice and Stamboul they had their troubles too. But their servants and grooms moved in threes and fours at large, free for the day and commenting in another tongue on any unfamiliar fashion or custom they did not understand. In York's streets not a wheel had moved all day. The guildsmen of yesterday, special constables for the nonce, were hurrying each to his station, with orders that only such as carried candles were to be allowed to pass. And Saint Mary's bell was now tolling alone.

When Gandelyn first heard the rumours he grimaced. Some of these would talk less lightly of sackings and pillage and ungoverned men let loose if they had seen what he had seen, but even when the reports became more particular they seemed in no way to concern himself. At two half-heard words indeed he pricked up his ears—the

words were 'Cawood' and 'Hexham'—but Mary's bell
rang again, and if she was to see the Progress it was time
they bestirred themselves. It was in Jewbury that he had
heard the Cawood and the Hexham, but as they approached
the Minster from that direction their way was suddenly
barried by a constable with a halberd. At point after point
he tried, for the press was now great, so back to the
Minster he turned. There luck stood his friend. Half York
was carrying candles, and a little way back along the
Minster's south wall a buttress was being repaired. Old
stones had been taken out, new ones were in readiness,
with staging and tackle for their lifting, and she could
climb Clementhorpe's walls when she had a mind. By
mounting first he could give her a hand. 'Up,' he said, and
stuck his heel stiffly into a gap.

He had found their coign only just in time. Already the
distant chanting of the *Te Deum* was beginning to swell,
the smell of the censing was borne on the air. Nearer the
chanting rolled, and now too there drew nearer another
hushed and indescribable sound, a sound such as a long
breaker makes when it is tripped from below, the sound of
successive waves of people kneeling. A cordwainer's
banner sank in obeisance as its guildsman-bearer also knelt.
Then he felt the tremor of her body and heard the quick
catch of her breath as, themselves the only two unable to
kneel, there appeared in an open space below them the
solitary priest who bore the Cross.

And those of the balconies saw only the splendour in the
moment of its passing. Those who knelt saw no more than
could be seen by the lifting of their eyes. Most indeed saw
only the moving tops of tall candles and sacred pictures
held aloft, the glint of a mitre, the gemming of a labarum
or pastoral staff. But the two braced up there in their niche
saw all. They saw the canopy and its pole-bearers, the
shrine beneath it, the cushion, the crystal sacramental box

it bore. They saw him who carried the crozier and the acolytes with the urceoles, the Archbishop himself, so massy in his mitre and chasuble of gold that but for the trainbearers and those who supported the weight of it on either side he could scarce have laboured forward at all—

They saw the secular great who followed in the wake of the ecclesiastics, those from the Archbishop's palace in their velvets and sayes and SS-collars of gold, the lords and their gentlemen and esquires and after them the stately merchant-princes from Italy and Muscovy and the Levant—

But they could also be as conspicuously seen, and suddenly he thought her foot had slipped, for she clutched him.

'See—there he is!' she whispered.

'Who?'

'The gentleman who spoke to me on Ouse Bridge.'

But the face Gandelyn's eyes had already found was not that of any gallant of the pavements and the shop-windows of the bridge. For the occasion the short soldierly figure was clothed in velvet of the richest midnight black. He carried the device of Lancaster only on his breast, and when Gandelyn had last seen that face it had been swollen with passion that whinyards and pikeheads should have been lifted out of a grave under his very nose. Be sure the earl Philip was not in York for Corpus only, and suddenly his eyes were raised to Gandelyn on his perch in hard-set recognition. Then again he heard the whisper in his ear.

'No, not the one in black—the other—'

Turning his head the earl Philip had spoken to a bearded man behind him. A few words were exchanged. Stephen Hurst also glanced up, started, and slipped aside out of the procession just as Echo Hartlip heard rapid directions spoken hoarsely into her ear.

'Grip well hold of my hand. I have my foot to free first. Do naught till I tell you, then take it carefully, and have no fear. Don't look down. When you feel my hold slacken you're within a foot of the ground. Have you got my hand? Then steady—lower away—'

But even when their feet were on the ground he gave her not a moment.

'Give me that curst flame of a shawl and into my cloak. This way, round by yon tenements. As quick as you can, out o' this!'

'But where? Why?'

'You, home to your mother as fast as you can get. Me, I've things to see to.'

So it came about that that day she was as early in rejoining her mother as she had been late the night before, but this time she did not go by way of the walls. At Lendal steps they were turned back; the walls after dusk were forbidden. At Ouse Bridge they found the guard doubled, and the lucklessness of it was that none of it was of their own bringing about. That afternoon, near the Shambles, an Italian with five words of English had taunted an Englishman, who had retaliated with his staff. A brawl had followed, orders from above had been prompt, and now to the rumours was added that in the Signor Battista's private chamber at the *Bull* deliberative beards were mingled over how the unfortunate occurrence could most hastily be composed.

And now hardly were the solemnities over before York was busy with its secular life again. To-night the foreign gentlemen were to be the guests of the city at the guildhall. To-morrow the great mart would open, and at the appointed places the steward's crier was even now proclaiming its ordinances. Pie-powder was a coming and going of the market-officers and their clerks, and for one who listened to Mary's bell a hundred gathered to hear the crier's 'Oyez, oyez, oyez!'

That night, as the warm darkness fell and in the streets

intermittent lights at different levels began to appear, with here and there the sputter of a link or the opening and closing of a door, Gandelyn walked York, trying to piece this and that together. That the gentleman of Ouse Bridge should have been none other than Stephen Hurst he set for the moment aside. There were too many excellent reasons why the sooner he was out of York the better and let them seek him at his hospice-lodging who pleased. The grossness at Calais too could wait, with his own evasion of the Lancastrian in Washburn's wood. York might have its fourteen thousand souls but it had only four gates. It needed only a general order, issuing from no matter whom, and he would be taken, asked questions he had no mind to answer, and so much for his being a free man.

For he had failed miserably in his mission, as for Ripon had given it hardly a thought. The men of Hexham and Cawood had done the business without him, and say his letter to the Archbishop had a line of commendation to these of the Lord's Prayer? He was to see the pageant-master to-morrow without it. He had one reason and one reason only for remaining in York. In York he could be most quickly married.

He was now not even sure in which part of the town he was. He had left Stonegate by an ill-lighted alley, his lodging at the Pavement was best kept away from, and somewhere he hoped to come upon some small night-church in which to sleep. Timbered and closely-shuttered houses almost met over his head, not a footfall but his own was to be heard, and had York been a French town he would have made sure of the poniard at his waist. Then suddenly he heard his name spoken in a low voice behind him.

Now who (he was the next moment asking himself) would have looked to come upon Peter Oates in a quarter such as this? The dark street was scarce two strides wide,

the watch itself might well avoid such a thievish place, and
the precentor's clerk too seemed glad of company. Now
Gandelyn had recovered from his surprise.

'Peter, man! . . . As well you didn't raise your hand!
My own was just feeling for something!' and as Peter
muttered Gandelyn wondered for a moment whether he
had been drinking.

'We cannot all be dining at the guildhall.'

'Is that where they are? I looked for you in the procession to-day, but saw naught of you,' and Peter muttered
again.

'Processions! With all *I* have on my hands! All day I've
had my nose at it. A man must take the air.'

'I tried the walls too, but I was turned back.'

'Ay, they'll have closed the walls,' and as they turned
into a street darker still, 'Did you find Master Crosby
where I said you would?'

He seemed somehow to take it in an injurious sense that
Gandelyn had been a swaggering soldier while he himself
had been teaching children and counting the precentor's
sheets of paper. It now appeared that the reason why Peter
Oates had not walked in the procession that day was that
his employment had been of the most pressing urgency.
This of Ripon for example: prisoners had been taken; when
they were safely lodged the soldier's work was at an end;
but not so Peter's, and suddenly he asked Gandelyn how
deep was his knowledge of the law.

'As deep as your finger-nail, if that,' Gandelyn
answered.

'The luckier you! All day it's been shovelled on me, this
and the other! Try 'em, says some, and that's easy said,
but who try 'em and for what?' and he began to mutter
again. 'Scarce a day old, and they're at it hammer-and-
tongs!'

But lawyers know how to keep their mouths shut,

which Peter Oates did not, yet Gandelyn was scarce able
to follow more than one word in ten of it. It seemed that
half England wanted to try them, all for different things.
The jurisdiction was the Archbishop's, but it was Ripon's
Liberty that had been infringed. Now Netherby would
intervene, the Duchy would not be denied, whereas if it
was treason, as Peter Oates more than inclined to opine,
who should deal with it but the King in Council himself?
He became even more mysterious.

'Oyer and Terminer, to me that's taken abstracts of four
Supersedeases to-day! Mark you, this isn't for all ears. They
haven't finished counting them they've got yet. But it's my
advice there'll be a good hundred of them safe behind bolt
and bar to-morrow, and yet not one of those they'd give
half their estates to get!'

'You can't mean this handful from Washburn?'

'Them? No! They'll be given their whipping and let go.
It's them you daren't mention they're after, and *we* know
the man for that!'

'Who?'

'Who? Who but Philip of Gaunt? He'll be in at *that* if
he has to stop in York a year for it!' and Gandelyn
pondered deeply.

'Isn't that him they call the Cooper of the Oise?' he
asked at last.

'I know not what you soldiers call him, but for myself
I'd as soon have the devil on my heels as him!'

'Where in York does he stay?'

'He's been at Bishopthorpe, but for a certainty him and
His Grace will quarrel over this,' and suddenly he sank his
voice to a confidential whisper. 'But that's enough of it for
to-day. Where are *you* going now?'

'To my lodging.'

'What, this way round to the Pavement?'

'I've changed it.'

'But it was in Sneak Lane I came up with you and your hand went to that at your waist.'

'I don't take you, Peter,' and from Peter Oates there came a jeering little sound.

'Which of them is it?'

'Truly I don't take your meaning,' and Peter became tetchy.

'Nay, as well a sheep as a lamb! They watch us close at the Minster but they cannot hold us all day and all night too! If it's Crosseyed Mark's I know a better ken than that, and here it is. Mine lives at the back of Jubber. She works for a girdle-maker, but I tell her I'm the one to girdle her! It may be she's not come yet, so I'll take a peep in first—Alison her name is, and for a pair of breasts like butter—'

His hand fumbled at the door of assignation, and across the street there crept a crack of smoky light. Not all of York's night-birds had been thrust forth from its gates. Gandelyn heard the suddenly-checked voices of both men and women, then Peter Oates's hoarse whisper.

'Ay, she's there, and Bessie's with her. They don't like the door kept open—come in—'

But Gandelyn had gone. He was seeking no advice of Peter Oates's on how in York he could be most speedily married.

VI

The *Keys* was far from being one of York's greater inns, but it suited Robin Crosby in that it saved him money. It stood not far from Tanners Row, the smell of tanning hung over all the surrounding streets, and Gandelyn had been told not to present himself too early. To kill the time he had idled about among the pits and yards, his thoughts straying back to a glade of stripped oaks and a bark-shed where once he had listened throughout the night to the rain. Now as he passed the *Keys* again, glancing upwards at a latticed window, a tapster in the doorway caught his eye and nodded.

The ground-floor passage by which he entered led straight on to the kitchen, but the pageant-master had his own chamber upstairs, all the service he needed below, and from the passage mounted the dark crack of a stairway. Not the first door he came to but the second, he was told. But he had to grope for it, and only at his third knock did an impatient voice within call to him to enter.

It was past midday, but the actor's repast still lay untouched on the board. But the stopper was out of a flagon of malmsey, and Gandelyn had forgotten the guildhall banquet of the night before. Still the pageant-master took no more notice of him standing there cap in hand than he had taken in Roger Wymark's garden, and loose among the food on the table papers were strewn. In the seat of the casement-window were more papers, and a litter of them had been tossed to the rushes that spread the floor. To call attention to himself Gandelyn first coughed, then spoke.

'You said don't be too early, Master Crosby, but Corpus is over,' he said, and the actor, looking up, recognized him. His hand began to sweep his bald brow again, but the burden of his song was still as before—never again, never again.

'Their banquets neither, none of them! I'll sing and tumble at fairs, but if ever you catch me at a pageant again—'

'I knocked, and you said Come in, Master Crosby,' but next the actor looked at the scatterings of papers.

'And so I did, but that lot in the casement was brought to me in my bed, and when you rapped "Here comes more of them," I said, and out o' the window you were going!

You cannot move for their bills and charges! Last night all smiles and smirks and flatteries, but when it comes to who's to pay the shipwrights say it's Trinity, and Trinity says it's Brid, and Brid—' and in the midst of it the looking-glass eyes flashed on Gandelyn again. 'Did you see it? Which play did you see? Did you see Baalam? Did you see Noah? What sort of a fist did that fool make of it in the end?'

And Gandelyn had neither slept nor broken his fast, and it gave him an ache to see that uneaten breakfast on the table, but he had not trailed all those miles after Robin Crosby to let him go again, and up went his eyes to the ceiling.

'Did I see it, Master Crosby! Did I see Noah! Shall I ever forget it!'

'Did the oaf mangle it?'

'Mangle it! . . . Never a slip or a stumble, Master Crosby! Every cubit pat, and when the dove came back with the lines about the mess the world was in you should have heard him! Never was such a picture of mud and ruin!' and the actor's hand went to the malmsey.

'The bowers and towers—never yet did he get those bowers and towers right—' and Gandelyn pressed eagerly on.

'They rang like a chime of bells, Master Crosby! So on I went to Baalam and his Ass, and when it came to the shoeing of it I thought their sides would ha' split, yet never a sound for reverence when the angels began to sing,' and as on he went the actor sipped his malmsey more thoughtfully.

'Ay, that's better hearing,' he said at last. 'It's something. But that ass of Baalam's eats Pharaoh's lean kine out o' the pasture by the bill they send in, and here a cope's to mend, and six nails missing from the Cross, and a devil's mask's cracked, and a rogue with lime on his fingers wants to charge a shilling for a touch of red and a pinch of plaster—I'll dance from here to Jerusalem before I'll touch a pageant again! I'm queasy from that banquet too! Would they'd give you more money and a quart or so less hospitality! And now you're here what do you want?' he demanded abruptly.

So it was now or never for it, but a poor pennyworth it presently turned out to be. As for the little box that locked itself with the pellet, the actor had played with such nursery stuff while Gandelyn had been in his cradle. With his dice-top he fared no better, a thieves-fetch, and when Gandelyn picked up the malmsey-stopper and began to make it appear and disappear he was only told that a watcher ten yards away would be asking what he was doing. But when it came to his own exploits the actor's pitchpipe was still in tune. The triumphs that had been his, the halls, the castles! That was why York had bribed so famous a man to let his own company go forward without him. But let him come up with them again—so once more Gandelyn tried.

'What's this of the Two-ways we can scarce stir for hearing of, Master Crosby? You've but to say "Master Crosby the actor," and they cry, "What, him of the Two-ways?"' and hoisting himself from his chair the actor sprawled his length along the window-seat, which even then was not long enough for him.

'Set that chair under my legs and shout down those stairs for a raw egg with mustard and vinegar. Did you say the Two-ways? Young man, there's rogues and impostors that have tried it, but they soon turn away when they hear of the lifetime of hard work that Two-ways has cost! Yet it's naught without it's parti-coloured, and the morning after a banquet's not the time. They're all in a chest in the next room.'

Later Gandelyn learned that he never let them out of his possession, the precious pack of costumes with which he made himself Robin Hood on one side of him and the curtal friar on the other, or one half an English bowman and the other glittering with the lilies of France. The weapons he fought with were different too, as when the pitchforked devil in red had his set-to with the goatskinned saint with the pincers in his hand. So downstairs Gandelyn went for the egg with the vinegar and mustard, and when he returned the player had arranged his window-seat and chair to his liking, and when Gandelyn picked up a sheaf of papers with a timidly questioning look he only nodded.

'Ay, if you're that make of a clerk. My own learning stops at a few plays and song-books. You'll find pen and ink somewhere,' and he swallowed his egg at a gulp and closed his eyes.

The hour was perhaps two o'clock in the afternoon, and about Tanners Row other industries too had their habitation, tentercrofts and drying-grounds, a piggery, a maker of haybands, a weaver, for from a street or so away came the muffled 'Addle-'t-and-*tak't!*' of a loom. '*To grease for greasing of the rollers,*' Gandelyn read on his topmost paper, but the sounds of people about their daily work mingled drowsily with the sea-like surge, half a mile away, of York's great mart now in full swing. A cat-nap would do the pageant-master good. '*To Margaret Harvey for darning of the cope with crimson silk and pressing of the same, 4d,*' Gandelyn read, and found little overcharge there. Fourpence. Within twopence it was as much as God was paid, who had made the whole world, and perhaps the crimson silk had cost her a penny, and she had pressed it too. She might be some old woman with only her trembling fingers left, or a young one with a mother to keep, and Robin Crosby in his window-seat could not have been wholly asleep, for without opening his eyes he suddenly yawned and spoke.

'My time's been so ta'en up with this and that and the other . . . what's all this talk I hear about Ripon?'

Gandelyn had started with the papers at random, the first that came. The item the question interrupted was *'Hay, straw, and to making of forty fathom of straw-rope,'* and plainly it would be best to get them into some sort of order before going further. But the place was strange, the noises unfamiliar, the 'Addle-t-and-*tak't!'* of the loom had stopped, and another sound had taken its place. It was the tramp and shuffle of men, advancing in silence. It came from the street's end, was entering the street itself. Raising himself on his elbow Robin Crosby had pushed open the casement, and now the sound filled the room.

But Gandelyn's heart had sunk like a plummet with the fore-knowledge of what it was. He heard the blusterous Lord Abbot's voice again: Were there no men in Cawood, all the men they wanted at Hexham? . . . They were the prisoners being brought in from Ripon, and of a sudden he too was on his feet, his face with the pageant-master's at the casement.

Peter Oates had said they hadn't been counted yet. It was furthermore likely they would be brought in in small numbers, not to attract too much attention. Ten pair of them were advancing below, fastened wrist-to-wrist. All night they had trudged, with spear-butts to jog them forward from behind, and now thrice their number kept them company alongside, sullen and silent in their sympathy, for who with his living to earn dared to raise his voice with he knew not who listening to take a note of his name? A horseman on either side was thrusting his animal among them to keep them back, but dispersed they fell in again. The thing that went to the heart was the muteness of these defeated men with sling-supported arms and head-bandages through which the blood had soaked and dried. One fell to his knees, but another with a glaive found a way to bring him to his feet again, and still a woman's shrill cry of 'Shame!' was the only sound to be heard.

And then came a space. It seemed that one among them was to be more specially guarded than the others, and Gandelyn had no heart at all, but only the aching bottom through which it had dropped, as he saw who the one so singled out was. Their eyes met, the eyes with all the gladness of life to come, the eyes that knew only too well what lay ahead. He still wore his green fustian cap, but the soldier's cape had gone and a patch of his shirt flapped from the band of his leather breeches. The cord about the galled wrists was cruelly wrenched from behind. His wrinkled old face was distorted with pain for a moment, but having given Gandelyn that slow look of farewell he looked up no more. The last prisoner passed and Tanner's Row was empty again.

Robin Crosby was on his feet, looking down on him, wondering what ailed the youth. One would have said he was a stout enough lad. He could take command of a funeral, answer back pertly when he had a mind. From France, and yet to sink down in a heap at the sight of a few prisoners! But there was malmsey on the table. He forced a gulp of it down the young throat. Then placing him along the window-seat he thrust a paper into his hand.

'Let on to be reading this while the drawer clears away,' he said.. Then opening the door he called loudly down the stairs. (Nay, swooning away like any girl!) And there is a tougher way of dealing with last night's potations than an egg with vinegar and mustard if a man has but the nerve for it. No sooner had the drawer gone than he broke into a series of the most extraordinary and violent gymnastics. Placing himself in the middle of the floor he elongated himself till his fingers were bent back against the ceiling, swelled out his rib-arch till it seemed to yawn, and then dropped like a stone to his heels. From this position he shot out before him first one long leg, then the other, several times, and then, taking his ankles in his hands, placed them about his neck. But Gandelyn did not see him, balanced upon his hands among the floor-rushes like a duck. Still he saw only that face upturned from the street for a moment, its sorrow-drowned eyes welling with affection and adieu. Then, crosslegged and at his ease again, the pageant-master looked up from his seat on the floor.

'Well,' he said, 'Corpus is over. My time's my own again. Some things are better out than in.'

Needs must when the devil drives. Gandelyn's late lodging was now the first place he would be sought in. He would not be found there, orders would be given at the gates, and in particular any woman whose company he was known to keep would be watched in her every coming and going. The whole truth was not his to tell. In what he did tell he was not interrupted. For all he knew he had now betrayed himself, for long after he had finished the actor kept a profound silence. It was not until this became too much for him was he on his feet again, suddenly as stormily irate as he had just been mute.

'The devil cross out the day I ever saw their York!' he cried. 'Their quorums and their adjournments, their funds and their filchings, not a finger but has its coin sticking to it! Broken banquet-meats for the actors and their sixpence for God . . . do you mean I'm to *hide* you now?' he cried.

There was no answer. All must be as it must.

'And you told me you weren't wed!'

'I am not wed. The other's as you please, but that has to come first of all'—and now Robin Crosby turned up his eyes to some God beyond the ceiling.

'*What!* . . . The knots he's tied for himself and the last knot a woman!' and down with a groan he sank to the floor again. 'Where is this bride-brat of yours?'

'At Clementhorpe with her mother.'

'That's a religious House. Do Mother Superiors have madmen and lovers in and out their doors?'

'She swings up a tree and drops over a wall.'

'She—I'll be bound she does! . . . And the other, this bearded man, that knows 'em again before the "Ahem" o' the first is out of his throat?'

'He's all to come. He started life as a pantler. Then he rose to be a steward. He always said a man has to better himself as he can.'

'I know one whose study seems to be to worsen himself! But I always think best in the air. If I'm to be saddled with you two get you to them papers and see you don't stir from this house till I'm back,' and tossing his feathered cap to his head he was gone.

See it, then, that upper chamber at the *Keys* in Tanners Row where Gandelyn sheltered for the next five days to come. Because the place was an inn it was open downstairs to all. Upstairs the actor's rooms were two, with a curtain to divide them, and in the inner one, which was the first of the passage-doors at the head of the stairs, he slept with his Two-way costumes. In the outer one Gandelyn had the floor-rushes to lie on, a table for his piles of pageant-accounts, a stool to sit on, a ledge for his ink-horn and the window for light. He was told that after dark he might stretch his legs for an hour, and of this liberty he availed himself that very first night. But he was unaware of the actor's tall light-stepping figure that followed him, thirty yards behind. At the end of the street, but away from York and towards the leather-pits, was a tentercroft. Then, beyond the piggery, came a line of willows, followed by a widish open space, and by that time he was half-way to Micklegate. But for whatever reason she was not at the place of appointment, and he reached the *Keys* again to find the pageant-master in a loose gown and slippers, waiting for him at the street door. Abruptly he ordered him upstairs.

'And from now on upstairs you stay,' was his curt order. 'By what the drawer tells me two not of these parts have been here, drinking in the back bar. One of them was asking if he could have a chamber here for a night or two.'

'What kind of a two were they?'

'I did not see them, but bear this in mind, that I live by favour of such as are the masters of great houses and castles, not shirtrags on their way to gaol. Keep away from that window too. As well we aren't overlooked from across the way!'

And Gandelyn heard him with dismay. She had not been there, to-morrow he would not be there, and in all he said Robin Crosby was entirely right. If he was looked for, so now was she. No letter would serve, for were he to write one she could not read it. The closing of the pageant's affairs kept Robin Crosby continually here and there, nor was this the worst, for again the actor came in with news. The inn was being watched by men in Lancastrian livery now.

'Two of 'em here at the street's end as I passed,' he said. 'One of 'em tried to be civil to me, so if you want anything don't go down the stairs for it neither. Tell me and I'll see it's sent up. I'd put a curtain at that window, knowing the sort you are, but that would be as good as telling them. How long are those accounts going to take you?'

But what cared Gandelyn now for roller-grease or hay-bands or Margaret Harvey's pennorth of red silk? Out in desperation he broke.

'I thank you for your kindnesses, again and again, Master Crosby, but out I'm walking,' he cried. 'If it has to be a hedge-priest then a hedge-priest it'll have to be!' and the actor began to flash like quicksilver again.

'What's that? What's that?'

'The priest of All Fools is better than him I was counting on! Him, he took me to a street at the back of Jubber, where they sell women's breasts at a groat a pair—' and the actor gave him another flashing look, then started on his brow-polishing again.

'And me in my simplicity, asking you if you were wed! Nay this poor Archbishop, who'd wear *his* mitre!' and now it was Gandelyn who flashed.

'What Archbishop?'

'Why, His Grace of York, without you'd have His Holiness himself marry you, with ambassies, and the College of Cardinals, and a brace or two of bishops and a few kings and queens standing by! Can you think of no middle way? And when you've thought of it, how are you going to get out of York?'

'If I have to steal a rope at Ousebank and drop her over these walls—'

'Fie on such baby-talk! Would you be ready to take her hand, before witnesses, not in a church but here in this chamber, and contract yourself to be her husband if, as they say, holy church it would?'

So God be praised for a man of inventiveness at hand when he is wanted. Before they went to bed that night it was fixed for the midday of the next day but one.

On the morning of the handfasting any would have said it was Robin Crosby himself who was going to be married. While Gandelyn still slept among his rushes he was moving about his chamber, his Two-ways bundle open, arraying himself in his guildhall-banquet garments, his brow like polished alabaster with the grease he had used for his side-hair. When he threw aside the curtain he had other attire also over his arm, and he roused Gandelyn with a stir of his foot.

'Have you shaved?' he asked.

Gandelyn had not shaved. He was as yet neither bearded nor shaven.

'I'll send the drawer up. It'll make you look less virginal. Has this lady-love o' yours aught to be wed in?'

'She'd do for me as she is.'

'That's to be seen. The drawer'll take out your night-stool and bring you water. Then get you into my chamber and wash yourself while he redds the place up a bit. I'll be back maybe in an hour. The Sister Superior's given her consent, so I shall bring them with me.'

So Gandelyn received his first shave at the hands of a tapster, who also cast an armful of clean rushes over the old ones. Comely-clean he looked with his newly-white chin and his page-bush of hair combed trimly out, and kneeling for a few moments at the casement out of which he must not look he prayed that Robin Crosby might be tenfold rewarded in heaven for every good deed he had ever done upon earth. Saint Mary's bell was striking noon as their feet were heard upon the stairs. They entered, a black-draped Efga Hartlip who spoke not a word, her daughter in her only wedding-gift, an over-cloak of faded purple from the Two-ways bundle. Except for Gandelyn's petition at the casement there was no prayer. The witnesses were the two drawers from below, and Robin Crosby removed only his feathered cap as he directed and prompted the proceedings.

'Are we all here?' he said. 'Then there's naught to wait for. You two, take one another by the right hand and say the words I say.'

The hands were joined, and from Efga Hartlip's shroudings there came a shaky sighing sound.

'Young man, you first. Say "Here I take thee, Echo—" '

' "Here I take thee, Echo—" '

' "To my handfast wife—" '

' "To my handfast wife—" '

' "To have and to hold, at bed and at board—" '

' "To have and to hold, at bed and at board—" '

' "For fairer for fouler, for better for worse—" '

' "For fairer for fouler, for better for worse—" '

'Echo, with your hand in his say "Here I take you, Robert—" '

' "Here I take you, Robert—" '

' "To have to my husband till death us depart, and thereto I plight thee my troth—" '

The words were spoken, all standing.

' "If holy church it will." '

Again they repeated it together.

'Now kiss. If I've left aught out holy church will see to it. Drawer, the cup. He drinks first, then he passes it to her—'

So they were united. She returned to Clementhorpe with her mother, but—wonder of wonders—only till midnight now.

For that same midnight was to see them out of York too.

Again the device was the actor's, and what could have been simpler? A Noah was to take back to Brid. Robin Crosby, who had brought her in, never wanted to see that ship again, the men had their wages, and in Roger Wymark's garden by Holy Trinity the gilded topcastle had gone from the mast. The mast itself had been unshipped, and now lay the length of the Noah's waist, lashed and bedded down on the great roll of wrappings that protected the splendid sail. So why not young Robert Gandelyn and his bride? Again there were letters to take, this time to the Brethren of Trinity and the shipwrights' guild in Brid. The departure was fixed for midnight, and early that evening the young bridegroom had his final instructions.

'The head-drover's name's Moxy. You'll find him a bit hard in the mouth, but he'll dress you a rabbit so you'd think it was a partridge. The tall one's Jonas. You'll find

me in Wymark's garden at half an hour before midnight.
I shall see you as far as Monk Bar, and then I shall wish
you god-speed.'

'And how if at the Bar they search us as they search
the market-carts?' but a disdainful look humbled him to
the ground.

'When *I* pick my friends I pick *my* sort, not yours!
There'll be no searching of Noahs with the pageant-master
there and two of the Lord's Prayer standing by. Keep
where I shall stow you, and see neither of you shows your
faces till York's three miles behind you. You'll find a
basket with a bit of breakfast in it. In Brid I stayed at the
Dotterel. It's a house you can take a woman to.'

But still it was not enough, for Gandelyn wanted to
know when and where he was to see the actor again, and
again he was answered as if from some lofty height.

'Again! Have I not had my bellyful of you? Again
forsooth!'

'Yet I have been thinking upon a device, Master
Crosby—it isn't table-tricks this time nor sleights that
cannot be seen five yards away—'

'I care not what it is, I ha' no time for it now. I cannot
settle all up in York under another week, and then I have
my company to find. It might be Pocklington, it might be
Nawood, I cannot tell. A company of minstrels is easy
enough to find. The rest's all seen to. All you have to do
is to be at Master Wymark's half an hour before Mary's
bell strikes twelve.'

And so it was. In the grass about the quintain lanterns
burned, the last pair of oxen were being yoked up. Into
the Noah like dunnage they were bundled down, side by
side. There would be no pausing before the dwellings of
the wealthy now, but by way of All Saints and its lantern,
avoiding the Shambles because of the beasts, and along
Goodramgate in a ship who had rumbled into York in a

painted palankeen. At Monk Bar they were expected, the great portcullis was already partly raised. All who were out of their beds wanted to be back in them again, and as the drovers struggled with the cattle only one sleepy jocular voice wished them a fair wind. The gate-men stood by at the chains, the officer of the guard gave the order. The last lantern passed through.

And 'Never again!' muttered Robin Crosby as he turned away in the direction of the *Keys*, to grapple with the accounts that Gandelyn had left unfinished.

Pie Powder

Away from you too scanty is delight;
Unless you bring it I desire no wine;
Yet sun wakes in my eyelids when comes night
Nor till I ope them sets this sun of mine.
I hear the words you say you have not said,
I think the thoughts you think you have not thought;
I read the book no other eye has read,
Dream on the unsung song, the kiss uncaught.
Yet O to hear the grave word as you say it,
To see the gentle thought break on your face,
To listen to your melody who play it,
The Thing Itself, the very Kiss of Grace—
Oh, stay not overlong! No man can say
How soon comes night that has no Inner Day!

I

The darkness grew less opaque, but the swaying and the lurching, the creaking and the straining and the knocking of loose objects continued. Twice or thrice during the night they had heard the sounds of passing voices, guttural greetings exchanged, and then the market-carts, York-bound in the night, had been on their way again. From time to time she stirred at his side, he heard her breathing, and there would be no more nightly returning of her to her mother now. When Efga Hartlip took her vows she would have no mother to return to.

The greyness broadened. They lay among cordage and rough bulky bundles, in some after-portion of the Noah shut off from the rest. Overnight he had seen the stern pavilion, its proscenium nailed up with boards and the end towards the waist curtained in. As the ship's great sail was rolled and bolstered up he judged that the bundles about them were her smaller stores and panoply of flags and pennons. She did not move as he got to his knees and left her sleeping there under his cloak. He groped his way towards the hanging and lifted it.

He could have laughed for the disenchantment of it. After the stateliness of the pageant, how shorn a galleon she was now! With its butt lodged against the fore-house her mast ran prone for the whole of the vessel's length. It continued through the pavilion he had left, it stuck out like a sprit astern. The proud topcastle, made in halves, was stowed in its two semi-lunes in the waist, and stores and blocks and tackle had been thrown in at the last moment, which would account for the knockings of the

night. But suddenly all came to a standstill. They had
found water, and the drovers were busy getting out buckets
and nosebags. Vast about him Yorkshire's leagues were
still hidden in the dawn's silver haze. In an hour it would
lift, the world would flash with dew, and Brid would be—
how far? Sixty miles? Five days at the very least, and he
looked at the disorder about him. If for five days he could
not make this ship a home for her, their first home—

Then he thought he saw the curtain move, and steadying
himself by the mast he clambered back to the pavilion.

As a bachelor he had never given it a thought that these
creatures they shared the world with had lives no less
continuous and packed with business than their own. In
their torn smocks and shawls and foresters' jackets they
came, went, and until they came again in a sort ceased.
Now in the half-light she too was up and moving about.
She had found the basket with their breakfast in it, but
Robin Crosby had said nothing about what else the basket
contained. Lifting the curtain he slipped in. In a pageant-
garment she had been married; now in the basket were
other sparings that would never be asked for again, scraps
of women's stuff, a needle for mending, a few loose pins
for her hair, a handkerchief, a plain kerchief to tie about
her head, what was left of Margaret Harvey's pennorth of
red silk. At the parting of the curtain she gave a little cry.
They clasped as they stood. Let her sew her seam. She had
washed dishes enough.

And as for the continuousness of lives, what better
continuity was there than that first morning embrace, as
often as they had a mind to kiss?

Old Moxy too remembered Gandelyn now. He was the
church-bred young sir who had made them all kneel
because a funeral was passing, and it was unlikely that
Moxy had bent a knee since, for it was not by any godliness
in him that he got the most out of his cattle. He began to

take his orders from Gandelyn that very morning, and it mattered nothing that not half of them could be carried out.

For he would have had the mast erected again, the splendid sail set. He would have had pipes and a ship's bell and a bo'sun's whistle, to announce to the world that here came two worth any man's eyesight. Why should pageant-pennons and Trinity flags waste in their bundle when a bridal bed waited for its canopy? Joined together again the two halves of the gilded topcastle would make a sort of oriole's nest for the pair of them, a castellated throne for the vessel's queen. But the cumbrous mast lay in the way of all. Even Jonas, who was called in, shook his head. The best that could be done was to block the two semi-lunes up aft, with the stage ladder to climb in and out by, and early that afternoon the rockings and the bumpings of their equipage again ceased. They had left York in the night, twelve miles in a broken day was not amiss. On a common the beasts were unyoked and tethered, and brushwood and last year's bracken were carried up for their own bed.

There is a bridal shyness that surpasses that of the virgin herself. Now she was abashed and timorous at finding herself among so many men. Moxy and Jonas slept in the forehouse, the others where the players had dressed, on the ground between the wheels. It would have taken a trumpet to rouse them after their day with the sluggish animals, but she was quite sure they could hear every word they said, and with the waggon again at a standstill he had come forward from his place, horsed astride the stern end of the mast with the road jogging past below. For the first time she had asked him where they were going.

'We're not going anywhere. We're *voyaging*. We're voyaging to a place called Brid,' he told her.

'And where shall we go after that?'

'Nowhere, at least not in this ship. To-morrow we come

to a port called Pocklington. In Brid we pay off the ship,
then we come back to Pocklington again, and then we
start looking for Master Crosby.'

But what was to happen after that he knew no more
than she, for Robin Crosby made nothing of his dice-tops
and ruby-boxes and not a deal even of his juggling. Like
the curriers, they would tew for their living he supposed,
and the art he was now turning over in his mind was one
he had only seen practised once. One day in France little
André, the tumbler who came and went between the camps,
had made him catch his breath at the sound of a cuckoo that
wasn't there. '*Tiens!*' the tumbler had suddenly exclaimed,
his face ecstatic and intently listening (for always the
attention must be diverted somewhere else), and as nearly
as Gandelyn had been able to make out André had given a
sort of cluck, far back in his throat, and from he knew not
where there had floated down the soft and placeless double
note. So if a Two-way Robin why not a Gandelyn with two
voices? But 'Get into that Noah,' the actor had ordered
when Gandelyn had tried to speak of it, and now Gandelyn
first sighed, then grumbled.

'It isn't me he wants, it's you. He calls me Robert
Glooms-and-gleams, and he wouldn't show me the Two-
ways because they'd made him queasy at the banquet, but
I've seen his costumes. One's all sky-blue down one side
with the silver lilies of France, but if it's Anthony and his
pincers then that half of him's as red as a firedrake.'

'He seems to have a lot of very rich things,' she
murmured.

'He has to have, because he says it's nothing without
it's parti-coloured. But before he could make you a dancer
he says, he'd have to pick you to the bone and mangle you
about till you were neither juice nor jelly.'

'It's to be hoped he'll ask me first!' she retorted.

'And André was only a tumbler, and he was going to

teach me, but I never saw him again. But when *you've* finished dancing the king will ask you what you'd like for a present, and you'll ask your mother, and I shouldn't ask for the Baptist's head if I were you because that put even Herod in a panic. I'd have—I'd have—now what would I have? No matter. There's bracken to lie on to-night. Have you nothing to say in my ear, but not so as all the drovers in Yorkshire will hear? Then we'll get the ladder.'

So on the bracken, with the pennons for Matthew and Mark and Luke and John about them, they slept.

Overnight they had seen the far-off skyline of the wolds, and the next day they began to climb without intermission. Not that it seemed to bring them anywhere, for the wolds sank out of sight again the closer they drew to them, and all they saw was foothills that rose to right and left, rough wastes scattered with gorse and heath and scented with thyme. And now if they descended to stretch their legs the ship was quickly overtaken again, and if they went ahead it was but sitting down to wait till it caught them up. But such was its length with its trail of labouring cattle in front and its pole-head sticking out behind that it needed a common to turn in, and it was Moxy's wont on approaching a township to do his halting outside it, feeding and resting his beasts, and then himself going ahead to prepare a way through without further stop.

But that day it was the two who were in Pocklington market-place first, and considerable as the place was she found little to see in it after York. It had a church and a manor-hall beyond, but Gandelyn would draw no wages till he came to Brid, there was the ship to wait for, so turning his back on the inns he had no money for he led her by a beck-side to the manor mill. There from a foot-bridge they listened to the growling of the heavy stones and watched the churning of the wheel in the water. But it was the first tumbling water she had seen since she had left

Washburn-in-the-Forest and the streamside with the
boulders and the handrope, and she fell into a brooding.
To make matters worse he called to a man who appeared
at a small door beyond the wheel, to ask him what else of
note Pocklington had to show. 'Ay, there was the nunnery,'
the man shouted back, raising his voice to make himself
heard, and emptied his bucket into the stream and went in
by the door again. Side by side, still in silence, they made
their way back to the market-place.

But he had the word of Peter Oates for it that the Washburn men would be given a whipping and let go, and there
was no need for them to visit nunneries who had left Efga
Hartlip at Clementhorpe, who would pass her presently on
to Lintham, who would pass her on to God. If the cattlemen
thought from their silence that they had quarrelled, let
them think.

But old Moxy, who could dress a rabbit so you would
think it was a partridge, had done better than a rabbit that
day. By some means or other he had laid hands upon a
hare, and they smelt it in the pot even as they mounted by
their ladder to the Noah again. Across a corner of their
pavilion she had rigged a cord to dry her bits of washing
on. Sad thoughts of Washburn and her mother were all
part of the strangeness of this ship-on-land, with the hillsides for its billows and a ladder for when they wanted to
get out and walk, and not for all the custards-royal in
France would he have exchanged Moxy's hare that day.
She too would have to learn to be an argonaut and take
things as they came. By Moxy's reckoning it was five days
to Brid, of which to-morrow would be the third, and as up
and up they laboured again the face of the land was
beginning to change. Nearer the high saddle the hills
became of a drier whiteness, the wayside flowers smaller.
A fresh wind blew steadily in their faces, and swept and
rippled over harebells and trefoil and patches of pale

purple thyme. It lacked only the shards and the sheep and—
strangest unreality of all—he himself might have been back
in the mirage of the chalk again, so little older as time is
reckoned, so much a man by any other reckoning. So short
a time ago, he had never seen her; now at night she lay
by his side. Then, carrying his black streamer before her
own father's body, there had appeared one day out of the
sunny bloom a ship; now in this selfsame ship they voyaged
together. In a few days the ship, too, would have gone, but
she would still be there, for fairer for fouler, for better for
worse, to ask him questions about this fantastic castle of
her birth, and this verderer-father of hers not even whose
name did she bear.

And when she did so, now or then or at any time, what
was he to answer when her questions became questions
about himself? Matthew Poole, unable to write his own
name, had at least contrived to raise himself to a knight's
degree; but Gandelyn, what was he? It was the lord John
who had put him to his schooling at Netherby, and that he
was of Westmoreland stock he was assured by every im-
pulse of loyalty and service in his breast. Yet had he been
any offspring of the lord John's it would long ago have
been acknowledged. It was true the lord John had had an
elder sister, rest her shriven soul, for once he had privily
seen her picture, and the pictured eyes had ever since
looked into his like his very own. Even if Brother Baruch
knew he would never tell him. So patience, duty and trust
till in his own good time the lord John should disclose
it all.

But she, his by handfast, and all else when holy church
it would—any day, at any moment, the unanswerable
question might come.

II

It was easier going for the cattle now. Many sheep dotted the hillsides, the inland gulls were blown about above them though the wind was light below. But now the skyline was on their left, and east and south the land lost itself in undulations of woodland and far-receding plain. Constantly afoot and ahead, mounting little hillocks for the first glimpse of this sea that twice he had crossed but she had never seen, they chased rabbits and picked unripe berries and grubbed for edible roots; but whoso looks closely at Robert Gandelyn's Arras now will find traces as it were not of first design, as if something had been hesitated over, unpicked, thought better of, and in the end stitched in again as before. Brid, for example, would bring them to the sea, but he lingers at Great Driffield, where they had much ado to get through because of the great wold-wains and the multitudes of sheep and young lambs. He was eager for the sea, but he delays again at Burton Agnes, where they had leave to picket the animals for the night under the trees of a vast park with wide stone gates. And after all what a man tells and does not tell is his own business. She spoke no more of her mother. Her small bundle of belongings was ready long before there was any need, and the drovers too wanted to see their homes again.

So, on a busy, sunny mid-morning, they came to Brid.

As before, it was best to leave the Noah a little way outside, and he went on to Trinity ahead. At Trinity however they were not ready for him, for the ship must be inspected before he got his wages and his quittance, and about Brid they wandered. Hardly in Hull itself had he seen so many jetties and warehouses and sheds and yards, and she clung closely to him for the confusion of the shouting and the odours of tar and brine, shy before the red-armed street-women with their crans and their baskets and their open-throated cries. The smell of nets and salt water and fish-heads reminded her of Thomas Twentyman and Ousebank, so down to the shipyards he took her, himself guided by crashes of ponderous and cannon-like music, with intervals that shook the very ground they stood on. Inch by inch, to the rhythm of brassy instruments, a hundred men with heavy beetles were lifting a ship. The multiple impact, every wedge struck at once, the great underbelly reverberating to the blows as if siege was being laid to a city—ah (he cries) there was music for the titans themselves! But it overpowered her, for she liked the ship with the wheels best, and she stuffed her kerchief into her ears, and when they returned to the Noah their business in the town had got about, for half its inhabitants seemed to be gathered there, and still the Trinity folk were not ready. The *Dotterel*, Robin Crosby had said, was such an inn as a woman could be taken to. He found it, and quickly discovered that the pageant-master had left an excellent name behind him. With gushes of civilities they were shown to their chamber, and it was the first bed with curtains she had ever seen. Water was brought that filled the room with its steaming, and she was drowsy with the noise and the rough and bawling voices and the salty seaweed air. So leaving her there off he strode to Trinity again, its brethren, its clerks, its tallymen, the Noah and its inspection.

One is nineteen and a bridegroom only once. Tearful kisses under elders or bob-apple ones as a topcastle lurches on its way, kisses on York's walls or in the *Dotterel's* curtained bed—from Trinity he now had his wages, and

could not keep his hand out of his pocket for the hole they
burned there. So with a wife to keep—the shops.

But again there were no shops in Brid like the shops of
York, and by the time he had come to his senses again he
found that the only sensible thing he had bought for her
was a pair of boots. His score would be to pay at the inn,
he must have more money, so having finished his business
with Trinity he turned to the shipwrights, rejoiced to see
their Noah again and clamorous to know how Corpus had
passed in York. The *Dotterel* was their accustomed meet-
ing-place. Into it they crowded, so now for a touch of
Gandelyn's quality. Going upstairs to their chamber to
look at the purchases again, she left him below, in the
middle of the floor, such a histrion as never was as he
rapturously declaimed *Noah* and the *Shepherds*, to up-
roarious applause. On the second evening came those who
had not been there on the first, this time with Moxy and
Jonas and two of the drovers to bear him out. Round went
his cap, and next out came his top and the box with the
ruby in it. Never in memory had the *Dotterel* done such a
trade, and for long afterwards they spoke of him as 'That
wick 'un that brought the Noah back.' Who had said that
money had to be tewed for as the curriers tew their
leather?

Never had summer skies been bluer nor clouds so nobly
up-piled than on that fourth morning, when half a hundred
of them accompanied them to the jetty-head to see them
off along the sands. In Brid the only thing he had bought
for himself was a strap to carry her bundle and his own
folded cape. 'Come and give us Corpus again next year,
Wickun!' they called after him as he dropped to the
mussel-crusted pier-footings, his house on his back like a
snail. In an hour the jetty became a distant thumb behind
them.

But she saw no sea such as he had a score of times

described, now lifting whole fleets to the skies, now engulfing them again. All she saw was a straggling triple wrack of brown weed alive with a myriad hoppers, jellyfish wasted half away, and as far as her eyes could stretch a flat immensity of drying sands. Low and far away these ended in a thin white edge that hardly lapped, and farther away still, not brown now, a rock over which broken water sometimes creamed lazily. But he stuck to his tale, that she would see.

'Noah's wife wouldn't believe it was going to rain,' he told her; 'take them boots off,' and when she had done so he slung them with his own from the roll that made a hunchback of him and herself suddenly slender and of a different balance by his side. Two small irregular tracks lengthened behind them as they struck out for the ebb.

Except that sooner or later Robin Crosby would be to find he had no plan. There was loose money in his pocket and nothing to spend it on. So far away from anywhere she had ever been before all places were the same to her, her feet were bare as when he had first seen them, and for them both life in its largeness lay open before them. His face was of a somewhat deeper brown than before, but her colour had little to change from, and she had wrapped her head in woman's oldest and ever-new tiring, her plain kerchief, knotted under her chin to keep her hair from blowing away. But even when they reached the edge where never-dry rocks laid bare their pools it was not yet the sea of his vaunting. It was a shop-window of a sea, a sea set out with wares, and she slipped and stumbled on the cushions of wet weed to peer down at the coralline stars and grey crabs and glistening jellies and the crystalline sea-flowers as eagerly as she had looked at the jewels and taffetas of Ouse Bridge. The reason he carried his bundle so high was the food with which he had loaded himself at the *Dotterel*. They would eat as they kissed, when they

H

were hungry, for what is dinner-time more than the time a man has his dinner? But the rocks among which they played meant that the sands now went no further. Instead there rose, almost close at hand, overshadowing white cliffs, mewing and screaming and racketing with birds, cliffs the tops of which seemed to run on and on till they were lost to sight. A thousand years made no difference to them, so set your clerking wits to work on that, Robert Gandelyn, and ask yourself how much youth it takes to make up a thousand years. Also when next you tell her about the rough and raging sea tell her too about its creeping stealth. Suddenly she gave a cry. They were islanded, with water all about them. He too had forgotten the deeper water about the rocks, and it would have been her turn to laugh at drenchings as into it he dropped, with her cramped to his pack for a double burden. But her eyes closed in fear as she saw nothing between her and the land but shoals of water, shining as it reflected back the sky.

And when from the safe foot of the cliff-way she looked back she saw no rock at all, but only a few curds of white, and a limitless shimmer of green that joined the sky in deepest, softest blue.

So with cliffs that a thousand years do not alter it matters little whether it was that day or the next when, high above it all, they thought to look down on it but could not. For the higher they mounted the more the sea rose with them, so that instead of a few close-in rocks they saw, small and many miles away, ships like specks, not with splendid sails, but in their workaday greys and browns, and some with nothing but thin poles, at rest on the water as if its level surface was their home. And for two days a man might walk that high rampart, seeing æons of sea, that did not creep and retire in a thin wash along the sands now, but came in in thunderous rollers, range after range, that boomed in the caverns beneath till

the promontory trembled and spilled it out again in seethings of white and green. To look down a dizzy ravine was
to see the birds battling drunkenly in the invisible back-
washes of air. It was to see the great boulders far beneath,
greening to emerald and deepening to blue until the next
oncoming giant crashed over them in a spread of surge.
In a place so heroic and primal he must needs play the
Proteus too, peopling its air with sprites and its depths
with sea-monsters, who (he shouted to her) must be
appeased with a living maiden every year. If the wind
carried half of it away it was something for the wind to do.
But it was in a turfy cranny, with the wind passing over
their heads and the tumult below by so much the louder,
that to annoy her he began one of his most fantastic tales
in the middle.

'So off this brave knight and his lady set to the Holy
Land, and after a long time they came to the Grecian sea—'

Her eyes seemed to have forgotten the colour of woods
as she asked him if there was a sea there too.

'Is there a sea in Greece!—But one day I'll take you
there. So one morning this lady was sitting thinking of her
lost sons—'

'You didn't say she had any sons.'

'Don't take folk up when they're telling a tale. She'd
three sons, but at a ford they had to cross a lion comes
raging out of a thicket and pounces on the eldest. So don't
say that I haven't told you that! And in a dark wood a
leopard runs away with the next, and soon after a unicorn
snatches the youngest, and three was all they had.'

'How old was she if she had three sons?'

'There weren't any old people in those days, and one of
her sons was nearly three yards high. So one day there
comes along a very old man—'

'You just said there weren't any old people—'

'He was born old, like me. There had to be that sort or

there wouldn't have been all these priests and soothsayers. And by the time this knight had become the most valiant knight in all the world—'

'Who makes them knights?'

'It's all laid down in the rules of chivalry. One knight makes another, but he has him to answer for. Now I have this tale to begin all over again. So at last there comes a day when his lady says to him, "My lord Sir Isumbras," she says—'

'You said before his name was Sir Robert—'

'I'm coming to that. Sir Robert was this youngest son of his.'

'But you said they were all dead," and he gloomed-and-gleamed again, as Robin Crosby had said. Dead, in *his* stories!

'They were no deader than I am! This unicorn I told you ran off with the youngest, just when this good knight was hard-pushed in a great battle one day, it comes galloping towards him with his youngest son on its back, in golden armour, and he'd grown up by that time—'

And as on he rambled the wind continued to sweep the grassheads above them and the water to churn and thunder in the chasms below.

They slept that night at an egg-taker's hut, a furlong back from the cliffs, but with the breaking of the sea still in their ears. And wild and lovely as the place was they could not stay there for ever, yet they were loth to leave it without having descended to the shore once more. The egg-taker, like the knight of his tale, had three sons to pay out his rope while he dangled and twisted among the birds in mid-air, and he knew a way down by a gully on foot, which he showed to them the next morning. They were welcome to stay another night with him, he said, so down the two who were now one descended to the giant boulders of the talus, where from the greatest to the smallest the

stones were scoured as round as eggs with their unceasing
grinding and rolling. The foam-ridged rollers were as
green as glass and twice as high as themselves, the sands
battered as hard as a floor with the massed tons of their
breaking, and there was neither Actæon nor hot and ruddy
David to spy. As the receding waters exposed the sand
again it was warm as a bakestone in the sun, and only the
shadow of the cliff at the end of the day told them it was
time to go.

The great headland still ran on and on, the gulls still
mewed overhead, but the sea that had climbed with them
disappeared behind them the next day. About them spread
a wide world of stunted herbage and heather, intersected
by dikes and sheepwalks and ancient entrenchments. And
now she was glad of the boots he had bought her, and once
she asked him how far it was to this castle in which she
had been born. The feet in the boots were bare, they were
as dusty and tangled and unkempt a bride and bridegroom
as could have been found, and now they could walk a whole
day and not see a living soul. But that was not to say that
sometimes she did not hear the most unexpected sounds,
born apparently of the empty air. Suddenly he would stop
as if tranced. Rapturously he would turn up his eyes, listen,
then point. 'Cuck-oo!' would come the dulcet hiccup, or it
might be 'Ec-ho!' for they are much alike, or it might be
a peewit, or the drumming of a frog, or a distant voice
calling on them to stop. She knew the sounds came in some
mysterious way from himself, but she could never quite
catch him at it, and now, as she set her hair after a night
in a fallen-in sheepfold or lying under his cloak beneath a
tumulus, he could not keep his eyes from her every movement. She had a way of fastening herself up at the waist
with her elbows sticking out and her hands fumbling
behind her that stayed with him half the day, and when
evening came again her eyes in the dusk reminded him of

those pools so clear that not the darting minnow is seen but only the flicker of its shadow below. Was it that that the bald actor had seen at the lifting of an eye?

But actors do not play to cromlechs and cairns, so they talked it over as for days they tramped, just a young couple the world never missed, of uncertain parentage both, wedded by handfast and the rest as holy church might confirm. They agreed however that Robin Crosby would not be found looking for his company in the heather. It had better be back to Great Driffield, a road with wains and fellow-travellers and inns where groats were to be had. They might come up with him at Pocklington, it might be Nawood.

'Do we stir ourselves?' he asked her.

'Yes, if Newbiggin's as far as you say, she answered, and again from aloft there came an airy 'Come, Echo!' as if Robin Crosby himself called.

Fraternities of players do not go about in hiding or unnoticed, but it was on a hearsay that they trudged half way to Malton, only to find they had been misinformed. As the farther north they went the wilder the country became, back they turned again, the money he had picked up so easily in Brid began to run low, and in Pocklington there were no shipwrights, glad to see their ship again and agog to know how Corpus had passed in York. At Nawood his spinning top came near to getting him into trouble, for one surly fellow knew its trick and muttered something about the watch-house, and already behind them were the days when if they did not want to do a thing they did not do it. In the end it was by no contrivance of his that, in a nowhere of a village called Tong-under-the-Hill, they came one afternoon upon a solitary harper, playing his harp to an empty street, with a nackerer ahead of him shaking a poke for nobody's money. The street had at one time been half-consumed by fire and never rebuilt. The half that remained was tumbledown, grass grew in the market-place. Yet lo, it was in this last place of God's making that their search was over, for no sooner had Gandelyn asked the harper his customary question than the harper stopped playing. He looked from one to the other of them. 'Are you the two from York?' he asked, and then pointed up the street to the place's single inn. They would find Master Crosby there, he said. It later turned out that somewhere in the region was a lead-mine. Occasionally, once a month perhaps, there passed down the blackened street a cart with a few sand-moulded pigs. For such a place one inn was enough, and in its single room, alone and with his head between his hands, Robin Crosby sat.

And never, never again was still his moan. A man's oldest companions were not to be trusted, none, not one. For it seemed that scarcely had he turned his back but his company had fallen at odds, quarrelled, and split up into two. The remnant he had come upon was that he could best have spared, and even Gandelyn's long narration about the Noah comforted him not at all. He, the renowned Two-ways Robin, was set back to the indignity of a market-stroller again, and he cursed York and his own greed for its gold that had brought him to this.

But the split-up of the company was Gandelyn's god-sent opportunity. The harper was Andrew, a noble-bearded man but grey and beginning to feel his years. The seceders had left him his tilt-cart, the donkey, and most of his costumes and effects, and of these Terence was in charge. The nackerer was the nackerer, and that evening Gandelyn counted them observingly up. Including the master-actor himself they were four. To these two more might now be added, and Gandelyn had been cunning enough to pack Echo for the present out of sight. Some-time during that evening Robin Crosby raised his head.

There at the door stood the girl. His eyes, resting on her, flashed like fifty lark-traps. He sprang to his feet, clapped his hands together, and shouted loudly for Terence.

'Terence! *Terence!* . . . Them fainthearts that ran away, have they left us aught?'

'Nay, if you mean the cart, Robin, they took no more than a mask or so and a rig-out apiece,' the costumier replied.

'Have they left Herod's crown and beard?'

'They're in the cart at the back.'

'The robe of flame?'

'Ay, ay, for thieves I've known worse,' and next the kindling eyes alighted on the nackerer.

'Nackerer! What's in that old tithe-barn besides rats?'

'Mice,' said the nackerer.

'Is it used?'

'I ha' seen few young folk here yet, but such as there is might tell you.'

'Have my skipping-board ta'en in there first thing in the morning. Then set up a couple of boards with a horse-blanket, or sacks, or what there is. Find fullers-earth if you can, and a drop or two of sweet oil. Them three would show me their backs, would they? Then by pie, it's to be seen what we can do without 'em!'

From all of which it was already plain to Gandelyn that she had been quite, quite wrong when she had said it was to be hoped he'd ask her first.

With Tong's disaster its church too had suffered, but the tithe-barn stood some way up the lead-mines road, as the places where hidden deeds are to be done are set apart. Because its door opened at a thrust the nackerer was stationed outside it, with orders to find some way of securing it by to-morrow. Only husbands were admitted, he said, and his business with her now came before any husband's business. For modesty's sake she might keep her shift, but off with the rest save for Gandelyn's cloak, nor would she need that by the time he had warmed her up. The planks were padded with sacking, the fuller's earth was ready. He dusted his hands with it. But 'Mary ha' mercy!' he cried as he laid them on her limbs, tough and indurated with leagues of walking whereas he would have had them softer than rain-water. 'The woman's made of cowhide! She's brawn with oak-knots in it! She could rive down the pillars of the temple! Who's to make any-thing of a piece of ironmongery like this?'

Yet it had to be tried, and for a dismemberer of women no more blushing blood than Robin Crosby's ever red-dened a cheek. Her husband would have to be taught to be her torturer, and for an hour that morning Gandelyn was taken into every secret of his beloved's fibres, the actor talking all the while without ceasing, that she might not know what dig or twinge was coming next.

'Yield yourself, girl, yield yourself!' he cried again and again. 'Let your breath out, don't hold it—would I'd had you between the millstones when you were in your cradle! Yet see, it's no more than a few bits of her that's got stuck together with striking on anvils in smithies! There's things she'd shriek at—there, that was one of 'em . . . now let her rest herself a minute. See, these bones of her back, young Glooms-and-gleams, they follow one another so. Dip your hands in this fuller's earth and start at her neck. . . . Ay, but get your fingers and thumbs deeper into her brisket, see, the same as I do! Lord, that folk will think they're given bodies to turn 'em into whipcord! . . . Now over with her, and loosen, woman, loosen, not stiffen, stiffen—'

Then, as she was ready to swoon for apprehension and numbness:

'Now like this, with the palms of the hands and a bit gentlier. She'll be stiff to-morrow but 'twill pass. Then let her sleep for an hour where she is while I see to that door. Ay, so, sit with her and hold her hand—'

A bar was set inside the tithe-barn door. Soon this or something like it had become their daily exercise. And now it was Gandelyn's turn.

But when Gandelyn broached his project of the two voices the actor's 'Never again' became the song of the loom when by mid-week it quickens ever so slightly: 'Time enough yet, time enough yet.'

'This of York's cost me half of my company, and I have to get going again while my name's in folks mouths. This you speak of I've heard of it, but I can tell you nothing about it,' he said. 'They say they begin with pebbles in their mouths. Besides, that was a French cuckoo. Let's see what's in that cart.'

For he would have no man in his company who at a pinch could not play an instrument or two, and from the cart he fetched out an old crouth, which he thrust into Gandelyn's hand. 'The nackerer'll show you,' he said, but in the cart Gandelyn found for himself an artificial marmoset with a short red jacket and a suit of such tinsel decking as the monkey wears when they set it on the mastiff's back. It opened and shut its jaws when it was pressed from behind, and Robin Crosby, with half a lost summer to make up, himself always seemed to have fifty different things on his hands. Money was scarce, they had the inn much to themselves. A garret had been found for the bride and bridegroom, and in the common parlour of an evening there was always some chipped sceptre to mend or a dagger of wood. For the shriller sound he would string Gandelyn's crouth with wire when he could come by some, but for the present he must make do with gut.

'You can suck your pebble while you're fingering,' he said, 'and you'll have a few parts to learn too. All must be able to play *Robin Hood* in their sleep, and a dozen more.

Would you be handy at writing a line or two in if need should arise?'

'I might,' said Gandelyn.

'Then let Echo get her needle and be running over these sarsnets. Nackerer, fetch the paints and be touching up these masks. It's time I was getting myself into trim too.'

His skipping-board had been carried into the bat-ridden barn. It had been the half-door of some pig-house or pen, and his rope was a rope like another, but let Robin Crosby cast his jacket on the ground, kick off his shoes, give the rope a shake and then begin, and you watched with all the eyes you had. Neither young nor old he looked as the rope slipped under the feet that hardly seemed to leave the board, and at first it flipped slowly. He turned with scarcely perceptible movements of his wrists, then as he began to quicken the tapping of the rope on the board became a rattle. Suddenly his feet left the ground. Thrice the rope had passed under them before they touched it again, and his next leap was a yard and more high, his feet twinkling of themselves with the rope flung out sideways and at large. They became the feet of a squirrel in a spinning cage as first he crossed the rope, then releasing it sent it snaking up to the cobwebby rafters. With shining eyes Gandelyn watched from an upturned bucket, and as the rope descended again a loop suddenly pinioned his arms to his side. It might as easily have been his neck. Then the dancer stood before him with his hands on his hips, not even breathed.

'Fifteen years ago,' he said, 'I could skip.'

Echo's reward for her daily racking came when Terence brought the costumes out of the cart. Their gold was not real gold, nor their pearls real pearls, but her eyes danced like brook water at the sight of them, and now she was beginning to crow it over Gandelyn that for all his manly strength she could do a dozen things that he could not. But the actor only shook his head. He could not make a dancer in a week or two nor yet in a month or two, he said. For the present the best would have to be made of a lick and a promise, but there were other ways. Give folk plenty of bustle and noise and something to gape at, tell them well what the miracle was going to be before they saw it, and they did the rest for themselves. The summer was slipping by. He had most of the charges to pay, his gains from York were becoming steadily less, and three who knew every trick of their trade were waiting for two beginners. June was almost out, and it was the winter that was on his mind. Already they had been in Tong-under-the-Hill over a month, and decked out in her pearls and gold that were not real, he drove her to it all day long in the barn. Then in the evening he sighed.

'We shall have to make do as we go,' he said. 'She's neither silk purse nor sow's ear, but we can lose no more time,' and Andrew the harper spoke.

'Where are we making for when the autumn comes, Robin?' and the actor stroked his head thoughtfully.

'Why, that's as it may be. But in York, when I could get away from those Solomons in their Guildhall, I spent middling of time with the vintners and grocers.'

'Why them?' the nackerer asked, and was fittingly answered.

'As well you have me to do your thinking for you! In this trade, wouldn't you want to know who's opening his house in York again for the winter and who's laying in provisions to spend it where he is? Isn't it meat and drink for us too he's buying?'

'To be sure, to be sure.'

'The next place to this is Layside, and we've no stage, but there's a green where they dance. At Cowhill there's a hustings where they hold the Pleas. That's how I came to find you in a place with only half a street left, because none of you thinks to find out which of the gentry's on the move!

If one of them has a daughter getting wed, Princeamour here'll be able to fit her up with a wedding-song. And Terence, I'm taking the costumes out of your hands. Blancheflower here will see to them better than you can. And to-morrow she goes into the red one.'

Yet because these had stood by him when the deserting three had not nothing should be done but by the consent of all, and on the morrow in the great mouldering barn she made herself Salome for the first time. For a beginning he bound her head with a mesh, not of rabbit-snare but of fine glossy silk to keep her hair within compass. On this he set a property wreath of flaming red poppies. Poppy-red too was the tunic he tightened under her compact breasts, but its lower part was leaved and lapping and counter-changed with white, in such a way that with her every bend and gesture purity and satanic flame seemed to writhe and contend for the possession of her. Her small shoes were black as cobs of coal, and Robin Crosby pointed abruptly to where he had set his skipping-board across two buckets to represent Herod's banqueting board.

'Beaumains — Princeamour — Gleams-and-Glooms or what your name is—you're Herod, sit you there. It's to give her a point to act on. But there's no reason why you should be wasting your time, so take these,' and into his hand he thrust a number of much-thumbed and stitched-together papers, a sort of prompt-copy of such songs and ballads as he possessed. 'Scan 'em over and pick out aught you fancy for Andrew to be knocking up a tune to.'

So while Echo twisted and turned under his direction, bending herself backwards till her scarlet coronal came within inches of the ground, he turned over the soiled leaves:

> 'Thou art, she said, a gentle knight
> And I a bride in bower bright
> And of high kin y-come,'

he read, but all the time he was listening to the actor's
tyrannical voice.

'You're losing your smile! Smile though the roof crack!
You're thinking of King Herod, and yet you're not thinking of him, if you follow me! He's aflame for you, but it's
your dancing keeps you afire! To-morrow we'll have
Andrew in. Your eyes will want a dab of paint and maybe
your mouth too. Again, and remember your smile—'

And:

> 'Maiden on the moor lay,
>   On the moor lay, on the moor lay,
>   Maiden on the moor lay
>   A sennight and a day,'

Gandelyn read:

> 'What was her drink?
>   The well was her drink,
>   The chilled water of wellspring,
>   Well was her drink,'

and then again the actor was hauling her, mauling her, his
own finger-tips arched over his head.

'Slacken, slacken, not stiffen, stiffen! The king's eyes
are on you! He's glowering in a frenzy for you! But you,
that's brought him to that, show him the more and give
him the less the madder you make him—'

But these things have to be when warm castles are to
be found for the winter and plenty to eat and drink and
soft lying for them all. There came the day when weeks
more of it would have taken them little further, and with
plenty of nackering to drown his false notes and a bit of
mountebanking thrown in Gandelyn could now stop a gap
well enough with his crouth. His other side-tricks would
suffice for the getting together of the first few of a crowd,
and for their good-bye to Tong's score or so of lead-miners
and their women they gave a noble performance of *Robin*

Hood in the tithe-barn, with cudgellings and batterings enough to gladden any heart. The nackerer played Maid Marian, for Echo had enough to do without speaking-parts. During the performance she was mending a flame-lappet of her fire-costume that she had tripped over at rehearsal. That red taffeta cost a shilling a yard.

The order in which they finally departed down Tong's fire-blackened street was as follows:

The donkey between the shafts of the hooped tilt-cart came first, and if it died of age on the way the nackerer would haul instead and at last somebody would have seen a dead donkey. Mounted on the front seat sat Echo. She was somewhat thinner in the face, and ate less than before, but it was easier to make yourself fat than thin again. She was there to be looked at, and the more diverse she made herself with her bits of shawls and fillets the better. Andrew, who came next, carried his harp in a green bag on his back, Terence and the nackerer followed, and Gandelyn brought up the rear. Often he fell some little distance behind, for his throat-cluckings and other extra-ordinary noises were his private business, and as for Robin Crosby, half the time he was not there at all. Striding ahead on his long legs he was their runner to spy out the land, their gatherer of information, returning with orders that they were to prepare themselves for the playing of this or that. Sometimes Andrew and Gandelyn sufficed for the entertainment, the harper playing, and Gandelyn juggling or miming as it might be; but at Layside there came an innovation. It was a market-day, and on the balcony where they had intended to perform the supervisor and his assistant had placed their table. *Solus*, Robin Crosby had decided to give them the Two-ways, this time the scimitared blackamoor and the christian with his short whinyard. But the innovation was this: that while the bout was at its heat, not far from the market steps a drunken red-nose in a smock began to make a hurly-burly, deriding the performer and bragging he could do as well himself. Nobody knew him, for he was no Layside man, and Robin Crosby, stopping his performance, challenged him to make his words good. Such however was the market-drunk fellow's buffooning and so clownish were his stumbles that presently the whole market-place was rocking with laughter, which changed to a roar of mirth at themselves as, with scimitar and whinyard together, he began to juggle with such dexterity that before he had finished the half-pennies were rattling into the nackerer's dish.

But Echo did not like to see her husband with a red nose, and sat at a distance in the tilt-cart, silently sewing.

But it was for Cowhill that the master-actor had laid his plans the most deeply. The Cowhill folk set themselves somewhat above all others thereabouts, for besides its market the place had a speech-hall and a leet, at which the lord of the manor was wont to preside in person. Returning from one of his excursions ahead Robin Crosby called them all together and under a tree addressed them.

'From now on one thing's got to lead up to another, each a step better than the last,' he said. 'By what I can hear this worthy magistrate's a Somebody hereabouts. Echo, are you paying heed to what I say? Into Cowhill we march in full fig, Herod and his lords, all painted and dressed. I ha' spoken with the bellman, and it's to be in the speech-hall. But you, Echo, you'll take your bundle in your hand, and there'll be a tiring-woman to meet you, and you'll slip in by the side door. I'll be there to trim you up, and when you come on you'll find us all at board, me in my crown in the middle. Then you'll see me make a sign. Andrew'll sing the words, and you'll see my face, all raging with lust and love, but take no notice. You dance the way you did in the barn, but remember it's for the

sake of the lordly gift I'll give you, not Beaumains. It
might be weeks before we get another chance like this—'
with a great deal more, which is omitted.

So there marched into Cowhill that afternoon five such
figures as the place had never seen, robed and turbaned
and bearded and jewelled with rubies as big as eggs, who
scowled and flashed their eyes and rattled their scimitars
as the bellman went ahead. But into a side-door of the
speech-hall there slipped a figure so dazed and shrinking
that only half of her seemed to be there at all. But it was
the half Robin Crosby wanted, and the raised part of Cowhill's leet-house was in fact a far more commodious
platform than any of York's pageant-stages. Its lawyers'
bench was set out as a feasting board. There was no
Herodias, and for all she knew her own mother was in
Lintham by this, but Andrew's chanted argument made all
plain. As Herod pledged his councillors and lords there
crept into the hall as it were a ground-fire blown in by the
wind, that stirred as Herod half rose in his seat, and then
suddenly leapt like a tree in flames. Her face was whitened,
her pale eyes sunk in sombre pits, the mouth that he had
reddened seemed that of a fire-eater. At a point Andrew's
harping broke off in the middle. She sank to the ground
again, a hearth of taffeta ashes that so lately had been
living flames, blank and aghast to find the head between
her knees. After that she would never be afraid to dance
Salome again.

But the true and secret intent of Robin Crosby's
scheming came after the performance. They were bidden
to sup and sleep at the manor-house itself, and as far as its
gates all Cowhill accompanied them. Andrew and Terence
and the nackerer supped with the upper servants. She was
still in a daze, but the lady of the house, supposing her
shyness of speech to be the exhaustion of her dance, praised
the maidenliness of her demeanour. Gandelyn was pre-

sented by the chief player as one who had served with the
lord John in France, of other guests there were only two,
Sir John the priest and a gentleman of the neighbourhood,
and no sooner had the dame and her charge left the board
than Robin Crosby took the floor. So lately in York, he
had news to impart, but far more to receive, of halls and
their owners, their diversions, their tables, which of them
had the longest purse. What one did not know another had
heard of, Gandelyn told his small tale of France. So the
evening passed, and their good host had not been so late
out of his bed these two years.

But that night Echo slept in the tirewoman's feather-
bed, and before she left the next morning she had been
given an almost-new kirtle stitched with silver thread and
two new fillets for her hair.

The road now found they kept to it. If it seemed a place
worth playing to, well; if it did not they held on their way.
The donkey slept as he walked, a net of hay was slung
beneath the tilt for its eating, and upstairs was the married
quarters. Besides its tilt the cart had an additional tenting
that could be pegged out behind, and here slept the rest of
the company. Andrew harped ahead, but there was no
more *Salome*. That was for better than market-crosses and
fairs.

And ask Robin Crosby now where he was going and he
had a half dozen great halls and houses at the tip of his
tongue.

So they came to Malton. Thence two days later they
passed to Hutton, where Gandelyn was once more the
drunken farmer who could do the Two-ways better than
its inventor, and from Hutton (crossing the Derwent) they
reached Filby. After Filby it was some other place of which
Gandelyn forgot the name, but it was at Sturton, where
they had not intended to stop at all, that there came another
opportunity not to be missed. So unlikely indeed was it to

recur that once more Gandelyn was told to make himself ready.

Before Sturton's single inn a horse-trough stood, and there a number of horses were being watered and buckets clanked and dogs lapped thirstily. The fence-season was over, a dozen men in various liveries were assembled, and a forester in green was questioning the innkeeper and other natives of the place. But it was no hunt in cry, breathing itself before resuming the chase. It was only (it appeared) that somewhere a stag had broken preserve, had been proclaimed, and now must be found and returned to harbour again. But there might be money for the players to pick up, and suddenly every beater and dog-ward turned his head at the sound of the nackerer's fair-ground voice.

'Room for them, pray, room, room! Good people, make 'em a space, for this time it is to the death! Through Syria and Arabia and Barbary they ha' sought one another, and it's in Sturton one of 'em's to die! Make a ring and gather round!' and into the space about the horse-trough there leaped as it were two men joined together, a paynim with a great scimitar and a christian with a short-sword and half a scarlet cross on his breast. To their combat they fell with 'Ha's!' and clashings, alternating with such speed and nimbleness that indeed one man seemed to be two. The dogs set up a barking, never had such agility been seen in Sturton before. But a bucolic clown, early in the day as it was almost too drunk to stand, was suddenly heard to bawl that he could do as well himself, and they would have put him into the trough, but there was a gasp of incredulity as suddenly the oaf was in possession of both the weapons at once. Up the scimitar shot into the air, higher than the eaves of the inn, with the short-sword after it. They were joined by yet a third weapon, a twinkling poniard, and before the inn, with a lad in charge of it, stood the horse of one who regaled himself inside. At the doorway this traveller suddenly appeared, wiping his handsome beard. His tasselled baldrick bespoke him as one of pretension in the world, yet he did not look like a hunter of stags. The next moment he was back in the inn again, raising his voice for the landlord.

'Who are those outside, and where do they come from and where are they going?' he demanded.

'They say a stag—'

'Not them in the liveries. I'm riding with them. Him with the red nose, juggling there by the trough.'

'I ne'er set eyes on him before.'

'Who's the parti-coloured one with him?' but Robin Crosby's fame was not so universal as he supposed, for the landlord didn't know him either.

'Then across the street there, the young woman in the tilt-cart? See, the one that's looking at herself in a hand-glass,' and again the innkeeper shook his head.

'They're none of Sturton, any of 'em. I heard there were strollers a day or two back at Cowhill.'

And Stephen Hurst might have been mistaken about the lithe man who twinned the christian with the paynim, or even the fat red-nosed one who played with swords and knives. But there was no mistaking the pomegranate shawl of the girl of Ouse Bridge, and Stephen called hastily for his reckoning. It only remained for his own baldrick and handsome beard not to be seen and recognized.

'Has this house a back door?' he asked the landlord.

'Ay, sir, walk straight through.'

'Have my horse taken round there and make haste with my reckoning.'

And to his reckoning that day he added a bounty of two pence, for if everything went as it should what were two pence to Stephen Hurst now?

Castle of Pleasure

Now for a monkey of a private mind
What gazed-on life is this? I cannot scratch
My scurf-dry skin but here's this humankind,
An orrery of eyes come round to watch!
Those horse me on the dog and sound the charge,
Set the choice morsel just beyond my chain:
Loin-tethered too, laugh at my season's urge
And quick contracted eyes indrawn with pain.
These have a sort of little thimbley Soul
They praise their faces with, but when I peer
To see what other ape invades my pole,
And spit and snatch behind, yet nothing's there,
I weep with rage and steal their silvery clue;
Now I've a little Soul to question too!

I

Bulmer Castle, rising on its grassy knoll above the tree-tops of Gaultres like an island from a forest sea, was not yet two men's lives old. In the days when we had been routing them in France a certain William Bulmer, of no very distinguished birth, had amassed wealth as a pur-veyor to the armies. Few built castles nowadays, but he had set his heart upon having a castle of his own to die in, and he had lived just long enough to see its last stone set in its place. Even so, this had left his son, the present Sir Thomas, with more money than he knew what to do with, so he had followed his father upwards by buying himself into the Lancastrian nobility by marriage. The lady Adela's family had seen to it that the purchase had been an ex-pensive one, and the couple, now elderly, contrived to jog on comfortably together as long as they were never left for long alone.

This they never were. So open a house did Sir Thomas keep that he always spoke of it as 'this inn of mine,' and as a strong-point any soldier would have laughed at it. To the west the swamps of Gaultres were its chief defence, to the east ran the Derwent. A pale or park to the north was a standing encampment for the servants and attendants of those who came and went, and where it looked over its treetops to York, a day's ride away, only the wall-piercings for the hoarding-timbers spoke of fortification or the possibility of assault.

But for victualling it could at any time have held out against a short siege. At the foot of a wide grassy slope the river was dammed for a fishpond, in the glades of

Gaultres meat was to be had for the hunting, the granaries bulged with their sacks and bins, the kitchen fires were never out. Passers-by of station invited themselves, and when the fence-season was past no sooner had one set of guests departed than another took its place. With their ladies they came, these also suitably attended, and in Sir Thomas's lofty hall sixty might sit down at once. Many he did not know fished his pond and were to be met in his stables and mews. Of salt and fresh they ate their fill, with by-eating at all times and dogs everywhere. and with his major-domo at his elbow Sir Thomas bustled about from his cellars to his butteries, from his greater guests in the inner court to the squires and pages and yeomen who camped at the palisades, superfluously asking them how they fared.

But alas, one thorn had planted itself in Sir Thomas's easy side, sticking the closer that because of his wife there was no getting rid of it. His castle had not been his own ever since the lady Adela's first cousin, the earl Philip of Gaunt, had quarrelled with the Archbishop and walked with high words out of his house.

Yet he had not brought with him any great train. Himself, Sir John Boles, Sir Emrys, Sir Maris and his own personal attendant, made no more than five, and as it happened the southern wall of the castle had been untenanted at the moment of their arrival. They were seldom even five, for if not Sir John Boles then Sir Maris or Sir Emrys was back and forth between Bulmer and York, three days away perhaps, coming and going, on what business Sir Thomas left it to his lady to ask. To the other ladies the lady Adela spoke vaguely of battle-knocks in France and the repose her cousin's hard service had earned. 'Let him sleep in a soft bed and rise at what hour he will,' she said. 'He'll take his seat at table with the rest of us when he's ready.'

Bulmer had no moat, and the earl Philip, alighting from his horse in the forecourt under the southern wall, had looked up at the piercings for the defence-hoardings and then turned abruptly to the hovering Sir Thomas.

'The last time I was here wasn't there a sort of watching-post jutting out?' he asked, and so indeed there had been, a light platform-cabin of wood and glass, perched up there for the sake of the wide view.

'Ay, Philip, there was, marry there was!' Sir Thomas had replied, rubbing his hands.

'Then run the timbers out and have it set up again,' the guest commanded. 'Let me have the chamber adjacent to it. See I have separate service till I tell you otherwise, and let only my own come near me,' and he cast his reins to a groom.

The chamber was made ready for him. Three steps led up from it to the eyrie outside, and by opening his inner door and stepping across the passage he could look down from a railed gallery into the great hall itself. His attendant knights were given the rooms on either side of his own, and now at his pleasure, looking southward over the miles of treetops, he could see in certain lights a faraway glitter on the horizon that was York, thin and faint in its haze.

For a pattern of fidelity and patience Stephen Hurst might now have been held up as an example to the world. Sir Emrys lost charts, but Stephen found things instead. Sir Maris excused himself that his writ had run out, Sir John Boles loved his own ease. Now Stephen would deal with these one at a time. It was irksome for the moment that he must flatten himself against walls when they passed and bend over his handsome stomach when they appeared at a door, but it was the way to the earl Philip's person. It was his master himself that he found the most out of balance, dangerous and difficult.

Gladly would Stephen have stayed behind in York, for

York in the summer was a place much to his liking. He
liked the air of the walls in the cool of the evening, to walk
with the fashion along its riverside, to show his tasselled
baldrick in Coney Street. The foreign magnificoes had
gone, those turned out had been readmitted, and it was
pretty to see them on Ouse Bridge, lifting their nymphs'-
eyes under their hair-nets and swinging their saucy girdles
as they walked. But more profitable to remain where he
was, ministering to a war-sick and in-growing mind. As
for this business of Ripon, let these insolent knights burn
their fingers with it. Stephen would be the dog at his door
and the whisperer in his ear, shave him, see to his wardrobe
and his medicines. In the afternoons that glass cage on
Bulmer's southern wall became as hot as a furnace, even
the nights were hardly cool. His master slept like a
common soldier, in his clothes, removing only the boots
from his hot feet, and through the wall Stephen could
sometimes hear him for half the night, pacing and
muttering to himself.

'My lord, you must shake this off!' he besought him.
'By all I see this is a house of good cheer and merry company! All day Sir John Boles hunts, and sleeps like a babe
at night! Your gentle kinswoman frets that you don't join
them at table! Let me lay out your blue velvet, my lord—'
but he stopped at the sight of the other's glare.

'Are there leeches in that pond below?'

'Leeches, my lord?'

'Ay, leeches, sangsues, aught to suck this heat out!
Shave me? Bleed me, man, that I may get ease! There's
traitors in York too for all their cloven mitres! Find me
leeches! Cannot you hear it, the blood singing in my
veins?'

'There's physician's in York, my lord.'

'There's a gallows too in York!'

And Sir John Boles could have bowed and withdrawn,

and the others always had some other way out, while here at his side Stephen must remain. Yet the great wheels cannot turn without the little ones, the sick soldier smelt policy and treachery all about him, and what were a few groans in an Ouseside dungeon if in the end a Clifford or two ceased to trouble or a Westmoreland head in a paper cap grinned down from Micklegate Bar? Again Stephen ventured to approach the dangerous question.

'The law must have its time, my lord. We have one batch of villains where they cannot get away. It is not for me to intrude myself, nor do I doubt your lordship is faithfully enough served. Yet there are ways and ways, and all of them have not been tried till the last has been tried. Were it your pleasure that *I* should go to the governor of this prison, as coming from yourself, to find out what I could—' but he quailed before the bloodshot look he got.

'*You* find out, that twice have failed me! You took me to a graveside, but only after what was there had gone! You let a knave in a wood get away, and again at the Corpus procession you said you had your hands on him, but in all York he was not to be found! You take your wages—'

'My lord, I have had none yet—'

'No, nor shall you, as I find you to be! I have a complaint of you from Sir Maris too, that even here things are ordered in my name, and your commanding of my cousin's servants, and even to Sir Emrys you have shown officiousness! Out o' my sight, before I whip you away!' and from his breast he snatched forth a short bundle of cords, wired at the knots, with which at his worst he was wont to flail himself.

Yet York it would have to be, by permission or without, and maybe his sun had risen a little too early bright. To Bulmer too he would have to return, for it might be that among so many other service was to be found under its roof. So borrowing a horse from its stables to York he had gone.

But all was to no purpose. When he presented himself at the prison, his beard clipped and a posy ready in his hand, it was only to be told that without authority the governor would allow none near his prisoners. He was down to the last of his small savings. In York it seemed to cost a man money to as much as breathe, and in the inns in Coney Street he had to affect to be waiting for some person of consequence who had not yet arrived. He entered into grave conversations, but those he talked with could not suppose that a man so informed, of such a presence and with such a horse in the yard, was still no better-off than a beggar.

So he had been half-way back to Bulmer again when he had come upon the party of forest-servants, in quest of its missing stag.

And even now dared he trust to a scent so faint? A girl across a market-place, sitting in a tilt, looking at herself in a little glass? Aniseed, aniseed, a woman's waft and gone! A juggler by a horse-trough, a fat fool in a smock and a fiery nose—

But it was that or nothing, and Stephen's spirits rose as he pelted back from Sturton alone, stopping at a ford with a trickle of water to let the animal drink. Drunken men did not juggle so! He had juggled with weapons, too, as the other had sat by a graveside in his glimmer of knives! As for the man in the coloured clothes, once on a hillside he had come upon a Noah, and the fellow with whom he had spoken had said he was Two-ways Robin, who could fight a combat with himself, and it was young Gandelyn himself who had bidden him question the tall man. Oh, it shone, it shone! Was that animal going to drink the stream dry? Back to Bulmer! He shook the animal up and pelted forward again.

They were hunting at Bulmer that day, and had not yet returned. A glance up at the southern wall showed him no earl Philip in his out-jutting cage of glass, and shouting to a groom in by the forecourt passage he strode. This passage led directly into the great hall, but half-way along it stairs rose to right and left, both flights giving access to the gallery and his master's apartments. The portal by which he entered divided that end of the hall into two recesses, and because of the three high windows of the outer wall one of these was better lighted than the other. It was no new thing for dinner to be late, and until the huntsmen should return maids and tiring-women often sat with their feminine occupations in the lighter recess, with a cup of wine sent by Sir Thomas to stay them.

But that day the dinner was spoiling in the ovens. John Cook declared it was murdering food, and even Sir Thomas was saying he would give them no longer than another half hour. In the recess half a dozen young women toyed with their needlework, down the length of the hall the tables were decked for dinner, on the dais the napkins and the ewers of perfumed water stood ready. But except for the damsels and the little Brigitta, a dark little bob-cherry of a child of eleven who was never for two minutes in the same place, the hall was empty when Stephen Hurst appeared upon its threshold.

But of a sudden there was a flurry and a whisking away of needlework. Skirts were disappearing hurriedly into the closet that led to the women's apartments, Stephen's own heart was in his mouth as he slipped quickly back into the second recess. Dressed in a crimson house-gown, red-eyed and unshaven, there had advanced into the hall the short-statured man for whom (for all he called himself a guest) even Sir Thomas must rise from his seat and every lady dip her knee in a curtsey.

It was the first time he had eaten in the hall. By his own

direction he had been served separately, and even so had taken his meals as a campaigner might snatch something from the camp-fire and devour it in the saddle. Now his sword-cut face was turned up to the high-timbered roof where the iron cart-wheels for the flambeaux depended over the tables. He was looking at the sunlight that streamed in through the high lozenged windows, at the half-extinct smoulder in the chimney-breast, at the empty benches and stools and the tables decked for dinner. And seeing not a soul there down the length of the hall he strode. He mounted to the dais where not a servitor stood. Seizing a tall silver ewer he dashed it violently against the wall, while the perfumed water flooded about his feet.

'The trumpets!' his voice rang harshly out as he took his seat on the dais alone and rolled his eyes about him. 'Is a man never to eat? Or is there no food in this Yorkshire but at a prating priest's table? The trumpets to dinner, and let me not have to call twice!'

Already they were running in haste to find Sir Thomas. This only incensed the formidable guest the more, and his face was as red as his crimson robe as again he raised his camp-hoarsened voice.

'In the Holy Name, what make of a house is this? Stir up that fire and throw herbs on it to make a savour! Light up the sconces and let's have a brace of cocks to fight! Where's that varlet of mine that's left me unseen-to these three days? The trumpets, and set all the meat there is in Gaultres before me!'

Everywhere there were runnings this way and that. Sir Thomas himself had given the huntsmen no more than another half hour, and for shame's sake he must affect to be master in his own house. In they flocked, a few men, a score of frightened women, and it was Sir Thomas who bade the trumpets sound, and called for a blaze to be made on the hearth on a sultry afternoon, and made the men on the stool-ladders hasten as the overhead flambeaux were smokily lighted in the rays of the sun itself. At the moment all the music he had in his castle of pleasure was a couple of fiddlers, of cocks he had none, and when the fiddlers came they were ordered to play their loudest. All the ghosts of her family were in the lady Adela's pale face as she watched her women, sitting as close to one another as they could press, laughing when she laughed, which she did to the verge of hysteria. Their voices became shrill as they asked one another over and over again what could have happened to the huntsmen, and only the little Brigitta dared to gaze openly at the man who, now that meat was set before him, tore it with his fingers and cast the bones from him.

It was the little Brigitta too who was the first to hear the noises of the return. Told too often and by too many voices all that she must not do she had ended by doing unchecked whatever she would, and from some garnishing on the table she had filched a peacock's feather and stuck it in the meshings of her short hair, where it nodded like the plume of a horse caparisoned for tourney. At the moment when the horns were heard in the forecourt she was clamouring to be told who had spilt the perfumed water and dinted the silver ewer, and as if the twanging horns had been calls to the field up from his seat the earl too had sprung. Into the forecourt they streamed, to the bayings of dogs who also wanted their share of the praise. The bearers set down their various burdens and the shaggy beast slung from its pole. The hall stood empty, the women had their male protectors again, the spoils must be admired, and the little Brigitta in her peacock's feather was almost overborne by the gambolling of the mastiffs. The kitchen-men stood by to take charge of the kill, and the little Brigitta released herself from the dogs just as a cook was withdrawing a broken-off arrow from the dead beast's shoulder. With its removal the blood spirted out again, and one of the women started forward as the child held up her hand in glee. It was imbrued with blood.

'Come you indoors and be cleaned at once!' the woman cried.

But the sprite had to be caught first, and she eluded them with ease, making sport with her reddened hand. Then suddenly her face changed. A little to one side of the archway the earl Philip stood, and in dreadful France, when a town was to be spared the worst, wise commanders would not suffer their own soldiery to enter it till a day had given their blood-ripeness time to die down. It may be that at no time would the earl Philip have harmed a hair of the little Brigitta's head. It was only a child's small hand, reddened with a smear, and the cooks had taken up their meat and departed and the huntsmen were calling for their baths to be prepared. But salivation was trickling down the sword-cut of the earl Philip's unshaven face. The little Brigitta gave a scream. She knew nothing of the war-worm and its gnawing, but she had seen a shocking thing, and had run to hide her face in the nearest robe.

And with a hideous night before him the earl Philip too turned away.

In their own chamber the lady Adela and Sir Thomas were in tears over what was to be done.

'You'll see—you can almost hear them through the walls now, getting their baggage together—by to-morrow we shall see Bulmer half empty!'

'Yet he cannot be shown the door—'

'By all accounts of it the Archbishop had to show him the door—'

'It is the crossing of the Archbishop that has brought it on—'

'In a man's own house—'

'It comes and it passes—his cousin Edward was so—it has its times and seasons—'

'Cannot Sir John Boles advise us how long they're like to stay?'

'As long as there's a buck to dislodge as well talk to the moon as to Sir John Boles—'

'Sir Emrys—Sir Maris—'

'They're about his business in York half their time—'

'Then what of that man of his that orders what meats are to be taken up to him?'

'He took the grey gelding, wherever he went on it—'

'But he's back—Huguette's seen him not two hours ago—'

'Then let him be sent for.'

But Stephen Hurst was not to be found. No more than the others was he minded to face his master that night.

II

Rest assured he would see that no harm came to the lad. At his age he should never have been let go to France, and it passed Stephen's patience to see some of these that came back, half finery half rags, stuffed with bad habits, taking the warmest corner of the hearth and expecting to be waited on, while younger brothers now as tall as themselves had kept all going while they were away. Besides, wars were owed, not paid for.

And let his master too take his rest, as why should he not in his wasteful castle? His eating and drinking cost him not a penny, lusty gallants and ladies with lurking eyes did as they pleased. Was it a resting-day from hunting? There in the stables and mews was plenty to occupy them, comparing hawks and horses, seeing to a dog's broken tooth or the mending of a girth. So again let Bulmer's castle of pleasure he broidered in as before, looked down on as the birds look down, roofs and interiors, forecourt and backcourt, with the bivouac of its palisades behind. The palisades are open to all, and friars with their pokes and bagmen with their packs, pardoners and kawkers of trinkets, any that come may eat with the retainers and sleep in the stables and byres. Relaxed in their loose gowns foreshortened little gentlemen out of perspective stray with ladies in the gardens and under the fruit trees, mounting to the belvedere that hospitable Sir Thomas had had erected at the instance of some bygone Italian guest. This belvedere is a sort of raised terrace, set with trellised bowers of briar and vine, so that even when it rains one may still sit there and watch the silvery fall. Always the forecourt is astir with something, and from it the broad grass ride descends to the fishpond where the anglers sit in the boats, and perhaps a lady has an instrument that she plays between throwing bread to the swans. Tilt up the roof of the great hall and see which of the damsels is sewing in the recess, or peep into the chambers at the siesta-hour and see how many are taking their rest. For after all not a guest has left. Fluttered ladies feel a little foolish to have got into such a state because a man grumbled that his dinner was late, and the hearts of the lady Adela and Sir Thomas are light again. He has not troubled the hall since, they say his fever is declining, and it is the lady Adela's opinion that the remedy a patient fancies for himself often does him the most good. Leeches and to spare had been found in the pond.

But few men have a mind to mingle in company with a clot of sucking black leeches clustered behind their ears, and the earl Philip had had a truckle carried up to his eyrie on the southern wall. There he lay without his doublet, and Stephen Hurst had been given leave to draw up a stool

at his side, and his tale, though lengthy, was not finished
yet, for he was still speaking.

'I'm saying no more than I saw for myself, my lord.
There by this horse-trough he stood, stuffed out with hay
and a nose like a carbuncle, as sodden as a bear at a fair—'

'Take off two of these sangsues and set fresh there,' and
the glutted slugs were salted off and dropped into the jar.
The relation continued.

'But the other makes no concealment of himself, more
than comes in the way of his trade. He's the same that
staged their pageant for them in York, and they're
acquainted this while back,' and the feverish man pressed
the leeches closer.

'Did they track my cousin's stag?'

'It's proclaimed, my lord. This of Ripon's been a lesson
to them, and one stag will neither make nor break Sir
Thomas. All's in motion, nothing lasts for ever—'

'It would seem this tale does.'

'—and all points the one way. Dressed as he was I might
have been mista'en in the youth. There's actors a plenty,
and girls with looking-glasses too. But I'm not mista'en
in the three of them together. There's six of them, moving
from place to place, and it would be but saying the word
to get them here.'

'The sun catches me. Draw that curtain and open the
other casement.'

'It's likely the youth has a good answer to it all, so my
advice to your lordship would be this. First have him here
and hear his tale. Then let me go to York and have a word
or so with the other where he lies. Then, but telling neither
of them, bring them of a sudden face to face and see what
comes of it.'

Yet still he promised himself that no harm should come
to the lad.

No more in Bulmer's castle than elsewhere had Stephen

yet found his rightful footing in the world. He had a master possessed of a devil, and he must bend his body before supercilious Sir Emrys and slow-witted Sir Maris. He was too consequential a man to be placed among the servants, yet he had no place in the hall. Therefore he ate with the major-domo, and as the hour of dinner was Jacques' busiest hour he supped frequently alone. Most galling of all, lest his isolation should seem to be not of his own choice, whenever he passed through the chattering hall he must do so with his head high, as if on important business who had none.

And now added to all this the dusky little pansy they called Huguette, who waited on the lady Félice, was beginning to trouble him.

So say it happened to be the dressing-hour at Bulmer's castle on its hill. There in the kitchens the cooks would be sweating, in the cellar Sir Thomas taking advice of a new pipe of muscatel. Restless as a sprite, in and out of chambers the little Brigitta would be, where ladies as bold and warm as robins helped one another with their lacing and thrust their feet into their smallest shoes. Stephen too should have been making business for himself about that chair the earl Philip had occupied only once, and it so chanced, a day or two after he had spoken his mind to his master, that the pair of them were being discussed by the damsels in the sewing-recess just as he passed to the major-domo's room with a paper in his hand.

'He's a fine, portly man. You'd think he might stop for as long as it takes to say a good-day,' one of them murmured as his back disappeared behind the screen at the dais-end that masked the service. 'Would you say he'd been a soldier in his time, Denise?'

'He's more the bearing of some councillor of state to me. I warrant he'd newly back from some ambassage.'

'It's his lordship that's the soldier, and ay me, what these wars bring some of them to!' a third struck in. 'They'll scarce drink but from a piggin nor eat without they snatch it off the spit!' but another was of a different opinion.

'Widower or no widower, their scars become them well. You're welcome to the other sort for me,' and the voice of the precocious child was raised.

'The one with the beard always looks to see if Huguette's here when he goes through, and if she hadn't got her falconer—'

'Somebody'll have her wrists well slapped in a minute—'

'It *is* the falconer, and she doesn't meet him by the palisades. She meets him in that little wood by the fishpond—'

'You mind lest you have a handkerchief tied round your mouth and your hands behind you!'

'Now here's the other coming back—just see if he doesn't look at Huguette—'

'Take you this taffeta up to the lady Félice, saucebox!' the child was commanded, but she capered off to see what was for dinner instead as again Stephen Hurst passed through the hall.

Again taking matters into his own hands, Stephen Hurst was in fact newly back from an ambassage. If all went well he would tell his master later, the more readily that this time he had fared somewhat better. Even to know what sort of a questioning the prisoner had been given would be something, and he had finally succeeded in seeing the governor himself. The man, he learned, had not been questioned yet.

'Sir, I am from Bulmer castle, in the stead of one who would be here himself but that he is on a sick-bed,' Stephen had pleaded. 'I come in all humaneness, and desire but a few words with the prisoner himself, in what presence you will. 'Twill be an ill day when any man is put to the question before he has been given a chance to speak—' and in the end his request had been granted.

Yet he was an older and frailer man that he had looked to find, grizzled and stubbly, with peering eyes that shone with fever. He smelt two yards away, so that Stephen was glad of the posy he all the time kept close to his nose, and for Stephen a stool was bought into the warders' watch-room, but the other could hardly stand for the weight of irons on him. Ten words would suffice for all Stephen wanted to know. The man refused to speak them.

'Yet consider,' he had urged him. 'Long heads have been at work on this. In such a matter those I come from scarce dare show the good will they gladly would. It can be pleaded for you that you were set on by others, as indeed you were, and their names known,' but the peering eyes never left his own.

'I know you not, stranger sir. Leave me to my lot.'

'It is but that the law must be satisfied. If it is the presence of the gaoler—friend, leave us a minute—'

'I may not, sir.'

'See, even the gaoler fears I come in too great friendliness! I will come even nearer you! Many fingers now in dainty gloves will be burned before all these chestnuts are raked out of the fire, but must *his* burn—I will not name him, for he is scarce a grown man yet, but he lodged in a certain inn in York, and last before that he was heard of in Washburn-in-the-Forest . . . ah! You change colour!' for the fetters had clanked with the sudden leaning of the man against the wall. He would have fallen, but they bred them tough in Ghent, and after a few moments he was master of himself again.

'Sir,' he whined, 'I am but a poor lollbrueder, this is my weary old body you see, but my soul is in God's hands. If these names are known they are known. If they are not neither do I know them. I beg you to leave me to my prayers.'

And with no more than that Stephen had had to come away. Now he had mounted to Bulmer's southern wall, where he drew in his breath deeply. It would be many a day before a posy of clove-pink and bergamot ceased to remind him of a prison ante-chamber and a wretch in irons who stank, and he hoped he had breathed in no infection. From his place on the wall he could look down on the roof of the out-jutting eyrie on its hoarding below, over this ragged world of treetops, this endless Yorkshire plain that tamed even its rivers as they ran. Where they tumbled the other way, Ribble, Irwell, Wyre, Lune, his master had wide possessions. O to be away! In the orchards the fruit was ripening on the boughs, he was weary of this York and its bickerings and its wrangles. He could have told that wretch in the irons that it was useless to keep silence, since he had already been informed on, but that might have been to harm the lad. Or he could still tell the lad himself that under question the other had broken down. But suddenly lifting his eyes to the waste of broken woodland that was known as Bulmer's End he saw something that moved across a patch of glade. It was hidden, but it came into sight again, nearer and making for Bulmer, and shading his eyes he counted them. They were six, one of them leading a donkey with a tilt-cart. At that moment the trumpet sounded for dinner and Stephen stirred to life. Of itself his luck had come.

They had come to a stand by the fishpond to rest the weary donkey. The light-looking bags on their backs contained their instruments, the rest was in the tilt, and now the castle that for so many hours had played hide-and-seek in the distance showed only its upper parapet over the hill's green rise. Shyly the one woman among them whispered to him who stood by her side.

'Is this it?'

'Yes, sweetheart.'

'A castle the same as Newbiggin?'

He did not answer.

'There's boats on the pond.'

'Yes,' and the one who led the donkey spoke.

'What's now, Robin? Do we give them a stave to let them know we're here?'

'Ay, if this were Tong-under-the-Hill, but it is not,' was the answer as Robin Crosby took off his cap to see to the setting of its feather.

For he who goes as a beggar gets a beggar's wages, but As-good-as-You walks in, and the master-actor proceeded to give them their instruction. Echo and Gandelyn were to keep at his side. The others were to take the way round to the back, there to make themselves at home, but to offer no music or other entertainment till he gave the word. If there was any washing of hands or faces to be done here was pond-water for them, and next he turned to Echo.

She was tired and dragging of limb, but about her brows was her gift of the silver fillet, and she had contrived for herself a sort of small hand-poke for her personal belongings. For the long day's trudge she had put on her second-best shawl, and getting out her small silver mirror she smoothed out the corners of her eyes. Her hands were shaped like her mother's, none would have dreamed that ever a tooth had touched a finger-nail. Ay, she would do, the actor nodded, and the three with the tilt were already on their way round the pond. As they climbed the grassy ride there rose into sight a close-masoned wall. It had a gate in it, but it was open and no porter stood there, and beyond it was a wide flagged yard, with men in various liveries, to one of whom Robin Crosby spoke. 'Bide you there a minute,' the man said, and through an open portal disappeared into an inner passage. Again she whispered to her husband.

'I thought they always bade you stand and stop.'

'In war they do. He says they're at their dinner.'

'I wish I was in my bed.'

'Me, I'd like my supper first.'

'In castles do they . . . Oh!' and so exclaiming she pressed closer to his side.

Jacques the major-domo was dressed in decorous black. About his neck was his silver chain, his wand of office was in his hand, his silver locks hid his ears. Advancing with hurried little steps, and bowing as he came with Robin Crosby behind, his clean pinkness seemed to ask to be kissed as at the threshold he bowed low again and entreated them to enter.

'Had Sir Thomas but known you were coming, he says! But he'll be with you the minute dinner's over, the minute they've finished! For the present I'm to set you in the recess, but better shall be done to-morrow—Sir?—This gentleman is married? Then a chamber'll have to be found! But we'll find one, and all will shake down! Pray you enter—'

The passage was dim, but beyond it an inner brightness showed and a babble of noises ahead was broken from moment to moment by lightsome laughter. In a lofty timbered hall that seemed a league long a multitude of people sat. Three high sunny windows showered light down on the tables that ran on and on and stopped only at a faraway dais that nodded with laundered head-veils. On the hall's other side a massive stone chimney-breast rose in lessening stages half-way to the roof, and at this point a carved wooden upper gallery stopped. The chatter lessened for a moment as again the seneschal bowed, showing them to an alcove or recess where a table was being prepared.

'All shall be mended to-morrow,' he said. 'Better shall be found, better shall be found. Sir Thomas was longing for some of your trade to come! Be seated, be seated and be welcome—'

She was glad that from their recess she could see a good half of the hall without being seen. The ladies on the far-away dais would be the greater ladies, those who sat under the windows the lesser ones seated in their various degrees. Should they remain here she would have to learn their names and stations and which lady each one served, and her hand went to the little bag she carried for her conveniences. She had thrown back her head-shawl to see to the set of her silver fillet. Andrew, Terence and the nackerer had already been lodged with the trumpeter and the two fiddlers, but they two were to be given a chamber of their own. In the middle of the dais was one empty seat, and she wondered whose it was, then turned her eyes to the ladies under the windows again. They were eating sweetmeats, and some had little dogs in their laps, and dinner was drawing to an end. Of a sudden there was a rustle of rising and curtseying. The laundered ladies were leaving the dais. An elderly gentleman in a resplendent robe was descending from it, making his way down the hall. It was the master of the castle himself, calling his major-domo to bring him to this famous Master Crosby, for indeed never in his life had he heard a pageant so lauded as that summer's pageant in York.

The gallery that stopped at the chimney-breast ended at a black low-arched door. To close this door behind one was to grope for some moments in darkness; then from somewhere round the back of the chimney a grey light glimmered. It was the stair-foot of the turret, and in the turret itself all was as light as needs be. Their chamber was on its midway floor. No swallows nested under its eaves, the rushes for its floor had not yet been carried in, and its stone slit looked out on an unsunned opposite wall. But it was sufficiently furnished, with a chest for clothes, a narrow table under the slit, two stools and an uncurtained bed. There were also several bulky bundles, carried up from the tilt and not unpacked yet, and his belly-stuffing lay in its bags on the bed. But hardly had the major-domo closed the door upon them before she was looking blankly about her, he upwards to judge the ceiling-height.

'Is this where we're to be?' she asked.

'Ay, but only for to-night he says. I was wondering whether maybe there's a friar's begging-staff to be had in this place.'

For mountebanks have to devise their impromptus as they go along, jugglers must be ready to juggle with what comes, and carters and ploughmen are not commonly to be found in castle halls. But get a begging-staff with a hook for its poke, have it loaded and balanced at the smithies, and his hands would have the feel of it in a very short time. But suddenly she sank to the bed with a little choke, and in a moment he was by her side.

'Nay, what is it, sweetheart?'

'Oh—I don't like here!' and taking both her hands into his own he began to comfort her.

'Tut! It's but that those last two hills were overmuch for you! All new places are strange the first day or two!'

'I cannot feel like settling here!' and he laughed.

'What, us that have settled in ditches and under the heather, and in sheepfolds with the lambs and the ewes to help keep us warm?'

'That one with the crimson hair-pads and her with the velvet shoes, when we were sitting in the corner, they went out of their way to pass us so they could have a good look at me—'

'At you? At me you would say!' and he dandled the hands again. 'Have you never noticed my gift that way?'

'And the gentleman with the silver chain—'

'What, the head butler? Pay no heed to any of them. It's that fine fillet of yours they were looking at! How many of *them's* had an admiral's topcastle to sleep in?'

'I thought castles—' and now both his arms were about her.

'Look up, field-mouse! Let's see those eyes! Indeed they were the first of you I ever did see, when I came upon you among the oaks, and the willow shook and there was scarce any telling which of you was which—'

'I was looking for little Judith, and you caught me in my rabbit-net, and my harden over my shoulders—'

'And if I did? Letting on to be covering up a child, and the next day putting truffles in a man's mead! Leaving shameless images behind you in pools like I told you—'

'You came of yourself—' she gulped, and he laughed again.

'And then up in the middle of her own dinner up she has to jump and run for the bushes—ho ho ho!' but even as he laughed he kissed her oak-brown hair with sudden tenderness. 'Nay, pretty, look up! Born in a castle and cannot give a pack of hussies as good as they send! Be mettlesome with them! A knight for a father, and that you haven't got by nature we'll call it art, and have you not got me? See, I've barred the door. Let's have a few of these bundlings on the floor. Then make half a foot of room—'

But in the moment of her turning to him there came a rapping at the door. It was the nackerer, summoning him to Robin Crosby, to discuss with Sir Thomas what entertainment they were able to provide.

The Lady Adela and Sir Thomas had been married for twenty-five years less only a very few days. To the union the one had brought the renown of her name, the other wealth enough to satisfy her every wish, and in the forestalling of these Sir Thomas found his chiefest delight. Now the arrival of the players came like manna from the skies, and it was for this that the nackerer had been sent to fetch Gandelyn from his turret.

No ceiling-sconces had been lighted in the hall below, no guest shared in the consultation. Sir Thomas was rubbing his hands briskly with pleasure.

'Had you been told of it it could not have fortuned better, Master Crosby!' he chuckled. 'It grieved my lady to miss the stirrings at Corpus, but York's too pent an air for her the physicians say. We get no younger, Master Crosby, none of us. It's a shortness of breath takes her, a sort of heartburn. And now to Bulmer there come as good as the King's Players themselves!'

'When is this fortunate day to be, Sir Thomas, and what are your desires?'

'Why, the wedding-day's three days from now, and it's what you have so it be your best! I have but my two fiddlers, Peter and Thomasson, and them she can hear any day. What do you bring with you in the way of music?'

'I have such a harper—'

'A harp? That's rare! I'd a harper once, but it was an Irish harp, Brian I remember his name was. And you haven't seen my belvedere yet, but up and down this Brian would walk, playing as he went, and the young folk in the arbours, such as were shy—and the truer their love is the

shyer they often are—let but this Brian start to play—'
and now Robin Crosby rubbed his hands.

'Then I'll warrant you Andrew's your man; and for
playing in the hall he has a white robe and a green
chaplet—'

'So! Bards have no better!'

'And if your lady takes any delight in dancing—'

'Five-and-twenty year back she doted on it—'

'Then there's this poetic young squire—' presenting
Gandelyn, who at that moment advanced, '—he could turn
you a verse, some sort of commendatory piece in the lady's
honour—'

'What, will it stretch to that?' cried the delighted Sir
Thomas, and as this same commendatory piece had been
on Gandelyn's mind these last three days, with Andrew
fitting the music as they went, they fell to a survey of the
hall itself, its dimensions, whether a stage would be
required, and other such matters.

But the gallery by which Gandelyn had descended was
curtained where the double stair-heads led down to the
forecourt passage, and one of the curtains had moved.
Little more than an hour before Stephen Hurst had been
on the point of giving up the whole enterprise. With no
horse of his own, he travelled with a small pack of hide
that he could carry on his shoulders, in it were a spare
shirt or so, a second pair of boots that had belonged to Sir
Matthew Poole, a knife for his meat and the brushes and
pots and razors for his valeting. In the ante-chamber where
he slept stood the bulk of his master's clothing and belongings, and entering it Stephen groped for tinder to light a
candle. But suddenly he stood still. In the adjoining
chamber a light was already burning. From within a voice
was raised.

'Who's that?'

A moment only Stephen stood still. Then he entered.

At the head of the three steps that led to the outer eyrie the last of the daylight still showed, but on the table below two candles had been lighted. His master was lying down, but fully dressed in his blue velvet. No leeches or their jar were to be seen, somebody had shaved him, and his voice, though querulous, was the voice of a man once more in his right mind. Only the red soddenness of his eyes remained, and from moment to moment he passed his hand over them as if he found the candlelight too strong.

'Is that Hurst?' he asked without moving his head.

'Yes, my lord.'

'Where have you been? You should have asked my leave. Yesterday I called, "Send Hurst to shave me," but another came instead.' Then, asking no more where he had been, 'Hurst,' he said, 'I have been ill.'

The astonished servant was struggling to recover his composure. That things should now take this of all turns! But his master's voice went on.

'It was a darkness, a redness, I know not what it was. It laid hold of me first in France, and I shall return there no more. Others can take up with soldiering for me. It is not the killing. That has to be taken as it comes. It is the sending of a man back a stranger to himself,' and Stephen Hurst cleared his throat.

'There is deep understanding in that, my lord.'

'To say naught of his home and all that's his, for when he comes back what is that either? Other feet are on his hearth, the young are grown up, strange faces sit at his board, he hears names he does not know. His fences have been set back, his woods hunted, his streams fished, his titles pried into. Lucky he if his neighbour has not moved the law against him while he was away.'

It was temperate, not to be denied, and never had Stephen Hurst been of any other opinion. Now the soldier went on.

'I have castles in Clitheroe and over Ribblehead, lands about Hornby and Lune. From twenty manors and half the Palatinate I get my rents. I have quarries and tolls—' he passed the hand over his eyes again. '—when was it they last hunted here?'

'My lord, I have been away—'

'I was standing in the court when they came back. Out of a stag's shoulder one drew an arrow, and a little child was standing by. A child, of no age. She held her hand up before me, a baby's hand, yet reddened with blood, and all that night—all that night—' he shuddered and a harsh sob broke from him. 'I cannot tell you, Hurst. It is not to be told. A prattling child—to that it had brought me—' and Stephen Hurst sank to his knee.

'My dear lord, I cannot hear you say this. Think no more of it. It was your sick dream. You shall have cooling meats, and music to ease you to sleep,' but the head from which the madness had gone only rocked from side to side.

'O to smell my own air again, and think of war no more, but sleep through the night, and beget a child, not a son to be a burner and slayer, but a lily-girl, with healing in her hands and peace in her eyes and benefits on her lips. . . . What time is it?'

'Past eight, my lord.'

'What is my kinsman Thomas doing?'

'Consulting with these minstrels, my lord, over your kinswoman's entertainment. She will have been married—'

'Ay. Adela married. It was at Clitheroe, in the chapel. I gave her to him. I have not given one in marriage since. Do you sleep in the next room?'

'Yes, my lord. I shall hear your least movement.'

'Then leave me with one candle, for I dare not sleep in the dark,' and putting out the second candle Stephen stole on tiptoe away. A mord-lust it has been called, this fiendish overspill of war before which the little Brigitta had covered her cowering eyes.

But Stephen Hurst, lying fully clothed on his pallet that night, could hardly close an eye for the hope newly-sprung in his heart.

Harm come to the lad? From what Stephen had learned in York he seemed to have got himself into a sort of marriage, which was no prudent thing to have done, else Stephen had seldom seen a gallanter lad nor one he would have been more loth to see in trouble. So away with York and its prisoners and its confrontations, and hasten, Lancashire, a new master and the stewardship of his lands! All that night the earl Philip did not stir. Towards dawn Stephen too closed his eyes for an hour, and when he woke it was to sounds of bustle and preparation. Stepping out to the gallery he looked down. In and out of the hall servants were carrying this and that, the major-domo was giving orders for the rearrangement of the tables, the pageant-master directing where the rushes were to be swept from the floor. The greater dogs had been tied up, the service-screen moved back, over by the chimney-breast carpenters were at work. In Bulmer's End a stag of grease had been reported, but he would keep for another day, and as the guests too issued from their chambers, from the palisades to the belvedere, from the forecourt down the grassy hill to the fishpond, a hundred rumours ran. The boats were to be decorated, there were to be illuminations on the water. A bear had been secretly brought in, which was why the dogs were kept from hunting, and between Jacques' room and a buttery that was to be used as a tiring-room strangely dressed figures had been seen to come and go. In the back-court a tall youth had been observed bargaining with a friar for the loan of his gabardine and staff, and all that day sudden snatches of music and recital seemed to come from nowhere.

The damsel they called Huguette was plump and
dimpled and seemed to bounce as if on springs whenever
she sat down. She had a pretty ear to whisper into, it was
often whispered into in an arbour of the belvedere when
she should have been within doors at her duties, but
nothing ever came of it but a mild scolding from the lady
Félice. Her handsome young falconer was a bird of passage,
whereas when he went the pretty Huguette would still be
there for somebody else to whisper to, and now she had
heard from somewhere, and told Rosanne, that this shy
dancer with the fillet who kept herself so to herself was
in reality a slip of birth, dropped by some vicissitude of
fortune into this. After that there was no stopping their
tongues.

'Have you not seen the way she moves herself? One
minute she's as smooth as cream, then before you can look
she's as taut as a hissing swan—'

'Yet with a sort of look in her eyes, a pretty tinsel—'

'She dresses but homely—'

'That's their art! They know better than to show it all
the time, and you never see those three together but they
have their heads together over something—' and the little
Brigitta put her word in.

'They aren't always together. Sometimes it's only her
and the tall one. Yesterday the young one was down by
the fishpond practising something with the harper, all
about blest beds, but they saw me and shooed me away—'

'As so they should, tittle-tattle, for what do you know
about blest beds?'

But singing 'Its tongue shall be slit' the child was off
and away.

And from the alcove by the door that had been reserved
for them Echo still hardly raised her eyes to these gentlemen and sirs and Mesdames and mesdemoiselles who wore
their clothes as if they had always worn them, whereas

Robin Crosby would not allow her now even her pome-granate shawl.

On the morning of the festal day itself the lady Adela came down as radiant as if it had been that same day five-and-twenty years before. Her noble cousin, she reported, was wholly recovered of his distemper, he proposed to take his place that day at table with the rest of them, so let any of them misdemean themselves at their peril.

By afternoon the great hall stood ready. The entertain-ment, once it began, might wear out the day, the ceiling-sconces had been lighted, and again the torches of wax and resin mingled with the sunny motes that slanted from the tall window-shafts in diagonals of gold. Between these depended the pennons of the knights, and before each lady's place was set Sir Thomas's anniversary-gift to her who sat there. It had been decided that no stage was required. The chimney-breast itself had been boarded up to make a platform, and here, for the nonce higher than the dais itself, stood Herod's mimic board. The space about it, swept of its rushes, was guarded by a light barrier. And commanding the hall as it were twice, once because of its central position and again because of the rampant silken lion that backed it, stood the earl Philip's high-backed chair.

Not every tree is fruitful, and the lady Adela had long since learned to content herself in the orchards of others She petted and adopted, as she had adopted the little Brigitta, she had an amiable husband, and now the family spectre was laid again in her formidable cousin's con-valescence. Most to the occasion of all, if only she could keep the order of the entertainment fixed in her mind, this discreet manservant of his now prompted the lady Adela too. Thus: at the first sounding of the trumpet every guest would descend. Her cousin would be ready waiting for her at the stair-foot, she would enter the hall leaning on his

arm, but no wine was to be given the earl Philip before
the wedding-song, and then only well tempered with water.
So it would be less marked if nobody had any wine before
the wedding-song—but no, that would be commented on,
for the wedding-song was not till the middle of dinner.
Then as she and her cousin entered the music would strike
up, and all would rise, and the harper's seat was to be
before the dais, and presently the dancing-girl would
dance, but only a little wine for the earl Philip, not to heat
his blood again. The actors had borrowed the largest
silver-gilt dish for the play, but it was only used for the
boar's head and no boar had been killed. After the epi-
thalamium would follow something to make them all
laugh, and the good-night didn't come till the end. She
had better say it all over again on her fingers, turning a
finger down for each—only very little wine for the earl
Philip, and that well allayed—

She was in fact doing so when the sound of the trumpet
woke all Bulmer to life.

Come all, then, and see that pretty rising of ladies with
their lapdogs in their arms, the dipping of gentle knees,
the backs of the gallant gentlemen as they bowed low with
their hands on their breasts. See the sarsnets and the
furred gowns, the starchings and butterflyings, the raised
eyes and the special smiles, as the harp struck a chord and
the two fiddlers echoed it, not for Sir Thomas, who stood
at the dais alone, but for the two who entered, the earl
Philip in velvet of deep violet-blue, with his ageing cousin
on his arm, as if to bestow her again as he had bestowed
her in Clitheroe's chapel five-and-twenty years ago. See
Andrew the harper in his green and white, his chaplet of
leaves on his head, and Jacques with his wand and his chain
and his side-curls, and Sir John Boles in a figured bravery
of brown that changed to gold as he moved, and Stephen
Hurst, suddenly relieved from scheming and contrivance,

and happiest of all that the leechings and the lettings had sucked away his master's dangerous overplus. Hurt the lad? Bless the lad rather, for Stephen would have had all the world as set on happiness as he. York and its nightmares were over. Fair Lancashire would not be long.

So the nuptial celebration began.

It was of Lancashire that the lady Adela was speaking longingly to her cousin, for he had broken it to her that he would presently be leaving them. She was begging him, if he might not stay, to take her heart back with his own to the Ribble and Lune of their childhood, when every dewy morning had seemed to be the first morning of the world. With her own jewelled hand she tempered his wine for him, drinking covertly from his cup herself whenever he turned to the lady on his other side, to make it the less. But down the hall most of their wedding-days were still to come, and as the babble broke out it was of the players and the plays many of them had seen from York's balconies last Corpus, and the gentlemen affected to covet the kennelling of the dogs in the ladies' laps, but the ladies were prattling and making little wagers over what their unopened gift-packets might contain. And so let them feast the golden sunlight out and the sconce-light in. A very little trimming had fitted Gandelyn's ode to the occasion, and its chanting was left to Andrew. His deep and moving voice ceased. Tears of remembrance streamed down the lady Adela's face that all this commotion of pagan Hymens and heavenly chorussing should have been on account of Sir Thomas and herself, all those years ago, and the ladies opened their gifts, and the busy servants came and went. They were making ready the table over by the chimney-breast, and now the three sconces crowned the hall with triple light. Andrew too had moved his seat away from the dais. The matching and comparing of presents was suspended as there entered from behind the service-screen a procession barbarously royal and a tall figure in voluminous purple and a towering rubied crown against the stone chimney-breast. He was followed by his cup-bearer, crackling with tinsel-gilt, and another with an umbered face, and two more who rolled their eyes. The lady Adela turned to her husband.

'What is it they enact, dear husband?'

'Listen, my love, the harper is telling you,' and again Andrew's voice was raised in rhymed epitome.

The earl Philip sat quietly attentive on the dais. That harper played well, and his head and finger moved to the time of it. He played more than common well, and if his good cousin could spare him he had a mind to take him back to Lancashire with him; he would have a word with him about it. But his eyes chanced to stray sideways. Behind the service-screen, on a great salver, there waited a grim object indeed had it been a real one. But the earl knew what story was to be played, and for all its ghastly pallidness and its beard of tow clotted with painted blood it was only the pasteboard head of him whose meat had been the locust and the wild honey from the tree. For a wedding-day they might have picked on some merrier play, and his hand went to the table for his silver cup. It was empty, his fingers made a sign, and it was filled for him. He was savouring it, a stronger drink than before, when Andrew's harp began slowly to pulse and sob. Along the hearth space cleared of its rushes a crouching flame was creeping.

Gandelyn had begun to gloom and grow hot that she must bedizen herself so. In a broad false beard he was seated on Herod's right, and he had known since yesterday who was to be there. But let not any Lancastrian mange think she was one of these wenches of France, to be had into his tent and out again with an ecu when the first cock woke the morning drum! Now as she crouched she was stirring into little flamelets, that trembled and quickened as if Andrew's harp had been a bellows, puffing them into life. The poppy wreath burned like a cresset on her head. Suddenly she was on her feet, her pale eyes fixed on Herod. And as she broke into little wandering runs to quicken the flaming Gandelyn muttered to himself all that he must not say aloud.

'In the trap, am I? It's to be seen! I come into no castle without knowing a way out of it! (Well danced, Echo: stir him, set him on his horse!) Herod catches. . . . Ah, what's this of t'other? His hand goes to his glass! He's seen it too, the fire that's the hotter when it kindles from the top! And I'm to dance after this, with a scimitar and a whinyard in my hands! (*"What was her bower? The red rose and the lily flower"*—red hot, white hot—well danced, Echo!) . . . By God, see that! One would say the snap of a finger'd fetch her to him! He knows not whether his cup is full or empty! . . . From that hearth where she dances, how far now to where he sits there? Overfar, overfar! Would my poniard were a warping-knife, to stick your ace at eight yards! See the salty soldier has no sleep neither, Echo! It's eyes at the back o' the head for both of us now—'

From Andrew's harp fierce chords had begun to break. Herod had risen in his seat, proffering his rubied crown in his hands. But, loud and full-throated, Andrew was now giving out the grislier trophy the dancer demanded, and Robin Crosby's countenance was a spectacle of woe and weeping and the rafters rang with his shuddering 'No, no!' But in the gory decapitation was brought on its silver-gilt dish, and many of the ladies covered their eyes, and the actors themselves descended with their heads bowed as if for sorrow that they had lived to see a spectacle so impious.

But in the tiring-room the pageant-master was growling that it had all taken too long, too long. Gandelyn in his friar's gabardine was tightening up his artificial belly, and as he looked round the room his brown eyes suddenly flashed. Swiftly he turned to the pageant-master.

'Where is she now? What keeps her? Why isn't she here?'

'Be speedy. She was called forward by the lady Adela.'

'Get you on and started. I was seeing to the head. You should have kept at her side,' he upbraided him, but Robin Crosby could be testy too.

'Young man,' he cried, 'I played the Two-ways before you were born, and but for a guffaw I cannot see your clowning mends it! When she or any of us is summoned forward, forward we go! *I'm* master here! Are you juggling to-night?'

'Get you on. I'll follow,' Gandelyn growled, but he growled it to the actor's parti-coloured back.

Because Sir Thomas's brach Luff was fifteen years old, and blind at that, every passing hand rumpled his ears or rested in passing on his shaggy head. He ate at his master's knee, and Luff it was who had accompanied the girl to the dais, where she stood still bewildered and panting, scarce daring to raise her eyes. Sweetmeats had been heaped together for her as a general gift, for they of the lower tables wanted to finger her taffeta, to ask her a thousand questions. But the lady Adela's command came first, and the dazed girl's answer was hardly to be heard as she was asked her name.

'May it please your ladyship, Echo.'

'Echo! The pretty name! Hear you that, Tom? Her name's Echo, and see how Luff huggles up to her!' and her husband was rubbing his hands with pleasure too.

'Nay, after such capering, let her sit and a quencher of wine for her! Jacques, that stool and a cup!' and Sir Thomas himself poured out the wine, while to everything he said his lady said the same.

'Cool yourself down with this, young mistress! It has crossed the seas! It is a wine from Chios, that an Italian gentleman brought me!'

'This is my husband, Sir Thomas, and the wine is from Chios, and an Italian gentleman brought it for him. What was his name, Tom?'

'The Signor Battista.'

'The Signor Battista brought it for Sir Thomas, from Italy—'

'Chios, my love—'

'From Chios, hard by Italy,' and as the dancer sat there in her poppies and now quiescent flames the blind brach snuffled her as if he smelt the woodland again. Sir Thomas was pledging her, but the earl Philip too was leaning easefully back against his silken lion, and Stephen Hurst at the service-screen, seeing his glass once more re-plenished, watched him anxiously. But there pushed past him a tall slow-moving figure who walked as if at his devotions, the hilt of his sword held before him for a cross. As he stepped from behind the screen all seated themselves again, but scarce had he reached the rush-swept space before he might have been Mahound and soldier-priest too, for his sword was a cross no longer as to his famous feat Robin Crosby fell. With clatter and thrust and 'Ha!' a christian fought a paynim beneath Bulmer's swaying rings, not a sound was to be heard in the hall but the rasping and clashing of the two weapons wielded by the one man.

But Stephen Hurst was reviling the curstness of life that a girl of Ouse Bridge should be sitting within a few feet of his master while he waited at the servants' screen, and now the earl Philip was beginning to flush again. His eyes were hard on the dancer, and Stephen had seen the mummery before and knew what was coming. Even as he cursed it came. The nackerer had raised his voice, loudly

demanding who was this who had forced his way in
from the palisades and calling for the dogs to be set on
him.

For there staggered from the service-screen to the
hearth a friar so drunk that he stumbled over his own
begging-staff. He was so fat he could scarce carry his belly
before him, and the hall would never have believed the
next but for seeing it with their own eyes. The performer
himself had come to a standstill, his face half-moustachioed
only, a weapon slack in either hand. He too stood gaping
as up shot the begging-staff half-way to the rafters. Before
it had time to descend he too was weaponless and his
sword and scimitar also were rising into the air.

But now Stephen Hurst had eyes only for his master.
Always these soldiers liked them best when they were not
too difficult to come by, and he had reached forward from
his silken seat. His hand had gone not to his own cup but
to the girl's. He picked it up and drank from it just as from
the hall there broke a general '*Ah!*' The juggler had
missed! No he had not, for he had recovered the whinyard
almost as it touched the ground, and now inch by inch he
was advancing nearer to the dais. The earl was summoning
the girl nearer with his finger. He would have had her at
his side, but there was no place, and that sudden drinking
from her cup had lacked little of embracing her across the
table. The begging-staff and the scimitar and the sword
continued to rise and fall. Again came the gasp as again
he seemed to miss. But he was half-way to the dais now,
and the next moment out had shot the earl's hand. He had
plucked the poppy wreath from her head to see her face
the better.

Suddenly a dozen voices broke out at once. He *had*
missed, with a clatter weapons and staff had come to the
floor together, and half the hall was on its feet. The blind
brach gave a whimpering growl as there leaped to the

dais a stripling with a monstrous sagging belly, a naked poniard in his hand, his arm about the girl.

'Get you away—leave me to this—' he panted.

But—a naked poniard, and in those hands! The earl Philip had leapt to his feet, still grasping the cresset of poppies. The hall was a bubbub of dogs and a commotion of gentlemen who had started forward, and it was no time for niceties of conscience now. Forward Stephen Hurst too had sprung.

'My lord,' he cried in a loud vouce, 'ha' that stuffing stripped off him! See for yourself if it is not as I said!'

The earl Philip alone among them was composed. There was a twitching of the mouth-cut that resembled a smile as he turned to Sir Thomas.

'Good cousin Thomas, have you often this make of cutlery at this hospitable board of yours?' and Sir Thomas's hands were a-shake like two leaves.

'Cousin—I could die of shame—let him be seized—'

But it was already done, and the blind dog leaping for the prisoner's throat had missed and was rending and threshing among the straw entrails instead. Stripped, dishevelled, panting, bound, Gandelyn stood revealed, and again the earl's slit mouth resembled a smile.

'So. I might have guessed. The letter-kissing young poursuivant of Calais, Bella Neville's bastard! Is the wench his wife?'

And now from informer Stephen Hurst must needs turn bawd too. His eyes avoided the darkly-flashing young face, but his zeal only possessed him the more eagerly therefor.

'Not so, not so!' he cried. 'I who trailed half York for him, should I not know? Tell me the church he knelt in, the priest who joined their hands! An alehouse among the tanyards more like, with two tapsters for witnesses and a pennorth of ale for their sacrament—'

But there had gripped him from behind by some secret

nerve, so that he bellowed with sudden pain, a fantastic chameleon of a man with half a moustachio on his face and half a red cross on his breast, whose wrathful voice drowned his own.

'And who's this, while he's a beard left for me to take him by? Is this him I had to lout to for leave to pass a dead man, one they'd trussed up like a faggot with their ropes and stones? And only an uninstructed lad to see he was carried with decency to his burial! Would you tell *me* they're not married, and her own mother there, that's a bride of Christ herself? See that belly of yours isn't the next to spill like this belly of straw—'

But it seemed to exhilarate the earl Philip that his presence had been braved and his life attempted. As if the poppy-wreath had been perfumed he sniffed at it as he turned to Sir Thomas.

'Cousin, you must give me leave in this. Unmannerliness to ladies must be reproved. Fie, on a wedding-day! Sir John Boles, take you charge of this young hornet of Westmoreland! See he has no second sting, and let his guards not leave him! Where's that harper? Them that's for bed let them go, and them that would seat themselves differently let them do so! There's a night-piece to come. . . . Bind him fast, Sir John, you ha' seen his nimbleness—'

But the poppy wreath was still in his own hands as six guards led Gandelyn away.

Cloisters of Pain

A thousand years of youth at golden stand,
Rosier than roses, dreamier than this dream
Of shining ebb and firmamental strand
And sky and sky inwove with scarce a seam—
Sun at noon's poise, the pulse the only clock,
The heart for hour-glass and the kiss for chime—
Then the trod grave, the footfall, the first knock
Of Pays Perdu and Once-upon-a-Time. . . .

Tempest and levin rend the skies to-night
As darkness brings the Here-upon-a-Now;
The thief i' the candle steals away the light
That should be taper to the What and How;
A thousand years of youth, shrunk to no more
Than one far sparkle, of one morning's shore?

I

It was in no sense to be called a dungeon, for it had air, light, and company outside and in. Bulmer's northern end was its least frequented part, and it was here at its back that he was lodged, two stories above the bivouac of the palisades. His indoor company was that of his two guards, who were changed every four hours. The single window was high in the wall, with a sill that sloped steeply inwards. His bed was fixed, and an earth-pail stood outside his door.

They had taken away his belt, but his wrists had been loosed again and he might talk as freely as he wished. If he pleased he might join in the game his custodians played to while away the hours, a game of finger-counting with both hands suddenly flung up, its stakes nuts from Sir Thomas's larder or whatever the trifle might be. But the barred window, looking north, admitted no direct sun. The cool grey light varied only with the gradations from dawn till noon and from noon till evening, when the bivouac fires tinted the stone vaulting above his bed. He did not suppose he would be there for long.

None the less he had already been there two nights and two days, none had been near him but his guards, and each day, towards evening, Sir John Boles. Formally Sir John Boles asked him how he did and if he needed anything, no more. It was his duty, he discharged it with correctitude, and Gandelyn knew the gravity of his offence and awaited what came. A brawl at a festal board, a naked poniard and himself proclaimed a bastard—there was nothing to do but to wait.

Not married! . . . But Robin Crosby would see to that,

and that at least was something that could be asked. But when he asked it, on the evening of the third day, Sir John Boles only shook his head.

'There is to be no communication,' he said.

'Yet hear me, sir. Innocent of intent we come to this castle. I cannot tell how it came about, and for my un-mannerliness I would sue to to this house's master and his lady. Let me be chastised. But do not wreak my offence on others.'

'It shall be conveyed to Sir Thomas. But build not on it.'

'Sir, have you been in France?'

'I have.'

'In the field it would have been a heinous thing. Maybe here it is no better. I will humble myself before his lord-ship. I will kneel, I will kiss his foot. Only let me have ten minutes with this player.'

'It is not my office, but I will report your words,' and with another headshake he left him.

Not married! . . . But trust Robin Crosby not to leave her side. He would be there to comfort her, he would set other things in motion, and as for this vomit of a servant, above all else he must now keep his head. These guards seemed simple fellows, bribeable it might be to carry a message. They were in the corner at their finger-game. Always make friends with guards. He joined them, and for an hour the nuts with which they played became bewitched.

But nothing came of it. When he let fall his hint they too shook their heads, and for all he knew passed it on.

Not married! . . .

It was in the early evening of the fifth day that Sir John Boles entered his lock-up accompanied by a man he had never seen before. The guards were ordered to place themselves outside in the passage out of earshot, but the door remained open, and this man whom Gandelyn had never seen before was a soft-moving, soft-spoken man who might have been a lawyer or might have been sent to confess him, so secret and insinuating was his voice. They sat on the guards' stools, and this man bade Gandelyn too be at his ease, but Gandelyn continued to stand.

'A nod would do, a word. You are under no pressure. Then you'll have heard the last of this of Ripon,' he said, but Gandelyn answered warily.

'Sir, I was never in Ripon in my life.'

'Nor was it asked you. That answer alone almost suffices. But blood has been spilt and men taken with weapons in their hands, and as for yourself, Netherby protects you. It will be seen you have all your proper privilege as a clerk.'

'I do not follow you, sir.'

'It is known the errand you were sent out on. It did not miscarry, and you are in nothing to blame that it was forestalled.'

Suddenly Gandelyn felt himself sickly-pale. 'Sir, with what am I charged?'

'No charge lies against you. It may be you tarried a little by the way, but that is no more than the lightest of penances, and at the hands of your friends. Moreover, the man has spoken.'

'The man—?'

'They hold themselves stiff up to a point. Up to the third peg they have been known to stand to it. But truth lies in the fourth peg. Show them that—'

In the palisades below the men had lighted their fire. One of them was singing a song, but before Gandelyn's eyes a web of greyness had gathered. Sir John had turned his back, but it was to Sir John that Gandelyn spoke.

'Sir John . . . does this mean I'm to be taken to York?'

'Would you were not.'

'To be—questioned?'

'Not as he means it.'

'When?'

'To-night, after dark.'

'Then, good gentleman, for it's to be seen you have gentleness—you know what I would ask—' but again the headshake.

'My directions are express.'

'Five days have gone by since I saw her face or heard her name—'

'She shall know you asked it.'

'There is still an hour—but ten minutes, five, a look—'

'These five days she too has pleaded for it. By what this gentleman assures you you'll soon be with her again. You will be fetched in an hour. Guard—'

The guard returned and the door was locked again.

The moon that night, rising over the fishpond down the hill, wavered and assembled itself again to every feeding fish that broke the surface. It lighted the glades of Gaultres where the animals stood stiffly at gaze at every rustle, but no forerunning of bells announced the seven riders, silver-washed on the open hillsides and shadows· again among the shadows, headed southwards. Four rode ahead, two by two, followed by one who rode alone. Then came Sir John Boles and the persuasive stranger. And had Gandelyn not been told that on sufficient occasion he might take a horse?

He had given no parole, but he had no thought of escape. A stupor of accidie had settled on him, and now that the last foreign merchant had left York there was plenty of room at the *Bull*. But at eight o'clock the next morning, having ridden all night, he crossed its courtyard as if he had never seen it before. He knew without further asking what he must prepare for now. His own dilatoriness was to be chastised lightly, if at all, and even in the lyng-house they did not deal in pegs and holes. But to another it had already been administered. He had endured to the third peg, but at the fourth he had broken, and the last time Gandelyn had seen this other had been from the upper casement of a house called the *Keys*, with a bloody clout round his head, cruelly goaded yet uttering not a cry. It was he who had talked to him at sunrise by a ditch, telling him to have nothing to do with it, root nor twig, for for him all the joy and sweetness of life were to come.

Accidie of the spirit is accompanied by no pain. Only a great desire to sleep descends upon the soul, to sleep until no matter what has passed, and if not to wake again perhaps best of all. It was well into the afternoon when he opened his eyes at the sound of Sir John Boles's voice. The knight was standing at the side of the bed on which he had cast himself, looking down on him.

'Is it true you are of Netherby?' he asked, in a kindly voice.

'It is true, sir.'

'Then hold stoutly to it should you need it. Do you know York's castle?'

'I was once there. I took news of a bequest to its prisoners.'

'I have yet to see the buck I would not break sooner than I'd break a prisoner! What's easier than to leave a door open and then look in the other direction? Would I knew more of this Master Vyner!'

'Is that him who came to fetch me?'

'I may not answer questions. Myself I have not seen the other man. It was left to Sir Emrys and Sir Maris. You have slept for four hours. Hold fast to Netherby and its benefit. Are you ready?'

'Sir, do you return to Bulmer?'

'To-morrow or the next day. You need not speak it. I will give her the best news I can.'

'There is a dog of a steward—'

'I know the man. *He* breathes no Lancashire air, as he hopes he may! Now you must come.'

Fifteen ordinary minutes, rubbing shoulders with ordinary folk along everyday-trodden Castlegate, bring a man to the outer ward. Seldom a day passes without some examination that never reaches the ears of the world, only a single guard stood at the outer gate, and a second admitted them to a gloomy corridor, at the farther end of which, beyond the governor's office, stone steps descended. They ended at a gaolers' room, where staves stood in a corner, iron keys hung on a wall-board, and on a shelf stood a number of lanterns. This had yet an inner door, where stood a man who did not speak but only stood aside for them to pass. It was Sir John Boles's second visit to the prison that day.

Again steps descended, turning twice upon themselves. The stones underfoot were slippery now, the walls smelt of mould and mud yet of heat withal, and even yet they were not in the examination-chamber, but in a sort of ante-room for witnesses, of whom three or four waited. So far occasional slits in the walls had glimmered greyly. Now the greyness became a shadowy murkiness of lantern-light, and intermittent voices could be heard, then a single voice, with pauses as if whatever was said was being written down. Once there was a clink of iron, a stool scraped, and somebody coughed as if at the heat and thickness of the air. Gandelyn heard slurrings and scraps of words, in several voices, one of which was raised somewhat above the others.

'. . . five years ago, at a place called Spilling in Essex . . . at daybreak under a hedge, with his throat cut . . .'

Apparently some answer was made, for again came the pause.

'. . . at Bourne, in Lincolnshire, on a Shrove Tuesday

. . . on the day Ozerley courthouse was burned, a lawyer . . .' then another voice.

'Admitted, admitted. Durham is admitted too,' and a query of false surprise.

'What, that so far has been so strenuously denied? Is then all this of Washburn-in-the-Forest admitted?' and a legal altercation broke out.

'Not so. Under advice he amended his first pleading. He utterly denies that he was in Washburn more than the one night, and then only to dig a grave, as his trade is.'

'It has been stated, by two of his own sisterhood—'

'Come, we lose time—'

Not knowing whether he was to be taken back to the *Bull* Gandelyn had brought with him his cloak. Because of the heat and stuffiness of the air he had taken it off again, but now many things began to happen all at once. First his shoulder was touched. The cloak was dropped by hands about him again and its hood drawn forward. The warder stood aside, Sir John Boles had retired, he was bidden to step forward, and doing so was able to see the whole dismal sight.

Into the subterranean chamber at least fifty people seemed to have been compressed, prison officials, men of law, clerks, a chaplain, a surgeon, several bare-armed men who looked like mechanics. By dint of counting they became perhaps thirty, but never fewer than twenty reckoning those who stood back in the shadows. At a table three or four scribes sat, with the prison-governor at the head, wearily watching the proceedings pursuant to his office. But beyond a low archway lay an inner chamber, and it was from this that the heat and the choking came, and for a moment Gandelyn's own breathing was checked. It had a hearth and buckets of water, with other apparatus, but that which had taken Gandelyn by the throat was the sight of the manacled man who leaned against the opposite wall, alone on that side of the room. He still wore his breeches, but over his upper anatomy a sort of prison-sheet was wrapped. He could scarce stand for the iron upon him, but lodged as he was in an angle the weight in effect held him up. His face was like the wall itself for its greyness of stubble and prison-pallor, and his upturned brow seemed to writhe with prayer. But the argument had been resumed and the pens were moving again.

'It is common ground that in Washburn he visited this holy man, for his staff and gabardine were found there. Then by his own admission he dug this grave. And the next we hear of him he's in Ripon and armed. For all there is in between—Sir Emrys, may we have it read?'

It was read. Utterly it denied that he knew anything of weapons in consecrated ground, likewise that any but himself had been at the graveside.

'Let the witness Grindrod be recalled.'

Before the table there appeared a paunchy man in forest-green. His face was florid with the open air, he looked this way and that, but not once at the exhibit in the prison-sheet who leaned against the gaol-dewed wall.

'You have told the Commission you are employed in the Forest, in the ride called Pennypocket?'

'I have watched its ride these five years, sir.'

'You have stated that you accompanied the Regard as far as Washburn-in-the-Forest and there made certain discoveries, a hare-pipe and what-not, little to the present purpose. You are now asked to take your mind back to Pennypocket alestake, on a midday about that time, when you would have detained one with a white staff and a Durham cross, by every sign a sanctuary-breaker,' and again the former testy voice struck in.

'Admitted, admitted.'

'Ordered out of the realm—'

'Sir Emrys, this can go on for a month—'

'Suffer me to examine my witness. You were about to apprehend this man but you were prevented. Tell the Commission what prevented you,' and the witness spoke boldly out.

'I was advancing upon him, sir, when of a sudden, I cannot tell you how, there stood there one in a cloak, who breaks into a great noise and riot. He said he'd been given safe-conduct of him, with much abuse of myself, and between them they made off with six eggs—'

'Speak no more than you are asked. They went off together?'

'Ay, sir, and that by a side-way few strangers know of.'

'Describe the manner of their going.'

'That I can, sir, for from tree to tree I followed them over a mile. Scarce were they out of the ride but the woods rang wi' their laughing and their ho-ho-ho-ing, unsettling the does—'

'As it might be two of a trade, their noses in the same trough, so that if one of them now denies that he knows the other it would be hard to believe?'

'Main hard, if I were anywhere by!'

'Would you know this youth's face again?'

'Among a thousand, sir.'

But from Gandelyn the lethargy was beginning to lift. Of these faces he knew none but that of the silent governor, but one of them was addressed as Sir Emrys, and young Peter Oates, who haunted Sneak Lane for a girdlemaker's wench and her pair of breasts, had opened his eyes to a little more. The wretch propped against the wall might have been there only for them to sharpen their legal wits upon, and now that he looked again, sagging and bloodless as the man was and ready to drop at the least unbalancing, he had little the look of a man who had already been stretched to the third peg. How so should he have been on his feet at all? Never had he found Jan Schmidt without his wile, the subtler the more he made himself a fool. At the bottom of the wrinkled eyes something was awake and alert. Had then that soft-spoken man lied? But the examining voice was raised again.

'I am seeking to establish before the Commission, that two men, one of whom denies knowledge of the other, are nevertheless deep in guilt together! This is no matter of two drowsy women at midnight, nodding as they stir their gruel—'

'Eggs, eggs—it is down they were beating eggs—'

'—but of a nimble and dexterous youth, quick of hand and trained in the wars to such enterprises—'

'We are not so directed, Sir Emrys. You trespass on the function of the court still to come,' but a new voice interposed itself, the voice as Gandelyn was now able to guess of Sir Maris, who left charts behind him.

'This is an *Inquirendo*, issuing from the crown. Must we be dragged from Essex to Lincolnshire and from Lincolnshire to Durham, to let the truth slip between our fingers when we find it? Tongues lie, but not face-to-face! Make an end! Gaoler, that lantern!'

But before a move could be made there was a deep indrawn sob and a rattling of fetters. Down in a heap the prisoner and his irons had tumbled together, and yet he played his bitter part to its end. His beggar's whine was heard through the soul-sickening chamber.

'Merciful sirs! There was no other, what need had I of another? I am but one they set the dogs on—we are no lollards but the lads pursue us with stones—we sing hymns and wash them for burial—'

'Higher, gaoler—his hood well back so his face can be seen—'

'I know what awaits me in yonder—it was told me I'd been informed on—draw me with cords if you must, but let me not die with false witness on my soul—'

'His cloak off too, and let him step forward. Forester, is this the man?'

'The same, sir.'

'Then stir the one on the ground—make him look up—'

But only for a moment did the lantern shine on the strained and unhooded young face. Gandelyn, who had derided Jan Schmidt for a skin-saver and a coward, was on his knees by his side. But it was the old man's choked and broken words that filled the stifling prison-room, protesting to the last.

'He had no finger in it! Always there's a grave ready and another half dug! Ne'er again shall I see such a picture of simple belief as he made—'

'What strange strangers are these?'

'—me with my spade in my hand and scarce an inch of earth between, ready to dash out the lantern if but a glint showed—'

'Heard you that, Sir Emrys?'

'But neither haft nor point did he see, the innocent—never did fledgeling yield itself so for plucking—'

'See, the other takes him by the hand—his ear is at his breast—yet they did not see one another before!'

'Still I object! It is *ultra vires* and beyond the terms of our Commission!' and out broke the bickering anew, for nothing is so profitable as an *Inquirendo* when all know the fish they angle for are not in the pond.

But from far away Gandelyn seemed to hear another captious and legal voice, in a cooler chamber than this. He was in the parlour at the end of the chapter-house passage again, and Brother Isidore was giving him his last instructions, and no Lord Abbot had been there this time to tell him that if he failed he must look elsewhere than to Netherby for his succour. And now he was on his knees before a prison-broken man, whose prayer-wrung brows

even so were more at peace than his own as he whispered
to him in a voice that hardly reached his ear.

'Youth of my heart, how have you fared since I saw you
last?' but Gandelyn could scarcely find a voice at all.

'I saw you brought into York—'

'Ay, I saw you at the casement, but it was no time to be
remembering folk—'

'Jan—'

'They thought to bring us both to confusion, you in
your hood and me fetched upstairs, but they bring me joy
instead. But they'll not leave us long like this. How have
you fared?'

'Jan, they lie—I have breathed no word nor syllable
against you—'

'I know it, I know it. I saw to it you'd none to speak.
All Aptrick could have marched past under your nose, ay
at midday, and I could have played with you so for a
month.'

'At the graveside itself I saw no weapon,' and for one
moment only did a changed glint come into Jan Schmidt's
eyes. If he had . . . even he . . .

'Yet I was sent out to take you by the heels, you or
whomsoever—'

'Quick, for I know the ways of these. Where have you
been?'

'That chamber with the casement—I was married
there—'

Jan Schmidt's mouth was half toothless, and his tongue
was a liar's tongue, but wet diamonds lighted in the depths
of his puckered eyes. '*What?* You are married?'

'These four months, but now they tell me—'

'As never since have I ceased nightly to pray?'

'Yet now they are saying—'

'As close to my heart as I can for these—let me take
you to my arms, for you'll ne'er see me again—'

But the stirring of the chains made an end of it, and Sir Maris's voice broke harshly out.

'Warder! Part those two! Who's to know what file or picklock's passing between 'em? Him on the floor, back with him where he came from. This other—'

At the table the clerks were writing again. A couple of warders were setting Jan Schmidt on his feet. But what to do with the other was the trouble, and both Sir Emrys and Sir Maris were for detaining him where he was. But already the governor had had thirty from Washburn thrust upon him without charge, whom after a whipping he had been ordered to let go, and he would have no more of it. The altercation grew hot.

'Bear in mind, sir governor, this is Duchy business,' Sir Maris warned him.

'Show me your warrant, gentlemen.'

'The name of Philip of Gaunt should be warrant enough.'

'Sir John Boles also serves the earl Philip of Gaunt. Sir John brought him here, and to him I will deliver him.'

'Sir John is no more than in personal attendance on him. He knows nothing of this,' and the governor rose.

'While I am custodian here no man teaches me my duty. If he stays here it is as my guest.'

'You shall answer it.'

The debate was settled for them, but it was not to the *Bull* that Gandelyn was returning. From the shadows there stepped forth the soft-spoken man who had come to Bulmer to tell Gandelyn that he was in the hands of friends. He was armed with a paper, which the governor read. Then he looked up.

'Are these chaplains here?' and there stood in the outer doorway two grave-faced figures, at whom the governor looked, and then at Gandelyn.

'It is in order. They are the chantry priests. You are to accompany them,' he said.

Up the slippery stairs again that turned twice on themselves: back through the gaoler's room where the staves stood in the corner and the keys hung on the board; along the stone corridor and through the guardroom to the outer ward; but the sunshine of Castlegate struck suddenly hard on Gandelyn's eyes, so that he drew forward his hood. His attendants did not speak, nor did he question them. He had an idea, but could have given no reason why, that the name of one of them was Ambrose, and they allowed him his own pace. It seemed strange to be in York again, even in unfashionable Castlegate, among people intent on their own affairs, strange to see the dogs and the pigs, the shops with wares in them, to hear voices that greeted, conversed, laughed. These citizens of York would have stared if they had been asked whether anything was happening in the castle. There the castle stood on its monticule, the castle that was always there, so what should be happening? None was taken there but for good reason. Now they were approaching the Pavement, where All Saints' lantern burned throughout the night. Ouse Bridge lay ahead, and in Gandelyn's head was running a song of Andrew's that he could not get rid of. '*It was in the waning that forth they went.*' That was the Philip of Valois song, when Sir David the Scot had been ordered to subdue all England, from Tweed to Trent, and suddenly, passing a mounting-stone, he asked leave of his attendants to sit down. They waited with grave patience, and it seemed a long time before one of them touched him lightly on the shoulder again and asked him if he was rested. Once more they moved forward, but a little further on, before a haberdasher's shop, he again wanted to sit down. They were approaching Coney Street, and suddenly it seemed to him that everybody about him was behaving in a most extraordinary way. No constable was in sight, but from the direction of Ouse Bridge half York seemed to be pouring. Fore-running, grinning lads pointed behind them, there were laughs and jeers and cries of 'Watch, watch!' Dogs were gambolling and yelping, surely not on Gandelyn's account, and he heard one of his conductors say 'Let's get past.' But suddenly above the noise a woman's voice rose, shrill, hard, shattering.

'Vowed to God yet still as quick as lime! Nay for pity's sake quench it!' and the street rang with derisive laughter.

'Hark at her!'

'Their cornered lawns and brazen stomachers and such talk as never! Who'd ha' believed it?'

'Tell us, mother!'

'Drunk after compline—'

'Ware the watch!' but the railing rose higher still.

'*Me* a penitent, ordered to my knees to pray! *Me* to be told they're their brothers and near kin, and half a dozen young lads about the place they vow are the washerwomen's, till another of 'em's brought to her bed and the next you hear's she's his godmother! A brew of graveyard worms over them all—'

Across Gandelyn's head his conductors were talking. 'What riot's this?'

'I did hear something. She was at Clementhorpe. They passed her on to Lintham.'

But Gandelyn had raised his dull head. Mobbed, applauded, urged on, he had a glimpse of a face with a mouth open like a mænad's but split into a white half and a black one by a muffle. From the muffle a mares-tail of grey hair escaped about her eyes, and again the scornful voice rose high above the hubbub.

'What the worse is the Abbess's bacon that she eats her breakfast with the steward? Truffles, for kindling rabbits? Nay, I'll back to my own trade! Herbs in the streets,

bogbean for your fevers, good folk, and foxglove for a
pretty girl's eyes! I've a crystal I'll read your dreams in!
I seek my daughter! Thirteen-and-fourpence was to have
gone with her to set her up in a proper trade, and there's
an honest married woman for you, not a holy whore!
Foxgloves for the eyes—truffles to set a man on his horse
and a woman in her grave—who'd see her sweetheart in
my crystal?'

One of the priests muttered. 'She'll not get far along
Coney Street that rant—'

'An hour'll see the branks on her—'

'Here—look to this youth—some of these haven't seen
what he's seen this morning—'

In the haberdasher's shop was a wooden bench. They
pushed back his hood and placed him on it. People were
being begged to stand back and give him air. But the next
thing of which Gandelyn became conscious was the smell
of burning feathers in his nostrils.

II

In Bulmer's Castle of Pleasure all wished the storm
would break and get itself over. The grassy knoll gleamed
green as an emerald under a sky as heavy as lead, the
birds had left the air, in the pond not a fish stirred. The
horses shifted uneasily in the stables, and those of the
palisades had carried their belongings into stalls and
laithes, to be ready for it when it came. In chambers as
dark as night lights burned. It was hard to believe that
somewhere above the standstill to-day's sun shone in
the sky.

Along corridors too the lights came and went, for many
of the ladies would not leave their rooms. Others moved

from room to room in search of company; when it came it would come from the south, and a party that had bidden farewell to Bulmer that very morning would ride straight into it. One of them was the dusky Huguette's handsome falconer, and she had loosed her stomacher for air and was snapping at the little Brigitta for bringing the blind brach into her room.

'I'll not have mangy dogs about me, filling my bed with fleas!' she scolded.

'It may be they haven't got far and will turn back,' another said.

'Sir Emrys and Sir Maris were to be here to-day, but if they're wise they'll have stopped where they are.'

'The players have started to pack up too, and it's on foot for them.'

But the dancing-girl's name was not spoken. It was two days ago, but the scandal of it, that to Sir Thomas's dais a brawler had leaped and had had to be violently seized and pinioned, was still in every mind. And what of the shame brought on the lady Adela, that two who had been allowed a marriage-chamber were now exposed as not being married at all? It was as fresh as ever, and it broke out again.

'Master Hurst durst never have said it had he not known it to be so!'

'But the actor said her mother was there!'

'Her mother wasn't with her when she was trailing about with five men, and only a cart to sleep in, and all the shifts *we're* put to to steal half an hour—'

'Rosanne says it was my lord had her up to their table, not the lady Adela—'

'Brigitta, off with you, this isn't for you—'

'Where is she now?'

'In that turret, with Master Crosby—'

There came a rapping at the door. It was the major-

domo, lantern in hand, passing from room to room. Sir
Thomas, he told them, had commanded that a fire should
be lighted in the hall for such as wanted the courage of
company, and for once the lady Adela would overlook it
if they came as they were.

Still the storm did not break. The heavens over Gaultres
were a darkness suspended upon a darkness, and to look
out from Bulmer's southern wall was to see a motionless
bolster, as black as ink, thunder-stuffed and ponderous
with its liquefaction. It was watched by two men from the
oriel built out on the hoardings, and on Stephen Hurst's
finger a ruby ring glowed. It was a gift from the earl
Philip, and he had always known it to be the way. Their
habits and humours must be a man's hourly study. If one
did not another would, and there was no more to be said.
There rolled a low mutter of thunder over York's plain as
Stephen spoke.

'That is ever best done that does itself, my lord,' he was
saying. 'When you cut see you cut with the grain.'

'You cannot cut what locks itself away.'

'It is not the time to attempt it, my lord. By your leave,
your lordship was wrong to snatch that wreath from her.
It may be for a day or two she'll not let herself be seen,
but they seldom weep long who weep alone, nor does Sir
Thomas fill his house with weepers. A pale melancholy
will follow, which will grace her well. Ever it is the
sweetest when it comes of its own motion.'

'You would seem to have chambered in your time,
Hurst, but that was something of a bay you let out when
the actor nipped you by the arm,' but a beard is all the
better stroked when a ruby ring glows at the same time.

'The youth's to be called before the Chapter. They
cannot have bearers of letters dallying with incontinence
by the way. He'll be disciplined, and when she hears of it
she will weep, and such as they cannot make their homes

in castles on their own terms. Let my lady have her among her own women. She'll be dancing again all in her own good time, and if I know aught of them, your lordship shall provide the music—'

At that moment the eyrie of glass broke into an effulgence of terrific and searing light. It had not ceased to blind when there followed a peal that cracked above their heads like a sledge upon an anvil. It had no echo, for it stunned the eardrums, and a sulphorous smell made vile the air. The cloud over Gaultres became a writhing of violet, that suddenly split its underpart like a sluice. Something struck a pane like a missile, and before breath could be taken the forecourt below could not be seen for the deluge that descended upon it.

The little Brigitta had buried her head between Huguette's breasts, but not even bedclothes could keep out the successive flashes that surely must be shaking down York itself. 'Wait for us!' the child cried as the major-domo's knocking passed to the next door. The kitchens were a pack of those who had crowded in from their bivouac, for into pents and sheds spread the pools and rivers of running water, and only once in a while did a swathed figure make a dash across an open space. No last gleam of watery sun would lift upon Bulmer's rain-dark walls that night.

But down in the high-raftered hall every ring and sconce had been lighted and the blaze of the hearth-logs showed an empty dais. The tables had been carried forward from the three great windows, for none wanted to sit beneath those panes that every few moments became cathedral-lights of infernal splendour. Hardy gentlemen came and went on errands for this or that that the ladies had left behind them in their rooms, but the ladies sat huddled together with their backs to the storm, half of them attired as the lady Adela had given them permission.

In loose gowns and cloaks they huddled about the great hearth, some propped against the knees of the ladies behind them, sipping their cordials with their little dogs in their laps.

They had music to cheer them too. As long as Robin Crosby ate Bulmer's bread he was its servant, and striding up and down under the illuminated windows Andrew the harper paced, fully robed and chapleted, while they showed slackened hems and edges and hair loosened in its nets. If they wanted more racket they could have the nackerer too. But Robin Crosby himself was hipped and in dudgeon at the seizing of one of his men. The major-domo had knocked at the door of the turret also, but he would not leave the girl, and there the two sat, the wall beyond their slit ringing them with a moat of light.

'They said he'd be back in three days, and I'm giving him another three, no more!' the actor swore for the twentieth time. 'There's other castles, and if I'd known when I was well off York and its pageant would never have seen my face! For a company what did I want better than John Cormorant, who'd swallow you a side-sword up to the hilt, or Will Bungay that would eat brands from the fire like puddings, or little Welsh Davy, to sing *penillion* till they tumble off the benches with laughing? There was a company! But I'll find them again, and three more days he shall have—'

She had wept till she could weep no more. No more than the pageant-master would she lift a finger again till he returned, and when she was left alone she barred her door.

But word had been brought her—it came from Sir John Boles—that she was to wait for him where she was.

Who under a good roof did not draw closer to the fire to think of York's plain that night, the treetops of Gaultres every leaf a drum, the bending of branches till they broke, the runnings and the seethings and the soakings below? What of Aire and Wharfe when they became muddy and brown, and Nidd when it broke its banks, and Swale when it swelled and Ouse when its course was not to be seen for the lakes into which it had spread? Its Bridge, not to be crossed, must have cut York in two. Foss too would rise round the castle on its monticule, there would be boats in the streets, and what of the prisoners when it soaked and sucked in where they lay? But in the chantry of Saint Leonard's there lay on a rope-framed bed a youth who at some sudden peal opened his eyes. The crack loosened as it were some inner keystone, and drowsily he half raised himself and looked about him. From somewhere not far away came a deep unison of men's voices, singing. He remembered a smell of burning feathers, and somebody had been to his side while he had slept, for at his bed was a stool with a cloth upon it, but no food. He was staring at a plaster wall, with a niche in it in which was a shallow dish of oil, with a wick that flickered and floated. Over it, dark against the pale wall, a foot-long wooden crucifix hung. But the wall-lamp was not the only light, for a doorless opening led to some outer but still inward passage, that leapt with a dull imprisoned flash. At the same moment the singing was lost in a more tremendous roll. Somewhere a storm had broken.

The outer lobby gleamed again. The singing had ceased, and there stood in the entry a tall tonsured figure, certainly not Sir John Boles, as certainly not the priest whose name he imagined to be Ambrose. The figure asked him whether he had called. He had no memory of having raised his voice.

'Where am I?' and a harder voice than Ambrose's answered him.

'This is the chantry of Saint Leonard's.'

'Who are you?'

'I am its perpetual chaplain.'

'Why am I here?'

'For the present you are committed here.'

'I cannot stay. I have business.'

'The door stands open. No force will be used. But this morning you gave your word.'

'To whom did I give any word?'

'To one of us called Ambrose. Is your stomach ready for food yet?'

'I want no food, and with such a deal on my hands I cannot lose time doing nothing,' and the figure pointed to the crucifix in its socket.

'Need you do nothing? Have you not that? You gave your word. None will stop you, but over by Greendykes Saint Leonard has a gallows. There is food for you when you desire it,' and when Gandelyn looked up again the perpetual chaplain had gone.

Sometime during that night downward the loosened keystone plunged, bringing the arch with it in its ruinous fall. He remembered, not piecemeal but all at once. With a cry he was on his feet. Where were his guards and their finger-game? He had no guards, and the days—how many were they? Five days he had been in that other chamber, keeping his tally by the bivouac fires on the vaulting over his head. Then they had told him to make himself ready. Out into the moonlight they had ridden, he remembered the *Bull* yard, the bed on which he had woke, Sir John Boles who stood there. His wall had no outer window, no light but that of the lightning in the door-less doorway, and he had got from his bed and was on his knees when the wall-wick under the crucifix smoked thinly and went out. His only light now was within himself, the memory-light of a lurid cellar, the inextinguishable light of two diamond-drowned blue eyes, that at a word had become as starry as if their owner had been bidden to a wedding only a little too late. All the sweetness and hope of life—

But the whitewash of the lobby where the dull lightning had played had become a grey pallor again, and they were bringing him his breakfast of fish and bread as before he had ceased to see a woman with a mænad-open mouth, who cried out on their holy whores, for all she sought was her daughter.

With the passing of the storm Bulmer awoke to survey its damage. It was less than they had feared. Some concussion had shattered the oriel of its southern wall, the hoarding-beams projected over the forecourt like a double gallows, and they would dismantle it presently. The fish-pond down the slope was the worst. The rush of water had torn a portion of its lower side away, to repair it every man-at-arms was summoned from the palisades, and the broken banking was a chaos of stakes and planks and stones and barrows of clay. The earl Philip, silent and moody, watched the men at their labour as if he had been back among his barrellers of the Oise.

But the beaten-down gardens would quickly repair themselves. Briar-rose grows apace, once those masses of pink pulp had been shovelled away from the arbours of the belvedere the hard green clusters of buds would grow the stronger for their thinning, and that very morning the windfalls were carried to the styes and the birds were again at the reddening fruit. But the storm had put many in mind of the drawing on of the year. Guests spoke of leaving, some of them were distances from their homes, and now the extent of the floods could be seen from the walls. Where faraway pastures had been tree-dotted lagoons flashed. The high ground would have to be kept, but it was marvellous, many said, what nature could do in a very little time, and on the third day there were already signs of an abating. On the fourth there came a pedlar in from York who, knowing the land, had walked dryfoot.

He brought news, too, of no great importance, but it helped Bulmer in its isolation. Thus, by way of his kitchens, Sir Thomas might learn if he wished how Thomas Twentyman, the eel-catcher of Ouse-side, had again had it for selling his eels over the licensed fishmongers' heads. He might hear how a certain young clerk of the Minster (from the precentor's own office some said) had got himself mixed up in a brawl between two women in Jubbergate, which was likely to cost the young fool dear, since he was the tutor of the three young children of John Wymark of Micklegate, whom Sir Thomas knew well. But the pedlar could tell them nothing of any Robert Gandelyn. He had never heard of him, and now Robin Crosby had been as good as his word and better. Three more days he had said. They had now become a week and more, and he discussed it with Andrew among the planks and clay-mounds of the fishpond.

But Andrew was getting old and slower on the road than he had been. Robin Crosby had promised him a castle for the winter, here in a castle he was, with small chance of a better in which to end his days. Now Robin Crosby too had his sword-swallower and fire-eater to find, and it was Echo who was the trouble. Her answer was still the same, that there he had left her, and there he would come back for her.

'Get you on your way, Robin,' she said. 'He cannot be long now.'

'And am I to look him in the face and tell him I left you behind? And what of my *Salome?*'

'I shall have Andrew, and they don't dance Salome in weeds,' she sighed, and turned away.

But she would have Andrew for company, Robin Crosby had done what he could, and the very next morning into the tilt-cart went the poppy-wreath and the costume of flames with the rest. It might be he would find another to wear them, and now the donkey was fed as he had never been fed, and she and Andrew accompanied them to the foot of the grassy ride.

'It's odds I shall have word of him in York,' the actor said. 'You shall hear, or those of the Lord's Prayer will let you know. Andrew old friend, we ha' covered many miles together—'

She kissed them all round, the nose of the donkey too, and when Robin Crosby went he went, without any turning round. The harper's arm was about her as at the fore-court she looked back. But already they were not to be seen.

Where the belvedere dropped to the stables and yards a small columbary stood hidden away. Few went near it, its path was knee-deep with weeds on either side, and its masonry consisted of three sides only, honeycombed to the top with small square cavities. To put a hand into one of these was to feel a nook on the left and a nook on the right, one apiece for the pair, and for as high as she could reach the little Brigitta had felt in them all. Now the birds paired higher, and a rough wooden bench was whitened with their droppings.

It was here that she began to sit, with the crooning of the birds for moan and comfort both. Sometimes Andrew sat with her, and for company at night she had the little Brigitta to share her bed. It was no longer in the turret that was reached by the gallery of the hall. Other young women in adjacent rooms were a better protection than a bar on a door, and the little Brigitta was too young to understand. But she avoided other company. They asked her no questions, but this was probably because they had been told not to do so, and she liked the doves and their healing heart-break the best. The doves and Andrew understood.

But the dark-eyed girl they called Huguette had a heartbreak too. Her falconer-gallant had gone, any heart that was pensive and sad might mourn in the columbary, and there were empty rooms in Bulmer now. In the afternoons the older ladies took their siesta, the younger ones were somewhat less difficult to talk to one at a time, and one afternoon, as she sought the doves alone, she found Huguette already sitting there. She would have withdrawn, but Huguette looked up, smiled wanly, and moved a little way along the bench. She was affecting to sew, for sometimes the lady Clarice gave her things she could make again for herself. Also Huguette wanted to make herself thinner, for though measured together she and Echo would have been much of a height she looked the shorter because of her dimpled plumpness. And Huguette was firmly of the opinion that the best thing to do with a trouble was to unbosom oneself of it.

'Your name's Echo, isn't it?' Huguette said.

'Yes.'

'I've so wished I could talk to you. I seem to have nobody to talk to now.'

And neither was it good for Echo to sit day after day grieving with the pigeons alone.

But she liked it less when the one they called Beryl joined them in the columbary. Beryl was as tall as a camelopard, talked too much about the number of times she could have been married, and asked her too many questions about herself. The dress that the lady Clarice had given to Huguette was a green one that had once been a maying-dress. It was prinked here and there with white like hawthorn-buds, and was so different from the flame-tongues in which Echo had so lately danced that it reminded Huguette of the other, which she had been longing to handle for herself. But Echo had to tell her that she no longer had the other, for the actors had taken it away, and now Huguette wanted to know all about the dancing instead, and how she made it twirl like that, first white flames and then red. So Echo tried to tell her that it was the dancer who made the dance, and how Robin Crosby had taught her, till Huguette's dark eyes became round with wonderment.

'What, with his hands?' and Echo flushed faintly.

'My husband was always there.'

'Could you do it to me?'

But the tall Beryl said 'Men's hands are different,' and said it in such a way that Echo got suddenly up. The throaty note of the pigeons was more consoling when only she and Huguette were there.

The battered hollyhocks of the belvedere had been cut to the ground, but this only made the banks of foxglove the more richly purple. Vine-leaves reddened the arbours, the marigolds spilled over the beds, and the briar looked like blooming till Christmas came. Now in Bulmer's End a stag had been dislodged, and the remaining gentlemen were bent on one more kill before they left. As Sir John Boles had not returned they took its ordering upon themselves, and there came a day when again Bulmer was empty of its men. But the attendant ladies had contrived their own diversion. For days past Huguette had been altering the lady Clarice's maying-gown for dancing, as Echo had danced in her flames, and for this the Italian terrace was the chosen place. Lest gardeners and domestics should pry the little Brigitta had been posted at the end of the trellis to give warning of approach, but at first Echo had shaken her head. Her heart was too heavy, she said. But all had protested that except under her direction their trouble would be wasted, and Huguette had wept on her breast.

'See—I've set a winterhedge in the corner for us to change behind—it's the last hunting-day we shall have—'

'I cannot, I cannot—'

'And soon you'll be going—any day he may come to fetch you away—'

So as they put it in that way she had yielded, and with the winterhedge to screen their tiring-room into it they had all pressed to see how the maying-dress was put on. The monkey chained by the loins to his house on its pole grimaced restlessly at them from his platform, now on four feet and now on two, scratching his dry skin and blinking his close-set eyes as she showed them the placing of their feet and the balance of their arched arms; and as they swayed and curved and postured the monkey too began to do the same.

'No no, Huguette—watch me, like this. Loosen, loosen, not stiffen, stiffen—'

'Oh, my knees—'

'That's only the first few lessons. Rest a minute or two. . . . No, Beryl, it's not because you're too tall—'

But in the middle of it all the hop-pole of a girl came down in a heap, and made a great to-do about her ankle, and again the monkey mimed them and rattled his chain, and they were not really very sorry, for they were a little tired of Beryl and all the husbands she could have had. But Echo had best not have joined in the laughter at her, for it was on her that the injured girl turned.

'A tinker can always mend a kettle better than others can!' she scolded. 'Dancing's your trade, and we haven't all trailed from door to midden with a pack of men! The ways of castles are to learn, for all my lady's taken you up—'

But of a sudden her voice sounded alone. The little Brigitta, a faithless sentinel, had wanted to see the dancing too, and a silence fell, and every knee was dipped in the curtsey they knew, as there advanced along the terrace, catching them in their disarray and the farther arbour strewn with their lawns and light discardings, the man whom Sir Thomas himself in his own castle might not command. Nor was there a deal of the courtier in the voice in which he spoke.

'What's coil's this?' he demanded, at a sudden standstill.

Only Huguette's lips moved. 'My lord—we were diverting ourselves—'

'Have none of you any duties?'

'It is the siesta, my lord—'

Yet to-day he too was differently attired. With his afternoon gown he wore a flat black cap, that gave him the look of a justiciary, and he was looking at the girl in green as if he hardly knew her for the one he had pledged in the Chaian wine. Only the monkey's chain rattled as he watched her with half-closed eyes. Then came the abrupt and pointing finger.

'Off to your duties, all of you. All but her. Let her remain.'

Without a word they gathered their swathings together and one by one filed past him with deep genuflexions.

But the one he had ordered to remain behind was trembling in every limb. He might have come upon them by accident, but he was staying of design, and now she had an angry question to answer.

'What long-shanked mare was that railing at you?'

'Her name's Beryl, my lord,' she got out faintly.

'Seat yourself. Where got you that gown?'

'It is not mine, my lord,' she answered more faintly still.

'To-morrow the quean shall be set to washing dishes. It sits on you prettily,' and so saying, and pointing to the nearest arbour, he placed himself at her side.

But it emboldened her a little that he seated himself at

a convenient distance, as if the better to see her. She knew he was a soldier, soldiers are like to have such voices and looks, and even the glimmer of a desperate hope was at her heart. So paramount was he in this place that he had but to lift a finger and he at whom it pointed was haled off to York; but that same finger could bring him back again, and now his gaze was alternately on the green dress and on her face, back and forth.

'Ay, it becomes you prettily. You should be sitting on a white palfrey with green trappings and a garland round your head. Have you ever ridden maying?'

'No, my lord.'

'Not out into the woods in the early morning, with the bells tinkling on the bridles and the dogs scarce to be kept down for their leapings and lickings?'

'No, my lord.'

'You know who I am?'

'All know who your lordship is.'

'And what they say of me? Pay no heed to it. It comes of too much soldiering. But you'll know nothing of soldiering.'

But seeing that he drew no nearer to her she was ceasing to tremble. His last words had been a question, and for answer she inclined her head and lowered her eyes.

'You do? As how?'

'From those that have been in wars, sir. They cry "God and Saint Denis," and ride up to his shield and touch it with their spear, and when the battle begins he's their man,' and the earl sat suddenly back.

'*Eh?*'

'And sometimes it's scarce to be called a war for their posturings and—and—and then the prisoners give their word, and they all go into the pavilion—'

'The pavilion?' and she grew bolder.

'Or it might be the castle, and those that were only

squires before are made knights, and they have a great feast, with gilded sucking-pigs—' and now she could almost feel the boring of the eyes under the flat cap.

'Do they so! And from whence have you all this?'

'My mother, sir, lived in a castle.'

'Your pardon! . . . And whereabouts in this castle have they shifted yourself to?'

'I am with the ladies, sir, in the chamber next to Huguette's.'

'And what did you tell my lady your name was?'

'Echo, my lord,' and he began to mutter, incredulously.

'It must be so, it surely must, for none would dare it to my face. . . . And in which part of this castle do *I* lodge?'

'Where the house of glass was, my lord,' and he locked his hands together, and looked at his feet, and then again looked up.

'Be it so, Mistress Echo, that can find such daintiness in war. But how of blood? Is there never a thimbleful or so to grace the tale?'

'They do not speak of it, sir.'

'Then neither will I. But if I were minded I could tell you how I'd bring this castle of my cousin's down with no more blood spilt than would breakfast a flea!'

'I have heard you have been much in the wars, my lord.'

'Fifty times I have done it, to pass the long day away, and not a wall breached, nor a burning timber to pin a man down in his mail till it becomes his frying-pan!' and for all her shyness she was a little frightened.

'That would be a dreadful thing, my lord—'

'Not to be spoken of, so no more of it. But over yonder is Gaultres, where to-day they're hunting. Ay, Gaultres will do, and there it may be I have set this pavilion of mine up. I take my ease, with a cup of wine to sip and soft music to listen to, none so at his ease as I. But mark well, I have my sentinels posted, and all the roads are mine, and I sigh for company. So they bring me (by your leave) some cook or turnspit, who presently falls a-prattling. 'Twould amaze you how anxious to please such become when they're brought to *my* tent!'

'But—company from the kitchens, my lord?'

'Where else? Did I not say I held the roads? None comes in or out of Bulmer but I know of it, and those who make a sortie or two have grown strangely lean and hollow in the stomach. So if this talkative fellow must be talking let it be of how the castle is provisioned and manned, and what sick they have, and how many are ready to treat for terms! Let him tell me how best a disease can be dropped into its well, and the fear of hunger spread within its walls! They cannot remember the last sucking-pig they gilded, but I, I have my music and my wine, and it may be they bring me another merry fellow, who tells me they've gilded their last rat—' and she turned suddenly pale.

'My lord, I fear to understand you—'

'Nay, I am but perfuming it a little, as they tell me is the way. So—Bulmer falls.'

But she was on her feet. At his ease, in cold blood . . . but now his eyes were beginning to glow.

'Neither fire nor blood, as I promised; but say it were a foreign town to sack, stuffed full of riches and other lasciviousness?' and his voice rose. 'Let them not speak of war that have heard no trumpet blown but their own! Towns are ta'en as best they can be, and what are a few clawings and shrieks in French if they end in any country's kiss? Nay, look not so pale in your mayings! Have we not all good healing-flesh, and shall I not be healed too? Soon, when we're all in Lancashire together—I see you start, but I have laid no finger on you—'

But she had seen the intention in his eyes, that she too was a castle of pleasure to be reduced, and suddenly she had cast herself at his feet, her fingers snatching at his gown.

'Oh my lord!' it broke from her. 'First they said a week—I cannot tell how many days it has been—and still he does not come—'

'Come? How come? I speak of going, not coming,' but her voice too rose.

'He designed naught against your lordship! His fingers do it with whatever they touch—it was not even up his sleeve, as many times I have seen him, but there for all to see—' and the cut face suddenly hardened.

'Ah! The young jack-in-boots!'

'Or let me come to him—I'll find him by myself alone— he's my husband—'

'It has been said not,' and now the monkey too set up a chattering and a rattling of his chain.

'Sir, I was never at school—he taught me as we went— but I can say the Credo up to *Homo factus est*, and in its blessed name I beg—, and the answer was rough.

'There's naught to be done. It is out of my hands.'

'Then in whose hands—?'

'Shall we say God's, or at least the hands of the godly? Cease your tears. He took it upon himself. He broke like a twig in their hands, all York was hunted for him and he was not to be found. When he was run to earth he was with a pack of players and clowns. They stretch it to allow him as much as they have. For his affront to me I promise you he shall not die. But he'll be the first who did not.'

But now her huddle was not of red but of green upon the ground as choked and strangled words broke from her.

'My mother was there—I said "I Echo" and drank out

of his cup—never did he cease to say if holy church it would—'

'Then how comes it that when he's brought in the presence of a proved malefactor he straightway falls to hugging and embracing him in his arms?' and he too sprang up. 'Enough! All is in hand! My fair Cousin Adela too longs for her own air! This Yorkshire's too rough, too far away! In Calais the young blade brought me a letter, and such a letter! I was to cease forthwith my pretensions to my castle of Ash in Denbigh! My pretensions! To what was my father's since Glyndwr's time! I was to cease my *pretensions!* . . . But he had his answer!'

She was following him on her knees now.

'My lord, he was not the writer of the letter—'

'What, and his sister's bastard! . . . But we shall see which is the Neville and which the Gaunt! Up, dainty, for there's no need to reduce castles that fall of themselves with the mouths that's in 'em! There'll be no wintering in Bulmer for Sir Thomas neither, for in three days we start! What, shall I tarry here while my castle in Denbigh is plotted against? And now, by the Virgin's Heart, we'll take justice with us too! I was in France too long! Virtue and good example shall be set on their feet again, and that's always best started while men still smell blood in the air! Beat cold iron when there's hot to hammer? We'll have a cleansing of the realm before they start flinching from it! Many shall rue their peace when it comes! There shall be inquisitions, there shall be tribunals! They'll not know their Cooper of the Oise with his justice's cap on! Up, grasshopper in green, and we'll see the caps of the Lancashire lads darken the air for joy at their lord's return! You shall have your harper too, for where's the heart with no music in it?' and in his hard voice he broke into a rough camp-song. '*A barmcloth for my bonnie*—' he trolled, '—oh, this makes me merry! We'll have cygnets and lark-pie for supper, and you shall have fine linen to sleep in, and when we get to Ribblehead you shall dance for me in white, the white of this pretty neck that the green peels off from like a filbert! Nay, I ha' held off my utmost! I must take a peep at it now—'

But now that he advanced his hand to her she was not there either to resist or respond, for she had swooned away.

III

The Chapter's daily order varied little throughout the year. A brief reading from the martyrology, the saint for the following day, a passage from the Canon and a commendation of the faithful departed; then they proceeded to other affairs.

But since the Chapter was also the See's secular court of administration these other affairs varied widely. Probate, trespass, incontinence, theft, debt, all came before it, so that with parties to the case, witnesses, and the interested citizenry, the Minster nave itself was sometimes hardly more public. And plainly that morning something out of the ordinary was afoot. The commonalty thronged the booths and shops that hemmed the Minster in, they pressed gossiping about the precincts. From the entrance of the chapter-house yard they had to be kept back by constables with halberds, for this was no such pronouncement as they heard every day. One had transgressed not only as a man but as a priest too, and upon judgment was to be handed over to the civil power.

The chantry-priests of Saint Leonards were bound by no rule of silence, but there was little of speech among them, and for the first few days Robert Gandelyn's solitary

daily exercise had been thirty yards along a buttressed
alley, a turn and back again, and so until the appearance
of a frocked figure in the doorway had told him his hour
was up. Then one morning the perpetual chaplain had
entered his cell, followed by the one called Ambrose, and
having looked at him they had conferred together in the
outer lobby.

'It is impenitence. His very kneeling mocks us. He is
morose.'

'It is some contagion he picked up in the prison.'

'Has he been medicined?'

'It does not stay with him.'

'Does he eat?'

'Little.'

'It is recalcitrance.'

'It is worse. It is apathy.'

'Well, we shall soon be rid.'

But as he slept little he had the less to wake from. When
he did wake it was only a passing from one listlessness to
another, and yet he remembered all. Now he lay abed,
waiting for the toll of Saint Mary's bell, and hearing
instead only the quiet inner bell that summoned the priests
to prayer was incurious of them alike. He ought to have
been feeling, suffering grief, bitterness, anger, illusions of
hope, no matter what. Again and again he told himself
what his feelings should have been. Winter would come,
but after that spring would return. As the year grew
warmer the world would break to life again, and somehow
there would be a new beginning. They were still there, the
sheepfolds and the dikes, the long-crested rollers, the
roads, the inns, the fairs. In the chapel they sang the
Miserere, but he acknowledged no transgression. '*Maiden
on the moor lay, on the moor lay, sennight full,*' chimed in his
head, but it brought neither pang or pain. Only time was
going on, that no man need wait for, and youth, of which

one quickly mends. He sometimes thought of time as his friend.

Then one morning Ambrose brought him his breakfast, at which he shook his head, and a bitter-tasting draught with it, which he swallowed. 'If you would kneel *I* should feel better,' Ambrose said wistfully, and if Ambrose would feel better for his kneeling it was little trouble to kneel. Then he rose again.

'They have come. They arrived in the middle of the night and slept in the Minster sacristy. Can you walk?' Ambrose asked.

'Who has come?'

'Your friends, I trust. Some of us have done what we could. Lean on me, and take your time.'

Yet even then Gandelyn barely wondered who these friends of his might be.

The Minster was no great distance away. On the way there he saw many faces but no face he knew, the other priest had joined them, and guards with halberds stood aside for the three to pass. They were entering a small grey yard, full of old stones and building-stuff and lidless cases from which the contents had been taken, approaching the Minster by the northern way. At a low inner door the sacristan awaited them, and to him the second priest spoke.

'What's the morning's order?'

'This sad business of William Cobb. Is the youth ailing?'

'He's not to call ailing, but if a chair's permitted him till they're ready for him 'twould be a kindness.'

'Have him in first. Then I'll see what can be done.'

The inner door opened on darkness. They stood within the wall itself, and Gandelyn lurched for a moment against vacancy where a winding wall-stair rose. But a second door opened, and he blinked his eyes at the sight of the noble octagon of which even the foreign merchants admitted that its like for a chapter-house was not to be found in christendom.

From wall across to wall it measured four full roods. The soaring vault to which it rose was as high and higher, a single gilded knop without other support locked its roof-timbers centrally together, and the air about him was nimbused with the many-coloured light of painted glass. In seven of the octagon's bays tall fivefold lights rose as high as the arch-springs. Continued in foils and cusps to the very groining, compartmented and diapered, they glowed and twinkled with devices and arms, so that no matter from which direction the light fell it stained the stalls of the canonry below with the tints of the rain-bow's foot. The stalls themselves, slender-pillared with marble, were canopied with baldequins of stone. They ran without a break round seven-eighths of the whole interior, and only on this eighth side no radiance of window-glass towered. Instead, over a lintel of silver Apostles plaqued with gold, a painted mitred figure on the wall, with a king and a queen for his supporters, thrust the butt of his crozier down the throat of the serpent he trod underfoot.

Furthermore, above the canopied stalls, but beneath the great windows, a gallery ran. It was for the privileged lay, the merchants and magistrates of York, the great of the guilds and their guests. But in the midst of the floor below a massive table stood. It was for the clerks and pleaders, the lawyers and their minions, and here a crimson rope cut the chamber in two. Now the space beyond it was packed with clerics of every grade. Shoulder to shoulder they stood in their several habits, priests, deacons, collegiates, clerks, curates from York's other churches, summoned this morning all to plenary and public Chapter. Even the acolytes had been brought from their duties for their edification and warning.

For the unhappy cause of it all had sinned as man and as priest too.

The terrible ritual was already in progress. Temporal power of heraldic glass, spiritual authority to weigh and judge, alone at the table he stood, his sentence already pronounced. Only breathings and sighs broke the emotional silence, lips that moved in prayer, and one mechanical voice, cold as that of an interpreter, that from time to time gave a direction. Gandelyn had been given a chair. It was in a corner by the rope, and he was trying to keep his eyes open, but he was glad to close them again. Only once had he seen a face writhe so, and no stalls of canonry had ringed that chamber round, but sweating walls and workmen with bared arms and a cachot with timbers and ropes and a hot hearth. Over those limbs a prison-sheet had been dropped, but this man still stood in his chasuble and stole, his lips apart and his hollow eyes turned up to the knop-pin of the painted roof. His patten and chalice had been taken from his hands. Now they clutched his Testament only, and again the cold voice spoke a single word.

'Proceed.'

And Gandelyn himself had taken no vows, but he knew that candles blown out in that august place were not lighted again, the book that closed there closed for ever, and now there came forward two priests. The first removed the stole from the man's neck, the other the chasuble from his shoulders; but when a third would have taken away his Testament he clutched it to his lips and breast and his bitter cry chilled the blood.

'Sirs, sirs—take the heart from my breast—'

'Proceed.'

It was part of the charge against him that he had comforted these rebels of Ripon, and sans Testament, chalice, chasuble and stole he was a priest no longer. But he was still a deacon, and for a moment a maniple was placed upon his wrist. It was removed, and thenceforward his name would not be found in the diaconate. But what had it all to do with Gandelyn? Why must he be brought to witness a sentence so fearful? It was warm in the chapter-house. Its sounds were like the murmur of the bees among the heather, loud for a moment in the ear and gone. And now an acolyte had brought a candle, and another a candlestick, and their faces were whiter than the candlewax as they were bidden by a sign to take them away again. Without taper or urceole the man was no longer an acolyte, not even a doorkeeper, for into his trembling hand the key of the church door was thrust, to be instantly plucked away, and again the directing voice was raised.

'This man, William Cobb by name, a stirrer-up of the people to disaffection to God and the state, was but lately a priest. Brought to discipline, he elected to plead the benefit of the vestments you have seen him successively stripped of. To Cæsar the things that are Cæsar's and to God the things that are God's. His case has been justly weighed. Now his privilege also is removed. From the street let a common cap be fetched and placed upon his head. Then let the marshal do his duty.'

But behind Gandelyn in his chair stood the sacristan, speaking in a low voice in his ear.

'Stand if you can till these are passed, then sit you still till you are called. Ambrose bids you be of a stout heart. Look not too much upon their faces, and answer them not. Let your only answer be *Mea culpa*. Put your trust in the Recorder, and stand, for respect.'

All about him was a surging and a pressing. One end of the crimson rope had been loosed for William Cobb to pass from one court to another, and under the mitred figure that trod the serpent under his foot the double doors stood open. They showed the outer vestibule, and Gandelyn saw the gleam of halberds and heard the rattle of butts on its floor. The vestibule communicated with the north transept, and the Minster's nave must have been full of people too, for a surge of voices reminded him of the sea. It died away, those assembled to profit by the degradation were pressing outwards like water to the orifice of a vessel, and from the stalls half the canons had descended. William Cobb had gone too, according as the next court used him to prison, or Greendykes or some other gallows.

'Be ready,' said the sacristan again.

His chair had been carried some paces nearer the clerks' table. About him voices were talking in low conversational tones, papers rustled and moved, but it all seemed a great distance away. Again he lifted his eyes to the painted archiepiscopal foot upon the serpent. No sinner was punished in this place of aloofness and solemnity, only the deadliness of the sin was kept ever before the eyes. He felt his head sinking. They would shake him when they were ready for him. He was not to scan their faces too closely, his only answer was to be *Mea Culpa*, and he was to put his trust in the Recorder. For a moment he wondered who this so-potent Recorder might be. Then he closed his eyes.

Sometimes, in the high bracken or the purple sweeps of the heather, they had played at losing and finding one another. One would count while the other stole away, but with their bundle humped on his back it took a bush to hide him, so one day he had slipped it off, and it had taken the pair of them an hour or more to find it again. But she could make herself smaller than he, often her clothes were the same colour as everything else about them, and she was sometimes almost as difficult to discover as she had been that first time among the oaks, when in the level rays she had seemed part of the glade itself.

But the loveliest had been the gentle plashing of the summer sea on the flat sands. It never quite ceased, but

sometimes there would come a pause so protracted that it
was as if a breathing breast had stopped. (They would tell
him when they were ready for him.) But one day there had
arisen a difference between them. When two marry a third
is presently to be expected, and Gandelyn had sometimes
trembled at the thought of that third, yet had above all
things desired it. But she did not desire it just yet, and
among her mother's herbs were those with subtle secrets.
She was no gipsy, she had said, to drop a babe under the
nearest bush, rest for an hour and on again. It must be
born in a bed, like that first real bed in Brid, and she
had nothing ready for it except one tiny faded garment
with a half-embroidered initial. (He was to put his trust
in the Recorder and say nothing but *Mea culpa*.) In
Cowfold manor-house too, where the lady had given her
her silver fillet, she had had a fire in her room. (At the
clerk's table half a dozen of them were talking quite loudly
now.)

It had been Robin Crosby who had settled it in the end.
She couldn't have babies and dance *Salome* too, he had said,
and among these clerks there should be one Peter Oates,
whom Gandelyn mistrusted in some ways, but undoubtedly
he was knowledgeable in others, and would be able to tell
him who this Recorder was. But whoever he was he hoped
they would get it quickly over. It was time he was back in
Bulmer, and after all what had he done? He had been given
a letter to take to the Archbishop. Unable to deliver it
into His Grace's own hands he had asked for his suffragan,
and in the end had given it to the precentor. What could
have been more regular or in order? But now from the
table the words themselves were beginning to reach him,
dry and difficult words, spoken with mincing precision.

'. . . by no procedure. Most evidently, that would be
to make the law narrower than itself, and furthermore
inconsistent with itself,' and a voice replied:

' . . . besides which it is to argue by an *ignoratio elenchi* . . .'

But Gandelyn had urgent business of his own, that had nothing to do with this jargon of which he could make nothing. On a good horse he could be there in half a day, and though he went to Bulmer on his hands and knees—

But now one of these voices was beginning strangely to resemble the soft and subtle voice of Master Vyner, who in Bulmer's castle had come to him one night and told him that his presence in York was desired, but only for a momentary recognition—a nod would do. Then again the voices:

' . . . as may be read in Leviticus Eighteen. It is to the man that these interdictions are formally directed, the woman being interdicted only by consequent, since a reciprocal act, impossible to be done by one only. . . .'

' . . . not so, Master Recorder. To that I answer that it is only after marriage that the man has the deduction of the woman *ad domum et thalamum*. . . .'

Gandelyn was becoming confused. This pourparler seemed in some way to concern himself. He did not know what *ignoratio elenchi* meant, but as the one voice was that of Master Vyner so the voice now raised was that of York's precentor, who had asked him where his lodging was and later had sought him there in vain.

'Examples must be made. This looseness becomes over-rife. We have yet another on our hands, my own late clerk, complained of by Master Wymark of Micklegate. Tutor to his three young children forsooth! A common street-walker, and another who calls herself a stitcher of girdles, and in the street they fall to spitting and clawing and crying out my own clerk's name—'

'He is your clerk. Deal with him. To proceed with the present business—' but the ecclesiastical voice rose still higher.

'As dealt with he shall be when I have had my say! The world grows godless before our eyes! Our holy houses themselves are defamed with ribaldry and revilings! No longer ago than a week past, in Coney Street, a ranting woman who had presented herself at Linthorpe—' but the other voice now only grew the softer.

'I have her in mind, reverend sir. Again, let the law take its course. But to bring unrelated matters forward now, prejudicially to this youth's interests—' and the answers and the rejoinders droned hollowly on.

But now Gandelyn knew who this man in whom he was to put his trust could only be. York's Recorder was second among the Twelve, the adviser and spokesman of the chief magistrate himself. Learned in the law both civil and ecclesiastical, even in a capitularium as supreme as this he balanced the one against the other, and now Gandelyn was slowly taking the scene in. The plenary session had become an ordinary one, it *was* of himself that they spoke. Save for one stall the pillared seats were empty. In that, as next in rank to the dean, the precentor sat, and canons conferred with the clerks at the table. The Recorder *was* Master Vyner, requesting now that the charge might be read. A clerk's flat voice obeyed.

' "*Dicitur fornicasse . . . mulier citatur non comparuit . . .*" ' and from the dean's stall the precentor's voice was suddenly peremptory.

'What! Charged, and he lolls in a chair!' and the sacristan spoke in excuse.

'It is thought he has a touch of gaol-fever, sir. He has been given a febrifuge.'

'Then we permit him to sit. But for one who has pleaded clerkship he would appear not to comprehend. Put it into English for him,' and the flat voice went on more slowly.

' "For that Robert Gandelyn, clerk, sometime of

Netherby but lately employed with the armies in France
. . . in York and elsewhere, about the time of Corpus last
and continually since . . . has lived in open sin and incontinence, to the public scandal—" '

'Sir precentor, I seek to compose our difficulties, but
you foment them—'

'Sir Recorder, you called for the charge to be read. Pray
interrupt him not.'

' " . . . and for that he alleges a form or similitude of
marriage to have been performed at the *Keys* inn, in this
city, the same not having been ratified or subsequently
acknowledged by any church—" '

'It is his present prayer, that it should be remedied
forthwith—'

'Who took upon himself this mockery of a Sacrament?'

'No priest it is true, yet a man of credit, much esteemed
by those of the Lord's Prayer, Master Crosby the pageant-
master. Furthermore, it had the consent of her mother,
present at the time—' but he had better have left that out,
for out shot the churchman's hand.

'Clerk, reach me those other depositions,' and he
frowned over the papers that were passed to him. 'There
you slipped, Master Vyner! By these attestations this same
woman, Efga Hartlip by name, over and above her present
offence, has already been publicly fustigated, in a year to
be ascertained, thrice round the church of Newbiggin in
Netherby Forest, branded and ejected from the parish!
What!' and he cast the papers aside. 'Whipped out of
Newbiggin—dismissed our holy House of Linthorpe—a
seller of herbs and a teller of fortunes, which comes close
to witchcraft itself! Heard to cry aloud in the streets, of
our own sisters in Christ, that they lived in sin, drinking
and unseemliness and carnal frequentings with men—'

It needed no Leviticus Eighteen to tell Gandelyn where
he stood now. His *Mea culpa* was ready on his lips, but of

Ripon there came not a word, only this monstrous charge! So the lyng-house if they chose, only let them set a term to it, and let him not go into sequestration as one whom holy church itself would not marry!

But as his lips moved to the *Miserere* he chanced to lift his eyes to the gallery above the stalls. There the window above was not of the more armorial glass, but one of emeralds and nacres and the lesser greens, and benignly there paced one of its lozenges the pastoral image of the Lamb of God. But the gallery, too, ran the whole circuit of the place, interrupted by clustered piers. A short passage behind each gave access to the next, and though he had supposed all the spectators to have gone, figures were moving there. If one of these was not Sir John Boles he strongly resembled him, and he was bending in attendance on a short lady hooded for a journey. But still the Recorder was persistently defending him.

'His name is not to be found in York's rolls. He is of no fixed domicile, yet he is not a vagrant. My counsel would be, sir, back with him to those that sent him.'

'Do they marry them in brotherhoods now?'

'He is their man. Let them settle it.'

But the lady and her attendant gentleman were not alone in the gallery. Others appeared to be ladies' maids, perhaps the ladies themselves, but he had little time to consider it, for now he was being sternly addressed, and at length. But he had only to say *Mea culpa* and not to look too closely on their faces, and at a command to answer he tried to get on his feet.

'*Mea culpa*,' he muttered.

'Answer what you were asked.'

'*Mea culpa.*'

'Your defence has been well and learnedly argued. Speak in Latin, that we may know the extent of your clerkship.'

'*Mea maxima culpa,*' and the drone now became an almost liturgical chant.

'Your petition may not be, for reasons which I will abridge. It is an ancient bone of contention that by Leviticus Eighteen the nakedness of the son is a prohibited thing, whereas that of the daughter is nowhere expressly prohibited. Others too have quibbled that after the Flood such prohibitions had the benediction of God, since all derive from Adam and Eve. But it is also plainly written, "Their flesh is as the flesh of horses and their issue as the issue of asses," and by Leviticus Twenty both so offending are to die.'

'*Mea*—'

'There is yet another reason. It is plausibly argued that a man cannot marry a woman and she not marry him, yet for the continuance of the world there must be issue. But of this unlicensed conjunction there is none,' and suddenly Gandelyn's raised voice startled himself.

'It was but for a little while, sir, till our slender fortunes—'

'From which it follows that there is neither bastardy nor perpetuation of the offence. Should later some man of worth come forward, willing to take her as she is, and able to set her up in some suitable station, as it might be his own household—'

But Gandelyn never heard the completion of the period. From behind the upper pier there had emerged two other figures, one of whom might have spilled from the coloured window itself. The shawl that hid her face was full of twinklings and playfulness. It was the shawl that even in her flight from the herb-kitchen she would not leave behind. Its Persian bowmen had ridden with her in a palankeen, heads had turned to look at it on Ouse Bridge, in Sturton market-place it had betrayed her in the opening of a tilt-cart—

But at this point his story checks and falters. For pity's sake (he says) he prayed that she had only just entered and had not heard those dire words about her mother. But he could no longer deny that he knew, had long known, almost from the beginning had foreknown. Suddenly she moved, uncovering him who stood behind. He was speaking to his cousin, the lady Adela, dressed for a journey. Now the Lancastrian mange had brought her here that she might hear it publicly pronounced that she was not married, that she was free to do what she would. And henceforward she would need no thirteen-and-fourpence.

And not love, but its brother-german hate surged in his drugged breast. O that he had buried that poniard to the hilt while he had had the chance! Born in a visionary castle, could it be that she did not see him for the splendour of the place in which they stood? Should he cry her name aloud among all this glory—Echo?

But the Gaunt saw to that too. He himself deigned him not a look, but with his hand he drew the shawl from her face, and their eyes met. Of a sudden her full voice broke into an anguished cry. He vows she would have cast herself down. But his *Mea culpa* was forgotten. In York's chapter-house he had struggled to his feet, among a score of shaven tonsures and the dry baldnesses of eld the only dark and soldier-cropped head there. He was on his knees before the precentor, and her cry was lost in his own.

'Sir, hear me! Could a priest have been found—there was no other way—she too has knelt at York's high altar, we knelt there together and she was in nothing to blame—I am no priest, yet I have administered unction and it was approved—' and her cry too was added.

'Bobbie—I cannot help myself—I am being made to do it—'

'Let there be order in this place!' the unpitying voice replied, and he was touched on the shoulder. 'It seems

York knows you not! To Netherby then you shall go! Are they here that were sent? Then let them take delivery of him!'

There was a slipshod shuffling of feet. Across the tinted floor there advanced the tall deaths-head figure of Brother Zachary. Another took him on the other side. As they passed under the plaqued Apostles and the painted Archbishop who choked the serpent with his crozier he flung up his impassioned face.

But the last watcher from the gallery had gone.

EIGHT PANEL

(*fragmentary*)

Kettles to Mend

The Mad Mare bolted with him through the night;
A hundred hornèd devils tore his eyne;
But all their bleeding shut not out the sight
Of him and her at play at mine-and-thine.
And he bestrides this plunging runt—and lo,
Stumbled the Mare, and thine-and-mine were one
As if a heavenly archer bent a bow
And lodged his arrow i' the gold o' the sun!
And shall he sleep whose every aching joint
Jars in his spine like a dismembered chain?
Deep i' the gold that arrow's burnished point?
Then what's this barb that festers in his brain?
Let him ride bleeding on; what must be must;
No heaven of love lacked yet its hell of lust.

There was no urgency now. Often Gandelyn wished he was as old as these old, old men among whom they had placed him, some of whom never left their beds, slept as much by day as they did by night, had their food brought to them and were passed over at the general bleeding. Others, professed these fifty years and more, only awaited the bell that was to be known from all other bells because it was hurried, irregular, and by day or night every brother who could walk must cease his occupation at the first note of it. Yet others sat more easily than they lay, because of aches and twitches and rheumatic knots and pangs. Even those able to rise had not to walk far, for the infirmarium was all in one, dormitory, refectory, and church by reason of the wooden pulpit against the wall, from which Brother Paul read the passage as they ate in silence.

The windows were on the outside, with the cubicles beneath them, but there were cubicles along the inner wall too. This abutted on other buildings, and the long narrow refectory table ran the whole middle length. Outer stairs gave access to the hospital building, and the stream, the closets and the mortuary lay directly below.

He had little idea of why he had been brought there, so far from the guest-houses and the infirmary of the lesser lay-brothers. But it was close to the kitchens, and it was the day-noises of these that told the old men the hour. For night they had the distant service-bell, when it was to be heard for coughings and breathings, tossings and half-heard prayers. Always at night a night-light burned, and by day or night the place had an unchanging smell of its own.

At the permitted times Brother Baruch came to see him. Sometimes he came at other hours too, and as these were likely to be between mattins and lauds, when Brother Baruch himself was on his way back to bed, Gandelyn was sometimes asleep when he came. Brother Baruch always applauded this. The young, he said, needed more sleep than the old. In case Brother Paul should overhear their whispering he had an innocent untruth always ready on his lips. 'Say you were repeating the *Laudate*,' he would murmur, as in his woollens he slipped away, leaving Gandelyn to praise the Lord upon the earth, the cattle and the worms and the feathered fowl, with strings and pipes and the timbrel also.

But now they were beginning to be a little negligent of whatever sickness it was that had brought him in. Twice at night he had been bidden to carry vessels downstairs, daily the floor had to be swept, and if he was not yet strong enough for these tasks it was time he was making himself so. Therefore Brother Paul, who read while they ate, ordered him daily exercise. This he took, not with Brother Baruch, but in the keeping of Brother Zachary, and it was a surgery that cut two ways. True he smelt the air again, but to pace in silence with Brother Zachary from the closets to the porter's lodge, back and forth, six times to the allotted hour, was to see little of Netherby's white queenliness tremblingly reflected in its stream. He was counting his steps again as he had counted them from buttress to buttress when he had lain with the chantry priests. They had not had him to Netherby to pamper him. It still had its lyng-house, and the thought of it became his daily dread. Lying down there, with a cord to lower his bread and water and the least confinement for a year, would be to be forgotten indeed.

But Sundays were the days when for a short space the rule of silence was relaxed. The monks, pacing the cloisters were permitted to converse in lowered tones, and on Sundays he had Brother Baruch again. And during his residence in the world Brother Baruch had been Harry Green, of Sempringham, in Lincolnshire, the birthplace of blessed Gilbert himself. There for a time he had been clerk of the leet, with other occupations besides, and in his sequestration he still remembered the world and its ways. But at Gandelyn's present plight he shook his sun-browned egg of a head.

'God requireth truth in the inward parts, and I fear you have not yet found it,' he sighed.

'I did not find it here before. I shall not find it here now', was the muttered reply.

'They may not purpose to keep you here. Some are sent to our House at Melrose instead.'

'I have another destination.'

'Where, my son?'

'In Lancashire.'

'What to do there?'

'It is a vow I have made,' and for a time it was Brother Baruch who was silent.

'All will pass, as it has passed with me,' he said at last. 'Somewhere there walks this earth one who in the flesh I called for a time my son. Were I to see him now I should not know his face. It may be that he has knocked at this porter's gate, lodged here for a night, and gone, like myself, unknowing on his way again. It is the dragging of the flesh in me that I think of it. Sometimes I fear to look on a strange face lest it should be his. And as any may be he, so gladly I give to all. So you will find it. The day will come when you will say "This was I" yet will not believe that it was you. You will say "Thus I did," but another will have done it in your place. So take not your present error too hardly. Men must judge according to trespasses, but God by the best that is in us. A shadow was there, and it has gone. A brightness was there—was there—and it remains. It is that, the brightness, that wrings the heart, that wrings the heart—' and, incomprehensibly to Gandelyn, Brother Baruch drew forward his cowl and shuffled with a queer sound away.

Should Brother Baruch fail him now he would be friendless indeed, yet that very thing came to pass. He came no more to his bedside between mattins and lauds, bidding him praise the Lord with minstrelsy and pipings. Yet still no summons came from the sub-prior, and now, as he counted his paces with Brother Zachary day by day, so among the old men he measured each day as it passed. O that it might be even Melrose, so it came quickly, before the sun rose too late and sank again too early in the day! They would have to conduct him there, and did they think that he, who had stalked France by night, would not be able to give a handful of monks and retainers the slip? To Lancashire, to Lancashire, and if too late to Lancashire all the more!

It put more heart in him than fifty febrifuges, but it was a quickening of which strict Brother Paul must be allowed to suspect nothing. Therefore he affected a mildness and an obedience. He swept floors and carried vessels unbidden, and, had he known it, it was proselytising Brother Paul who had him lodged where he was, hesitating to trust him yet at large among the lay-brothers. So, broken and penitent, he was to be brought to Grace. In Brother Paul's opinion Brother Baruch's way was not the way, nor was Brother Baruch's own ardour always to be trusted.

So, as Gandelyn made himself the least and humblest of them at the bottom seat of the refectory table, Brother Paul, observing his meek demeanour as he read the passage from his pulpit against the wall, judged that the time had come.

The infirmary of the lay-brothers was a furlong away, some of these too were old, but the lyng-house and the mortuary did not lie immediately beneath. Also it was a stride nearer to the outer world and its multifarious trades. The pied monks were still busy in the kitchen-gardens as he and Brother Zachary passed, and not for Ripon or anything else had a mason been taken from his work on the central tower. Beyond the footbridge lay the guest-house, with the porter's lodge in between. Again no parole was asked of him. But the lyng-house was still too near.

Had he been a shoemaker he would have been given their shoes to cobble, a tailor their habits to mend. Even to be under Brother Baruch's gentle restraint he no longer desired to be set to work in the scriptorium, and Netherby had no occupation for a juggler and crouther. So because in a sense they owed him the horse he had had no occasion for he asked to be given the task of keeping the stables clean.

But upon deliberation they put him among the butchers instead.

II

Because of its disturbing noises the killing-house stood at the farthest limit of the outer north-eastern wall. It would have been unseemly that one who had been a soldier should be turned into a common slaughterman, Netherby had no need more than of the two it already had, and for killing they stripped to the waist. But Gandelyn was given a greasy sleeveless garment of rough blue frieze and a leather apron for his middle. His business was in the carcase-house, among the haunches and sides, the quarters of beeves and cleft sheep, the heads and shanks and tripes and the offal in the pails, and let who would sing of the beasts and cattle when the bell rang daily for lauds. He had looked down on industry and the 'Addle-t-and *tak't!*' of the loom. Of merchanting he knew nothing, of the law he had had enough. But he could fetch and carry and wheel a truck between the killing-house and the carcase-shop, and under instruction could make a cut where he was told.

And now, lacking his poniard, like Jan Schmidt he knew where to lay his hands on a knife.

There were four of them in the carcase-house, and except for the comings and goings of the cooks and the necessary noises of the occupation silence reigned there as elsewhere. All needs were known, whether of the Lord Abbot's private kitchen or the guest-house, the infirmary or the salting-house; but with these Gandelyn had little to do. He washed the covering-cloths and saw to the fly-strings that dangled like Thomas Twentyman's eels from their ceiling-sticks. He weighed ribs and briskets and emptied the buckets and scoured the heavy blocks with sand and turned the stone for the knives. He liked the sound of the whetting steel, and now he was a cadaverator too, for offal was to bury or burn, and Brother Baruch was quite wrong when he said that everything passed with time. Brother Baruch was old. It was the young who remembered, and Brother Baruch had no killing-houses to visit nor had he to watch them cutting up sides and quarters all day. The master-butcher was the eldest of the lay-brothers. He had his own knife, which dangled with its hone from his belt, and Gandelyn too wanted a knife of his own. Sometimes, waiting for the master-butcher to lock up for the day, he was left alone to do the final sluicing and setting in order of the place. The knives and cleavers hung in a row on the wall, and now and then, taking a couple or so of them from their hooks, he juggled with them as few ordinary fleshers could have done. Once in a Forest a flying arrow had killed a king. But an arrow would mean carrying a bow, and other things than arrows could be made to fly.

It would have to be a warping-knife, a knife to fling from the hand. With other knives the man himself could not always get away in time. He was seized, overborne, and it all came of acting in hot blood instead of laying his plans in cold. But a warping-knife sped on its way at the same time as its thrower. He did not even ask himself what it would remedy to throw a knife straight—now.

On Sundays the butchery closed and again he could walk with Brother Baruch. It is well, when you meditate a journey from Yorkshire to Lancashire in the shortening days of the year, to gather what information you can, and since he had left Sempringham Brother Baruch was said to have travelled much. It might be that he knew the ways over the Pennines too. But now in Gandelyn's eyes Brother Baruch was getting to look older every time he saw him. But the older he got the surer he felt that he knew all about the young. He wandered from the point, and when Gandelyn wanted him to tell him the ways to Lancashire he talked about blessed Gilbert instead.

'As a boy, I knew the House he founded,' he said. 'It was in Sempringham, behind Saint Andrew's church, and he set up a Rule for seven holy virgins against its wall. The boys would write impudent things upon it. They say he always took his rest in his chair, like Brother James in the infirmarium when his aches are on him, and he only ate pulse himself, but ever at his side was a dish he called the Dish of the Poor, where all the best morsels were placed. . . . Lancashire? What of Lancashire?'

'I've heard it's all forest.'

'I was never there. But after his death Gilbert was carried to many places, and wrought many notable miracles, so it may be he was there.'

'They say the rivers run the other way.'

'The rivers? They run west in Lancashire. But I looked for you at Mass this morning and didn't see you in your place.'

'I sit with the butchers now.'

'I cannot see so far. It is these years of copying, and I am beginning to make more errors than Brother Francis. Once he wrote "commons" for "commote," but I have forgotten what it was about. Where in the Church do the butchers sit?'

But the bell struck its single note, the hour of converse was up, and now Gandelyn trusted that next Sunday would not find him there. He had his knife. It was a broken one, which in some sort lessened the theft, and shorter it would be the better for the purpose. In the smithies at Bulmer he had had a friar's begging-staff loaded, but this, cutting down its handle, he had loaded for himself. He could practise as he went, and how and when to get away was now his study. The dormitory of the lay-brothers was over the cellarium, and he knew he was watched. But need it be by night, as had been his first intention? By day he had the liberty of his occupation. Comings and goings were frequent, and each butcher-brother would suppose he had been sent on some errand by one of the others. He would have liked to take his cloak, but it would be missed from his bed, and if he attempted it and failed he could hardly hope to escape the lyng-house now.

Then as he lay one night turning it all over in his mind he remembered Jan Schmidt, who also had purloined a knife. Day had been breaking, and the gravedigger had sat by a dry ditch with his clayey hand on his knee. He heard again his very words: bring them good news and they would feast you, but bring them bad and hungry you would go till you brought them better. '*Is one living that should be dead?*'

Have no fear! The leaves would be brown, but his cloak

was brown too. Oak-galls would darken his face, he would
see he did better than Jan Schmidt had done. . . .

But at the joy and sweetness of life to come he utterly
broke down, and by the time he was master of himself
again it had only advanced his departure by a day. That
very night he intended to be gone.

And even so all was wasted, for it was not that way it
came about. He had risen the next morning, haggard and
unrefreshed. He had dressed as he dressed daily, for the
butchers' shop, but this time he had contrived to convey
his cloak to a niche in the cellarium stairs. Leaving the
dormitory he had turned his face to the row of sheds, the
saddlery, the salting-house, the laundry. Then suddenly he
was overtaken from behind by Brother Zachary, who
pointed the way back, and for once Brother Zachary
spoke.

'Take those off and clothe yourself. You are to see the
sub-prior.'

And it was the last time Brother Zachary was his con-
ductor. Round to the chapter-house he led him, along its
cool passage. At the door of Brother Isidore's parlour he
knocked, listened and entered. Brother Isidore was seated
at his table. But also seated at the table with him was
Gandelyn's own Lord John.

The lord John was going a-wooing. True he was past
the first flush of such things, thirty and more, set of brow
and with grey and restless eyes, and he, too, had been
absent too long. For fifteen days he had been on his homeward way from France, the last three of them without
stopping in any town, and it was not his lands in Yorkshire
and Westmoreland, or his baronies of Wharram and
Wickware and Tollington and Wyke that had brought him
back in such haste. Time for a look perhaps, time for a few
orders, and then away again. His Grace of York himself

had appointed him to the deputy-wardenship of the Middle
Marches of Wales, which was better than an expiring
war.

Therefore the lord John was going a-wooing, for while
he was about it what ailed the castles of Briniau and Coed
Isaf, Coed Uchaf and Quellyn and Gwlad, to say nothing
of the disputed lands in Denbigh and Flint? What odds
was it that their mistress the lady Margaret was his elder
by a few months or years? By that time they had got their
green-sicknesses over. They had not to be watched as some
of the younger ones had, and it was not as if the lord John
had never set eyes on the Lady Margaret before. He had
seen her once, if not twice, when she had been say twenty,
and for a homely wench even then he had seen worse. So
the lord John was going a-wooing.

But at the sight of Gandelyn his brows met, and even
before he spoke to him his grey eyes were bent mistrust-
fully on the sub-prior.

'What's here? Is this boy ill?'

And scarce two years before what mimicry would Gandelyn not have made of it for the mirth of the choristers!
Cautious, captious Brother Isidore, at whose appearance
even fifty yards away they had always scattered, trying to
keep his balance between two stools now! For there still
rankled in Brother Isidore's breast a certain *Quare impedit*
and the harmful Welsh precedent it had set. The interest
and friendship of one on his way to the deputy-wardenship
of the Middle Marches was a consideration to be borne
well in mind, and Brother Isidore answered with smooth
and allaying words.

'It is true he is but lately newly out of our infirmary,
where he has given us much anxiety. Indeed for his better
nursing I had him placed with our own brothers, under the
particular care of Brother Paul.'

'He was hale and well enough when he left France.'

'My lord John, it was his eagerness and zeal. He offered himself for a certain office, perhaps a little beyond his years and experience, but remembering your lordship's affection for him we entrusted him with it. Then word was brought to us that he was in some sort of trouble in York. Straightway we took steps on his behalf—'

'How, trouble in York?'

'Till he had his health back we have forborne to question him. Now your lordship has come—'

'I have much to say to him, and we stay no longer than the night. Can he be placed in the guest-house with me?'

'Gladly. It was our intention.'

'Robert, can you travel?'

And Robert Gandelyn said yes.

But it was the lord John, on wooing bent, who did most of the talking in the guest-house across the footbridge that night. For others their oak-glades frittered their gold in the sun and suddenly a willow-palm moved; the lord John's mind ran on the domains between this river and that, on castles at strong-points, on rentals and harvests and market-grants and tolls of corn and ferry and mill. Younger than he might lose their time over a few players' ribbons and skirts that fanned to flames; he was for Quellyn and Gwald, Coed Isaf and Coed Uchaf and the deputy-wardenship of the Middle Marches, and it was long before he turned to Gandelyn's affairs. Then:

'They tell me Matthew Poole, to whom I sent you, is dead?'

'Yes,' said Gandelyn.

'And what have you been up to since then?'

'I'll tell you as we go,' said Gandelyn.

For in a sense, and in their several ways, he and the Lord John were going a-courting together, and from Wales to Lancashire was not far. At daybreak the next day they set out. Two more days in the Riding perhaps, and then west. But as they left Netherby's fretted pinnacles behind Gandelyn did not even turn his head.

The lord John did not travel across peaceful England alone. He was accompanied by a score or so of well-armed men, and as such a company was too large for any inn they were likely to come upon they carried a couple of tents, and at night the men slept about their fire on the ground. But now Gandelyn was thinking twice about unbosoming himself to the lord John as they went. It seemed to him that either he or his master had greatly changed since they had last met, and were he now to disclose all there were fifty good reasons why it would be immediately and peremptorily forbidden. Even to begin would open a door dangerously wide, and had the lord John told *him* all? Indeed he had not! Bella Neville's bastard! Not yet had he been told one word about that! . . . So no. For the lord John the sweetness and joy of lands and castles and the deputy-wardenship were all to come. He would tell when the lord John told, and by that time his business would be over.

So they clattered and jingled their way nearer and nearer to the lower foothills of the Pennines.

'Robert, man, be of better cheer!' the lord John did not cease to urge him as they rode. "What, so merry in dolorous France and so gloomy now our fortunes lie ahead!'

'I shall be merry again,' Gandelyn would mutter.

'I misdoubt something weighs on your mind, but am I to present you before my lady Margaret with *that* graveyard face?'

'It will clear,' said Gandelyn, and to save himself further questioning fell behind.

Now the savage hills lay all about them, and one night the sun went down extinguished by mists that shrouded the weeping woods. The tents were pitched and the fire lighted, but Gandelyn sat apart listening to the sounds of their supper being prepared. In a windowed chamber glorious with colour and light she had cried down to him from a gallery that she could not help herself, was being forced to go—she would have cast herself down—

But an arrow had killed a king—

So bless and save us, what heeltap stragglers intrude now, their faces peering into the leaping light just as their supper was ready? They were lean and ragged, yet their hunger-bright eyes had the look of men who were free even in their vagabondage. And was it to be believed that one of them was so famished that, striding to the fire, he snatched a brand from the flames and crammed it into his mouth, breathing out fire as if from a furnace, while another's belly so cried cupboard that he drew a half-sword from his belt and inch by inch to the hilt eased it down his throat?

But Gandelyn had humped himself still further away. Fifty times he had heard of John Cormorant who swallowed the whinyards, and Will Bungay who ate embers like puddings, and little Davy the Welshman who sang the *penillion* till tears of laughter ran down his hearers' cheeks. They were the remnant of Robin Crosby's company, earning their bread as they went. They would not know Gandelyn, but Gandelyn knew them, and had no desire that afterwards his face should have been seen and in a luckless moment remembered.

And it was yet another reason for saying nothing to the lord John.

There were four of the men. Fresh fuel was heaped on the fire, and when they had been given food the ring was widened for them to display their antics. One played a zither, another nackered, and the little one sang *penillion*, and the lord John's heart was growing lighter every hour, and again he called to Gandelyn, sullen in the shadows.

'Rouse you, Robert! You're missing the cream of the sport! Come and laugh as you used to!'

But once before Gandelyn had sat with armed men about their fire, his fingers busy with crosspiece and twine, turning a boarspear into a ceremonial cross. Now again they were busy. His new poniard would be the gentlemanlier weapon, but one must be ready for whatever comes, and now the other was nicely weighted and balanced to his hand. He had made a little pocket for it inside his right boot, and such a point and edge as it had! But another whetting would do it no harm, and himself good, and it flickered for a moment in the firelight as again he stroked it lovingly along the leg of his rawhide boot.

So, like the spectrum, it emerges from the darkness, violet at first, glowing with summer awhile, and expiring in its morbid red. Now the worn web itself begins to fray, the shot weft to grow hueless, the warp to slacken like an unstrung harp, so that between its wreck of strings the stones of history show forbidding and grey. Of the war that followed a war the roses are still to pick, but every root is there. It is nowhere on record that ever a Gaunt was found in a Lancashire wood with a warping-knife accurately lodged where the leeches used to suck, but then as now, the less recorded the sooner mended, nor has it any place here. A few loose verses have been thrown in, of no relevance except to set the panelling a little further back. One man enters the Forest, another comes out. A laughing youth sets foot into an Arras, without a laugh he leaves it. With no matter what to fill the gap between, which of us does more?